MW00872717

CHAMELEON

Moyes Capehart

Especially for Brenda.

OTHER BOOKS BY

Noyes Capehart

Capehart is best known as a visual artist.
For more about his work and current projects
visit his website
www.capehart.org

THE PRIVATE DIARY OF
NOYES CAPEHART

WALKING THE WAY OF SORROWS
with Katarina Katsarka Whitley

DEVIL'S MARK

CHAMELEON

A NOVEL

Noyes Capehart

Scotch Hall Publishing
Boone, NC

Scotch Hall Publishing
Boone, NC

2015 © Noyes Capehart

Cover Painting: *Purring* by Noyes Capehart
Cover Design: Becca Jett
Text Design: Luci Mott

Chameleon is a work of contemporary fiction. Names, characters, events and circumstances are either the product of the author's imagination or they are used fictitiously. Any resemblance to actual persons, living or dead, business establishments, events or locales is purely coincidental. No part of this book may be reproduced or transmitted in any form or by any other means: electronic, recording, or by any other means, with the exception of limited quotes for review, without the permission of the author.

ISBN-13: 978-1522841388

ISBN-10: 1522841385

for Suzie,

our children and
our grandchildren

CHAMELEON

PROLOGUE

She lived in the fashionable and exclusive Beacon Hill section of Boston. Wife of the late Bruce Mellan, celebrated Boston attorney, she was a principle player in the city's social world. At fifty-two, she had lost none of her beauty and, if anything, had attained a sensual depth that resonated with every adult male she met.

In her modest but elegant solarium, Zoa Carrin-Mellan nurtured exotic plants from around the world. A Botany major at Swarthmore College during the late 60s, her passion for collecting rare plants was second only to that of collecting art. In 1971, she married Mellan, seventeen years her senior. When he had the solarium added to their splendid Greek revival row house, cost was not a consideration. Initially, her collection ran the gamut of conventional selections from ferns to orchids, but shortly after Mellan's death in 1993, Zoa's botanical priorities changed. She began collecting deadly plants from around the world; castor bean, rosary pea, wolfsbane, nightshade and, her favorite, *Dionaea Muscipula,* better known as the Venus flytrap. On those days following her husband's death when she succumbed to bouts of melancholy and isolation, she would fix herself a cup of herbal tea and spend hours in her solarium, stroking her white cat Dagmar and patiently observing the flytraps until an insect would unknowingly crawl onto the hairy surface of the plant. As the trapping mechanism was triggered, sealing the fate of the visitor, she would smile contentedly. Dagmar, it should be noted, was named for an infamous baby serial killer from Copenhagen during the early part of the twentieth century.

On this day, the early morning sunshine bathed the solarium.

Across the hallway, some twenty feet away, the nude body of Zoa Carrin-Mellan shifted slightly under the weight of a single lavender sheet. An overhead ceiling fan moved the already heavy air. She rolled over onto her left side and inched closer to the back of her sleeping companion, a gentleman from Denmark she had met only two days earlier at a lavish opening at the Boston Museum of Fine Arts, a charming man by the name of Ankiel Thorssen. Zoa could hear the deep, guttural purring of Dagmar, curled up at that moment next to the chest of her new friend. "I believe she likes you, Ankiel," she said softly. "She is usually quite anti-social." She moved her warm body closer to him. "Won't you change your mind and stay a few days longer?" she whispered in his ear. "I don't want you to leave."

The man she knew as Ankiel Thorssen, Theo Volmer in reality, turned to face her. His hand found the small of her back and for the next few moments he stroked it gently, gradually intensifying pressure with his fingertips as they moved up her spine to the base of her neck. Soft, indistinct murmurs of pleasure resonated from deep within her being. "I must," he said simply. "I cannot postpone my business in Nashville any longer."

"And after Nashville? Do you promise to return to Boston?"

"You have my word on it."

In the solarium, a jade-green fly perched on one of the fronds of a Raphis fern. After rubbing its front two legs together in an ecstatic fashion, it flew to the surface of one of the Venus flytraps. A moment later, the lethal enzymes of the plant were activated and in seconds the visitor was trapped, destined to a slow, agonizing death.

Volmer took a cab from Zoa's home to Logan airport, arriving shortly before eleven a.m. He was met in the Barclays VIP lounge at the terminal by his personal pilot, Ernst Fromm, a long-time and trusted employee.

"*Ich bin fertig, wenn Du's bist.* I am ready when you are," Herr Volmer," Fromm said in crisp German. "*Wir haben die Abflugerlaubniss becommen.* Everything has been cleared for our departure."

"*Ausgezeichnet! Ich mochte starten.* Excellent! I'm anxious to be underway."

The Learjet quickly reached its cruising altitude, its destination Nashville, Tennessee. As the sleek aircraft flew high above a carpet of

silvery clouds, an attractive young flight attendant wearing a conservative dark blue skirt and a starched white blouse with a ruffled collar
approached her only passenger from the rear of the cabin. "May I get
you something to drink, Herr Volmer?" The simple question was laced
with respect. Her smile was radiant.

"A Bloody Mary would be nice, Idonna. Thank you."

"Perhaps a few oysters on the half shell?" she asked. "I'm told these
are especially good."

"Sounds delightful."

"With the usual wedge of lime, I suppose?"

"You know me well, my dear."

Volmer repositioned himself in the seat. He closed his eyes and
allowed himself the luxury of not having to think about anything of
more serious consequence than the oysters. With his right thumb
and index finger, he made subtle adjustments to the sound level of his
headset and then, satisfied with his efforts, melded with Samuel Bar-
ber's *Adagio* for Strings.

Several moments later, the attendant returned and gently touched
him on the shoulder. In his half-awake/half-asleep state, he fancied the
hand belonged to Largo Kopacz. "Your oysters and drink, sir."

A smile came to his face when he saw the oysters. Savoring them, he
returned his thoughts to Largo Kopacz and the intensity of his physical attraction to her from the moment they first met. His sexual conquests over the years had been impressive by any standards, and they
included some of the most beautiful women in Europe, but Largo had
presented him with an unexpected problem; she didn't succumb to
his charms. Perhaps it was that elusiveness that made her all the more
desirable. In that most private zone of his inner self where his darkest,
lustful fantasies played, she was its vortex, a spinning center of white-
hot prurience. Initial interest had become attraction. Attraction had
become desire and now desire had morphed like a demon into blind
obsession.

For Volmer, everything he pursued from art to women to power
itself was predicated on the same end game: possession. The thought
arrived like a soothing tropical breeze, *One day I will have you!*

Other thoughts followed, scattering the seeds of his carnal desires.
Notwithstanding the official certification that he had perished in the

massive fire at his Fiesole home three months earlier, he knew that some were left wondering if the declaration were true. He would have to be doubly cautious from this point on in his travels to make sure that his disguises matched up with his bogus passports. During his long tenure as director of the Uffizi Gallery in Florence, his face was frequently in the public eye. There, he was easily recognized if for no other reason than his height. At roughly five feet four inches tall, he was noticeably shorter than the average German, or northern Italian. However, as he often reminded himself, he didn't need to look far to find giants of a similar stature. Fellow countryman Ludwig Beethoven stood just shy of five-four, Ghandi was five-three and Picasso an even five-four. Insoles helped. In Anghiari, Italy, he had read, the average male was more in line with the men of southern Italy where five-eight was about par.

For a while, anyway, he would have to avoid major museums and social events that could endanger and reveal his true identity. The necessary self-imposed exile had been carefully orchestrated however, and it was now underway. Yes, there was the element of risk, but that only heightened his desire to play the game. He was now a chameleon in the aromatic game of deceit.

Though a distant second to his obsession with Largo, Volmer was quietly amassing a fortune from investments he'd made in U.S. companies: Microsoft, in particular. When Microsoft stock went public on March 13, 1986, Volmer invested heavily. Flushed with millions from his highly successful art forgery empire from the late 1960s to the early 1980s, he quickly became one of the largest individual Microsoft investors outside the United States. Little did he know as he soared high above the earth on that July day, that his fortunes were about to increase dramatically. Microsoft was four months away from announcing that the Board of Directors would approve a 2-for-1 stock split.

Six months earlier, under the name of Ankiel Thorssen, he rented a spacious condominium in Copenhagen, Denmark. There he had waited patiently for the right time to visit Nashville, a few miles from the home of Porter Blue and Largo Kopacz in nearby Franklin, Tennessee.

After Fromm landed in Nashville and was taxiing to the terminal, Volmer told him that he wanted preparations to be made promptly for the return trip to Copenhagen, two days hence. He spoke in English. "Ernst, when I have completed my business here, it is imperative that we depart Nashville without delay. And Boston will not be on our flight itinerary," he added, glancing at his wristwatch, steadying himself as Fromm guided the aircraft over the tarmac for the final few yards of its journey. "I'll be meeting a colleague in the terminal in a few minutes," Volmer continued. "Afterwards, we will be going to the Renaissance Nashville Hotel on Commerce Street. Have a cab ready."

Arrangements had been made prior to Volmer's departure from Boston for him to be met at Nashville's International Airport by a Danish security specialist, Arnar Bjorn. They first met at a film festival in Venice the previous summer. Aware of Bjorn's gambling addiction and his expressed need of money, Volmer had presented a proposal over drinks that the man couldn't refuse. It entailed a two day trip to the United States, for which all expenses would be covered, plus a lump sum payment of twenty-five thousand dollars.

Bjorn, a trim man in his late thirties with smooth, olive skin and dark, wavy hair that curled up at the nape of his neck, was waiting for Volmer in the Delta lounge, as per his instructions. Dressed in tan slacks, brown loafers and a cream dress shirt open at the neck; he could have passed for a professional golfer. For ten years he had worked with Danish intelligence, rising quickly through the ranks to become one of Denmark's most accomplished security experts. As he saw Volmer approaching, he shifted his position on the bar stool and drained the last of his scotch and soda.

Volmer smiled as he approached Bjorn in the well-lighted concourse. His eyes studied the Dane as if he were a medical specimen. "I trust you had a nice flight from Copenhagen, Arnar," he said extending his well-manicured hand.

"A very pleasant flight, indeed," Bjorn replied, returning Volmer's firm handshake with one of equal pressure. "I slept most of the way."

Volmer noticed his empty glass on the surface of the bar. He motioned to the bartender to refill it and then placed his order for a *Dewar's* on the rocks. When their drinks were served, he turned to face Bjorn. "Now, my friend, let us share a nice drink together and discuss the particulars of our mutual interests."

Fourteen Months Earlier

PART ONE

In the crucible of life, the propensity
for deceit smolders within each of us.

—Noyes Capehart

CHAPTER ONE

Best Friends

May 6, 1996
Florence, Italy
10:27 a.m.

To the casual observer in the Piazza della Signoria, the mustachioed man in the loose fitting khaki trousers, thin maroon sweater and floppy brown canvas hat was one of about fifteen tourists from the Balkans on the covered Loggia di Orcagna.

The late fourteenth-century structure, initially designed to provide members of the Signoria—the governing body of Florence—a preferred place from which to watch assemblies and public ceremonies on the spacious piazza, was now home to about a dozen works of marble and bronze sculpture, a haven for hippie musicians and an ideal refuge for those needing to escape unexpected showers, like the one falling on this day.

For Theo Volmer, the man in the rakish hat, the object of his presumed interest at that moment was the rear view of Benvenuto Cellini's imposing bronze sculpture of Perseus standing above the decapitated body of Medusa. In actuality, he had positioned himself behind the sculpture in order to be as close as possible to the main entrance of the Uffizi Gallery, no more than thirty paces to his right. He knew that Porter Blue and Largo Kopacz would soon be concluding their appointment with his successor, Interim Director Lucca Palma. The flowers and his accompanying note to Largo had been delivered to Palma's office by now. At any moment, they would be exiting the venerable museum. He wanted one last look at her. He wanted to see the expression on her face that would assure him that He had wracked her inner core. If he was any judge of character—and he considered himself to be among the best—he knew she would be emotionally reeling when she realized he was still very much alive, that he had not perished

19

in the flames. More than that, he wanted her to know that she was central to his most sexual thoughts and feelings.

The note that accompanied the flowers could pose a serious risk, but Volmer had done two things to make it all but impossible to prove it came from him: he had the florist print the note in a generic script and he had been careful not to touch or sign the card. Largo could go to the police if she wanted to, but without proof he had sent the flowers it was unlikely they would take the matter seriously. Even if the police took the trouble of tracing the flowers to a specific Florentine shop, the florists could only say that they never knew the name of the customer. It had been a cash transaction.

His wait was not a long one. Blue and Largo exited the Uffizi and entered the narrow Piazzale Degli Uffizi, the paved open area between the museum and the loggia where the mimes would begin assembling in a few hours to undergo their remarkable transformations. Her body language reflected his expectations. She walked unsteadily, her head lowered, as if her shoulders were supporting a great weight. Tears had come since leaving Palma's office. Mascara streaks were clearly evident.

"I'll never be far from you," he whispered aloud, reciting the final six words from the note she had read moments earlier. A smile formed on his thin lips.

He waited until they had passed and then moved to the front of the loggia where he watched them cross the crowded piazza and dissolve in the shadows of Via Dei Calzaiuoli.

Volmer then turned and began walking toward a waiting limousine at the distant end of the Piazzale Degli Uffizi, high above the Arno River. He was leaving Florence for an indefinite period of time, perhaps forever. His decision to leave Florence was not a capricious one, quite the contrary. Even before the fire that destroyed his Fiesole home in early April, he realized that Scotland Yard's investigation of a London art forgery could ultimately connect the dots to his highly successful forgery scheme during the decade of the seventies. Never one to leave anything to chance, he directed his private attorney at the time, Mario Drago, to begin squirreling away large hunks of his vast fortune in faux businesses throughout Europe and in prime land in Germany and France: anonymous assets that could quickly be converted to cash, if circumstances dictated. Through contacts of his own, Volmer opened coded accounts in a Swiss bank and one of the off shore sanctuaries in the Caribbean.

Knowing he was about to embark on a self-imposed exile that would first take him to Anghiari, Italy, before going to Copenhagen, he spoke with Drago over drinks one evening about his meticulously crafted plans. The astute attorney had been in Volmer's employ as far back as the sixties when Volmer was a mere curator at the Thyssen-Bornemisza Museum in Lugano, Switzerland. At the time, he was considered one of the most brilliant, if not at times shady, attorneys in Europe. Volmer had stepped in to prevent his disbarment over his involvement in an election scandal by bribing a key official in the Swiss Judicial system. Drago had never forgotten the gesture and his loyalty had been unimpeachable.

"I will be assuming the name of Azzo Gatti while in Anghiari," Volmer said. "I have already established a modest bank account there."

"I like the name. It has a nice ring to it."

"Yes, I thought so, as well. I selected it from a Florence telephone directory a few weeks ago."

Both men smiled before Volmer quickly shifted gears. "I need you to create a similar account in Copenhagen at the Spar Nord Bank in Copenhagen. Use the name Ankiel Thorssen."

Drago nodded. He understood the situation well. "That can easily be arranged. I have reliable contacts there."

"When trouble arises, my friend, everyone tries to follow the money," Volmer said. "You have done well in hiding mine."

Patting his abundant belly, Drago replied, "You are well positioned to easily access your treasures, should costly circumstances dictate. All you have to do is contact me when significant operational funds are needed and I will make sure your needs are promptly satisfied."

In a typical Volmer maneuver to deflect any trace of suspicion, he had appointed Drago as his temporary power of attorney shortly before the Fiesole fire. Knowing that he would officially "perish" in the conflagration, he directed Drago to remove all but a million lire from his Florentine accounts at the Deutsche Bank and the Palazzo della Banca D'Italia. As per his instructions, Drago was to then make a grand show of dispersing these funds to several Italian charities. What was a million lire to Volmer, after all?

Should anyone question Drago's actions, he would make sure that Volmer's personal accounts in Florence reflected little more than prudent money management by a successful museum director. Drago, after all, was as innovative as Volmer was thorough. The three hundred thousand dollar bonus he received for this most recent tending of Volmer's financial garden did not come as a complete surprise.

As Volmer approached the limousine, he took one last look at the walls of the Uffizi Gallery where he had spent so much of his professional life. An unexpected surge of anger then came upon him with the intensity of a thunderstorm.

The small, walled town of Anghiari, Italy, nestles high atop a steep hill in the province of Arezzo, near the border between Tuscany and Umbria, a little over a hundred kilometers from Florence. Dating from medieval times and surrounded by thirteenth-century stone walls, it looks down on the fertile plains of the Tiber and Sovara valleys. Under the summer sun, its angular stone buildings, narrow streets and salmon-capped tiles created a marvelous abstraction of geometric shapes and patterns, calling to mind some of the modern Cubist works of Pablo Picasso and Juan Gris. On this day, a visitor was arriving, a scholar by the name of Azzo Gatti.

A fraudulent passport had been prepared, one showing him with thickly framed glasses and a well-trimmed moustache. Contacts had changed the icy gray eyes to a bland hazel. His close-cropped hair, normally a blend of silver and black, showed the results of a recent trip to his stylist; the gray was gone. Clear glasses helped. In the months to come, his hair would grow much longer, eventually enabling him to wear it in a ponytail.

Upon his arrival, Volmer checked into the La Meridiana, a small, unpretentious hotel located in the city center. Prior to his departure from Florence, he made arrangements though a local realtor to view properties for rent or short term lease, preferably within walking distance of town. As he explained his wishes to the realtor, "I am looking for comfortable quarters that will allow me to pursue my research without interruption."

The following morning he met with a young and aggressive realtor with whom he had previously discussed his needs by phone. The realtor had asked about his research interests.

"It relates to a book I intend writing on the Battle of Anghiari," Volmer replied in a casual manner. "You are no doubt familiar with the siege?"

"Familiar? Yes, very much so," the man replied, pride showing on his handsome face. "It is the reason our charming town is on the map, *signor* Gatti."

As the accommodating realtor listened to Volmer's description of his intended research project, it raised no curiosity. Gatti was not the first academician to visit Anghiari with interest in the battle made famous nearly a hundred years later by a major blunder by Leonardo da Vinci.

Volmer was well aware of the details surrounding both the battle and da Vinci's disaster. The battle occurred in 1440, a fierce clash between Milanese forces and the Italian League led by the Republic of Florence and a strong contingent of Papal forces. In 1504, da Vinci received a commission from Gonfaloniere Piero Soderini of Florence to decorate the Hall of the Five Hundred in the Palazzo Vecchio's Salone dei Cinquecento. His chief rival at the time, Michelangelo Buonarroti, was selected to decorate the facing wall. Leonardo chose the Battle of Anghiari for his theme, while Michelangelo chose another celebrated Italian battle, the Battle of Casina. It was a contest doomed from the start. Experimenting with oil colors and beeswax, instead of the more traditional technique of fresco, Leonardo's painting began to drip and ooze before it could be finished. Thinking that intense heat would hasten the drying of the pigment, Leonardo positioned several charcoal braziers in front of the mural. The result was calamitous. The waxy oil colors began sliding down the wall, creating a large slimy residue on the tiled floor. Michelangelo, disinterested in the project from the start and eager to return to his sculpture, left Florence after doing little more that registering his cartoon on the wall. Both works in their incompleteness remained on the walls until 1515, at which time they were removed to make way for more conventional decorations.

As director of the adjacent Uffizi Gallery, Volmer had been to the Salone dei Cinquecento on numerous occasions during his lengthy tenure at the celebrated museum. He seldom did so without looking at the massive walls and marveling at the breadth of da Vinci's mistake. How could the man who gave us the parachute, the submarine and the helicopter be so misguided in believing that oil colors could be forced to satisfy the technical demands normally associated with mural art?

Volmer selected Anghiari as a temporary place of refuge for three reasons: it was less than an hour away from Florence. Should circumstances dictate a hasty departure, he could easily reach Fromm. Secondly, the population of Anghiari—under six thousand—ensured needed anonymity. Few of the locals, he discovered early, could afford the more expensive life style in Florence, nor did they strike him as being especially cultured. He doubted that few, if any, had ever stepped foot inside the Uffizi Gallery, or dined in one of the city's many fashionable restaurants. The likelihood that anyone would connect him with the Uffizi was remote, at best. Thirdly, and of marked significance, his fabricated research interests in the famous battle provided perfect cover for his larger reason for being in Anghiari.

For three days, Volmer was shown several attractive properties that matched up favorably with his expressed needs. He settled on a small but elegant stone house with an intimate courtyard and a stellar view of Sansepolcro. The furnishings hardly matched his tastes, but its location was perfect; fewer than ten kilometers from the center of town. The opportunity for regular exercise was appealing, but of greater importance the location provided critical privacy. The remoteness of the site comforted him like a glass of port on a cold night.

Within days, he acclimated to his new surroundings. It was essential that nothing about his intended brief stay in Anghiari call attention to himself. His finely tailored wardrobe was shelved in favor of the clothing worn by the locals; cotton corduroy trousers, white shirts buttoned at the neck and the ubiquitous heavy walking shoes. A low-brimmed black hat and a walking stick added to the impression he wished to convey. In making his first explorations of the intimate town, he appeared to be just another contented resident going about his daily duties. Given his language gifts—fluency in Dutch, Danish, French, Italian and his native German—he was viewed from the outset without suspicion. He found a tiny hole-in-the-wall place where he could get empty wine bottles filled with surprisingly good red table wine, a small but superb market and several accessible, if not exceptional restaurants.

It was during these first days in Anghiari, that he made the acquaintance of Dona Albrecci, a young and quite pretty woman in a small, neighborhood bar. In typical Volmer fashion, within two hours he had lured her to his bungalo. After several glasses of chilled white wine, they were lying naked under the sheets. A tantalizing breeze was teasing the curtains.

As Dona rolled over and positioned herself atop Volmer, an unprecedented thing happened: he was unable to reach an erection. In those excruciating moments, Volmer found himself confronting for the first time the same problem that men of the world have experienced since the beginning of recorded time.

Dona seemed unaffected. "It's no big deal." She suppressed a yawn before returning to the softness of the bed. "This happens sometimes."

"It is a big deal fucking deal to me!" Volmer shouted, frantically trying to arouse his sleeping staff with an obliging left hand. "This has never happened to me before."

Troublesome thoughts of those moments with Dona Albricci took him back in time. He was midway through a physical examination in April of 1982 when his physician commented on an issue of concern, something he discovered while viewing the results of some recent blood work. "Theo, we may have to take some measures to reduce your cholesterol. It's higher than it was this time last year."

Volmer listened to his doctor's words with broad indifference. He was in his forties and had never felt better.

"Your blood circulation is acceptable," the physician continued, "but as you get older the plumbing—if I may use that analogy—is likely to get more sluggish. In time, plaque could begin building up in your arteries and—"

"Are you saying I need to be on medication?" Volmer interrupted.

"Yes, I would recommend it."

Volmer was less than judicious in taking his meds, and in 1984 had to undergo bypass surgery. A change in doctors allowed him to step back from his medications, but by 1990 he was confronting hypertension. Another doctor put him on new meds and, like it or not, Volmer complied.

"I'm just telling you like it is, Theo," the young physician said. "Maintain your current habits and you stand a very good chance of having a stroke, or worse."

Things gradually improved—stabilized would be a better choice of words—for the next six years.

Then, on the evening of March 21, 1996, while having dinner at his home with Porter Blue and Largo Kopacz and his old friend Sarto Carpaccio, he blacked out and fell to the floor. All that Carpaccio knew of Volmer's medical condition was that he was popping pills for arrhythmia, the rate or rhythm of his heartbeat. Volmer had never shared with Carpaccio the severity of the risk of stroke or death that lurked within the shadows of his daily life.

Nearly two months after establishing residency in Anghiari, satisfied that he had avoided recognition and had blended in with the locals, he broadened his domestic explorations. On the recommendation of the town's baker, he visited a small, but charming, restaurant near the town center, The Verrocchio. The twelve-table trattoria was named for the Florentine painter and pupil of Leonardo da Vinci, Andrea del Verrocchio. It quickly became Volmer's favorite, not only because of the cuisine and ambience but its charming owner and chef.

The Verrocchio was owned by Astrid Borgmann, an appealing German woman who came to Anghiari in the late 1980's. Her distinctive Nordic features stood in marked contrast to the darker complexions of her Italian neighbors, but her high level of language proficiency allowed her to blend in effortlessly. To most of the locals, she was considered something of a mystery. No one seemed to know why she came to Anghiari or, for that matter, how she got there. One day she opened the doors of her restaurant and by nightfall her name was the buzz of the town. The gossip tattlers were quick to notice that she wore no ring. Most of the residents assumed she was unmarried, or perhaps no longer married, widowed perhaps.

Given her striking looks, it was puzzling—titillating would be a more accurate choice of words—that she was rarely seen in the company of a man beyond the confines of her restaurant. More than one Anghiari resident drew the conclusion that she was a lesbian.

From day one, Astrid proved to be among the most gracious and welcoming of the town's restaurant owners. She made a point of greeting first-time diners with a complimentary glass of wine and assisting with any questions they might have about her gastronomical specialties. By their second visit to The Verrocchio, she addressed them by name. If they were residents of the community, she was prepared to chat with them about their children or grandchildren, their vocations, even their aesthetic or political persuasions. Few failed to feel a grand sense of self-importance in the face of such flattery.

When Theo Volmer—that is to say, Azzo Gatti—first entered her establishment and overheard her talking with guests at a nearby table, he immediately picked up on the subtle German accent that flavored her flawless Italian. The overtone was like a distinctive herb, there to complete a delicious sauce but not overpower it. He guessed she might be from Bavaria, perhaps Munich or Nuremburg.

A moment later, his presence caused her to turn in his direction. A broad smile followed, like a bride's train. *"Benvenuto al Verrocchio.* Welcome to The Verrocchio," she said, extending a milk-white hand. "My name is Astrid."

"Good evening," Volmer replied warmly in the native tongue. "I'm Azzo Gatti."

They talked for a few moments, each drawn to the other. Volmer sensed something familiar about her, as if their paths had crossed at some point in the past. Before he could process a possible connection, she turned and motioned to a server. "Carmelo, please seat *signor* Gatti near the doors to the courtyard." She glanced at Volmer and added for his benefit, "It affords a splendid view of the night lights of Anghiari. It's my favorite seat in the house."

Throughout his meal, Volmer watched Astrid as she mingled with her guests, wondering what it was about her that kindled such strong feelings of connection. She was trim and quite lovely, no doubt a gorgeous woman in her younger years. The reels of his mind flashed back to the 1940's and his first encounter with the Hitler Youth. She could have been one of them, he thought, recalling the comely boys and girls who so epitomized the *Führer's* fetish for Aryan supremacy. The blond hair would have been braided then, strands of gold that would have glistened in the sunlight. For a moment, he felt himself caught in a passing wave of melancholy, a painful sensation of grief that such times had not brought the thousand years of glory promised by his father and by Hitler.

But the subtle lines that now etched Astrid's face suggested that the more recent years had not been easy ones for her. If asked to guess her age, he would have put her a few years younger than himself, though she could easily pass as a much younger woman. As the evening wore on and the restaurant began to empty, he moved to the small bar. He was just about to place an after dinner drink order when she entered through a door from the kitchen.

"I'm delighted you are still here, *signor* Gatti. When I saw your empty table, I assumed you had departed."

"Yes, I am still very much here. My exquisite meal called for a night-cap. I wonder," he paused, "if you might honor me with the pleasure of your company? I do so hate to drink alone."

She had been doing her homework on him during the course of the evening, to the extent her duties allowed her to do so. Her initial impression of him, favorable certainly, deepened as she observed his deportment. He might be wearing the clothes of a humble villager, but the man in her presence exuded a sense of sophistication, confidence and superiority not often seen in her restaurant.

"As a rule," she began, noticing her all but empty surroundings, "I don't mingle socially with my customers, but today has been a long and difficult one. My most experienced server could not be here due to an appendectomy, and I've been on my feet since we opened. I would very much enjoy a drink, thank you."

She motioned to a table in the corner of the room. "Might we move over there?" she asked. "At the risk of being indelicate," she added, spearing him with another smile, this one a bit more flirtatious, "My shoes are coming off the minute we sit down."

"I can certainly live with that." Volmer drained his glass before leaving the bar.

When they were situated, he asked, "What is your pleasure, *signora*? A cognac, perhaps?"

"Let me suggest our lemoncello. We make the best in all of Italy. It is truly exceptional."

"Then lemoncello it is."

For the first ten or fifteen minutes, they talked about Anghiari, the charm of its serpentine streets and the absence of offensive commercialization. When she asked him why he was in Anghiari, he replied simply, "Your famous battle, of course."

Cups of espresso followed the lemoncello as their conversation shifted to their respective back pages: where they had lived and what they had done with their lives; the usual first steps taken by strangers in getting to know each other. It was when Astrid made a casual reference to having lived as a child in Meran, Italy, that Volmer drew the connection.

"You lived there? When?" Flashes of cemetery headstones and the scent of gardenias formed in his mind.

The abruptness and intensity of the two questions momentarily startled her. She took a slow sip of espresso before responding, studying his face. "During the final years of the war. If memory serves me correctly, my mother and I were there from nineteen forty-three until nineteen fifty."

"I, too, lived in Meran during the forties and early fifties," Volmer replied quickly. "My father insisted that my mother and I leave Munich as the war came closer to Germany."

Thoughts of his father brought other, darker recollections: the many nights when his strong military fingers slid like serpents beneath his pajamas and fondled his penis ... his father's warning that he not make a sound, lest the enemy find and kill them ... the tears that soaked his pillow ... the constant fear of the returning fingers and the stinging admonition, "to make your soldier strong and big." Above all, he had continually wrestled with deeply seated feelings of guilt that he had somehow failed his adored father.

Astrid took a quick glance in the direction of the kitchen. "I'm puzzled. The name Gatti ... is it not Italian? How was it that your family was living in Munich at the time?"

Volmer was seldom caught off guard. He made it a practice to always be prepared for the unexpected. For a moment, he felt like he had been snared by a gaff, like a fish that had been pulled to the side of a fisherman's boat. Survival gears kicking into gear, he laughed before drinking the last of his espresso, gaining a few precious seconds with which to fabricate a response that would cover his error. "My mother took the name shortly before we left Germany." His face showed no expression. "She believed it was best to do so."

He observed a slight frown form on Astrid's face. "Let me put it this way," he added with an avuncular smile as he placed his hand on hers, "I was perfectly content with the new name. As my father was an ardent Nazi, a member of the SS to be precise, I felt ashamed to carry his name."

Her reply was swift. "I can readily identify with that. My father was with Rommel's Afrika Korps. He died in the Second Battle of El Alamein in 1942. It was a terrible time for us, as well." She hesitated for a moment and then asked, "The family you and your mother lived with in Meran ... do you recall the name?"

Volmer smiled. "Certainly. Bernard and Heide Thum. Don't tell me you knew them?"

"Knew them? Bernard Thum was my uncle, my mother's brother! We went to their home frequently. They lived next door to a large church."

The connection blazed like a white light. Memory fragments floated past his eyes, none staying long enough to grasp. A church near a cemetery, a large bank of swings near a statue, children everywhere. "The church? Do you remember its name?"

"St. Nicholas," she replied. "When I was older, nine or ten, perhaps, I played on some swings near the cemetery."

Volmer's mind began to give form to vague recollections. "Yes, I remember those swings. We could have played together. I also remember a girl in a dark blue dress with white stripes. Her hair was in ribbons ... red, as I recall."

"*Mein Gott!*" Her hand flew to her mouth. "I had a dress just like that. It was my favorite." She paused. "There was a boy not much taller that I."

"That could have been me," Volmer replied, unable to restrain a soft laugh. "I've never been much taller than anyone."

She looked deeply into his eyes as a warm glow covered her. "I do remember being at first so frightened of the boy. He seemed so much older, so much wiser." Slowly, the expression on her face changed. "What was your German name, if I may ask?"

He had come to the edge of the precipice. His father's name, Ulrich Brunner, would have meant nothing to her, nor would Volmer, the name his mother took from a packet of Dutch tissues before leaving for Meran, but his instincts told him to back away. He would keep those names in his pocket.

"Bateman," he said without hesitation, recalling the name of an engraver in Munich, a close friend of his father.

She sensed his hesitancy. "Sorry, I shouldn't have asked that question. Please forgive me."

"No harm taken," he replied, this time forcing a smile. "I've never been asked that question."

"I like the name Azzo Gatti." Her tone was soft, respectful. "Should I speak with anyone in Anghiari about you—and I will, you know because you are a charming and fascinating man—I will refer to you as Azzo Gatti." She hesitated briefly. "I like the feel of your warm hand, by the way."

"Good! Then we can be best friends."

"Best friends?" Her scarlet tongue emerged like a serpent from a cave and slid seductively across her lower lip. "I like the sound of that."

CHAPTER TWO

Issues

For Porter Blue and Largo Kopacz, the return from Florence to the United States brought some mixed issues, the most immediate being the resetting of their body clocks, the reestablishment of their respective circadian rhythms. Both encountered sleeping difficulties for the first several nights and neither cared for the taste of their familiar coffee, nor the local wine options that seven months earlier had seemed fairly upscale. After struggling for several days to readapt to Franklin, they came to realize what many visitors to Florence experience: its charm can change lives. Their lives had most certainly changed.

One issue, however, transcended Largo's physical adjustment and that was her deepening anxieties about Theo Volmer. The flowers and accompanying note he had delivered to the Uffizi while she and Porter were enjoying their conversation with interim director Palma had hit her like a violent blow to the solar plexus. They were meeting with Palma in order to finalize Blue's decision to leave the precious gift of Contessina de' Medici's fifth diary with the museum, the book they had stumbled upon just a few days earlier while visiting a bookstore in Siena. Contrary to Italian police reports and especially the Florentine Press, she felt all along that Volmer had not died in the fire in his Fiesole home.

It was more than a feeling. She had seen him after the fire; she was certain of it. It happened near the Santa Maria Novella station in Florence while she was on a morning run. It was a matter that she chose not to raise in her conversations with Blue, for she knew he held his own painful and troublesome associations. Although halfway around the world from Florence, her deepest fear was that Volmer would reenter her life at some point, that somehow he would find her and the torment would continue. The intensity of her feelings triggered a long-buried situation, one she'd never shared with Porter Blue or for that matter, with anyone outside her immediate family.

She was eleven at the time. The year was 1973. Her family lived in the south Pittsburg community of Bethel Park. The Thanksgiving holidays were approaching and members of her class were putting the final polish on a short play scheduled for the last day of classes. As her home was a short distance from the school, Largo and her best friend Kietha Miller usually walked home together. On this particular day, Monday, November 19, Kietha had to leave school early in order to accompany her parents to the viewing of her Aunt Edna and the funeral services at the Westminster Presbyterian Church.

Largo left the school about four-thirty for the twenty minute walk home. About halfway there, she was aware of a man in a dark brown overcoat walking a comfortable distance behind. At first, she thought little of his presence, but within a few minutes he had closed the distance between them. As she began walking faster, he quickened his pace.

"Don't run, Largo," the man called out. "It's me, Mr. Beane. Let me walk the rest of the way home with you. I'm not sure it's wise for a young, pretty girl to be on these streets alone."

She quickly recognized him. He was the choir director at their church, a quiet man in his forties but looking much older. Her mother, a veteran member of the choir, had said only good things about him. Largo stopped and waited for him to reach her. He lived two houses down on their street.

Beane was not a large man, at most about five-ten with thinning hair and a splotchy complexion that gave the impression that he was sickly. His thick lips always seemed wet, as if he had just licked them. "There, that's better." Beane wheezed slightly as he neared her. "You don't mind a little company, do you?"

"No, sir, I guess not."

"Good! We can have ourselves a nice chat."

She had not said much during the walk. Just before parting, Jasper Beane touched her on the arm and asked, "Do you usually walk to and from school alone?"

"Sometimes."

"I take my afternoon walk along this very street," he continued, "but I don't recall seeing you at this time of day."

Largo was feeling increasingly uncomfortable in his presence. "It's usually earlier."

"Of course," Beane replied. "I prefer the late afternoon."

It happened again several days later after the Thanksgiving holidays. This time Kietha Miller was with her. Largo noticed him when Kietha stopped briefly to tie her shoe. "Do you know Mr. Beane?" she asked.

"You mean the creepy, old man?"

"Yeah. I don't really know him. My parents do."

That evening over dinner, Largo told her parents about her recent dealings with Mr. Beane. "I think he's weird. I don't like being around him."

"That is totally absurd," her mother replied. "Mr. Beane is a respected man of the community. He's the choir director, for goodness sakes."

Her father looked up from his plate and volunteered, "You should be ashamed of yourself, Largo. I hope you did not show such an attitude when you were with him."

It was later in November after parting with Kietha, that Largo entered her home and found a brief note from her mother.

Hope school was good today. Fix yourself a snack and I'll be back soon. I'm over at Margit's, helping her with some things for the school bazaar.

The Kopacz home was a modest split-level dwelling built in the fifties. The front entrance opened to a flight of six carpeted steps that led to the lower level and the back door. After Largo processed the brief note, she put her books down on the sofa and started walking in the direction of the kitchen. As she did so, she heard something from the lower level that sounded a bit like a muffled cough. She walked back to the stairs and saw Jasper Beane, standing near the base of the stairs. "What are you doing here, Mr. Beane?" Her voice reflected her mounting anxiety.

"I've come for a little visit," he replied as a polished black shoe appeared on the bottom step. His left hand was clutching the railing.

"Please don't come up here, Mr. Beane. Please go home."

"Just a little visit, Largo." His feet were now on the second step.

From her position, she could see the fireplace and rack of metal tongs on the hearth, just a few paces to her right. She quickly grabbed the poker and returned to the top of the stairs. Beane was now one step away from the top level and had a clear view of the poker.

"Be a good girl, Largo, and put that down. Don't do anything foolish."

Without thinking or weighing the consequences, she lashed out at him with the poker, striking his right shoulder.

Beane cried out in pain and stumbled down the stairs. Before she could think of what to do next, he bolted from the back door.

Trembling with fear, she sat on the top step for several minutes, both hands gripping the poker. As she had done earlier, she told her parents that evening about this most recent incident with Jasper Beane.

"You must stop this right now, Largo!" Her father's anger was palpable. "I'll not have any more of these slanderous accusations, is that clear?"

"But look at his shoulder, Daddy! Go look at it."

Her father scowled at her. "I'll do no such thing. You go to your room, young lady, and pray to God to forgive you for saying such terrible things. Lying like this...well, it's simply reprehensible!"

Largo went to her room as directed, but as for seeking God's forgiveness she had no intention of doing so. Her mother and father, Jews by ancestry, left the synagogue when she was a child. The family joined the Presbyterian Church, less out of religious convictions than social opportunities. True, she might have said some less than kind things about Mr. Beane, and she had popped him with the poker, but she was not about to ask for God's mercy. Beane was the sinner, not her.

Assistant choir director Jacopo Panela presided over the next practice. When Largo's mother discreetly asked him if perhaps Jasper Beane was ill, the man's reply had startled her. "He called a few days ago to say he was leaving Bethel Park for a few days, something about a last minute decision to visit his sister in Texas. It seems he'd taken a bad fall and had injured his neck, or shoulder, something like that."

The disturbing incident burned a hole in Largo's young psyche. Mr. Beane was never again discussed in the home, although Largo's mother soon started picking up the girls after school. As she told Mrs. Miller, Kietha's mother, "It may be silly, but I just feel better about keeping our girls out of harm's way."

Even when Largo reached her adult years, her surveillance of her surroundings continued in high gear. She was consciously on guard for men like Jasper Beane. The mere mention of words like *stalker* and *predator* carried chilling connotations.

Another matter confronting Largo and Blue was where they should live now that their Italian adventure was over. It had been one thing for her to join him in Italy during Balfour's spring break; another altogether for them to return to the conservative college in middle Tennessee and continue their intimate relationship in his home. He was, after all, a professor and she was still a graduate student. Aside from a small element at Balfour—Blue's closest friends and colleagues—most of the faculty and most certainly the administration could be expected to hold critical positions on such a relationship.

Largo was visibly upset. "Well, I, for one, don't give a rat's ass what the people at Balfour think. If we love each other, I don't have any problems with sharing the same bed with you. Just because most of your colleagues are past sex, doesn't mean we can't enjoy ourselves. It's not like we're under age, for God's sake."

Blue shared her perspective, but he also knew the mindset of small, Southern towns like Franklin. Cohabitation outside of marriage was not exactly looked upon in a charitable light. She was only a semester away from completing her master's degree and would not be taking another course from him, but the most pious of the town's moralists could and likely would make life difficult for both of them. Blue was quick to say he was on her side, but Largo was not totally convinced of that. They decided they should begin looking for new quarters before the fall semester got underway.

Upon their return from Florence, Largo took the first steps in contacting each of her professors to find out what she had to do to resolve the grades of incomplete she'd received at the end of the previous semester. Her ethics and philosophy professors had been most understanding and gave her the assigned projects she would need to complete in order to resolve the matter. Both told her that she could have the remainder of the summer to complete the work.

The lone obstacle in the matter was Dr. Roberta Summerhill, the senior professor of Art History under whom Largo had been taking an independent study course on Coptic painting. A staunch evangelical, Summerhill's views on pre-marital sex had long been chiseled in stone. She had not known bedroom pleasures before her marriage thirty years ago; ergo, no woman should, certainly not one of her students.

Those faculty in the Balfour inner circle suspected that Summerhill had not enjoyed such pleasures since 1971 when her husband Devon left Balfour College with the secretary of the Biology Department. When Largo called her from Florence the previous March to explain her circumstance and to request the incomplete grade, Summerhill was not thrilled. "Are you calling to ask me if I will condone such immoral behavior, Ms. Kopacz?"

"No, Dr. Summerhill, I'm not asking that at all. I'm calling to request a grade of incomplete so that I might handle an urgent personal matter that has arisen here. I will promptly make up my assignments upon my return." Summerhill's stinging indictment of her moral character prompted a closing post script. "My personal life, if I may say so respectfully, is none of —"

"See me when you return to Balfour. We will discuss the matter at that time." Before Largo could counter, the indignant professor hung up the phone.

"Bitch!" Largo had screamed into the receiver before throwing one of her sandals across the room, narrowly missing a vase of sunflowers.

Largo met with Summerhill in Balfour's Grayson Hall five days after returning to Franklin. Earlier that morning while reviewing her remaining degree requirements, she saw that a grade of F had already been assigned. She called Summerhill, requesting an appointment to discuss the situation. With reluctance, the professor granted her a ten minute session, her schedule being too busy to provide more time.

After Largo respectfully asked for an explanation, the professor replied curtly, "Your academic interests are best served by repeating the course. I had no alternative but to register a failing grade for the semester. Now I really must bring this discussion to a close. I'm expected in the chairman's office in five minutes." Summerhill closed the meeting by summarizing her reasons for assigning the failing grade. "In the long run, you will appreciate my judgment here."

As Summerhill spoke, Largo noticed three framed Teacher of the Year citations hanging on the wall behind her teacher's large, leather chair. The irony was striking. She composed herself before opening her mouth. "Your decision has nothing to do with my academic interests, Dr. Summerhill."

"I beg your pardon!"

"This is about my sleeping with a Balfour professor. It goes against your spiritual grain. Why don't you just say that? Why can't you be honest with me?"

"Well!" Summerhill continued with a grand show of indignation, "Let me just say this, young lady, Dr. Blue would do well to study the Balfour Faculty Handbook. At this institution we have our standards."

"How dare you take such a judgmental position with Dr. Blue!" Largo thundered. "He did not force me to go to bed with him. I'm thirty-four years old, Dr. Summerhill, not some naïve, nineteen year co-ed who thinks nothing about swapping sexual pleasures with a teacher for a good grade. My sex life is my business and most certainly none of yours." Largo rose from her seat and walked towards the closed office door. Just before grasping the knob, she turned and looked at her professor before hurling a final dart: "You must be so proud of your teacher of the year awards, Dr. Summerhill. Having had the opportunity these past few minutes of experiencing your high degree of professionalism, it is no wonder you are considered such an asset to this department." She walked out of the office, leaving the door wide open.

"Close my office door," Summerhill barked.

"Close it yourself!" Largo countered, not caring whether Summerhill heard her, or not.

As she walked down the hallway, Largo realized that the independent study course would have to be repeated in order for her to meet the hourly requirements for graduation in the spring, but it didn't have to be on Coptic painting, and it most certainly didn't have to involve Roberta Summerhill.

But there was a larger academic issue confronting Largo than mere graduation. During her time in Florence, surrounded by some of the world's most significant human accomplishments in art, philosophy and letters, she began to give thought to a doctorate degree. She was good, very good, in her field and she knew it. She had an unquenchable thirst for learning and instincts for art that transcended the ordinary. The question was what she would do with her talents and creative energies once she completed her studies at Balfour. Where would she go? What would she do? If she wanted to teach or do research at the university level, the PhD would be a necessity. One problem with such thinking was that Balfour did not offer the advanced degree and even if they did she would want to go elsewhere for it. She'd seen too many students go straight from a baccalaureate degree to a masters, some even staying in place for their PhD. Where was the growth and experiences between each level of study? That was more like seven or eight years of college.

She was determined not to travel that road. She wanted her mind to expand with new experiences and more challenging academic demands. There were a number of fine institutions in the United States where she could realize a doctorate on her terms, but one place kept cropping up when she thought about the subject: Krakow. She could go to Poland and study at the Jagiellonian University. She'd spent time in the library researching the venerable institution.

The Jagiellonian was the second oldest university in Central Europe, first opening its doors in 1364. A smile came to her face when she read that Copernicus had studied there. The international value of such an educational experience could be enormous. While not fluent in Polish, she commanded an acceptable base. She would be able to pick it up quickly. Krakow was not only the site of the Jagiellonian, but it had been the home of her great-grandparents before they were herded off to Auschwitz and gassed by the Nazis.

Such thoughts, however, triggered a second, more complex problem: Porter Blue. Living on separate continents was not the best way to deepen a relationship. And there was the rub; did she see a future for them or, for that matter, did he? It pained her to even consider it, but was that what either of them wanted? She was very happy with him. She certainly respected him, and the sex had been good, but was she—were they—confusing love with infatuation? Did they have enough in common to sustain the kind of union it took to go the distance?

What if they married? Would she be content to remain in Franklin and live in his shadow? The thought of another divorce did not sit well, either. She buried the matter for the moment, knowing, however, that it would smolder like a hot coal until the two of them addressed the future. Perhaps right now was not the time for doing that. Nothing had to be done today, but there were bridges that eventually had to be crossed. A lone tear rolled down her cheek as she exited Grayson Hall and headed for her car.

As the oppressive summer ran its course and the fall semester approached, Largo completed the work for her incomplete grades while Blue struggled to bring his novel to completion.

On the advice of a colleague in the English department, Blue placed a few chapters of his manuscript with a woman in Nashville with strong editing credentials. Gretchen Michaux was not at all like the woman he'd envisioned when they initially talked by phone. For one thing, she was considerably younger than he expected, scarcely a day over thirty. For another, she had a gritty voice, a way of expressing herself that carried a layer of toughness. Listening to her speak, he found it hard not to draw a parallel with the raspy voice of Lauren Bacall. The woman was not pretty in the conventional sense of the word, but she had striking blue eyes to go along with a voluptuous body. By the end of their first meeting, she had impressed him as someone who rarely stood on formality, someone who knew how to have a good time and someone who took little crap from anyone, especially men.

A week or so after leaving the first two chapters with her, she called to provide her first impressions. If he was expecting gushing praise from her, he didn't receive it.

"I finished the material you left with me. It has a strong academic flavor—there is no mistaking the fact that you are an art historian—but I found that your way of presenting your story prevented this reader from feeling a part of it. There is an old axiom in our profession, Porter, 'Show, don't tell.' Put simply, give your reader more dialogue between your characters. Let us hear their voices."

She absorbed his uncomfortable silence, surely knowing from experience he was not prepared for her initial findings. "What I am trying to convey is that sometimes it is not a matter of what you are wanting to say as much as it is how you are saying it, if that makes sense. You know your material, there is no question about that, and the story line is quite interesting. I believe it has all the makings of a wonderful read. All I am saying is that the first words we put to paper are not always the best words to use. The bottom line is this: Good writing is rewriting. It's as simple as that."

Blue struggled for a long moment before he could respond. He expected her to find some rough edges, but he was not prepared for such a blunt salvo at the start. "I can't quarrel with your criticism. Most of my past writing has been non-fiction, so I suppose I relied too much on that approach. I hear what you are saying."

"Let me make a suggestion. Why don't you re-visit these first two chapters and get back with me when you've done so. If you're comfortable with letting me look it over, I'm only too happy to do that."

For two weeks, Blue sat on proverbial pins and needles as Gretchen Michaux reviewed the revised chapters with a fine-toothed comb. On a steamy September morning, she called to tell him she had completed her work. "I would like for us to find a time of mutual convenience to discuss your work. Overall, I found it quite improved, but a few passages here and there probably need more attention, uppermost among them the title. *Contessina's Diary* is about as bland a title as I can imagine. It sounds like *The Cookbook*, or *The Telephone Directory*. You'll need something with a bit more spice, if you want to draw a reader to this book, especially a woman."

"My schedule is fairly open right now. Once my classes get underway, things will tighten up. Why don't you look at yours and pick a date that works for you."

Her reply was registered with little hesitation. "How about ten o'clock Thursday? That's the nineteenth. Will that work for you?"

Blue quickly scanned his pocket calendar. "I can do it in the morning. Where would you like to meet?"

"My office, if you are agreeable."

"It works for me."

"Good, I'll look forward to seeing you."

Thursday, September 19

Largo arose early and slipped into her running shoes, careful not to awaken Blue. On Tuesdays and Thursdays, his first class was not until one o'clock. Her only class of the day was an hour later. The forecast called for a hot day and if she was to get her run in, she needed to do it before things heated up. It was already sixty-two degrees and a quick glance at her bedside clock told her it was just six-thirty.

In the early morning light, she could see the small Memling painting next to her bed that had once belonged to her Polish great grandparents. Hermann Göring's thugs confiscated it in the late 1930s along with their modest art collection. It was finally discovered in a Stuttgart warehouse earlier in the year. Uffizi curators in Florence had crated and shipped the painting to the Atlanta High Museum. They had been happy to serve as the receiver of the valuable fourteenth century painting, thereby minimizing issues with customs until Largo could retrieve it. Reflecting on its tortuous journey over time from the Netherlands to Krakow and then to Tennessee, she took daily comfort in its presence. It was like talking with her deceased ancestors. They had given the world her grandparents and her own father who, in turn, gave her the breath of life.

She knew even before leaving Italy that the day would come when she would have to part with the valuable and fragile painting of men at prayer. Her decision to gift the Memling to the Atlanta High Museum came after a lot of soul searching, but the fingers of practicality actually pushed the button. When she and Porter decided to hang the work in their home, they were astonished at the cost of insuring it. A simple rider to Porter's home policy cost them several hundred dollars a month, not to mention the cost of installing a top of the line security system. And there was more; a five hundred year old painting needed a controlled environment in which humidity and light concerns could be constantly monitored. A private residence in humid middle Tennessee hardly provided such care.

After discussing the matter at length with Blue, both agreed that a reputable museum was the best place for the picture. The Atlanta High Museum had been kind enough to assist her in getting the painting to the States, so it seemed only right to ask them if they were interested in one day acquiring the work. One good thing about that was proximity; it would be close enough for her to visit it frequently.

Initial discussions with the museum had been very encouraging. Its director, Norman Geller, had voiced an immediate desire to have it. "I'll not only assure you that it will be well cared for, Largo, but we will display it with all the respect it deserves. It will become the centerpiece of our European collection."

It was important to Largo that he not misunderstand her offer. "While I know it deserves the care that only a museum can provide, I am not yet ready to part with it. That time will probably come near the end of the summer."

"Of course," Geller replied. "You take all the time you need with this. We are just thrilled that you would consider us."

"When you do receive it, there will be one condition."

"Certainly, and what might that be?"

"At some point in time, I would like for the picture to be placed on loan to the National Museum in Krakow. I have very strong personal reasons for insisting on this. The work was stolen from the home of my great grand-parents by the Nazis."

"They lived in Krakow, I presume," Geller replied solemnly.

"Yes. I owe this to them."

"Then rest assured, we will not only be happy to comply with your wishes, but at the appropriate time we will initiate dialogue with our Polish counterparts, if you desire. Such a connection can only be good for both museums."

"Thank you. I will get back in touch with you as soon as I am ready to release it."

Geller smiled. "Largo, the Atlanta High Museum has been here for over ninety years and barring a disaster of some kind we'll be here when you are ready to part with your treasured painting. Take all the time you need."

Porter Blue's follow-up conference with editor Gretchen Michaux went well. Her criticism of his title was softened by the words of support she had for the manuscript. "Your story evolved nicely from a juvenile romance to a powerful inside look at key personalities of Renaissance Florence. I was able not only to understand but to empathize with the tragic life of Lorenzo de' Medici, to see the father and not just the skilled politician. If I may say this without offending you, Porter, I had not expected such a tender story from an art historian. Most historians are so goddamned dry."

"I appreciate your comments in that regard," he replied. I wanted the story to have the historical setting, but I was far more interested in the characters and their interactions with each other.

"Ah, yes, the characters," Michaux spoke with a charming lilt. "Would you like to know my favorite?"

"Certainly." Blue smiled for the first time.

"Contessina, hands down. I wanted to put my arms around her at times and comfort her, especially after her father died and she had to proceed with her wedding to Piero Ridolfi, and what a shit he was! You did a masterful job of crafting him, but I just hated him to the bone. As for Michelangelo, I had trouble at first comprehending how a boy of thirteen or fourteen could possess such talent. However, the deeper I got into the story, the more I connected with him. I thought the way you colored him in the final part of the story was special, the way he concealed Contessina's most private diary behind one of the walls in the papal apartments. I came to feel really sad as he approached his final days." She folded her hands and brought them to her chin in a reflective way. "You made some nice improvements, Porter. My problems with your story are few, mostly surrounding grammar and typos, easily fixed concerns. I've made notations throughout the manuscript. I do want to commend you on your syntax. Except for a few passages, and I've noted them as well, the pace of the story is very effective. Let me ask you," she asked, shifting the focus of her remarks, "what do you plan to do now with your story?"

The question brought a momentary flush of embarrassment. "Ideally, I'd like to get it published, but what publisher would be willing to gamble on an unknown author like me? I mean, my name doesn't have the clout of a John Grisham or a David Baldacci."

"You're absolutely correct about that," she replied. "Publishers these days are not inclined to drop big bucks on novices like they used to do in the past. Were this fifteen or twenty years earlier, your chances of snaring a lucrative contract would be much better. But times have changed; you're absolutely right about that." She saw the muscles at the rear of his jaw ripple and the look of defeat in his eyes. She knew the course of the conversation had not been an easy one for him to process. "I'm giving a little party on the evening of September 24th, a Tuesday. I wonder if you and your wife would like to attend? A dear friend of mine, a well-known New York literary agent, by the way, will be there. Perhaps you and he could chat over a drink together. I have the feeling he would be willing to read these initial chapters of your story, especially if I tell him he has no choice in the matter. What do you say to that?"

"I'm not exactly married," he said, "but we would like to attend."

"So, then, you are currently involved with someone?"

"Yes."

"Man or woman?"

"A woman, of course." He thought about defining Largo as a former student, but stepped away from that. "I have a girlfriend."

"Then bring her, by all means! What's her name?"

"Largo, Largo Kopacz."

"My, what an absolutely beautiful name. Is she?"

"I beg your pardon?"

"Beautiful. Is she?"

Blue smiled. "I tend to think so."

"Then I shall look forward to meeting her."

CHAPTER THREE

High Risk/High Reward

Friday, September 20
Anghiari, Italy

As the verdant valley below Anghiari changed to shades of brown, Volmer carefully cultivated his relationship with Astrid Borgmann. The warm days of early fall were peaking in cadence with their developing relationship. What began as quiet talks in the bar of The Verrocchio soon gave way to more private moments and more substantive conversations. On those rare days when she could get away from the restaurant for an afternoon and evening, they took day trips to nearby villages; charming places like Lucca, San Gimignano and Siena. It was in San Gimignano that they spent their first night together.

For Volmer, the most refreshing thing about these excursions with Astrid was the return of satisfying sexual intimacy. Thoughts of Dona Albrecci hovered in his mind during these moments of love-making, taunting him relentlessly. The fear of another erectile catastrophe always lurked in the shadows. While those first few times triggered anxiety on his part, he began to relax in Astrid's sensual presence. It felt like old times. He wanted to believe that the meds he had been taking recently had helped. All he knew was that he was back in the saddle. As her trust in him grew, she gradually opened like the petals of a flower and he drank the nectar. Once again, sex became a positive, not an intimate moment to be feared.

One afternoon in Cortona while looking at Fra Angelica's *Annunciation* in the Museo Diocesno, she surprised him with a question. "Why is it you've not asked me why I live alone? Everyone else in Anghiari wants to know that."

"I assumed you would tell me when you were comfortable in doing so," he replied, letting his fingers explore the surface of a nearby marble carving. He luxuriated in the varied tracks left by the sculptor's chisels, feeling as if he were touching the very breath of the carved figure.

"I was married before coming here." Her words floated in, as if from a far-away voice. "My husband Fritz died in 1987."

"Were the two of you living in Germany at that time?"

"Yes." She studied his face for a moment before continuing, "There is something I need to tell you about Fritz."

Volmer was checking the nails on his left hand. "And what is that?"

"Two years before his death, my husband was involved in a major art theft in Paris."

"Was that by chance the Musee Marmotton Monet?"

"Why, yes, how did you know?"

"I was in Florence at the time. It was all over the news." He failed to add that the celebrated theft—five masked gunmen walking away with nine paintings—caused the Uffizi to carefully re-examine its security procedures. For a moment he was back there, back at the Uffizi. Theft of irreplaceable works of art was a constant concern. Security measures were evaluated and modified at periodic intervals. More than once during his tenure as director, he played the mentally challenging game of devising ways of sneaking something out of the museum; a small Egyptian bronze or a Della Robbia ceramic platter, even a small rug. It would not be that hard to do with just a modicum of insider knowledge.

To prove the feasibility of his imaginative planning capability, an hour before closing time one winter day he dropped in on the lead curator. While the man was momentarily distracted by a telephone call, he picked up a *Temporarily Removed* label from one of the work tables. Ten minutes before the formal closing of the Uffizi, he called the maintenance department and asked for a workman. Five minutes later a squat, balding man arrived at his office carrying a small bag of tools, looking not unlike a doctor making a house call. Together, they walked to one of the fifteenth century galleries where he instructed the workman to remove a small egg tempera painting by Sasseta, an Italian painter considered one of the most important in the Sienese Renaissance. As the man went about his duties, Volmer chatted with a guard whose primary thought at that moment was finishing his day and going home.

The workman gave Volmer the painting and watched as his superior placed the *Temporarily Removed* label where the painting had been positioned. After the workman departed, Volmer returned to his office, draped his overcoat over his left arm and walked out the main entrance with the valuable painting concealed inside. After all, no one would dare question the director.

The following morning, he arrived earlier than usual and placed the painting and a small printed note on the same work table from which he had taken the label. When the assistant curatorial staff started arriving thirty minutes later, one of them noticed the painting and the note saying it was ready to be returned to the gallery wall. The conscientious employee supervised two members of the maintenance staff in re-hanging the work, and no one gave the matter any additional attention.

When the guards made their initial rounds minutes before the ten o'clock opening of the museum on the following day, everything seemed in place. No one had a clue that the small picture had spent the night atop Volmer's bedroom dresser next to a jar of hemorrhoid cream.

"If memory serves me correctly," Volmer said, rejoining Astrid Borgman in her world, "one of the stolen pictures was Monet's celebrated *Impression Sunrise.*"

"There were six Monet pictures, in all," she added with evident discomfort. "Also one by Renoir and another from the hand of Berthe Morisot."

Volmer smiled as he recalled the details of the case. "They were all recovered, as I recall, in Corsica."

"Yes," she replied.

Volmer shifted the conversation back to Astrid's late husband. "How did Fritz die, if I may ask."

"Lung cancer. He had been a heavy smoker."

"He was one of the masked thieves?" Volmer asked, almost casually.

"Yes." She hesitated for a moment and then continued with something of a smile. "You know, it's almost funny now, looking back on those days. Before the Marmottan robbery, Fritz and the others met often at our home to discuss the final details. They were very concerned about leaving evidence behind, fingerprints, and the like. Fritz had read an article in the paper a few days before that meeting about a rape case in England in 1986 that was solved by means of DNA, a relatively new tool in crime fighting. I'll never forget what he said about it, something to the effect that they can identify a person from a single hair!"

Volmer nodded, somewhat surprised by her sudden show of animation. "Yes, DNA opened the eyes of the world to genetic coding."

"But do you know what ultimately led to the capture of the men?" she asked.

"No," Volmer replied, "but I have the feeling you are going to tell me."

"Stupidity! Two years after the robbery, one of the men got drunk in a Munich bar and boasted of the heist. An off-duty policeman heard every word and it wasn't long before all four of them were arrested." She looked away for a moment and then returned her eyes to his. "Fritz would have been arrested, had he not died."

Volmer said nothing.

"Anyway," she continued, "Fritz had been diagnosed with the cancer in 1983, two years before the robbery. He was being treated and we tried to be optimistic about his chances, though in truth my optimism exceeded his. When he first told me about the planned theft, we both wrestled with the moral, not to mention legal, consequences of his involvement and mine as well, if you look at the bigger picture. As he put it to me, 'I may not have much time left. We'll take our cut and see the world, do those things we have always dreamed of doing. It's not like we're planning to kill someone, you know.' When I considered that the paintings would likely be recovered one day and returned to the museum, I had no trouble accepting his rationale. He was my husband. If I was going to be losing him to cancer, I wanted those final memories." She looked away for a moment and then said, "Tell me, Azzo, does it upset you to know that my husband and I were criminals?"

"No, not in the least." He placed his hand on her shoulder and gave it a gentle squeeze. "There are far worse things in life." Knowing that his response might have sounded too cavalier, he added, "I know it's been hard for you."

"Yes, it has been difficult. I've been lonely for a long time." She reached up and put her soft palm atop his hand. "You are a kind and understanding man, Azzo. Your presence these past weeks has been a blessing."

"I enjoy my time with you." He looked at her and asked, "Another delicate question, if I may. Were you disappointed to learn that the thieves were caught?"

She could feel her breathing becoming a bit more forced. "Yes. Why would I not want the others to enjoy the spoils? That might have been wrong of me, I know, but ..."

"You don't have to say anything more. Let us put this subject to rest." He placed his arms around her and pulled her close. "I will be here to support you; how's that?"

"You don't know how much that means to me, Azzo." As they walked out into the sunshine, she snuggled close to him and asked, almost in a whisper. "Will you hold me throughout the night?"

"It will be my great pleasure to do that and more." After walking in silence for a long minute, or two, he said, "I want to ask you a hypothetical question, Astrid, and if you don't want to answer it that will be fine."

"What kind of question?"

"Well, again hypothetically speaking, if I were to come to you next week with a proposal to relieve The Prado or The Louvre of one of its most valuable paintings—say, a prized work by Velazquez or da Vinci—would you consider joining me in the venture?"

"You can't be serious!"

He smiled. "Of course not. I'm just letting my imagination romp in a field of daisies. But think about it. Wouldn't it be fun?" He could feel the tingling needles of excitement at the mere thought of such a daring move. Not since he orchestrated the first of the forgeries in 1964 had he experienced such exhilaration over an idea. His mind returned to that day when he scribbled a diagram of his forging concept. He had drawn an equilateral triangle on a scrap of paper. At the top, he wrote the word artist. On the bottom left point he added the word scholar. Next to the third point, the word technician. For his plan to work, he would need an artist skilled enough to make convincing copies of a wide range of artistic styles. A scholar was needed to provide air-tight provenances and a technician was essential in making absolutely sure that the materials used were in consonance with the materials of the time.

It had worked beautifully. From 1964 until well into the eighties, he had amassed millions of dollars. And he had shown the good sense to dismantle his empire before anyone could connect him with the operation. It was that kind of adventure he craved again. And it wasn't for the money. Like the mountain climber who challenges Mount Everest simply because it is there, he had master-minded the forgeries because he could; all in order to enjoy the sweet taste of adventure. Now at fifty-seven, he wasn't ready to slip into life's slow lane and simply grow old. "High risk—high reward ... think of it!" he added.

A sparkle came to Astrid's eyes.

"We could do it together and then disappear," he said. "We could live the rest of our lives in Buenos Aires, or Jamaica, go to an opera in Milan one evening and then hop on my plane for breakfast in Nice, or Monaco! Make love in the glow of a Venetian sunrise and then walk naked that afternoon on a beach in Greece. How does that sound to you?"

She laughed. "It sounds like you've been in the Chianti!" She pulled herself even closer to him as they walked. "Do you know, I haven't laughed like this in a long, long time. I'd almost forgotten how to do it." She looked away for a moment and then said, "My answer to your question a moment ago was not entirely accurate."

"Oh, what question?"

"You asked if I would join you in a caper like that."

"Yes, but I was only speaking hypothetically. You know that."

"It doesn't matter. I would, you know."

All the while she was revealing her soul to him, he was recalling the days with Sarto Carpaccio, Derek Heath and Ampelio Ragonese when they were filling their pockets from forged paintings. "And I would do the same thing were the circumstances reversed, dear Astrid. Were you to ask me that same question, my response would be an immediate yes."

She squeezed his arm and added in little more than a whisper, "I'm having a lovely time today."

CHAPTER FOUR

Different Twists

Tuesday, September 24
Nashville, Tennessee

Gretchen Michaux lived in the community of Belle Meade, one of Nashville's older and more affluent communities. The rear of her large, Georgian home, set within a pocket of vintage maples, fronted the seventeenth hole of the respected Belle Meade Country Club. On hot summer evenings just before twilight, her husband Wade could usually be found in the middle of the fairway with a small bag of balls harvested from his backyard, his eight iron, and a scotch and soda. For the highly successful insurance CEO, it was his way to unwind after a tiring day in the office. On many evenings, he was content to simply stand on the well-manicured grass and sip his drink, watching the birds dart about in the golden light above the well-bunkered green.

On this particular evening, he had no sooner reached the fairway than he heard Gretchen calling from the back patio; guests were coming and she needed him.

Porter Blue and Largo Kopacz arrived shortly after seven. A valet met the car as it came to a stop near the front entrance. After assisting Largo from the car, he whisked the vehicle to an inconspicuous parking area, but not before palming a crisp ten-dollar bill from its owner.

Largo was at Porter's side less because of a desire to attend, than duty. Two hours before leaving home, they had argued about her expressed need to extend her studies in the field of art history.

"I don't have a problem in the world with your pursuit of the doctorate," he had said, searching for a favorite pair of khaki trousers in his closet, "but I don't understand the rush. Why all of a sudden?"

"It isn't all of a sudden. I've been thinking about this for a long time."

"Really? I don't recall you ever mentioning it before yesterday."

She left the room without replying, leveling a parting shot as she passed through the doorway to the bathroom. "I most certainly have referenced it, but you've been so engrossed in your damned book you haven't heard most things I've said." A moment later, she called out, "You did say casual, didn't you?"

"That's what she said." His voice was flat, like a Kansas road.

The drive from Franklin to Nashville was an uncomfortable one for Blue. He felt very much on the defensive. She was right, he had been spending almost every free moment trying to improve his story and bring it to closure and, yes, he hadn't been paying much attention to her. If she had spoken about the PhD, then obviously he'd not tuned in on it. But she had been on the moody side for several days. Everything wasn't his fault.

"Look," he began with an apologetic tone, "I'm sorry if I've not always been as attentive as I should have been since we got back. I know you have your own priorities and I wasn't trying to be indifferent to them. It's just that ..."

"I know, Porter. The book is important. I'm proud of you for doing it and I want to see it published as much as you do, but I finish up at Balfour next semester. I have to begin making plans for what I want to do with my life. I'm not saying I have to do anything right now. I can put the doctorate on the back burner for now, but we'll have to talk about it soon. Okay?"

"Yes, I promise." He knew that whatever she chose to do with her professional life would mean a separation of some kind.

They were met at the door by Gretchen Michaux, all five feet three inches of her poured, it would appear, into a lime green tank top and white slacks. Not so surprisingly, she was barefoot. She flashed a huge smile when she saw Largo. "You're even more beautiful than Porter said you were! You two come on in. Wade is tending bar out back. Hope you like ribs."

Largo gave Blue something of a smile as they walked past their hostess. "Just what lies have you been telling her about me?" She reached for his hand and gave it a loving squeeze.

The patio was filled with guests, most with drinks in their hands. Wade Michaux spotted them when they stepped onto the patio and gave a big wave. "Get your butts over here. The bourbon is flowing!"

He watched Largo closely as she moved in his direction, her hips swaying in a rhythmic, appealing way. As for the man at her side, he was as attractive as Gretchen had said. They were a handsome couple, a welcomed addition to the party.

When Blue approached, Michaux shook his hand with gusto. "You gotta be Porter," he said, stealing another glance at Largo. Michaux gave her a polite hug. "I'm delighted you and Porter were able to come. Now what can I get you to drink?"

Largo was the first to respond. "I'll have a Chardonnay, please." She glanced around the spacious patio and surrounding garden. "I love your place."

Michaux smiled. "How about you, big guy?" he said, turning to Porter. "Something with a little more kick to it?"

"I think I'll have some of that flowing bourbon, neat."

"That's a serious ass kick, my man!" Michaux replied much more loudly than was necessary. He grabbed Blue's shoulder like a father might grasp the shoulder of a son. "I think you and I are gonna get along just fine!"

For the next thirty minutes Porter and Largo drifted about the patio, meeting many of Nashville's movers and shakers. With the exception of the conductor of the Nashville Symphony, a splinter of a man with enormous ears, most of the men seemed cut from the same cloth; businessmen somewhere in their fifties, most overweight and balding. The women with their facelifts, breast enhancements or reductions and glittering jewelry resembled sorority sisters at their college's thirty year reunion. Just when Porter thought that Gretchen's literary agent friend had been forced to cancel, he arrived at her side.

"Porter and Largo," Gretchen cooed, "this distinguished gentleman is Damon Kirk, one of the most successful literary agents in New York City,"

Kirk's appraisal of Largo approached a leer; Blue stepped between them and extended his hand. It wasn't surprising that Kirk appreciated Largo's toned arms, her raven hair and flashing emerald eyes, but Blue wanted it clear who she was with. "Kirk met Blue's stare with a knowing grin and met Blue's hand with a warm handshake. "It's a pleasure to meet you both." Turning to Blue, he said, "Gretchen says you're working on an interesting book."

"Porter's a very good writer," Largo said, her arm now tightly entwined around his. She looked into Kirk's eyes, knowing that he had been undressing her for the past few moments. She sized him up with little effort: *he loves power and thinks he's God's gift to women between the ages of seventeen and forty.* "The story is quite interesting."

Gretchen was eager to give Kirk some time alone with Blue. "Largo, while these two boys talk, let me show you our modest home. I would very much like your opinion on the new bed linens in our guest room."

"I'm glad for this opportunity for us to chat," Kirk said in the wake of the ladies' departure. "So, you are a writer?"

"I want to think I am," Blue replied, pushing his initial negative impressions of Kirk aside.

"Ah, modesty," Kirk countered, draining his glass. "I'm always a bit suspicious of that in a writer. Why don't you join me while I get a glass of something. I'm eager to hear about this story. Gretchen said it's a romance with a different twist. I like different twists."

They took their drinks to the distant end of the patio, far enough from the others so they could talk. Kirk was the first to speak. "Let me be blunt, Porter, and save both of us some time. I told Gretchen I would read the first chapter of your book. If it grabs me by the nuts, I'll read the second chapter. Fair enough?"

"That's more than fair. I appreciate your willingness to read it."

"Don't misunderstand. This is how I earn my living. It's more than a willingness on my part to read your book. If it's as good as Gretchen seems to think it can be then I would like to see us both make a shit-load of money from it. I can be as greedy as the next guy. Let me put it this way, my friend: I have some very good contacts in the publishing world. It's a cut-throat business, but I know how to play the game. I know where and how to pitch a book, if I like it. You sell me on your story—the title should help—and we'll get it published."

Blue took a deep sip of bourbon as his eyes scanned the spacious great room through yawning French doors. Kirk surprised him.

"I don't blame you, pal, I'd be looking for her too."

"I'm sorry?"

"Largo. I assume you are wondering which prick has zeroed in on her."

"She can handle herself," Blue replied, trying to suggest his thoughts were elsewhere. Kirk was saying exactly what he was thinking. Wanting to make the most favorable impression, he returned to the subject of his book. "So tell me, Damon, if I may speak frankly, assuming you like my story how is the game played from that point?"

Kirk smiled, bemused by the naivete of the professor. "Well, I'll call a few publishers, the ones with whom I've enjoyed successful business relationships. I'll exaggerate the strong points of your story, conceal the weak ones, and tell them if they don't jump on this one, they'll regret it. Of course, most of them will tell me their publishing schedule for the year is booked, but I know where to fish. I'm not worried about finding a publisher, but the key is—"

"I know, you have to like it."

"That's it, dude. Now, if I were you I would get some more bourbon in that glass and rescue that good-looking woman who came with you."

Both Largo and Blue were in a better mood as they left Nashville for the twenty-two mile drive to Franklin. The drinks probably helped.

"Did you enjoy yourself tonight, babe?" Porter asked, his eyes set on the road ahead.

"It was nice. I think Gretchen is cute and very sexy. What's your take on her?"

"She does have nice equipment. I'll give her credit for that."

"Yes, and you haven't tried it out yet, have you?" She saw the oncoming headlights frame his face and reveal the evident frown. "I'm just teasing, Porter."

"What do you take me for?" he asked in a playful way. "Do you think I'm some kind of philanderer, Ms. Kopacz?"

"You'd better not be."

The next mile rolled by in silence. As Blue passed the Franklin city limits, she asked, "You've not said anything about your conversation with Damon Kirk. How did that go?"

"Fairly well, I believe. He'll read a chapter. If he likes it, he'll probably read the whole manuscript."

"And then what?" She struggled to conceal the prickly needles of irritation that she'd been experiencing of late.

"He'll float it by a few publishers. He sounded like he knows the business pretty well."

"I bet he did."

He stole a quick glance at her. "What does that mean?"

"Nothing. If you like him—trust might be a better word—and he delivers, then I'll celebrate with you. I just don't want your hopes dashed to the ground."

"But you believe the book has merit?"

"You know I do. My gut feelings about the man aside, I think he'll like what he reads, Porter. I'll go even further and say that I will not be surprised if your story gets published within the year and that movie offers don't follow. Your book reads like a movie. I think you are on the cusp of making it to the big time, lover."

"I like the sound of that ... the lover part, I mean."

They lay in the darkness as their breathing gradually returned to normal. She knew he would likely be asleep within the next ten minutes. After sex he usually drifted off like a baby. There was no good time to talk with him about it, but she knew as the minutes ticked away that she needed closure of some kind on her desire for a doctorate. Even if he disliked what he heard, she needed to say it. She rolled over in his direction and placed her smooth hand on one of his. His breathing was already making those first few telltale sounds. "We need to talk about something, Porter."

He shifted his position and yawned. "Talk about what?"

"You know, this doctorate thing. I don't want it to be a problem for us. I didn't present it the best way earlier this evening, before we went to Gretchen's. There's something I should have mentioned."

"I'm listening."

"Before you entered my life last December, I had a roommate, one of my girlfriends. Her name is Carol Kramer. I ran into her at the library a few days ago. As we were getting up to speed with each other, she mentioned that she was dating an assistant professor in the Art Department at Vanderbilt. It sounds like she's pretty smitten with him."

"And what does all this have to do with a doctorate?" Another yawn.

"I'm getting to it. Carol said that her guy was recently bitching about his teaching schedule. It seems he had to give up a favorite drawing course and take on a new section of art appreciation in order for the department to handle the increase in demand. Anyway, he told her that the department is going to be hiring one or two adjunct faculty next January to cover these courses. She urged me to apply for one of the positions. I've given it some thought and think it might be good for me to do it."

"Yeah, you could teach a fine course."

"Here's the way I see it," she continued, pleased by his receptiveness. "It's a short commute to Nashville. I could take advantage of the opportunity to take a post masters graduate course during the semester. The hours would probably help when I do apply for my doctorate. I'd make a little money. I might even take a course in CPR. What do you think?"

Blue was quickly taken back to a night a little over a year earlier. Largo had just arrived in Florence on Balfour's spring break. They had been invited to Theo Volmer's home for dinner. Sarto Carpaccio, Volmer's effeminate friend, was there. Shortly after dinner, Volmer experienced a heart-related problem that required immediate medication. Largo was on her way to the powder room, so Carpaccio called to her to get Volmer's meds. "His tablets! They're in his bathroom ... a small green jar." The thought arrived: had Largo not returned with his pills, would Volmer have died? Blue darted around the CPR issue. "Maybe I could toss in an appealing suggestion, one I've been thinking about."

"What is it?"

"Well, we've been concerned about this idea of living together without being married, what people around here might think and all that shit. What if we look for a place in Nashville? I wouldn't mind the commute to Franklin three days a week. We would be spending our days apart, but it might defuse assholes like Summerhill. What they don't know wouldn't hurt them. It might put out the fires."

"You'd be willing to do that?"

"Why not? This will give you a little time to reach a decision on where you'd want to go for this damned doctorate, and when." He laughed. "Just teasing."

"Oh, Porter, that would be perfect!"

"Good, now can we go to sleep?"

"One last thing to say. I know where I want to go."

"Where?"

"Poland. I want to study at The Jagiellonian."

It was really none of Blue's business, but he asked the question anyway. "You are looking at an expensive package."

"I'm not asking you for anything, if that's what you're thinking." A harsh tone colored her words.

"No, no it's not that." Blue quickly realized the insensitivity of his remark. "I just meant ..."

"My grandmother left me some money before she died," Largo interrupted. "Her parents—my great-grandparents—were able to get her and her new husband out of Krakow just before the Nazis invaded Poland. It wasn't a fortune, but it was invested carefully. As a result, I have the means of attending a university of my choice, either here or abroad. I want that to be the Jagiellonian." She hesitated for a moment. "It was Grandma's hope that the Memling painting would one day be returned to the family. I think she would approve of my decision."

"I'm sure she would."

After an uncomfortable period of silence during which Blue realized she was not about to leave him any time soon, he found her hand beneath the sheet and gave it a loving squeeze. "I want you to do what your heart tells you to do, sweetheart. If that means going to Poland, then so be it. I will support you, whatever you decide to do."

CHAPTER FIVE

Teeth Feathers

Monday, October 7
Anghiari, Italy

At first, Volmer enjoyed the dramatic change in his lifestyle. He derived a great deal of pleasure from passing as a local, and the more he realized that he was being taken as a man of Anghiari the more he put himself into his new role; it was all a new game. But as time passed, he grew increasingly irritable and bored. The sudden burst of anger he experienced on the day he left Florence was followed by other days and nights when, for no apparent reason at all, he would experience waves of acute emotional strife. As he tried to explain the feelings to himself, the only plausible explanation was that he was trying to get even with someone for his fall from the pinnacle of power.

It failed to register that the root cause of his discontent was Largo's rejection. For the entirety of his adult life, no woman had ever walked away from his charms. He had been the one to discard his lovers when familiar replaced anticipation. He was the one who called the shots, the romantic playmaker who notched more than one belt with his sexual conquests. Knowing of this developing propensity for anger, he was careful to maintain his composure when in Astrid's company. At times, the torment felt like knives were being thrust into his back.

There was a second cause for his unrest, although impatience was probably a more fitting word. Shortly after settling in his new environment, he began browsing newspapers and the Internet for major contemporary art exhibitions in Europe. In much the same way that he used the 1964 Venice Biennale to find Derek Heath and jump start his long and successful art forgery empire, he once again needed the services of a highly skilled painter. There was one last forgery to make.

Unlike those days in the 1960s and 1970's when he could phone associates or those who owed him favors, he had to continually remind himself that he was officially dead and a loose tongue from any such contact could bring dire consequences. He would simply have to be patient. There was no need to rush. He would find the right artist.

As if Providence was aware of his need, Astrid talked tirelessly during the following week about an upcoming art festival in nearby Arezzo. She had invited Volmer to her home and planned to treat him to a home-cooked meal. "It might not match our Munich Oktoberfest celebrations, but throughout Tuscany this is considered a big deal." She held up the glossy cover of a regional magazine that contained a lengthy article on the festival. "I seldom buy anything, but I love to shop around. Sometimes I find something that I can use in The Verrocchio. Artists from throughout Italy will be there, as well as musicians and highly skilled crafts persons. I think it might be fun." It seemed obvious to her that he held little interest in the festival.

While she busied herself in the kitchen, Volmer poured himself a glass of dark red wine and moved to her small and intimate veranda. On his way from the kitchen, he picked up the magazine Astrid had earlier referenced. He scanned the publication and was about to place it on a nearby coffee table when his eyes fell on an article about one of the featured artists at the festival: Pieter Bajek of Ravenna. As the article explained in depth, Bajek was a person with quadriplegia who had developed into an area favorite. A reproduction of one of his works—a blue heron standing in marsh grass—showed remarkable attention to details. Volmer read the article, concluding with the thought that he should pay the artist a visit. Something about the young man struck a chord within him; he was curious to meet him and see for himself the scope of his works.

Five days later, Volmer rented a new Fiat and under perfect skies they set out for Arezzo. The drive should take less than an hour, giving them most of the day to experience the festival. Volmer knew the outing would bring a smile to Astrid's face and help to push back the noxious subject of her husband's crime and subsequent death. His willingness to attend the outing was sweetened by the article on Bajek. While she was exploring the booths, he would be free to visit the artist and see if he was a fit for his grand plan, the very reason he chose to come to Anghiari in the first place.

The size of the event exceeded Volmer's assumption. Patrons by the hundreds entered the turnstiles, and almost everywhere he looked he saw white tents jammed together like bricks in a wall. Keeping up with Astrid proved difficult, for when she made an impromptu turn to enter a tent he was easily separated by the moving crowd, forcing him to reverse his direction. She could see his level of irritation rising.

"Why don't we meet back here in an hour? I feel badly dragging you along. You can't be interested in most of this stuff." She saw an emergency tent a few paces to her left. "Let's meet back there. It's now ten-thirty. What about eleven-thirty? Will that work for you?"

"I'm fine with that. You have fun. I'll see you in an hour."

For the next few minutes Volmer floated on the surface of the crowd like a leaf, drifting aimlessly but careful to maintain a sense of location. He would, after all, have to return to the medical tent in less than an hour's time. As he neared an intersection between exhibitors, he saw several large paintings hanging on the side of one of the corner tents, each stunning in its capture of detailed realism. He had found Pieter Bajek.

Forcing his way across the lane of pedestrians, he entered the tent to find the most improbable spectacle: the artist, a young man in his late twenties or early thirties, propped upright in a motorized wheelchair, painting an exotic bird on the limb of a tree. The remarkable thing about it all, the paintbrush was clenched between the artist's teeth. His hands appeared to the strapped to the arms of the wheelchair.

An attractive young woman was standing at the side of the artist. "Please come in. Pieter will want to personally greet you."

Volmer took a few hesitant steps in the direction of the artist. As he did so, his eyes went to the canvas. The feathers of the bird and the bark of the tree limb looked so real that he couldn't believe they had been painted. He then noticed a small photograph of the subject taped to the easel above the canvas. It looked as if it might have been torn from the page of a magazine. The detail in the painting far exceeded that in the photographic image.

By slight movements with his head, the artist was able to control a small, pointed brush. He paused when Volmer reached his side and the young woman removed the brush from his mouth. The top end of the brush, Volmer noted, was inserted in a clear, plastic mouthpiece, a mouthpiece not dissimilar in appearance to those worn by an athletes to protect their teeth.

The artist tried to turn his head in order to face Volmer, but his restricted mobility prevented eye contact.

Volmer saw the difficulty he was having and moved quickly in order to position himself within Bajek's scope of vision.

The young man smiled and said, "Good Morning, I'm Pieter Bajek. Thank you for visiting today." A second, more infectious smile followed.

"It is my pleasure," Volmer replied. He realized that the man spoke with evident difficulty, as if the muscles of his throat were resisting basic speech patterns. "Your work is astounding."

The nodding of Bajek's head reflected his embarrassment.

While they were talking, the young woman cleaned the brush in a cup of gray water and dipped the point in a jar of cerulean blue liquid acrylic. When the artist was satisfied with the amount of pigment on the brush, he asked for it.

Volmer watched as she positioned the mouthpiece and he brushed in a faint hint of the blue on the bird's leg. After the young woman removed the brush, he said to Volmer, "This is an underpainting for the bony legs. I'll follow this by dry brushing a blend of magenta and umber to get the desired illusion of skin."

"Fascinating!" Volmer was genuinely impressed with Bajek's skill. He turned his attention to the young woman, now positioned so he could see her more clearly; petite with soft, shoulder length auburn hair and pale blue, distinctly lidded eyes, eyes that reminded him of photographs he had seen of Marilyn Monroe. She wore little makeup, only a trace of lipstick on a small, but nicely shaped mouth that carried a trace of a pout. To Volmer, she was deceptively seductive. "I'm sorry, I didn't get your name."

"I'm Fela, Pieter's wife."

"And I am Azzo Gatti from nearby Anghiari." He hesitated for a moment and then added with an engaging smile, "I'm assuming neither of you is Italian."

She laughed. "No, we are from Poland. Krakow."

"I know Krakow well," Volmer replied, buffeted by thoughts of Largo Kopacz whose lineage had its beginning there. "A beautiful city."

He looked back again at Bajek's painting, mesmerized by the quality of the picture. "Does he always paint his pictures from photographs?"

"He can only work from photographs now. Being confined to this chair makes it impossible for him to work comfortably from nature. I used to pose for him and he did some wonderful figurative works, but that's become quite difficult in recent years."

Volmer's thoughts of a naked Fela glowed. He drew the immediate conclusion that she was sexually starved. "I take it you are no longer posing for him?" The question carried a slight edge of impropriety.

Bajek had been following their conversation. "I'm quite content to use photographs," he volunteered. "The way I see it, I'm luckier than most men to be blessed with the gift for painting. It matters little to me that I have to use my teeth in order to get something done."

Volmer noticed that others had gathered in the tent wanting to see Bajek paint. He would have enjoyed conversing with the talented young man—even more the opportunity to enjoy Fela's scent—but it was time for him to leave. Bajek already had the brush back in his mouth. Before leaving, Volmer turned to her. "Will you and Pieter be returning to Krakow after the festival?"

"No. Pieter is not suited for the climate there. It is much too severe in the winter. We are now living not far from here, in Ravenna, near the Adriatic. In nice weather, we spend a lot of time at the shore."

Volmer could picture her lying on a beach towel, glistening in the sun. "As I am something of a collector, might I come to Ravenna and see more of your husband's paintings?"

"Why, yes of course. We would be delighted to have you do so."

"Then may I ask if you have a card? I would need the address and contact information."

Fela pulled out a small drawer on the lower part of the easel and removed a green and white card. She gave it to him, saying, "*Signor* Gatti, please do not hesitate to contact Pieter. He is always happy to have the chance to show off his studio."

"I will look forward to seeing him again ... to seeing you both again."

Volmer exited the tent and immediately entered the river of humanity. As he secured the card in the pocket of his trousers, he darted around a slow moving woman with enormous ankles, pondering for a moment how she could maintain her balance. He continued briskly in the direction of the emergency tent, humming the strains of Wagner's *Die Meistersinger*. He could not be more pleased with his discovery; he had found his artist.

On their return to Anghiari, Volmer said little about his day at the festival. His mind kept replaying the magical skills of Pieter Bajek and the alluring presence of his desirable wife.

"You're very quiet, Azzo." Astrid's eyes were on the passing landscape. "Are you angry with me for ruining your day?"

"No, no, quite the contrary. I thoroughly enjoyed myself today. I saw some very interesting things during my little walk-around. I was just thinking about the beauty of this part of Italy. Having spent most of my life in cities, I never really took the time to explore the natural splendor of my rural surroundings. We should do this more often. In fact," he said after a brief pause, "I think it might be fun to visit the eastern coastal area, perhaps Ravenna."

CHAPTER SIX

A Glowing Thought

Tuesday, October 15
Franklin, Tennessee

From his bathroom window, Porter Blue surveyed the entirety of his back yard. He enjoyed the first signs of change in the color of the leaves and the hint of browning grass. The maples, among the first to undergo the metamorphosis, were now spotted with dots of yellow-orange and crimson. The stubborn oaks would not be yielding to the pressures of fall for another few weeks. Of the four seasons, the fall was his favorite. He loved the first, crisp changes in temperature, the opportunity to wear sweaters and, of course, the arrival of college football.

On this morning, as he ran the hot water spigot and began the ritual of his morning shave, his state of serenity was jarred by the intrusive sound of his bedside telephone. With a grunt of annoyance, he left the sink and picked up the receiver before it could ring for the fourth time. "Porter Blue," he said, more mechanically than pleasantly.

"Porter, this is Damon Kirk. We met recently at Gretchen Michaux's home. My visit to Nashville is coming to a close. In a few days, I'll be returning to New York."

"Yes, of course," Blue replied with a much warmer tone, recognizing the voice of the literary agent. "Good morning!"

"And a good morning it is," Kirk said. "I read your stuff. Gretchen was right. You're quite a story teller."

Blue smiled as he recalled Kirk's words when they first met. *I'll read the first chapter and if it grabs me by the nuts I'll read the second chapter.* "So," he said with a trace of a chuckle, "the family jewels are a bit sore. I'm glad to hear that."

"I'm ready for another few chapters," Kirk said, choosing not to continue the discussion of bruised gonads. "How soon can you get them to me?"

Blue tried to contain his excitement. "What about this afternoon?"

"That'll work for me. I'll be tied up in meetings until about three, but we could meet around three-thirty for a drink, if you are up for that?"

"Surely. Just tell me where and when and I'll be there."

"I'm staying at the Hilton Nashville Downtown. How about the bar there? It's usually pretty quiet until around four. It's on 4th Avenue, near the Convention Center. Do you know it?"

"I do."

"Good! I'm looking forward to chatting with you about the story. I'm not an art person, exactly, but I'm a big history nut. I'm looking forward to reading some more of the manuscript. Don't forget to bring it, by the way."

"I'll have it. See you later."

When Blue entered the bar, he saw Kirk hunched over a bar stool, in conversation it seemed with the bartender. As he neared the bar, he said, "I see you've gotten a head start on me."

Kirk turned, flashing a big smile. "This is just my first one." Looking back at the bartender he added, "Keep my tab open and add whatever he drinks. We're going to grab a quiet booth." The bartender acknowledged Kirk's remark with a nod. He was much more interested in the closing frames of a televised bowling tournament.

When the two men moved to the distant end of the bar and claimed a booth, Blue handed Kirk a thick manila envelope he was carrying under his arm. "Here's the rest of my story. I hope I haven't kept you waiting." He slid into one of the dark green leather seats. "The traffic was a bit dicey out near West End."

"No problem," Kirk replied. "I've only been here for a few minutes. What's your pleasure?"

"Bourbon sounds good. On the rocks."

Kirk relayed the drink order to a leggy waitress who followed Blue to the booth. "And bring me another one of these."

For the first few minutes, they talked about things unrelated to Blue's book; the recent party at Gretchen Michaux's home and the chances of Bill Clinton defeating Bob Dole in the coming election.

Blue sensed from Kirk's comments that he held strong Republican leanings, so he skirted around the issue of party affiliation.

Kirk's initial impression of Blue was a positive one. Kirk had known his share of writers over the years and, for the most part, they were more than full of themselves, seldom interested in hearing what others had to say. Blue seemed different and he liked that. "Okay," Kirk said, taking a deep breath, "the first chapter got my attention. It needs some work, but I think you might have something here with the story, itself." He paused for a moment and then said, "Before we get into this book of yours, my thoughts and all that stuff, let me share with you a truth I've learned over the years."

"Certainly." Blue began gearing up his defense mechanisms.

"Pitching a story like to this to New York publishers is a little like fishing for crappie in a big lake. There are any number of places where you can stop and drop a line, but if you think you can just go back to where you caught your limit yesterday you're crazy. Crappies are fickle. So are publishers." He hesitated for a moment. "Both Gretchen and I think you need to come up with a different title for your book and I may have come up with something. What do you think about *Tuscan Secret*?"

Blue was not expecting such a question. "I like it," he said, his voice reflecting less than complete approval.

"Well, think about it. The Tuscan part was easy. The secret part of the title is much more subtle and, I believe, more enticing. I got the idea from Michelangelo planting Contessina's diary behind a wall in the papal apartments. It contained the secret of most concern to him and Contessina, the secret he thought would be buried forever." He waited a moment for a response from Blue. When he realized the writer was not about to challenge his suggestion, he took a slow sip of his drink. "I need to tell you something, my friend."

"Fire away."

"I've courted big time publishers and more than a few small ones. Emerging writers like you without name recognition don't stand a chance with the big dogs. That may sound shitty, but that's how the game is played. My recommendation, assuming I have an overall positive feeling about your book after I've read it, is that we approach some of the smaller, more independent outfits that specialize in historical fiction. Your stuff isn't hard core history, but it does provide enough of that to make it appealing. Throw in the romance between one of the world's most famous artists and the daughter of Lorenzo de' Medici and it's a grabber. Are you good with that?"

Blue's brow creased in thought. "I don't know how to answer that question. Until I met Gretchen and you, I didn't entertain serious thought about ever getting my story published."

Damon Kirk smiled. "That's as good an answer as any. Publishers, all of them, even the small ones, are seeing profit margins getting smaller and smaller. That's the downside to all of this. Only the big ones have the jack to launch big promotions and all that jazz." He took a sip of his drink before he continued. "You'll have to cover a fair share of the expenses."

Blue nodded, but said nothing.

Kirk took another quick sip of his drink. He could see the cloud on Blue's face. "Let's say for the sake of argument that I can interest some of the smaller publishers. I know a few in California, one in Chicago and another in New York, Gladiator Publishing. My friend Worth Manion is the head man at Gladiator."

"Tell me a little more about Gladiator." What he was hearing about Gladiator sounded good, but he wanted Kirk to be more definitive.

"They may be small, but they're as professional as they come, believe me. They are one of the good guys. If they gave out a Nobel Prize for ethical and sensitive publishers, Gladiator would get one."

"What do you think my chances might be with them?"

"That depends on how solid your stuff is when Worth looks it over. Based on what I've read so far, the beginning of your story seems to have good bones, but I'm not sure you're ready to make your pitch to them. As the saying goes, you have one chance to make that favorable first impression. My suggestion is that you stay with Gretchen Michaux for a while. She's a good editor. Your stuff doesn't have to be perfect when you knock on Worth's door, but it has to be damned close. If he's willing to take a big chunk of his time to read your manuscript, you want it to leave a good taste in his mouth. At best, he'll still want to put you with one of his editors, but that applies to almost all publishers. The path can be a long one from writing a book to getting it published."

Kirk hesitated for a moment before continuing, wanting to read

Blue's face for his reaction. "Compared with major publishers, their promotional approach would be decidedly more low key; local and regional events—book clubs, libraries, college programs and that sort of thing. It's not likely they would push national or international events. They would put some money into the promotion, but not like publishers have to do with the big boys and girls; none of the flashy tours and that kind of jazz. Only the heavyweights get the rock star treatment."

"So, I'd be covering most of those costs?"

"Yes, something like that."

Blue was less concerned about the size of Gladiator Publishing or the amount of money he might make than with Kirk's blunt assessment of the world of big time publishers. He had not written his story simply to make a lot of money, nor to be popular. He viewed his story like a painter might consider a difficult and demanding canvas. The last thing he wanted was to have some hatchet man come in and dismantle his story for commercial reasons. For him, the choice was easy. "If Gladiator seems receptive, let's put our marbles there."

"*Your* marbles," Kirk replied.

"Yeah, my marbles."

Kirk glanced at his watch His monthly poker game was less than four hours away and he needed to recoup his losses from the previous month. "Get back with me when you're ready to make a run at Gladiator and I'll help make the arrangements. If your story proves to be as good as I think it can be, I'll want to talk with you about courting Worth Manion."

"And if you are not all that pleased with what I'm leaving with you?" Blue asked.

"Then you'll need to find a new agent, I suppose." He dropped a fifty dollar bill on the table and added, "I've gotta piss real bad. I'll be calling you." Before he turned to leave, Kirk asked, "I haven't taken all the air out of your bubble, have I?"

"No. You were candid, and I thank you for that. I need to know how deep the water is." Blue watched him disappear into the restroom, realizing that the next few weeks were going to be long and difficult ones.

Blue reconnected with Gretchen Michaux three days after his

meeting with Damon Kirk. She was open to his request for editorial assistance, but made it clear up front that she would not mince words in responding to his story. If Kirk had reservations about placing Blue's manuscript with Gladiator Publishing at this time, then she was going to double-down and make sure it would pass their litmus test at some point in the future. She also told Blue she hoped he had deep pockets, for her services were not going to be cheap.

CHAPTER SEVEN

An Enigma

Friday, October 18
Ravenna, Italy

The directions to Pieter Bajek's home in Ravenna were easy to follow. Fela had made detailed notations on a map sketch she sent to Volmer. He was already quite familiar with Ravenna, having been there on several occasions during his tenure as director of the Uffizi.

One of his more memorable visits occurred in 1978 when he personally delivered to the *superiore*, the mayor, a fine Cezanne, one of Derek Heath's most successful forgeries. The corpulent politician was so thrilled by his acquisition that he insisted that Volmer join him and his beautiful, much-younger wife for dinner at a fine restaurant just off the Piazza del Popolo.

The evening was capped by assisting the mayor's wife in getting the inebriated man to bed, and then joining the delightful woman in another one. Life in those days, he thought as he negotiated a narrow driveway flanked by towering cedars, had its rewards.

Fela Bajek met him at the door, a forced smile doing little to conceal her distress. "Please come in, *signor* Gatti."

As he passed her, she noticed he was carrying a black notebook that looked like a photo album. "This has not been a good day for Pieter. At the moment he is sleeping, but he gave me explicit instructions to wake him when you arrived. He is so excited about your visit today."

"Perhaps this is not a good time. I'm happy to return when he is feeling better."

"No, please ... please come in. I was just about to fix a cup of coffee. We can visit for a few minutes before he wakes up. I'm sure that when he hears us talking, he'll call for me to come and get him. How do you like yours?"

"Black, please."

Volmer followed her into a small living room and sat in one of two upholstered chairs flanking an old television set. Three vintage lamps provided limited illumination.

She noticed Volmer's eyes exploring the room. "I'm sorry the place has not been picked up. I fully intended to have it all spruced up by the time you got here, but as I said ... today has not been one of our better days."

"No need to apologize. You should see my home. It is always in a state of disarray."

Her smile was one of doubt. "Have a look around, if you like, while I get our coffee. I won't be but a minute."

The walls were covered with Bajek's paintings, each showing meticulously rendered images; exotic birds, leopards and the like, all set in mysterious landscapes. There was only one figure painting, a small one of Fela. He moved closer in order to better examine the brushwork. The likeness was superb. Bajek had painted her with light coming in from the side that carved her delicate features in crisp *chiaroscuro*.

As Volmer often did, he looked for nuances of style that matched up with other artists. It took him only a moment to make the connection. The little picture projected the same sense of silence he'd seen in Vermeer's paintings of figures set in distinctive interiors. Bajek's work lacked the compositional mastery of the Dutch painter, but it was obvious he had taken more than a casual look at Vermeer's mastery of light and the way Fela took it. As he studied Bajek's treatment of Fela's breasts, he was struck by the contradiction—the name Fela in Polish means lucky. To his way of thinking, the name didn't fit her situation.

Volmer picked up on something else while going from painting to painting. Four small paintings were completely different in style and manner. They were, in fact, more professional in appearance. He was examining one of the smaller works—a moody still life—when Fela returned with a tray containing two cups of coffee and a plate of biscotti.

"You don't need to waste your time on that one," she said, placing the tray on the seat of a straight-backed chair. "It's one of mine."

"You are much too modest, Fela. Your paintings strike me as being not only expressive in character, but very well composed. You have had formal training, have you not?"

"Yes, years ago." The three little words sounded a bit hollow. "I attended the Academy of Fine Arts in Krakow. But," she paused long enough to brush a few strands of hair from her pretty face, "I haven't had the time in recent years to paint. I stay quite busy with Pieter."

Volmer nodded, imagining her without clothes. "I can well imagine."

A long moment of silence followed before she spoke. "I should probably take this opportunity to tell you about Pieter. You must be wondering about his circumstance."

"I assume he experienced an accident of some kind, that or an illness."

"The former. Pieter was an accomplished platform diver. It was his passion. His major goal was to represent Poland in the 1992 summer Olympics in Barcelona. One weekend in the summer of '91, he took a break from his training and insisted I join him for a weekend at a small resort near Krakow. While we were swimming near a floating dock, he said we should take off our bathing suits and lie on the boards for some sun." Her smile was radiant. "It was such fun! We were both nineteen, full of adventure." She took a cautious sip of coffee before continuing. "When the sun began to dip low in the sky, we put our bathing suits back on and started to walk back along a narrow walkway that connected the dock with the land. Pieter stopped, cupped his hands around his mouth, and shouted, 'And now, diving for Poland is Pieter Bajek!' He turned and began racing down the walkway and across the dock towards the water. He arched high into the air—in slow motion as it now seems—before disappearing from my view. I heard the splash, but couldn't see him. I waited a minute or two for him to appear on the dock's ladder. Just as I began to grow concerned, I saw two men running towards me on the walkway. When they raced passed me, I heard one of them say, 'He's floating!' By the time I reached the dock, they had pulled Pieter from the water. He was lying on his back and they were administering CPR."

"Your husband injured himself in the dive?"

Her words were softly expressed. "Yes, he struck a submerged part of a piling from an earlier extension of the dock. It caused extensive spinal damage and Pieter ... well, he has been in the wheelchair ever since. He is paralyzed from the neck down."

Before she could say more, both heard her husband calling from the bedroom. "Please excuse me," she said, rising to respond to his call. "We'll be out in a few moments."

Volmer took the opportunity to examine more closely some of Pieter's paintings. As he inched closer to the surfaces, he marveled anew at the extraordinary approach to painting; everything, feathers and all, had been done with his teeth.

Pieter and Fela entered the room just moments later. He was dressed in khaki slacks and a lightweight lime-green sweater. His handsome face beamed as she wheeled him close to Volmer's chair.

"It is so good to see you again, *signor* Gatti," Bajek said, as Fela positioned the wheelchair so that he could make eye contact with his visitor. "I couldn't believe her when she told me you were coming."

"It is a pleasure to be here," Volmer replied, sharing his smile with her. "I've been admiring your work." He paused for a moment. "And Fela's, as well. You are both quite talented."

Bajek glowed with pride. "Fela is a wonderful painter. She is a lot more creative that I."

"I might respectfully argue that point," Volmer replied. "While your styles are quite different, both of you bring a refreshing degree of creativity to your pictures." They talked for a few minutes before Volmer inched closer to the real reason behind his visit. Intuitively, he picked up the notebook and placed it on his lap. "I understand from Fela that you have experienced a difficult morning, Pieter, so I want to be very careful not to overstay my welcome. I have come to your home for two reasons: one, I would very much like to purchase one of your paintings." He looked at Fela. "And one of yours as well, if they are for sale. My second reason for requesting this time with you is to ask if you ever do commissioned work?"

Bajek appeared confused and asked with hesitancy, "Commissions?"

"Yes, paintings done for a client for payment, of course."

Fela sensed her husband's difficulty. "Pieter's work is very personal, as you can see. If he has taken on commissions, I don't recall them."

"Then may I take a few minutes and share with both of you a situation I am confronting? It may hold some financial interest."

"Please," Fela said, studying his eyes while brushing back a few strands of hair, "we would like to hear what you have to say."

Volmers fingers caressed the notebook before he spoke. "A member of my family, a great aunt to be specific, is suffering with Alzheimer's. Her condition reached the point recently where the family had to place her in a facility where her daily needs can be met." It was an outright lie, of course, but he could tell from their reactions that they bought every word. "In speaking with her recently—the facility is in Florence—I asked what, if anything, I could do to make her more comfortable. We had been very close. She said that she would like for me to bring her a small painting that for years hung in her home in Florence, a depiction of men at prayer. It was destroyed in the terrible flood in November of 1966."

Volmer paused for a moment. "But of course, neither of you were even born then." He continued, sharing with them one of his last conversations with his aunt. "She was talking of her worsening mental debilitation—she knew her mind was atrophying—and she said in little more than a scratchy whisper, 'It is my very favorite painting and I want it with me while I die.' I've never forgotten the depth of despair in her voice."

He opened the notebook and removed a color photograph of the painting and handed it to Fela, one of several dozen photographs he had made at the Uffizi while the painting was in his possession. She studied it for a moment and then returned it to him without comment.

"This painting," Volmer continued, "was done by Hans Memling, a late fifteenth century painter from The Netherlands. It is an oil on wood."

It was Fela's turn to be confused. "I'm afraid I don't understand, *signor* Gatti. Are you asking if Pieter can make a copy of the painting?"

"Yes, if he is comfortable working with oils."

"I am familiar with the medium," Bajek interjected. "The only reason I'm not using oil paints with my recent paintings is the drying time required. Acrylics can be marketed much more quickly."

Fela returned to the monetary aspect of the commission. "As you raised the financial issue, *signor* Gatti, we are very dependent on the sale of Pieter's pictures. Pieter receives a small government hardship check each month, but we have no other means of income, other than the occasional sale of a painting. Acrylics allow us to set prices more within reach of the average buyer."

"Then let me be quite specific." Volmer knew the two fish were already in his net. "I will pay Pieter handsomely for the completed picture, but there is one important condition: it must be as accurate and convincing as he can make it. I know that my great aunt will never care one way or the other about this qualitative concern, but it is of the utmost importance to me that the work could pass for the original. I owe that to her. She practically raised me. I want her to truly believe her cherished painting is back in her possession."

Volmer realized that a final issue needed to be addressed. "Should either of you have concerns about what I plan to do with the picture after her death, please put them to rest. I will be happy to return the painting to you, if you would prefer that. Quite obviously, my conscience would not permit me to display it or even try and sell it as an original, not to mention the illegality of such actions. As it would not carry your signature, Pieter, I assume you would not want it to be passed on to others after it has served this purpose. If you and Fela wish to destroy it, for example, I would have no objections at all."

Fela managed a smile. "We would like to consider your generous offer, *signor* Gatti. May we have a few days to discuss it?"

"Absolutely." Volmer rubbed his hands together with manufactured enthusiasm as he raised himself from the chair. "I was serious a few minutes ago when I said I would like to buy a painting from each of you. I assume they are for sale?"

Fela looked at Pieter before replying, "Yes, of course. It would please us to know that our works are in your collection."

"Then let me show you the two paintings I have selected."

After they returned to the living room, he pointed to Fela's somber still life and then to a striking painting by Bajek of two cranes in high reeds. The feathers were exceptionally convincing. "I love both pictures."

Fela conferred with Bajek for a moment before scribbling out the prices for each work on a paper scrap and then giving it to Volmer.

He reviewed the figures impassively. "Your prices are more than fair. I trust you are comfortable with cash?"

She registered an awkward nod in the affirmative. "We thank you."

Volmer left moments later with a painting under each arm. As he neared his car, Fela following, he said, "I would like to call in a few days for your decision. If Pieter wishes to take on the job, I'll provide him with the size of the painting and a few other necessary details." He placed the paintings he had purchased on the ground next to the car and made a gesture with his hands. "The painting is about the size of a medium-sized book."

On his return drive to Anghiari, he mentally revisited the events of the day, quite satisfied with the results. One or two things were very different about this situation than what he experienced with the earlier forgeries. Most noticeably, there was no need for a provenance, the formal bit of paperwork that verified the bloodlines of the painting. For another, he did not have to worry about someone eventually discovering that it was a copy.

Whereas his colleague Ragonese had been quite obsessive in cherry-picking the pigments for their forgeries, Volmer was content to let Bajek select his own materials. In fact, such a course of action all but insured that a discovery would likely be made at some point in time. That was the beauty of it all; the painting Bajek was being asked to execute only had to fool Largo for a short while. Once she realized it was bogus, she would already be in his trap.

From his earliest awareness of the small painting by Hans Memling, Theo Volmer knew it held special importance to his father. While young Theo never fully understood the full extent of his father's patriotic allegiance to Hermann Göring, he was old enough to realize how essential that loyalty had been to Germany's greater cause. He believed, even though his mother tried to convince him to the contrary, that his father was a war hero.

As he grew older, his admiration for his father flowered. When his mother died in 1956 and Theo assumed ownership of the painting, his feeling of possession intensified with the passing years. Of all the stolen paintings that came down to him, it was without question his favorite.

One of the first things Theo Volmer did upon assuming the reins of the Uffizi Museum in February of 1971 was to have the small Memling painting photographed. Whatever his reason for doing so—and it could have been as simple as his desire to flex his new power as director—he directed his staff to take close ups of the gold-leafed frame, even the back of the painting. The wooden panel on which Hans Memling had painted the image had been cross-braced, as was common in earlier times to prevent warping. In those days, framers rarely covered the backside of paintings.

He knew the work had been taken from the home of Levi and Zohara Nowak in Krakow, shortly after Hitler came to power, so it came as no surprise to find a dated label between the cross-bracing that confirmed his assumption that the Nowaks had the work reframed at some point after it came into their possession. Although the name of the frame shop had been partially obscured by what appeared to be ink, he could clearly see an address and a date:

————orski Oprawa Obruzow
Ul. Senacka 3541
Krakow, Poland
11 March, 1931

Next to the label, on the other side of the bracing, was a faded orange sticker about the size of a large postage stamp with four black numerals: 7002. Volmer assumed this was an inventory number, perhaps from the gallery where the Nowaks had purchased the painting. Detailed photographs of these specific particulars were in the black notebook.

As before, Fela met him at the door. "Thank you for coming back, *signor* Gatti." This time her greeting carried less warmth than before. "Pieter and I have discussed your proposal and he would like the challenge of trying to provide you with the painting you desire."

"Splendid! I was so hopeful he would view my offer in positive terms."

Hers was a hesitant smile. "You're catching Pieter on a much better day, I'm glad to say. He woke up at five o'clock this morning, as excited as a young child on Christmas morning!"

"That's music to my ears. To tell you the truth, I had just about given up hope of finding an artist with the skills needed to execute the painting I desire. The two of you make a formidable team, Fela. I have no doubt I will be very pleased by your combined efforts."

"We will do our best, let me assure you of that." She led him through the narrow hallway to the small living room he remembered from his last visit. Pieter Bajek was seated in his wheelchair in front of an easel supporting a recently started picture. He was wearing a lightweight jacket which seemed unnecessary on such a warm day, but Volmer quickly realized that his paralysis probably carried circulation problems. Fela pulled up a chair next to her husband and positioned it so the two men could again experience comfortable eye contact. She then repositioned the remaining chair in the room between Bakek and the window.

After a few minutes of comfortable conversation, she excused herself. "Let me prepare a cool drink, *signor* Gatti, while you and Pieter enjoy each other's company. I won't be but a minute."

Volmer nodded.

The two men spoke in very general terms for the first few minutes before Bajek addressed his confining condition. "Fela said she told you of the accident that led to this," he said, making slight twists with the few muscles in his neck that responded to signals from his brain.

"Yes, a diving accident. How tragic."

"It is what it is." Bajek flashed a hint of a punished smile. "But," he continued with an upbeat tone, "it brought me to painting and that has been my salvation. It took a while for me to gain the necessary control needed to approach detailed pictures, but as you can see I do fairly well at it now."

"You are far too modest, Pieter," Volmer replied. "I know of few painters today who can match your performance, and I'm talking about artists with full use of their limbs."

Bajek basked for a moment in the compliment, before saying, "My only hesitancy in accepting this commission is my ability to fully satisfy your expectations."

Volmer emitted a rare, high-pitched laugh. "I thought for a moment that your concern might be with the price I am willing to pay," Volmer countered. "We've not addressed that if my memory serves me correctly."

"No, we haven't."

"Let me ask you, Pieter, now that the financial issue is on the table, would you like me to speak to that, or wait until Fela returns?"

"Feel free to do so now, if you like. My brain is the only part of my body that functions as it should."

"Well, of course," Volmer replied quickly, "I meant no disrespect."

Bajek smiled. "None taken. You would be surprised, however, at how many people see my physical condition and assume I'm a mental vegetable, as well. I know you were not thinking along those lines."

Volmer clasped his hands together, as in prayer. "For a completed painting from you, Pieter, regardless of its quality, I will pay you 40,000,000 lire. If your painting matches the degree of accuracy and attention to detail I consider essential, I will double that figure. Does that sound acceptable to you?"

For a long moment, Bajek was speechless. "I'm more than pleased with your offer, *signor* Gatti. You are talking about more money than I've made from the sale of all my paintings combined. It is more than generous."

"Wonderful!" Volmer replied, clapping his hands. "Then we have a deal, young man."

Fela heard the clapping as she approached the living room from the kitchen with a pitcher of iced lemonade and three glasses. She looked at her husband before asking, "My, am I missing a celebration of some kind?"

"I was just sharing with Pieter the financial details of my proposal," Volmer offered. "I'll let him fill in the details for you."

The expression on Bajek's face radiated such pleasure that for a passing second Fela experienced an unexpected wave of uncertainty. Ever since the day of the accident, she had devoted herself to her husband's every need, careful always to protect him from any harm. It wasn't that she held any specific reservations about Volmer, but life had dealt them a devastating surprise and instinctively she distrusted anything that seemed too good to be true. "So, my husband, just what are you beaming about?"

Volmer, sensing the shift in Fela's mood, studied her face as Bajek summarized his offer. When he referenced the specific amount, the muscles in her face tightened. It was obvious to Volmer, if not to the handicapped artist, that she did not share her husband's excitement.

"That's a lot of money," she said evenly as she handed Volmer a glass of lemonade. "Why so much for a copy?"

"A fair question, my dear." Volmer repositioned himself in the chair. "I'll give you two reasons, but first something of a confession." He paused for effect. "I am a very wealthy man, Fela. At the risk of sounding boastful, I have more money than I can possibly spend in this lifetime. I'm not married and I have no children or heirs. I intend leaving a substantial amount to my favorite charities, of course, but to think that I might be able to permit my aunt to live out the remainder of her life with this picture ... well, there is no price too high for that." Of course, he never mentioned that his vast fortune came from his art forgery empire.

For Theo Volmer, the essence of a convincing lie was not the deception being created; rather, the skill—the talent, as he saw it—in framing the prevarication. In coloring his fictitious aunt for someone as intuitive and guarded as Fela, he reveled in the layers of nephew love he was able to invent.

However, as he carried out his well-crafted charade, he experienced an unfamiliar emotional sensation as he looked into the eyes of Bajek; a surprising sense of admiration bordering on envy. Here was a man so severely handicapped that life's most basic functions were all but impossible to perform without constant assistance. And yet, rather than languish in self-pity and resentment and blaming others for his condition, he seemed enthralled with the act of painting and the gift for imaginative fulfilment.

By contrast, Volmer's life had been one of privilege, certainly after attaining adulthood. Where had he ever tasted the depth of a passion like this? Not in making his fortune or the conquest of women or even the run of successful forgeries; none of that had delivered such rewards. His eyes returned to Fela. "My other reason for making such a financial offer lies in my hope that your lives may be made more comfortable by the additional income." And then, as abruptly as he had experienced his emotional epiphany, he changed course. "But of course I will be more than glad to downscale the offer to a figure more in keeping with your comfort level. In reality, it makes no difference to me. I can certainly spend the excess money elsewhere."

Fela said nothing for a moment. She walked over to Bajek and kissed him tenderly on the forehead. "I will leave the financial decisions to Pieter. He is the one, after all, who will be doing the hard work."

Volmer shifted his full attention to Bajek. "Very well, I will be sending to you by post a prepared oak panel measuring exactly sixty-three and one half centimeters by one hundred and twenty seven centimeters. It will be backed with ribbing, much like support panels were made four hundred years ago. The surface will have been primed with several thin layers of sanded rabbit skin glue. The top layer will be smooth and white. The only condition I am compelled to make is that the painted surface be free of any brush marks. The package containing the panel will contain a number of high quality photographs. I will ask that these be treated carefully and returned with the painting. Do you have any questions, so far?"

"No, sir."

"As for the time frame, I would like to receive the finished painting by the end of December. Does that pose any problems for you?"

Bajek's head seemed to wobble for a moment. "No, I should have no trouble completing the painting by then." Bajek looked at Fela, expecting her to register approval of the venture. To his surprise and disappointment, she offered no response. "Would you like for me to mail it to you when I finish?" he asked, now more than a little concerned at the unexpected change in Fela's demeanor.

"No, that won't be necessary. I'll be happy to return for it. I would enjoy another visit with you and Fela, if you have no objections to that."

"That would be nice." Bajek's voice sounded tired.

"Well, let me ask you, Pieter, what is your preference on the financial matter? Are you all right with my offer, or do you wish for me to reduce it?"

Bajek wished that Fela would address the question. When it was clear that she had no intention of doing so, he said, "We deeply appreciate your suggested offer. My expenses present a constant problem, as you can imagine."

"Then so be it! I will get the panel prepared and in the meantime leave a few photographs with you so you can begin to appreciate Memling's fine eye. He then turned to Fela. "If you will be kind enough to see me to the door, I will take my leave."

"Of course. Thank you for coming. Your visit has been like a tonic for Pieter."

Volmer moved closer to her as they neared the door. The shift in proximity to her excited him. He could smell the faint trace of perfume. "Your husband is an exceptional young man. If I may say this without offending you, Fela, I would gladly give up every kopeck I own to have a wife as lovely and devoted as you. Pieter is a fortunate man."

For a disturbing moment, she feared he might touch her. She could feel her breathing accelerate. *Surely, he will leave without creating an incident.* To her relief, he did so, pausing only briefly to thank her again for her hospitality.

She watched from the door as he walked away, wondering what he was really like. She searched for the word that would best describe the man who moments earlier had been in their home and placed a treasure at their feet. The word floated into her mind as Volmer turned the distant corner and disappeared: he was an enigma.

That evening as she prepared their meal and Bajek floated on the wings of his imagination, she began to see Azzo Gatti as so many pieces of a jig saw puzzle; charming, gracious, cultured, mysterious, generous, kind and articulate. Why was it then, that he evoked such uncertain feelings in her? As she stirred the pot of potato soup, the answer bubbled up abruptly: she didn't trust him.

On the twenty-second, four days after his visit with Fela and Pieter Bajek, a package arrived at their door. It bore no return address. After opening it, Fela found a folded note from Azzo Gatti taped to a sealed cardboard box.

Please contact me, Pieter, when you have completed the painting. I can be reached at The Verrocchio, a charming restaurant here in Anghiari. One day it would be my pleasure to treat you and lovely Fela to one of the many specialties that tempt me every night. Ciao!

The box contained several items, among them a small wooden panel with an extremely smooth, white surface, a manila envelope containing containing several photographs of the painting, including selected details of the composition.

She glanced at the photographs for a moment before taking the box to Pieter. Removing the manila envelope, she showed him each of the photographs. "These are for you if you are still interested in this commission."

Bajek studied in silence the wooden panel she had placed on his easel. Since the accident at the lake, he had not been able to provide much in the way of family support. Fela had worked part-time where she could, but aside from his infrequent sales—and they brought in far too little for them to make any appreciable advances or climb out of their pit of debt—he knew that Gatti's commission could provide them at least with a chance of escaping the world of poverty that had become their way of life.

Fela was not happy with the arrangement, he knew that, but this was something he could do, something that could help both of them down the financial road and, not insignificantly, shore up his faltering self-esteem. Did not everyone know, did not Fela know, the feeling of complete dependency that had come to characterize his life? Who, after all, would fault him for trying to escape such a sentence? He looked at her for a moment before replying softly, "I don't believe I have any choice. I need to do this."

Fela said nothing. She simply turned and walked away.

CHAPTER EIGHT

A Forced Smile

Thursday, November 7
Franklin, Tennessee

After Largo's class ended at two o'clock, she made the twenty minute drive from the campus of Vanderbilt University to Franklin with bittersweet feelings.

Her meeting with art department chairman Gene Hagen went better than she expected, although she had difficulty following him at times. He was an introvert—she realized that quickly—and when he spoke there were times when he almost disengaged from the conversation. He would stop in the middle of a sentence and look away, as if the action might cause her to disappear, thus allowing him to return to his internal world where all was bliss. After what seemed to her to be a protracted prelude, he offered one of two adjunct positions for the coming academic term in January. He acknowledged a modest salary, so modest that Largo realized if money was the primary reason for applying, she could do much better waiting tables.

But the position did mean that she didn't have to make a major change in her life at this time, one that most certainly would have a negative impact on her relationship with Porter Blue.

Although she had tried to explain to him that a big part of her desire to go to Poland and study at the Jagiellonian was rooted in simply wanting to experience the space in which her great-grandparents had once lived, he had not seemed to fully grasp its importance to her. She knew he was not ready for their relationship to end, so the position at Vandy should alleviate a lot of that tension, at least for the time being. Wanting to see the glass half full, she would focus on the positive aspects of the assignment: the opportunity to teach and that the experience could be invaluable at some point in the future and also, the position had a beginning and an end. It only carried a one-semester commitment. By the end of the semester, she would be free to make the move to Poland. She would walk on Bracka Street and once in Krakow make the difficult drive to Oswiecim and the death camps of Auschwitz and Birkenau. It was a trip she had to make if she was ever to find the closure she needed with the deaths of her great-grandparents.

As she pulled into the driveway, she was surprised to see Porter's car. On Thursdays, he didn't usually get home until after six. He had been surprisingly quiet following his session with Damon Kirk, so she braced herself for a worsening of his mood.

"I'm in the den," he called out, after hearing the front door close. "I've got two glasses of wine, one with your name on it. It's celebration time."

Largo had reminded him that morning that she was going for her interview, so the upbeat tone of his voice did not come as a complete surprise. She took a deep breath, put on a convincing smile and entered the den with her thumbs up. "Just call me professor Largo. They offered me one of the positions."

"I knew it; I knew it," he warbled, meeting her at the door with a big hug. "Tell me all about it."

"There's not a lot to tell. I'll have two sections of art appreciation. They call it art survey"

"Did Hagen say anything about the summer?"

"No; he said nothing about it, nor did I ask."

Blue could not prevent the smile from forming on his face. "What did you think of Hagen? Is he a piece of work, or what?"

"He was a bit obtuse, but underneath his awkward manner he seemed like a nice person."

"Well, I've never met him, but from everything I've heard he's one hell of a painter. His creativity is off the charts."

She wondered for a moment why such a right-brained person like Hagen was assigned an administrative position and the even larger question of why he would even want it. She let the thoughts die. The bottom line was that she didn't care one way or the other. "You're home earlier than usual." She ran her fingers through her long, dark hair, thinking it was about time to re-visit her stylist. "You didn't get fired, did you?"

"No, quite the contrary. Afternoon classes were cancelled so students and faculty could attend a special lecture by Maya Angelou, part of Balfour's Artist and Lecture Series. I'd forgotten about it."

"So you didn't stay for it?" she asked.

"No. I probably should have, but I have a briefcase full of papers to grade. At any rate, it was probably a good thing that I didn't attend. I got back here around two-fifteen and guess who called shortly after I got here?"

"I have no idea," she responded with little animation.

"Damon Kirk. You remember him, don't you?"

"Oh, yes," she replied in a chilly tone. "The schmoozer." She could see his face drop. "And what did Mr. Kirk have to say?"

"He liked the changes I made with the book. He read the revised manuscript and was genuinely pleased with the improvement. He feels comfortable enough now to place it in the hands of Worth Manion at Gladiator. I suppose we'll know pretty soon what he thinks of it. That's why I had the wine waiting." He handed a glass to her, delicately clinking it against his own. "Cheers!"

Her smile concealed the thought: *So it isn't to celebrate my good fortunes at Vanderbilt.* She swallowed a sip of wine and then replied with fabricated excitement, "Why, Porter, that's absolutely wonderful!"

She'd no sooner uttered the words that she regretted letting her petulance show. His book had been a sensitive issue for both of them, but there was no reason to be mean-spirited about it. "Look, sweetheart, I've given this a lot of thought. I know I've shown my bitchy side over your book, but I'm thrilled to death it might be published. I mean that."

"Damon said that if Gladiator buys it we'll start appearances close to home; within the state, then the bordering states and, if everything goes well, end up with some key cities ... Chicago, San Francisco, New Orleans before winding up in New York City.

A wistful smile crept over her face. "New Orleans, did you say?"

"I did. Will you go with me?"

"If I'm still here, I'd love to go."

For Blue, the *if I'm still here,* stung like nettles.

Tears began welling in her eyes. Not wanting him to see them, she turned away and began walking towards the bedroom. "Give me a second to freshen up. I want to hear everything he said." It was all she could do to get the words out of her mouth.

Blue sensed her abrupt mood change, but had no way of fully comprehending the basis for it. He did realize that by focusing on the good news about his book he had essentially negated her accomplishment at Vanderbilt. Had he looked deeper, had he been more in tune with her hopes and dreams, he would have understood that Largo did not view the Vanderbilt position as something to be celebrated, but rather as a postponement of her intentions to go to Poland. At that instant, he felt small and very ashamed.

CHAPTER NINE

Ringing In

Monday, November 18
Anghiari, Italy

Although it had been little more than a couple of weeks since Theo Volmer mailed the supplies to Pieter Bajek, he was already itching to receive the completed picture. His time at Anghiari had about run its course.

He was ready for a more cosmopolitan environment, but the larger reason for his desire to vacate Italy was twofold: Astrid was becoming increasingly demanding of his time and attention. Talk of marriage was becoming as much a part of their time together as pasta. And secondly, always lurking in the shadows of his mind, was the fear of being recognized. He had come to feel that he was sleeping with one eye open. Having given Bajek until the end of December to finish the work, he knew his impatience was unrealistic; still, as the days ticked by he wondered how he was going to process the coming six weeks.

He spent the morning walking the streets of Anghiari. As was his custom during such strolls, he stopped at a small coffee shop and read the daily paper while enjoying a robust espresso. After devouring the front page, he turned to page two and found an in-depth article on ten of Europe's most celebrated private collections of art, among them the Gade Collection in Copenhagen, Denmark.

As the article acknowledged, Anders Gade founded his impressive collection in 1902 while living in Ostende, a collection known for its eclectic selections. Gade not only focused on the upper tier of old masters from da Vinci to Rembrandt, but he was equally at home with the emerging moderns, van Gogh, Cezanne and Picasso. Anders Gade died in 1951, with the keys to the collection passing to his only son Nils when he turned eighteen in 1957.

Volmer first learned about the collection during his early days at the

Uffizi. In May of 1976 when he was invited by Nils Gade to attend a lavish museum reception in Copenhagen for the late British artist, Ben Nicholson—the occasion, a ten year memorial exhibition.

Quite by chance, Volmer found himself in Gade's company near the end of the reception, and within minutes the two men were engaged in museum talk as if they had known each other for years. Gade was openly impressed with Volmer's surprising grasp of museum operations and wondered for a fleeting moment if he might be interested in moving to Copenhagen. He could use someone with innovative ideas and a strong work ethic.

When asked by Volmer to talk about his collecting background and instincts, Gade spoke freely about his first encounter with the world of fine art and its effect on his current philanthropic endeavors, favored among them was Denmark's alarming child pedestrian accident rate, the highest in Europe at the time. "Following my father's death—I was only a child at the time—I soon found myself having to take the reins of the family business. I had developed an appreciation for my father's acquisitions, but my sole interest at the time was music, cello to be particular. My sights had been set on orchestral performance, but that dream came to an abrupt halt when I confronted the magnitude of my responsibilities."

"That must have been a difficult situation." Volmer wanted to give the impression that he too had known the consequence of inheritance. "When my father died during the war, I came into possession of some valuable works of art—nothing on the scale of yours, I must say—but I nevertheless experienced the same kind of required adjustment with my life goals."

Gade registered a sympathetic nod.

"Your collection," Volmer continued, "was moved, was it not, from Ostende to Copenhagen a few years ago?"

"Yes, you are quite correct. In nineteen sixty-nine. There was little to keep me in Ostende. I had always loved Copenhagen, so it seemed perfectly natural to make the move. I purchased two charming eighteenth century townhouses in Nyhavn on the waterfront. Are you familiar with the area?"

"Only slightly. I was there a few years ago, but just overnight. What I recall about Nyhavn is the charming row of colorful buildings by the harbor. I remember thinking that they resembled colorful books on a bookshelf; yellows, blues, oranges—all quite lovely. And the old boats in the harbor," Volmer continued, "I just loved them."

"Yes, absolutely! If you like vintage boats, you will have to return in August. A huge boat festival is scheduled every ten years around the middle of the month. The harbor will be a true spectacle, looking very much like it did in the mid-sixteen hundreds."

"How fascinating!" Volmer chirped.

"As regards the townhouses I purchased," Gade continued, now quite excited by the opportunity to treat his new acquaintance to the richness of his passion, "I had some major renovations done to make the two structures function as one. I do hope you will try to attend the festival."

"I would like to do that, my schedule permitting."

Volmer motioned for an espresso refill as he recalled his return visit to Copenhagen in August of 1986. At the time he was putting the wraps on his highly successful art forgery empire.

Gade treated him to a full tour of the harbor and the city before giving him a complete look at his collection. It was while they were strolling about the galleries that Volmer registered a provocative observation, one that might have seemed out of place had he not been affiliated with a museum and its inner workings. "I am surprised," Volmer began, eyeing a portrait profile of a young girl with a blue head dress, "that you retain so few guards. I would think a priceless collection such as this would necessitate a larger protective staff."

Gade had observed the path of Volmer's eyes and how they lingered on the image of the young girl. "We only recently purchased her. From the provenance, we know that she was painted by Vermeer around 1660 and remained in Dutch hands until 1875, at which time it was purchased by a French industrialist. In 1901, it was sold to a prominent businessman in Ghent. At the man's death, my father acquired the portrait at the estate sale. She is quite lovely, is she not?"

"Yes, indeed. Did the provenance identify the sitter?"

"No, the work is a tronie." Before Gade could elaborate further, Volmer let his host know that he was, indeed, familiar with the term.

"Yes, a seventeen century Dutch term for a painted head not meant to be a portrait of a specific person. How fascinating!"

Gade smiled. "We believe it is one of several studies Vermeer made for *The Girl with the Pearl Earring*," the collector replied, pride flavoring every word. "Surely, you've seen the famous painting in The Hague?"

"Yes, of course. I make a point of doing so every time I'm in Amsterdam. The tilt of the head is very similar." Volmer paused. "Don't you just love the way the eyes look up at you?"

Gade shifted the course of their conversation without responding to the girl's eyes. "As to your comment a few moments ago about our guard staff, we've found that our visitors much prefer us to keep our armed employees as insignificant as possible. In great part, our ability to function with a limited number of guards is due to the renovations we made to the two buildings at the time of purchase."

"Oh, in what way?" Volmer asked, wanting to convey polite curiosity.

"We eliminated several points of entry and egress, thereby minimizing the chances that someone could walk away with our treasures. The heavily barred windows, as you might suppose, do not invite intruders."

"A wise move."

Gade basked for a moment in the compliment. "The biggest improvement we made came at my insistence four years ago when we installed an enhanced electronic surveillance system. That, as much as anything, has kept us quite secure."

"In this day and age," Volmer said, "One cannot be too careful with one's pictures."

Gade was finding Volmer more than a bit charming. It had been a long time since he had conversed with anyone so savvy about museum operations. Intrigued by the fact that Volmer was selected at such a young age to direct the Uffizi, he wanted to capitalize on the opportunity at hand to get to know the man better. Without giving it much thought, he said, "My wife has gone to be with her sister in Aalborg for a few days, Theo. I'm wondering if you would join me tonight for dinner at one of our finer restaurants?"

"Why, I can think of nothing I would rather do. What a kind invitation."

Gade noticed that Volmer's eyes shifted to an attractive woman at the end of the bar. "Excellent! I have a meeting this afternoon with the French ambassador, but I don't expect it to last very long. It's more of a formality."

Volmer nodded politely.

Gade suddenly felt unsettled by his impromptu overture, as if Volmer might not be that interested in Danish cuisine. "I can't promise that our meal will match what you're accustomed to in Florence, but contrary to conventional thinking, our cuisine has improved considerably over the past few years. I don't think you'll be disappointed, at least I hope not."

"I would consider it a privilege to share your company, Nils."

"Good." Gade was relieved to be past the awkward invitation. "Why don't I pick you up at your hotel around seven? You did say you were staying near Nyhavn?"

"Yes, at the Phoenix."

"Of course! It is one of our best. Over three hundred years old."

Volmer nodded. "I was told that when I phoned for reservations."

Gade arrived at the Phoenix just a few minutes before seven. To his surprise, Volmer was sitting in the lobby, his hands folded in his lap. "I trust I'm not late," he said, glancing quickly at his watch.

"No, no." Volmer arose to meet him. "I much prefer lobbies to hotel rooms. It's a deeply seated practice, one going back to my first days at the Thyssen-Bornemizsa. One never knows what celebrities one might miss by remaining in one's room. And the bar is much closer and so much friendlier."

Gade registered a smile of relief. "Then why don't we take advantage of our proximity to the bar and have a drink before leaving. I'm ready for one."

"Well, yes, why not," Volmer replied spiritedly. "And this will be on me, I insist. What is your pleasure?"

"A Scotch would be superb."

"Wonderful, you are playing to my hand!" When they reached the bar, Volmer ordered two *Dewar's*. "I'll have mine neat," he said to the bartender. "Nils?"

"Make it two of the same," the Dane replied with a gracious smile.

The two men took their drinks to a secluded section of the bar for the next few minutes, each using the occasion to feel out the other. By the time the second *Dewar's* arrived, they were chatting away like fraternity brothers, the substance of their conversation being the world of pictures.

"If I may say this without offending you, Nils, I have always envied men with impressive art collections such as yours."

Gade registered a hearty laugh. "And you, Theo, sitting on your vast holdings, your Titian and da Vinci paintings! My collection pales to that."

"Yes, but let me say this," Volmer replied, raising a finger for emphasis, "I don't own those paintings. That is a huge difference."

Both laughed.

It was becoming clear to Volmer that Gade must have imbibed before coming to the Phoenix. Perhaps a round, or two, with the French ambassador. Seeing a golden opportunity before him, he suggested a final drink. "And then I'll be ready for your special Copenhagen meal."

By a nod of his head, Gade acquiesced.

"I think you are to be commended, Nils," Volmer continued, "for maintaining such a low profile with your guards. Such sensitivity to the public is admirable. How I wish the Uffizi could be so accommodating, while at the same time providing needed security. Our numbers make that virtually impossible."

"This may surprise you, Theo, but my greatest fear is not theft. I am much more wary of forgeries, especially those of more modern artists. It was just recently that a fake Giacometti showed up in London. It was in all the papers."

Volmer smiled inwardly, knowing Gade was referencing one of his "children." Had Derek Heath not been so stupid during their association, the Giacometti would have never been discovered in the first place and everything would not have unraveled, as it did. "Yes, I read something about it." Careful to maintain his even demeanor, he added, "It seems that more and more museums and galleries are facing that problem. And we're not immune at the Uffizi, let me say."

"Of course," Gade replied with a hint of a slur. "Ours is a unique situation. We are more like a family. I cannot share this with many," he continued, "but as you are a museum man you might find this little tidbit interesting. Our night-watch force consists of just two men."

"Two men? Are you serious?" Volmer flashed a convincing show of incredulity. "We have over two dozen."

"Yes, but here again we rely on our electronic security approach. There are twenty-two stations in the building, each connected to the Danish Police. As our two men make their nightly rounds, they must "ring in" at these stations no more than five minutes before a designated time and no later than five minutes after that time. Any variance whatsoever with this protocol—even a few seconds—is immediately interpreted as a problem of some kind and the police are here within minutes."

Volmer feigned ignorance. "This ringing in? I don't quite understand."

"It's really quite simple," Gade offered like a man giving away his fortune, "Our men carry large, brass keys that resemble the end of a gun barrel, tubular. When they reach a station they insert the round key and give it two turns. This sends the signal to the police that all is well."

As a child might do, Volmer clapped his hands. "How fascinating! I'm always looking for ways to beef up our security. We have a few cameras, of course, but nothing to match your more sophisticated system."

"That's surprising," Gade countered after a slight belch. "I would have thought the Uffizi was fully state of the art."

"The sad thing here," Volmer volunteered with a self-deprecating laugh, "is that we Italians are always the last to implement new technology. I sometimes think we fancy ourselves back in the middle ages, relying on daggers and clubs." He hesitated for a moment and then asked with disarming innocence, "Have your watchmen ever missed their check-ins?"

"Well, of course," Gade confessed with an expression on his face that Volmer read as embarrassment, "but only a few times. Our employees are most conscientious."

Volmer's curiosity led him to ask, "How do the police announce their presence when they arrive? I'm asssuming the entrances are tightly secured."

"There are only two doors at the rear of the building, one large enough for us to receive crates of varying sizes and the other clearly marked for staff only. Both doors are always locked at all times. The front entrance is unlocked during the day, of course, but it is securely locked after closing. The watchmen know not to admit anyone except uniformed police. If they have mistimed their check-ins—and they will know if they have done this—or there is an emergency in the area; a fire, for example, in the immediate neighborhood or something of that nature, they will be expecting the police to ring a bell next to the smaller rear entrance. Our watchmen slide open a small panel near the top of the door that enables them to identify the caller through a pane of bullet-proof glass."

"Yes, of course." Volmer wanted the man to continue.

"As for the police, they make a cursory examination of the collection and usually leave without much fanfare. Mind you, I don't like it when it happens, but these incidents are very rare and always of more embarrassment to our watchmen than a concern to me. As I view it, incidents like these come with the territory." Gade paused to scratch a spot below his left earlobe. "What I can tell you is that we have never had a theft at the Gade Collection in over seventy years, a record most museums and galleries would love to possess."

"Seventy years," Volmer replied. "Most impressive."

Gade was now in high gear. "Yes, seventy-two fucking years to be exact!" he answered in what could be described as a defiant manner.

"Have you ever considered upgrading your system?" Volmer asked.

"Upgrading it? Why? If the process works why change it?"

Volmer smiled, sensing the man's developing inebriation.

Dinner never came.

Volmer and Gade ordered sandwiches from the bar before concluding their evening with cordials and black coffee. Volmer helped Gade into a taxi and then returned to his room, more than pleased with the information he had harvested. That night as he donned his pajamas, the thought glowed like a hot coal, *Only two watchmen.*

As Volmer continued with the article, he made special note of a planned city celebration in February of 1997, just a few short months away: Copenhagen's seventh century as a recognized city of the world. The gala would feature a large retrospective exhibition by artist Harald Giersing who helped to bring classic modernism to Denmark during the first two decades of the twentieth century. Volmer knew nothing about Giersing, nor did he care to, but perhaps he would attend the celebration, notwithstanding the risk involved. Nils Gade would now be approaching sixty, if he was reasoning correctly, but not likely to remember him from their last meeting twenty-four years ago, should their paths cross.

His close-cropped hair at the time he met Nils Gade had now become a ponytail and the signature icy gray eyes that Gade might well remember were now a nondescript hazel, thanks to contacts. The trip to Copenhagen would afford him his first real challenge of passing unnoticed in the art world. What better time than this to step away from Anghiari and Astrid's clutching fingers and allow Azzo Gatti to step off stage.

When he finished the article, he paid his bill and walked out into the delicious sunshine of Anghiari. Luxuriating in its warmth, he headed for The Verrocchio. As his feet negotiated the cobblestones, he thought about the Gade Collection. If its essential operations had not been changed appreciably in the past few decades—and he doubted they had—then the well-endowed Gade Collection was as vulnerable as a beautiful eighteen-year-old virgin, ripe for the picking. A tantalizing plan formed in his mind like the arrival of the first spring crocus and he smiled.

Tuesday, November 26
Ravenna, Italy

Silence surrounded Pieter Bajek as he guided the tip of his brush to the pointed end of a man's beard, a man at prayer. The painting had finally turned the corner and the artist was beginning to feel confident for the first time that he would be able to realize a compelling likeness of the Memling. After days of struggling to simply position the subject material on the prepared panel, it was beginning to breathe. He still had much more to do to bring the picture to completion, but looking at the calendar he felt confident he could complete everything by the end of December.

Since beginning the painting, he had bonded with the phalanx of men, each on their knees in homage to God. He wondered what it would be like to simply kneel again, but on a larger scale what it was like to be devout. Even before his accident, well before that afternoon at the lake, he had experienced little in the way of spiritual nurturing from a church. Yes, he had prayed for healing in the days following his spinal injury, but seldom had he approached an altar with prayers of thanksgiving or intercession for others, even more rarely had he attended church services in order to become one with a community of sinners.

His spiritual travel had always been alone, and if he was truly honest with himself he would have to admit that if he had received little in the way of nurturing returns from the church, he had given less. He would have to admit that he had no real faith. His life was not God-centered. These thoughts brought forth a number of disconcerting self-views, but one shone with the light of a hundred suns: guilt.

Fela's arrival with a hot cup of tea was a relief. He motioned to her that he needed the break and she assisted him in the removal of the mouth wedge that held his brush. He ran his tongue over his lips, feeling the crusty ridges that had come from two hours of continuous painting.

"They're chapped," she said with a trace of irritation. "I'll get some lip balm."

Bajek sat back in his motorized chair and intently studied the emerging picture and the three detailed photographs of the Memling that Fela had earlier taped to the edges of his easel. Since beginning the commission, he sensed that the little picture had created something of a wedge between them. Fela was still as attentive and loving as she had always been, but he could see the subtle mood changes that were beginning to arrive like the first blush of rust.

"Is something bothering you today, Pieter," she said, gently moving the small canister of lip balm over his lips, the same lips that used to come to her in the dark. He would trigger her arousal by smoothly pressing them against the raised nipples of her breasts and then crushing her own mouth when their passion screamed; all so long ago. "No, I'm fine. It's just that working on this picture has caused me to think about my own spirituality, that's all."

She walked over and stood behind him, draping her slender arms around his shoulders before kissing the top of his head. "Is this something you want to talk about?"

He could feel her breath on his neck. "Fela, do you think I am a good person?"

"What a silly question, Pieter! Of course you are a good person. Why would you ask such a question?"

"I don't even go to a church, or tithe. I'm not prayerful like these men," he said, looking at the intensity of expressions on their faces.

"Pieter, you have given these men the gift of piety. You have taken your brushes and paints and made their faith seem so real. That insight had to come from somewhere within you where righteousness and good lives: your spiritual core. A bad person couldn't paint a picture like this."

He hesitated for a moment before asking, "You don't like him, do you? Gatti, I mean."

She released her arms and stepped away, feeling a knot form in her stomach. "It is not a matter of liking Azzo Gatti. I don't trust him, Pieter."

They had talked on several occasions about Gatti. He knew of her developing reservations about him. The last thing he wanted to do at this moment was upset her. "Well," he answered with as much cheer as he could manage, "the good news is that we won't have to see him ever again."

"Yes, sweetheart," Fela replied with a heavy heart, not believing for a moment they would soon be cutting ties with Gatti. "What about some lunch," she asked. "I picked up some nice ham at the market. I think you'll like it."

Fela had not noticed it. In the lower left hand corner of the painting four men in long robes with stoles stood under a clump of trees that provided shade. Pieter, for whatever his reason—and it might have been to gain the keys to salvation—had painted the face of one of the holy men to resemble his own image. It was scarcely noticeable, but if one looked carefully one would see his handsome countenance.

PART TWO

"To the man who only has a hammer,
everything he encounters begins to
look like a nail."

—Abraham Maslow

CHAPTER TEN

Going to the Show

Friday, November 29
Nashville, Tennessee

The call from Worth Manion came as Blue was preparing to leave for Balfour. "I spoke with Damon Kirk earlier this morning. He sent me a copy of your manuscript. I haven't completely finished it, but I think it's time we talk about this book of yours. I'd like for you to come to New York, if your schedule permits. We'll cover your expenses, of course."

Blue tried to sound nonchalant, as if he received calls from big city publishers all the time. He listened as Manion summarized the situation with Gladiator. "The bottom line is that Gladiator is interested. Let's take it from there."

"I'm happy to hear that. I'll look forward to meeting you." When he hung up the phone, he made his airline reservation without consulting Largo. She had made it clear that before the spring term started at Vanderbilt her time would be spent preparing for her classes in January.

Monday, December 2

Blue's parting with Largo had been strained. They had argued again the night before over her insistence about going to Poland. Of late, their quarrels had become more frequent.

"I took the damned position at Vanderbilt," she had snapped angrily, "so that we could be together, but don't believe for a minute that I'm going to ask for more than the one semester. You have your book— and I'm happy for you—but my life and aspirations are important, too."

"Of course," he'd said, placing his arm around her waist and feeling her stiffen. "I want you go to Poland if it's that important to you. Who knows, by the summer I might be able to join you. I would like that."

She had never positioned him in the equation. This was something she wanted to do by herself. "You just don't understand, do you? I've loved being with you and living with you. I think I love you, but I don't see Poland as something we will do together."

He was not expecting her perspective. "Really?"

"Porter, think about it. Your plate is going to be soon so full with book things you wouldn't be able to go, even if I wanted you to."

"So, that's it, is it? You don't want me to go in the first place. You'll just call everything over and go your merry way. That's great!"

"It doesn't have to be like this, Porter. When you left to go to Florence last year, it wasn't with me. I cried over that for three or four nights, but then in March we got together. Separations in a relationship happen all the time. It doesn't have to mean the end of everything."

He had walked out of the room. They didn't talk again until going to bed.

When he awakened just before dawn and reached for her, he found nothing but her pillow. An hour later, after showering, shaving, and dressing, he found a folded note from Largo on the granite counter top in the kitchen near the coffee pot. The brief message felt cold and clammy:

*Have fun in New York. Call me when you know
your return flight particulars. Love you.*

American Airlines flight 3207 descended through a mantle of pewter clouds over New Jersey and eleven minutes later touched down at JFK Airport. Blue deplaned shortly before 2:00 p.m., secured his one suitcase at baggage claim and made his way through the terminal, all while replaying the previous evening with Largo. He stopped at a pay phone to call her, but received her recording. He left the message that he had arrived safely. It ended with the three words: I love you.

A drizzling rain was falling when he finally found a taxi stand. He tossed his suitcase across the backseat, climbed in and said to the driver, "The Premiere, on Park Avenue."

The drive through Queens provided little in the way of exotic scenery until the cab entered the Triborough Bridge. At its crown, Blue got his first good look at the skyline. A full serving of jitters came with it. He was still having difficulty believing his book was about to be birthed. He knew, or rather expected, that Gladiator would want some changes made. Damon Kirk had said as much. Following that conversation, he had talked by phone twice with Worth Manion who had seemed genuinely positive in his comments about the story. Still, Blue's comfort level at the moment was far from reassured.

Blue glanced at a folded note in his trouser pocket. Manion would be waiting for him at three-fifteen in the atrium of The Premiere, one of two adjacent mid-town hotels built in recent years by billionaire Hayward Crowne. Blue had seen Crowne a few times on television, never able to get past the obvious comb-over. Glancing at his watch, he was relieved to see it was just past two-thirty. He should make it with time to spare.

Manion was sitting beneath a huge potted philodendron when Blue entered one of the highly polished revolving doors at street side. He watched as the author approached, measuring his stride and assessing his outward appearance. Good-looking was the first descriptor to form in his mind. He should do well with the public, eye candy for the ladies. That should convert to good publicity and sales. Yes, he thought, as Blue drew nearer, we may have a winner here. When the writer was about fifteen paces away, Manion pulled himself up from the comfortable chair and crafted a welcoming wave. "You have to be Porter Blue," he said through gleaming teeth. "I'm Worth Manion. Welcome to New York."

He was not far in appearance from the man Blue had envisioned. He had a head full of prematurely gray hair, well styled, and a tennis player's body on a six-foot frame. The thought formed quickly: *a gym fanatic.* "I like your digs," Blue said, gesturing to the opulent surroundings, consciously wanting to convey the impression that he, too, was sophisticated enough to appreciate such surroundings.

"My office is not all that fancy, I assure you. Crowne put a ton of his money in this," Manion replied, motioning with both hands to the glittering atrium. "It's all about appearances." He paused for a moment and then said, "I'm looking for a martini partner. What do you say?"

"Why not," Blue countered. "I'm not driving."

For the next hour they talked in the elegant bar, Manion addressing Blue's story in very general terms. It seemed clear that the publisher was not yet ready to toss an attractive contract on the table. If anything, Blue took his manner to suggest that the publisher had some problems with or reservations about the manuscript.

Manion could see the anxiety in Blue's face. "Let me offer a few thoughts, Porter, about your story. For starters, I agree with Damon Kirk's assessment: you have taken a unique approach to this book. There are tons of books on Michelangelo, but I don't recall ever seeing one that focused so tightly on his teenage age years and his feelings for Contessina de' Medici. I like that. I believe average readers, especially those with art interests, will find the story appealing." He shifted slightly in his seat. "Not to mention the romantic denominator. If there is a concern at our end—let me be perfectly honest and say my end—it is that what you have is not ready to go into the oven. I understand from Damon that you're working with an editor and have rewritten aspects of the story. That's good, but it still needs tightening. I'd like to put a couple of our best editors on this. They'll work with you, if you're good with that. The sooner we can polish this just right, the sooner we can begin thinking in terms of publishing and promotional concerns. And by the way, Damon told me that the two of you have come up with a title: *Tuscan Secret*. I like that." He paused for a moment, wanting to make sure that Blue understood that his story was very much alive. "Speaking of Damon," Manion continued, "has he mentioned that we will be looking to you to hire a publicist and come up with some local or area venues where you can talk about your book—libraries, book clubs and the like?"

"Yes, he mentioned that. I have a number of academic contacts who should prove helpful in that regard. One in particular is a fellow graduate student who is now on the English faculty at Memphis State University. I've talked by phone with her and she's offered me a slot on a panel discussion in early January. There are three other writers eagerly awaiting the publication of their first novels. Is that the kind of venue you are thinking about?"

"That's a perfect example. Several of those would be nice, indeed." Manion paused for a moment. "Do you know what minor league baseball players say when they get the call to come to the majors?"

Blue smiled and replied, "Something along the lines of 'going to the show.' I've always liked that phrase."

"Absolutely! I think you might well be on your way to getting such a call one of these days." Manion took a long, deep sip of his martini and then said, "I don't know if Damon told you or not, but I'm close friends with Hollywood filmmaker, Bernie Wildenstein and his wife Lucrezia. From time to time he calls me to see if I know of a good story that he might consider for a movie. I mention this because I have the feeling that Lucrezia might like your story. She is not just an Italian, but a Florentine. What's more, she's a descendant of one of Florence's most celebrated families, the Pazzi, I believe. I take it you are familiar with her bloodline?"

Blue's reaction was intentionally subdued. "Yes, I'm quite familiar with the family. In Renaissance Italy, the Pazzi, the Strozzi and the Medici were the dominant forces of the day." What he didn't tell Manion was that the Pazzi hired an assassin to take out Giuliano de' Medici in the cathedral in Florence, the Duomo. While Giuliano and Lorenzo de' Medici were celebrating mass on Easter Sunday, 1478, the man rushed to the altar and stabbed Giuliano nineteen times. He died instantly. Lorenzo was injured, but recovered. Swift reprisals followed, and the Pazzi family was disgraced. "I'm not sure that Lucrezia Wildenstein would view my story in a sympathetic way," he replied tactfully, "but I would certainly love for her to read it."

Manion said little more about the matter. His allotted time for Porter Blue had about run its course and he had other pressing matters begging for his time. "I trust your return to Nashville goes well. We'll be in touch."

Blue walked away from the world of Hayward Crowne realizing that he might actually be getting the call. He suddenly felt like he was standing on the top of a mountain ledge with the vastness of infinity staring him in the face.

CHAPTER ELEVEN

The Last Supper

Tuesday, December 17
Anghiari, Italy

A Ravenna-stamped letter to Gatti arrived at The Verrocchio during the early afternoon. Astrid gave it to him when he arrived shortly before six. "This came today." A discernible tinge of suspicion flavored the disclosure. She had observed the postmark. "I take it you've been to Ravenna recently."

He'd said nothing to her about Ravenna following his off-hand remark on their way back to Anghiari from the festival in Arrezo. The comment had been very general in character, something about them perhaps making a trip there one day. "Yes, I went there to talk with a local artist about making a painting for me, a commission, if you like. He has now completed the picture."

"How nice. Will you be going back to pick it up?"

"I thought we might do that together."

"I'd love to, if I can. We're approaching Christmas, though, and you can imagine how busy we are going to be until the first of the year. You may have to go by yourself."

"Yes, if I must."

Two days later, a cold one, the sky was absolutely clear when Volmer left Anghiari for Ravenna in a silver Audi, his choice at the car rental agency. He smiled at the thought that Astrid had been unable to join him and that he would not be placed in the situation of having to explain to her anything about the painting. He had told her it was a commissioned work; that was all she needed to know. With the painting in hand, he would soon be exiting Anghiari.

Fela Bajek met him at the door. This time, however, there was no welcoming smile.

"It's good to see you again, Fela." He leaned over and caught her by surprise with a kiss on the cheek. "I hope this is not an inopportune time to be calling?"

"No, this is fine." Her voice sounded hollow as her hand instinctively touched the spot on her face where his lips had been. "Pieter ... Pieter and I have been looking forward to seeing you again. Please come in."

Volmer entered the small hallway that led to Pieter's studio. "Something smells good."

"Cannellini soup. Pieter's come down with a bad cold. Soup is all he wants. I hope you won't pick up the bug."

He sensed the concealed message: *I hope you will be leaving soon.* "I won't be here long enough for it to snare me. I've just gotten over a bout with my sinuses. I appreciate, however, your concern for my welfare."

Pieter Bajek was positioned in front of his easel, in the center of which he had positioned the faux Memling. When Volmer's eyes saw it, he took a double-take. The copy was astonishing, down to the smallest of details. "I'm not believing this! You have done an absolutely superb job, young man."

Pieter's face lightened. "I am glad you are well pleased." He tried to control an evident jerking of his head.

Fela moved quickly to her husband's side, knowing that he didn't need to be talking. The illness had tired him and he should be in bed. She surprised Volmer with a question. "And how is your dear great aunt, *signor* Gatti? I trust she is resting comfortably."

"She is doing about as well as can be expected," he replied, feeling Fela's emerging hostility towards him, as a wild animal in the field might catch the scent of a predator in the high grass. In a strange way, her mood change excited him. As before, he saw her through purely sensual eyes, delighting in the bloom of her youth, no doubt craving sexual pleasures that he could deliver in ways she could not imagine. "I thank you for asking, but regrettably, she has slipped a bit since I was last here. But," he added, pausing for effect, "she still asks about her painting." He took another look at Bajek's copy. "She will be so pleased to have this."

Fela excused herself on the pretense of needing to check on her soup.

Volmer took the opportunity to shift his attention to Bajek, thinking how delightful it would have been twenty years ago to have such talent at his disposal. Derek Heath had produced some good forgeries during those years, but his skills paled in comparison to Bajek's mastery.

With Fela out of the room, Volmer quickly shifted to the matter of Bajek's compensation. "I believe when we initially talked of our business arrangement," he began smoothly, "I said I would pay you a fixed sum—40,000,000 lira, as I recall—for a completed picture, regardless of its quality, and double that amount if the work fully matched my needs and expectations. Am I representing things accurately?"

"Yes," Bajek nodded, "that was my understanding."

"Well," Volmer continued, "it pleases me to say that I am prepared today to give you the full measure, 80,000,000 lira. I am more than pleased with what you have accomplished."

Fela returned to the room just as Volmer referenced the commission.

"I trust this figure meets with your approval, Fela." Volmer enjoyed the blended expression on her face of surprise and suspicion and even more the position in which he had just placed her. *Let me hear you say no to that, little pussy!* "As far as I'm concerned," he continued, "the two of you have earned it." He reached inside his jacket and withdrew a large white, sealed envelope. "I hope you don't mind cash."

Fela took the envelope only because Bajek couldn't. It felt warm, repulsive.

"And now, Fela, if you will be kind enough to wrap the panel and return my photographs, I will be on my way. I know Pieter needs his rest."

"Of course. It will only take a second."

Volmer took the final minutes to commend Bajek again on the depth of his visual ability. Fela returned to the room just as he was saying, "There is a parable in the *Bible*—I'm not sure I'm quoting it correctly—that one shouldn't 'light a lamp and put it under a basket.' I feel that way about your work, Pieter. It needs to be seen."

"Matthew five-fifteen," she said flatly. She handed Volmer the painting and photographs as if they were contaminated. "Your knowledge of the *Bible* comes as something of a surprise, *signor* Gatti." She no longer cared if he picked up on the sarcasm that dripped from every word.

Bajek looked at his wife with an expression of confusion. She was showing a hostile side of herself he had never seen.

When they reached the front door, she turned to Volmer and said, "Am I correct in understanding that when your great aunt passes, you will return the painting to Pieter?"

"Why of course, Fela. That was our agreement. Of what possible use would his copy then be to me? I much favor the original paintings I acquired from the two of you recently. They hang in places of honor in my home."

She was not ready to let go. "When that time comes, I will ask that we meet at a public place somewhere between here and Anghiari for the transfer of the painting. I never want you setting foot in my home again."

Volmer surprised her by taking her right hand and kissing it. "Let me make this easy for you, Fela." His warm hand continued to hold hers. "When my great aunt dies I will send the painting to you by special courier. You will never have to see my face again." He released her hand and smiled. "Let me leave you with another passage from Scripture, one you would do well to ponder. It comes from Hebrews thirteen-two, 'do not forget to show hospitality to strangers, for by doing so some people have shown hospitality to angels without knowing it.' I trust you and Pieter will have a blessed day."

With Bajek's painting mere inches away on the front seat of the Audi, Volmer returned to Anghiari immensely pleased with his good fortune. Notwithstanding Fela's closing shot, which he took in stride as a reflection of her fear of and desire for him, it had been a glorious day. The Memling copy far exceeded his expectations.

When he returned to his home in midafternoon, he rewrapped Bajek's painting with a portion of a felt blanket and placed it in a small, leather suitcase he'd purchased for just this purpose. His next step would be to have the work framed, and for that he would need the skills of a specialized framer. He then opened the envelope containing the photographs he'd left with Fela and Pieter. He counted them. They were all there.

He quickly filled a second suitcase with selected personal belongings, happy to leave behind most of the tasteless local clothing and his half-used toiletries. That done, he showered, dressed, and took the two suitcases to the Audi. It was now a little before five, time to go to The Verrocchio. Astrid would be expecting him and a full account of his trip to Ravenna. He would have a drink and then enjoy an early dinner. As was their custom, he and Astrid would have the obligatory lemoncello in the bar afterwards. She would ask him—as she almost always did—if he wanted to wait for her to close and come to her place. This night he would elect not to do so. He would tell her he had picked up a sore throat.

Parking in the area of The Verrocchio was seldom available in the evening. Knowing this, Volmer left the Audi in a parking lot not far from the restaurant. The five minute walk would be nice, an opportunity to play sexual mind games with Fela Bajek. He passed a closed tourist office. In its window was a tempting display of Milan featuring Leonardo da Vinci's *Last Supper*. The caption on a large poster read, Come Join Us! Volmer smiled, pushing thoughts of naked Fela Bajek aside. *Thanks, but I'll be having my own last supper at The Verrocchio in just a few minutes.*

Three hours later, Volmer made his way out of Anghiari and turned the Audi north; his destination, Copenhagen, Denmark. As of that moment, Azzo Gatti no longer existed.

CHAPTER TWELVE

Nyhavn

Friday, December 20
Copenhagen, Denmark

Volmer left Anghiari with the intention of driving until fatigue became a factor. An hour out of Zurich, he stopped in order to phone ahead and see if a room was available at the Steinburger Au Lac, the elegant hotel in Zurich he first visited in 1964. It was there he met with Derek Heath, the artist who helped him launch his forgery empire in the late sixties and then became too greedy for his own good. He was disappointed to learn that the hotel was temporarily closed for renovations. The person to whom he was speaking recommended the Hotel Eden Au Lac.

As Volmer, now Ankiel Thorssen of Copenhagen, pulled into the well-groomed grounds of the recommended hotel, his eyes traveled to one of the canals that surrounded it, reminding him quickly of the canal on the grounds of the Steinburger Au Lac in which Heath's body was found a few years later, a bullet lodged in the back of his skull.

When he reached the front desk, he found a young woman wearing an I.D. plate above her left breast showing the name Moira. He handed his passport to her and then asked in a voice that reflected his lassitude, "I would like a wake-up call at seven, please."

She smiled as she made a notation in a large ledger. "As you wish, Mr. Thorssen. Enjoy your stay with us."

By nine-fifteen the following morning, Volmer had showered and dressed. He took the elevator down to the main level, enjoyed a satisfying breakfast of poached eggs, shad roe and black coffee and then paid his bill. He was soon back on the road. A new life in Copenhagen was a little over five hundred kilometers away. By his calculations, he should be there by late afternoon, or early evening.

s Volmer was driving north, Astrid Borgmann was walking the short distance from her home to Volmer's rental bungalow. After knocking on the door repeatedly and getting no response, she inserted a key he had given her and entered. To her surprise, several of the lights were on. "Azzo, are you here? Are you up?" Not getting an answer, she ventured in the direction of the bedroom, fearful that she might find him dead.

Finding the bed unused from the night before, she redirected herself to the kitchen. "Azzo, please answer me. Where are you?" She continued to probe the villa before returning to the bedroom. He was clearly not at home. For the first time since she entered the dwelling, fear crept into the marrow of her bones. Several coat hangers littered the floor of the bedroom closet and one of the dresser drawers was wide open. Had he gone? Had he left without even saying goodbye?

When she went into the bathroom, she saw several personal items on the sink; a hairbrush with a cracked handle, a used toothbrush in a small, ceramic holder and a half-filled jar of shaving cream. *If he has gone, he left quickly.*

At that moment she recalled her husband's comment about the DNA importance of a single hair. She looked again at the hairbrush. Several dark hairs were lodged within the bristles. On impulse, she picked it up, made one final pass through the empty house and then returned to The Verrocchio. If Gatti did not contact her before the day was over, she would accept the inevitable. Salty tears found the edges of her mouth as she left the residence.

Volmer had pre-arranged a rental condominium in Copenhagen during his final days in Anghiari, one not far from the charming seventeenth-century waterfront district of Nyhavn. As he had earlier told the real estate agent by phone, he was only planning to be there for a few months and desired a short term lease.

"We can do six months," the man had replied, "but nothing shorter."

"Six months will be ideal. I would like to take occupancy on the twenty-second, if that's possible."

"We will have everything ready." The man's response oozed cordiality.

Volmer arrived in Copenhagen around four p.m., darkness beginning to envelope the city. He'd all but forgotten how early the sun sets in Scandinavia during winter. He took a room in a small inn and enjoyed a meal of braised neck of pork with rye and onion-apple compote, complete with a bottle of chilled rosé. Ankiel Thorssen was turning the first page of his new life. That night he slept well.

The following morning, Volmer assumed occupancy of the condominium. He took the first few minutes to put his few things away, generally pleased with his accommodations. It would be home for the next few months. He made a list of things he needed to pick up while he was out. At the top of his list, underlined in red, was a visit to the Gade Collection. In parenthesis, the hour it was scheduled to open.

There were few people in the Gade Collection when Volmer entered shortly before eleven. Not surprisingly, there was no sign of Nils Gade.

For the first few minutes, he strolled from gallery to gallery, admiring the quality of the collection. The first thought to cross his mind was the similarity between this collection and the Phillips Collection in Washington, D.C. He had seen the Phillips on two occasions; in 1970 when the Alte Pinakothek sent him to Washington to examine a work about to be placed at auction, and the second time two years later when he attended an international meeting of museum directors. Like Duncan Phillips, Gade displayed his collection in rooms that still retained much of their original flavor. Prized works hung above fireplaces and behind stuffed sofas. There was an intimate feeling to the place, as if one had been invited into the collector's own home.

One of the first works he saw was the Vermeer study of the girl with the earring. It was followed by exquisite works by Degas, Cezanne and Monet. Each wall contained treasures, most of them modest in size due to the architectural parameters.

Taking a pen to a small pocket notebook, he began making quick layout studies of the galleries; the locations of doors, windows and selected paintings and, of course, the positioning of the electronic stations Gade had referenced. It was not lost on him that a guard followed his actions closely when he moved close to a painting by Gauguin. From a second floor window, he gazed out at the harbor. Looking to his right and then to his left, he noted the last object he could see in either direction: a yellow boat to his right and a large trash bin to his left.

An hour later, he left the Gade Collection. The sun was beginning to peek through a thin layer of clouds. Perhaps it would warm the gray December day. A few people were sauntering about, all warmly bundled, as was he. Playing the role of a tourist, he ambled up and down the waterfront, enjoying its uniqueness, stopping frequently to sit on one of the many available benches. Of particular interest to him was the presence of uniformed police. He jotted down the particulars of the uniforms he could see beneath calf-length heavy, black coats. He saw numerous signs announcing the February first tribute to the seventeenth-century composer Dietrich Buxtehude. Several large boats were at anchor, many of them new, reminding him painfully of the yacht he lost when he fled Florence, *The Parsifal*. He had such plans for Largo on that vessel.

In exploring the waterfront, he noticed that directly across from the building housing the Gade Collection a flight of stone stairs lead down to the water. When he walked over to the edge, he saw that the stairs ended on a narrow rock ledge just above the water level. It appeared to extend for approximately fifty feet in both directions. As any curious tourist might do, he descended the stairs for a more detailed look around. After walking only a few feet to his right, he noticed what appeared to be an open tunnel. On closer inspection, he saw a heavy iron gate, some ten yards into the cavity. Only the front portion of the space was accessible. The part he was in appeared to be empty, save about a dozen thick, flat stones that were stacked against one of the walls. After he returned to the ledge, he removed the small pocket notebook and registered a few notations.

From the waterfront, he explored several of the small streets that led to it. One, in particular, held special interest: the one that ran directly behind the Gade Collection. The two doors were there, just as Nils Gade had said. The passage of time had apparently not brought about any changes with the building.

That evening, Volmer enjoyed a quiet dinner at a nearby restaurant and returned to the condominium. It was time to call a friend.

CHAPTER THIRTEEN

Merging Tracks

When Volmer's father Ulrich saw that the war could only end with disastrous consequences for Germany, he contacted a boyhood schoolmate, a dairy farmer in Stuttgart by the name of Werner Fuchs. For a price, Fuchs agreed to store the paintings Ulrich had received from Hermann Göring in compensation for his devoted service. Put simply, Fuchs permitted him to place the paintings in an unused root cellar until the end of the war, at which time Ulrich could come and remove them. Before Ulrich could do so, he died at the hands of Hermann Göring and the war ended. Werner Fuchs died in 1960, at which time the farm went to his son, Gunther.

After Theo Volmer removed the paintings from the root cellar in Stuttgart, he and Gunther Fuchs maintained contact over the years. In the mid-sixties, Fuchs was arrested and charged with larceny. Volmer, then a rising star at Munich's Alte Pinakothek Museum, placed a few well-placed bribes and had the charges against Fuchs dropped because of insufficient evidence. From that moment on, Gunther Fuchs, like Mario Drago, was completely devoted to Volmer. They had shared each other's company on a few occasions between that time and the present. Fuchs, a handsome man, had stayed in shape, carrying little fat on his six-foot frame. At each such get-together, he always offered to be of service to Volmer, should he ever need him.

❧

Tuesday, December 24
Franklin, Tennessee

Notwithstanding Bing Crosby's best efforts, snow was not predicted for middle Tennessee on Christmas Eve. Largo and Blue spent

117

the morning in Nashville trying to make the most of things, visiting the life-sized replica of the Parthenon in Centennial Park and shopping in the affluent neighborhood of Hillsboro Village. He bought a red scarf for her and she countered with a hardback copy of David Baldacci's new book, *Absolute Power*. They returned to Franklin after lunch and enjoyed a glass of wine while watching the last few minutes of *Braveheart*. That evening they returned to Nashville for dinner at Virago's, the site of their first date.

"It seems a hundred years ago that we were here," Largo said moments after they were seated. "Does it seem that way for you?"

"Yes, in a general sense. A lot has happened since then, hasn't it?"

She nodded before taking her first sip of wine. "It's been a good year."

"The best." Blue replied. He looked at her, thinking back to the day she arrived in Florence. He never expected her to come, to leave Balfour for the brief spring break. When he thought about what happened so soon after her arrival: meeting Theo Volmer, finding her great-grandparents' stolen painting in his home, her abduction to the fishing village of Choggia near Venice, nearly dying in the car when flames erupted; everything carried a surreal flavor, including the fact that they consummated their love for each other in Florence. And now, he feared that everything he had come to cherish and value was about to evaporate.

He caught her eyes glistening in the candlelight. "I don't know what the future holds for us, Largo, but I've loved every minute we've spent together. I want to think we are just entering a new chapter, but more than anything I want you to know that I want to grow old with you."

How could she counter such a declaration? Did she not feel the same way? Yet, both were poised to go in opposite directions, he with the currents of his book and she with the primordial desire to reconnect with her genetic forebearers. They were at a critical crossing in their lives, and the last thing she wanted to do was say something convenient. "Can we just say, my adorable friend and lover, that I want to take that proverbial walk in the sunset with you, but we both know that neither of us is ready at this time to make that kind of long-term commitment. Neither of us would be happy with ourselves, not to mention each other, if we shelve the unknown and lapse into a life of security, conformity and boredom.

"I never want you to be bored with me, Porter, and I'm convinced you feel the same way."

His pensive expression softened. "Let me ask you this—and I'm not arguing with what you just said, for I feel much the same way—if I go chasing the big book in the sky and you go to Poland in the fall in search of your roots and that doctorate, do you see the day down the road when we will get back with each other?"

"Of course I do! How could you even ask such a question? Haven't you heard the phrase, 'Absence makes the heart grow fonder'?"

"I'd like to think that's the case." In his gut, he feared she would find someone else.

That evening as they undressed for bed, Largo's eyes fell on the Memling. It was still so hard for her to believe that the painting had been found and returned to her, that it was hanging next to her side of the bed, that it was the last thing she saw before turning off the light and the first thing she saw in the morning—the little men at prayer.

She had Mason Creed to thank for that, the Scotland Yard investigator who worked so tirelessly to make it happen. She had thought of him often during the past six months, wondering if he was back in London and if he was dating anyone. In her eyes, there was something very appealing about Creed. While not model handsome, he was a nice-looking man, a man whose inner strength and character had spoken to her. Were she not involved with Blue, she could easily be attracted to a man like Creed.

Thoughts of him drifted away gently, replaced by those of Poland in snow and train cars filled with doomed Jews. She probably needed to get back in touch with the Atlanta High Museum. Arrangements would have to be made. "Do you know, do you really know, Porter, how special this little picture is to me?"

"I do, sweetheart."

It had been a long time since Volmer's name had been mentioned in their home. It was if both of them viewed his name as a sinister virus, one that could only inflict a serious illness if spoken.

"Where do you think he is?" She removed her earrings as the question was asked.

Porter pretended he didn't understand what she was asking. "Who are you talking about?"

"Him, of course. Volmer."

They had been down this road before. She steadfastly believed she had seen him near the train station shortly before they left Florence last July. Blue was less certain. When he had voiced doubt in the past about her claim, she usually got angry. "I don't know, but if he's alive, then he's a million miles away, darling. Theo Volmer is a dark part of our past, but not likely to ever cross our paths again. I want you to believe that." He hesitated for a moment and then added, "It's time to let go of this, Largo. You're only punishing yourself."

Her thoughts were hurled back to Jasper Beane. Three months after striking him with the poker, he was arrested and charged with child molestation. What if the poker had not been on the hearth? Would he have violated her? *He can't understand. Porter wants to be loving and protective, but he can't begin to know the feelings that ran through my body when Theo kissed me in his home. It felt like I was being kissed by the devil. It was both repulsive and electrifying.* "You are probably right," she lied. "I'll work on it."

There was something else on Largo's mind, something that had been lodged there after initially meeting Volmer. "I want to ask you a question."

"What is it?"

"It's about Volmer."

"What about him?"

"Have you ever considered that he might have gone both ways sexually?"

Blue thought for a moment. "His relationship with Sarto Carpaccio always suggested there might be something between them, but to be honest about it, I never really questioned his sexual priorities. Like most people, I assumed he was screwing every good-looking woman who crossed his path. I take it you have some questions?"

"Yes and no. There was just something about him; so fastidious and suave. I've wondered from time to time, that's all."

"That's interesting," Blue replied. "Now that I think about it, I know what you are talking about. Maybe he enjoyed a full plate. He wouldn't be the first to do that, you know."

"I know."

When they climbed beneath the covers, he reached for her and pulled her close. For a moment they were completely still, his face buried in her hair. Then, just as he was about to set his hands in motion and enjoy the Rodin-like beauty of her naked body, he felt the trembling and then heard the gentle sobbing. "Please, Porter," she said with difficulty. "Tonight, will you just let me hold you? I am so afraid."

"Afraid of what?"

"Him."

They didn't know it, but outside the first few flakes of snow were falling like silver dust from an angel's wings.

Wednesday, December 25
Copenhagen, Denmark

It was snowing hard in Copenhagen when Volmer placed a call to Gunther Fuchs from his condominium. He'd been able to secure the telephone number from a tax official in Munich. The phone rang four times before Fuchs picked up.

"Yes?"

"Gunther, this is Theo, Theo Volmer."

"Theo?" There was a long pause. "I thought you died in a fire a year ago. It was in all the papers."

"The world thinks that," Volmer replied casually. "But I'm very much alive at the moment, I assure you."

"Where are you? Are you here in Munich?"

"No, I'm calling from Copenhagen. How are things?"

"I can't complain. My knees are giving me trouble, but aside from that things are good."

"The price we pay for getting older, my friend." Volmer hesitated for a moment and then continued, "Is this a good time to talk?"

"Absolutely. My God, Theo, I can't believe it's you!"

"I hope this doesn't come as too much of a shock."

"No, no, I couldn't be more pleased or excited. What's up?"

Volmer wanted to play the next card carefully. "I would like for you to come to Copenhagen, if you can. I want to discuss a very profitable business opportunity with you, one I think you will find attractive."

"It sounds very interesting. When do you want me there?"

"Saturday, the twenty-eighth. Can you make it?"

"No problem."

"Excellent. I'm living in a condo near the waterfront. Do you have a pencil handy? I'll give you the address and phone number."

"Fire away."

Volmer provided the needed information. "And Gunther, I'll ask you to do a few things before coming."

"Anything."

"First of all, no one should know about this call. Your word on it."

"Of course, Theo. My lips are sealed. What else?"

"From this moment on, I will ask you to address me as Ankiel Thorssen, not Theo Volmer. I will explain all this when I see you."

"Okay."

"Finally, this enterprise will call for the services of two additional participants. We must be able to trust them completely."

"I understand."

"Are you still trim and fit?"

Fuchs was surprised by the question. "For the most part, yes. Why do you ask that?"

"I have my reasons."

There was a moment of silence at Fuchs' end of the line. "I'm sorry, Theo ... Ankiel. That was a thoughtless question of mine."

"It's all right. I would have probably responded the same way. The point is, one of the two men we need should be in his thirties and about your height and size."

"And the other one?" Fuchs asked with some hesitation.

"He needs to be a good swimmer and know explosives inside out. Remember, both men must be totally trustworthy. I cannot stress that too much."

"Copy that. I'll be there on the twenty-eighth. I'll take the morning train."

"Call me from the station when you arrive." He paused and then added, "And Gunther ...."

"Yes?"

"*Frohliche Weinnachten!* Merry Christmas!"

A wave of relief washed over Fuchs. "And a Merry Christmas to you, Ankiel!"

Volmer hung up the phone and fixed himself a *Dewer's*. He sat in the dark, looking out at his new surroundings. It was a little over five weeks before game time. *Ankiel Thorssen has a lot to do between now and then.*

Gunther Fuchs arrived in Copenhagen on the twenty-eighth at 10:47 a.m. He promptly called Volmer and an hour later they were seated at the kitchen table in his condo, enjoying kippers, mixed cheeses, black bread and beer. As he had been directed to do, he came with the names of two men.

Volmer was direct. "And you can trust them?" A trace of skepticism flavored the question.

"Completely." Fuchs munched on a cracker. "I've known both for years."

"Tell me about them."

Fuchs took a deep sip of beer. "Ilyus Bager is our explosives man. He worked for the past nine years with Dietmar Shipyards in Bremen doing underwater demolition, clearing the harbor, that sort of thing."

"Before Dietmar?"

"German Navy from nineteen seventy-eight to eighty-two. Submariner."

"And eighty-two to eighty-six?" Volmer was curious about the four year gap.

"Free-lancer."

"Explosives?"

"Only the most difficult assignments. He was in high demand from the Baltic Sea to Le Havre."

"How old is he?"

"Forty-six. Born in nineteen-fifty." Fuchs studied Volmer's face for his reaction.

"What have you told him about this?" The question carried a sharp edge.

"Only that he's going to be able to play with his toys and get rich at the same time."

"I'll be briefing you on his mission. Tell him to pack accordingly."

"I will."

Volmer took a brief break to urinate. When he returned to the kitchen, he removed two cold beers from the refrigerator. "What about the other guy?"

"Jannik Eriksson, a gym instructor in Frieburg. Born in Stuttgart in sixty-two. We've stayed in touch over the years. He's been in and out of jail since nineteen eighty, mostly petty stuff. Nice looking, right at six feet, always chasing women. You'll like him."

"I don't have to like him," Volmer replied curtly. "If he can do the job, that's all I'm concerned about."

Fuchs was silent for a moment. "He's reliable."

"Good, that's all I need to know. One final question, Gunther, can both be ready to leave Germany on short notice?"

"That should not pose a problem." Fuchs got up from the table and walked to the window, just as several large, black birds dropped from the sky to the yard below. "May I ask a question, Ankiel?"

"Certainly."

"Exactly what are we about to do?"

"That's a good question, Gunther. I was about to get to that." He joined Fuchs at the window. "You and I, with the help of your two friends, are going shopping very soon."

"Shopping? I don't understand."

"We are going art shopping, my friend, and we can leave our money behind. It won't be needed."

"I like the sound of that."

Volmer did not like the idea of Fuchs leaving Copenhagen. "Is it imperative that you return to Stuttgart tomorrow?"

"I must. I have people coming to look at the property on Monday."

"You're selling the farm?"

"I think so, but I can return whenever you like."

He placed his hand on Gunther's shoulder. "I would like you back here no later than the second of January. That will give you a couple of days to take care of your business at home. I'll make a hotel reservation for you. You should plan on being here for at least a month. I will be covering all of your expenses, of course. You and I will have to use the time between now and February to do a lot of serious planning."

Fuchs listened intently.

"And our demolition man," Volmer continued, "we'll want him down here by January fourth. We'll need to thoroughly brief him on his role."

"You have obviously put a lot of thought and time into this," Fuchs said. "Why is it I am not surprised?"

Volmer smiled. "Now, come back to the table with me, Gunther. I have some things to share with you that should make the selling of the farm easy. It's time you know everything."

CHAPTER FOURTEEN

The Bigot

Tuesday, January 7, 1997
Memphis, Tennessee

The three-and-a-half-hour drive from Nashville to Memphis was a comfortable one. A few days earlier I-40 had spotty areas of ice, but the weather conditions had improved and the skies had cleared. Blue left Nashville around noon and used the time on the road to consider the things he wanted to say at the panel discussion at Memphis State. If everything went well, he could tweak his remarks to match his format at other pit stops. He found the Rose Theatre Lecture Hall on campus without difficulty, shared a few private moments with Madeline Herzog and at the appropriate time took his position on stage.

Moderator Herzog thanked the participants and welcomed the attendees, saying that for teaching purposes the program would be taped.

It took but a cursory glance for Blue to realize that he was the oldest of the four and certainly the most conservative in dress and manner. Dressed in charcoal slacks, a white turtleneck and a black blazer, he could have easily passed for a television anchor. Two of the other three participants were young men, looking more like disheveled college students than serious writers. One, the taller of the two, had a scraggly black beard, dreadlocks and wore dirty red tennis shoes. He had written a vampire novel. The other young man, more athletic in build, wore a long-sleeved yellow dress shirt opened down to the fourth button, pressed jeans and loafers with no socks. He mumbled rather than spoke, leading one to believe that his desired macho image and second-rate James Dean impression were of more importance to him than his story, one about a Mormon missionary who became a drug dealer in Detroit. The lone female writer, anorexic in appearance and as pale as death, was dressed in an all-black outfit. Her book, as she would tell the audience in a voice so soft it was all but inaudible, was a metaphor on life.

126

Blue was the last to speak. Herzog introduced him as an art historian at Balfour College in Nashville. After her introduction, she invited him to share with the audience an overview of his book: how he came to write it and the challenges and rewards he experienced during the journey.

He began slowly, more nervous that he expected to be. As he began establishing the time frame for the novel, he felt the nerves beginning to dissipate. "My fascination with the Italian Renaissance began years ago with my first visit to Florence," he said, looking out at the sea of faces. From there, he talked about the artists of the period and then the extraordinary opportunity afforded thirteen-year-old Michelangelo to come to the Medici Palace and study in Lorenzo de' Medici's Academy of Ancient Art. "It was in the Palace that he met Contessina de' Medici, a beautiful girl of eleven." He paused briefly for a sip of water. "There have been numerous books written about the art of Michelangelo—hundreds probably—but few to my knowledge touch on his personal life at that young age. I wanted my story to embrace his relationship with Contessina, a youthful love affair, if it may be called—"

The interruption came without warning when a short, hawk-nosed man in the fifth row stood up to face Blue. His three-word question came like a shotgun blast. "Was Michelangelo gay?"

Herzog responded quickly and asked the man to sit down. "Please, sir, your question is as rude as it is out of order. I will ask you to hold your questions until Dr. Blue has finished."

The man dismissed her as one might discard a gum wrapper. "No, I want to know if the dude was queer. A simple yes, or no, will do."

Blue paused for a moment. "To be completely honest with you, sir, I don't know the answer to that insensitive question. Michelangelo lived over five hundred years ago. If there are unimpeachable records that attest to his sexual persuasions, I'm not aware of them. I don't believe I can accurately address your question, or that aspect of his character."

"Character!" the man exclaimed, as if he were spitting out rancid food. "He was a pervert, and everybody knows it. Just look at his art— it was immoral, through and through. Pure pornography. And please, don't try to play games with me by suggesting he liked girls."

For a moment, the auditorium was deathly silent.

"So," Blue asked calmly, "are you saying that Michelangelo's Sistine

Chapel frescoes and his *David* are immoral? Would that be correct?"

"You're damned right! All that nudity—who wouldn't object to that?"

Blue thought for a moment and then replied without expression to the man's question. "Only an ignorant bigot, sir."

The man raised a clinched fist high above his head and, waving it erratically, shouted back, "No one speaks to me like that, certainly not some wannabe writer!"

"Well, I just did," Blue replied. He reached down, picked up his glass of water and took a long, slow sip.

Were it not for the presence of two security guards who restrained the man from rushing the podium and then led him from the auditorium, the closing moments of the program could have been electric.

And then, to Blue's surprise, a most extraordinary thing happened. Almost to a person, the audience stood as one and applauded him. Madeline Herzog came to Blue's side quickly and tried to restore order, but by this time some were walking down the aisles towards the stage. The closing moments of the program resembled the end of a football game when home fans rush onto the field in celebration.

By the eleven o'clock news, televisions stations throughout Tennessee, east Arkansas and northern Mississippi were airing clips showing Blue in verbal combat with the irate man. Like the spread of a virus, late night news programs throughout the southeast picked up the story. From her bed, Largo watched and listened in joyous disbelief. The following morning the front page of *The Commercial Appeal* displayed two photographs of the bizarre encounter under the heading,

Writer Takes Down Bigot

In mid-afternoon the following day, Blue received a telephone call from Worth Manion. The story was spreading like a wildfire.

"What you did last night is worth millions! I've received more calls in the last two hours than I can count, asking about you and this book. You couldn't have done a better job in launching our promotional blitz, Porter. I don't know how to put it any other way ... *Tuscan Secret* is going to be a blockbuster!"

Largo called him at his hotel around midnight, eager to know how everything had gone. They talked for nearly an hour.

A few days later, someone else caught a television clip of Blue's encounter with the bigot, a man most interested in Blue's literary visibility: Theo Volmer. Blue had indicated in a follow-up interview which ran as part of the Memphis event that he and Largo were looking forward to their first real vacation since returning from Florence. They planned to be in Cabo San Lucas, from July 10th to the 20th. Smiling, Volmer scribbled the dates on a small notepad.

Tuesday, January 14
Nashville, Tennessee

As he had offered to do, Porter Blue spent most of the day in Nashville looking for a new place to live, Largo at his side. Both welcomed the opportunity to step away from their respective paths and the issues that came with them. Largo was particularly pleased. It was the first weekend after the start of classes at Vanderbilt and she needed some downtime. As for Blue, Gladiator was ready to put things in motion. He could now say officially that his book would be published. Details were being sent to him.

In discussing their domestic preferences, Largo and Blue felt they could be comfortable in a two-bedroom place, be that an apartment or a condo. From Blue's perspective, knowing that he would soon be looking at substantial travel, the most essential concern was security. While he had to be away, he wanted Largo to feel comfortable, protected. After looking at five places, all in metro Nashville, they went to Virago's for sushi and some much-needed unwinding. Over a couple of drinks, they reflected on the day and the options before them.

"What's your top choice?" Blue asked, looking into her eyes with something of a melancholy feeling.

"That's a tough one. Probably the condo near The Ryman Auditorium. I've forgotten the name."

"The True Opry, the one on Church Street?"

"Yeah, it's a crazy name, but I really liked it. Just think, we could walk down to the Cardinal Cafe in three minutes and listen to the best of the best in country music. The place is legendary. What about you?"

"I'm good with that. Actually, I could go with any of the five."

She looked at him in silence for a moment. "I know you're doing this for me, Porter, and I do appreciate it."

"You're welcome. I think we are both ready for a change."

After a wonderful meal, Blue knew he'd had one drink too many to make the return drive to Franklin, and Largo wasn't about to drive for the same reason. They spent the night at the Renaissance Nashville Hotel. She had no way of knowing it, of course, but she and Porter spent the night next door to the very room Theo Volmer would occupy when he arrived from Boston in July, just six short months away.

The first few days of the semester had been somewhat bumpy for Largo, but by the second week she had squarely planted her teaching legs. Given the nature of the art survey course, she had been relatively free to approach essential course objectives in her own way.

Her basic philosophy about a course like this was that hard facts were not nearly as important to a student as the much deeper issue of why; why do artists paint and sculpt? Was it for the money, the fame or prestige, or do artists respond to some inner force that can't be quantified? She wanted her students to think, not memorize, to empathize with an image, not merely observe it. Was there a distinction between seeing and looking? When she lectured—and the survey course was, by definition, a lecture course—she was much more likely to stop in the middle of a sentence and solicit a student's opinion than to mechanically follow prepared notes.

Her performance had not gone unnoticed. One of the department's tenured professors, Dr. Gerald Saltzberg, had interacted with Largo during those times they were in the slide room making selections for their classes. In talking with her, he had been impressed not only with her maturity but her in-depth knowledge of modern art history. He had known many adjunct instructors over the course of his twenty-five years on the faculty, but few with more than a general command of the subject material. Largo was decidedly different.

He had shared his observations with Chairman Hagen and he, in his diffident manner, approached her a few days later with an offer to continue, if she would care to do so. "So," Hagen said as they journeyed upward in the elevator, "Saltzberg says that ... what ... you want to return in the fall? Is that right?"

"I beg your pardon, sir?"

Hagen tilted his head back for a moment and counted the acoustical tiles in the ceiling. "Seven times twelve would be eighty-four, if I am correct. I'm sorry, you were saying?"

"Sir, I never talked with Dr. Saltzberg about remaining after the semester's end. On those few occasions when we chatted in the slide room, we only discussed ..."

"Well, of course. If it's the money, I can speak with the dean." He cocked his head sideways and winked at her. "But you know our dean. He's such a pussy willow when it comes to money."

"Mr. Hagen, I believe there is a misunderstanding here. With all due respect ..."

"So, you will think about it? Good. I have always felt that Picasso's use of color was terribly underappreciated. Your thoughts?"

Before Largo could respond, the door opened at the third floor and Hagen floated away like a cloud. As she walked to her office, she pondered the oblique offer to continue past the summer. Were it not for her strong desire to experience Poland, she would love to swim longer in the waters of education. She would at least think about it.

Beyond the classroom, she and Porter Blue were trying their best to keep their relationship on track. The move from Franklin to Nashville was having a very positive effect on their relationship, and the evenings at the Cardinal Cafe were every bit as special as she had hoped. For Largo, long a fan of jazz and country music, the opportunity to catch performers like the Marty Crum Jazz Trio, the David Coe Duo and Brian Ashley Jones was beyond exciting. She and Blue were there when Jones released his *Come Out and Play* CD, a blend of country, blues and pop.

Most of Blue's time was spent on the phone with Manion and the staff of Gladiator, addressing the many things that accompany the publishing of a book. For days, Blue had been pondering Worth Manion's comment that he would need to obtain his own publicist and come up with approachable venues. It would be awhile before he had copies of the book. The important thing was to establish public awareness of the book. To "get word of it out there," as Kirk put it.

Not only did Largo's shift to a more positive mood bring cheer to Porter's heart, but good fortune chose to smile on him, as well. Franklin's own Lippman-Crowne Realty called to say they had sold his house to a young couple from Kingsport. The buyer was an aspiring young country musician, ready to show Nashville that Tim McGraw was just another singer.

Porter and Largo took occupancy of the condo in True Opry on the twenty-fifth. As for the good Christians in Franklin, they put away their swords of righteousness, pleased that the moral fiber of their evangelical community was still very much intact. Blue left for Charleston, South Carolina, on the twenty-ninth for the funeral of a close college friend. He wanted a few days to himself so he could prepare for his next presentation and review the contract he'd received from Gladiator. Largo had encouraged him to take all the time he needed. To her surprise, she had not really missed him.

CHAPTER FIFTEEN

The Gade Collection

Saturday, February 1
Copenhagen, Denmark

By mid-day, the temperature was one degree centigrade, cold but not uncomfortable.

For most Scandinavians, the day was a very pleasant one. The streets of Copenhagen were filled with people, many of whom had come from considerable distances to celebrate the musical genius of Dieterich Buxtehude. Colorful flags festooned Nyhavn and boat horns chorused, as if in response to Herbert von Karajan's magical baton. The concert was about eight hours away.

Bager and Fuchs had arrived on January ninth, so that Volmer would have ample time to talk with Fuchs before briefing Bager on his part of the operation, a critical one. Eriksson arrived later, on January 27th from Cologne.

Volmer's initial impression of Bager was a positive one for two reasons: one, the ex-German seaman was short in stature, scarcely taller than himself. Secondly, Bager spoke only when spoken to. During his initial conversation with Volmer, his responses were laced with formality and respect, as if he were addressing his commander.

While Bager was short in height, he was powerfully built. Nicknamed *der Feuerhydrant,* fire hydrant, his 156 pounds were all muscle. Bager was snub-nosed with a firmly set jaw and small, suspicious eyes that constantly scanned his surroundings like a searchlight. He had disproportionately large hands and, as Fuchs had previously told Volmer, he'd previously killed three men in bar fights, each with a swift, hard jerk of the neck. His hair, brown in color, was cut close to the scalp.

A horse of a different color was Eriksson. At nearly six-two, he had a lean body and nicely sculpted facial features. He had long, thick, black hair, combed from the front to the back. The first turn-off for Volmer was the grease used to hold every hair in place. What piqued Volmer the most, however, was the man's sullen manner and evident narcissism. He gave the impression he was bored with everything. At his first opportunity Volmer shared his less than favorable impressions with Fuchs who took an understandably defensive position.

"I'll agree," Fuchs replied. "He's not the most pleasant person to be around, but he is totally dependable."

"I hope so."

The better part of the afternoon was spent at a sparsely populated skating rink some distance from the harbor. The recruited players listened carefully as Volmer covered every minute detail of the plan he had been shaping for months. From time to time, he would face one of them and ask a pointed question; anything less than a completely satisfactory answer drew his scorn. As he was bringing the meeting to a close he said, "Do each of you fully understand your role tonight?"

Receiving no outward response, he turned to Fuchs. "Gunther?"

"I understand. I'm good with it."

"And you, Ilyus?"

Ilyus Bager replied, "I do, sir. I have everything I will need."

Volmer then turned to Eriksson. He was trusting Fuchs' judgment, but at that moment he had reservations about the man. "Are you ready, Jannik?"

Jannik Eriksson nodded, but said nothing.

"I'll take that as a yes." The six words seemed laced with acid. Eriksson's demeanor galled Volmer, but he remained calm and showed no change in his facial expression. He took a quick look at his watch. "It is now four-twenty p.m. I suggest we return to my place for a nice meal together and grab a few hours of rest. In a little over five hours it will be show time."

A short while after arriving at the condo, Volmer assembled his team at the dining room table. Before he could begin, Eriksson surprised him with a question. "When do I get my money?"

All eyes turned to Volmer. "Thank you, Jannik, I was just about to get to that." Volmer clearly resented the question. He made eye contact with everyone before he responded to Jannik. "Aside from what I am about to give each of you in a few moments, you will receive the balance shortly." He looked around the table and added, "That comes with the completion of a successful operation."

He paused for a moment. "If anyone else has a question, I would like to hear it now." Hearing no response, he smiled and distributed sealed white envelopes to everyone. "Before you open this, I would like to say a few words." He hesitated for a moment until he was sure that he had their attention, especially Jannik's. "Later tonight, each of you will perform a vital service for which you will be paid handsomely. I believe Gunther has already spoken with you about the financial aspects of this service, and I am satisfied from our session earlier today that you understand your respective roles."

Heads nodded affirmatively.

"What I am giving you now is to be considered a bonus, one I trust will show good faith on my part, while rewarding you at the same time for your commitment and loyalty." Turning to Bager and Eriksson, he said, "Gentlemen, I need to be emphatic on this: after we complete our business tonight and the two of you board the train for Hamburg, we will not meet again. Is that understood?"

"Yes," they replied in unison.

Volmer smiled, pleased with their responses. "Then let's pretend this is Christmas morning. You may now open your envelopes."

Each man did so, finding 20,000 Deutsche Marks in new, crisp bills. Smiles quickly ringed the table.

Not long after the meal, cigars followed.

At 7:45 p.m., Bager walked to the chair in which Volmer was seated and said in a low, respectful voice, "It is time I leave, sir."

"Yes. Do you have everything?"

"I do, sir," he replied, patting a black, zippered shoulder bag.

"The key to my condo and your ticket to Hamburg?"

"Yes, sir. I have them."

"Fine, now check your watch. I'll do the same. It's critical you and I synchronize to the second."

When the adjustment was made, Bager said, "I'm on your mark."

"Good! Now go safely and take a taxi to the station immediately after you finish. I will drop off Jannik once we leave. Just adhere to the procedure we discussed earlier today. Everything must go as timed, especially the last few minutes."

"I understand, sir."

Bager walked briskly from the condo to the waterfront in five minutes. As Volmer had instructed him to do, he located the rock stairway across from the Gade Collection and quickly disappeared from view. He found the open end of the tunnel and entered it. Aided by a small flashlight, he changed from his street clothes into a wet suit from the shoulder bag. Aditionally, he removed flippers and two of his toys. Bager then checked to make certain that a hand-held remote control device was still in the bag. Satisfied that he had everything he needed, he stuffed the flashlight, a heavy jacket and his clothing and shoes in the bag and zipped it shut. In seconds, he slipped into the water like a muskrat from a wet rock, disappearing without a sound.

When he had concluded his work, he returned to the tunnel and removed the flashlight from the bag. Placing it on the ground to provide adequate light, he then removed the wet suit and quickly dressed. He took the remote control device from the bag and put it in one of his trouser pockets. That done, he stuffed the wet suit and the flashlight in the bag and took it to the water's edge. Leaning over carefully, he filled the bag about half-full with water. He then placed three heavy, flat rocks in the bag, zipped it shut and lowered it quietly into the water. After watching it sink, he climbed the stairs and began slowly walking away from the waterfront.

From the time he entered the water until that moment, twenty-seven minutes had passed. As he walked under a streetlight, he checked his watch. It was 8:27 p.m. If anything, he was a few minutes ahead of schedule. Volmer had instructed him to take a taxi to the train station after finishing his work, but Bager was thirsting for a drink. *Ten minutes is not going to make much of a difference.* He left the waterfront and walked a short distance to a small bar. He ordered a whisky sour and sat in a darkened corner, keeping close watch on the time. It crept.

As Bager was downing the last of his drink, Volmer, Fuchs and Eriksson were seated in a non-descript gray cargo van parked behind the Gade Collection between a delivery truck and a small sedan. Fuchs and Eriksson were dressed in police uniforms, complete with the long coats.

A check of the time told Volmer it was now 8:49 p.m. Unless the protocol had changed, one of the night watchmen would be ringing in shortly. He mentally replayed Gade's description: *From five minutes before the hour, to five minutes after the hour.* Fuchs and Eriksson were poised to leave the van at Volmer's signal.

At precisely 8:51 p.m., the first of two bombs in the harbor exploded with a violent force, illuminating the night sky. An empty barge that had been at anchor for three weeks was ripped to pieces by the blast. Billowing smoke and fire followed.

Inside the Gade Collection, one of the watchmen, Magnus Clausen, was walking by the windows of a third floor gallery. By chance, he was looking out at the harbor the moment the blast occurred. The concussion caused the windows to shake violently. He had just checked the time and knew that he would need to be ringing in within the next few minutes. He took a walkie-talkie from a holder on his belt and contacted his partner who was on the ground level, screening the bank of monitors. "Get up here, Liam! You are not going to believe this. Hurry!"

Liam Kordt, the man downstairs, had felt the explosion, but replied, "I can't leave my post, Magnus. You know the rules."

"Screw the rules! This could be terrorism!"

Kordt left his post and bolted into the gallery thirty-five seconds later, startled by the intensity of the fire. Before he could speak, the second explosion occurred at the other end of the harbor. A 38-foot yacht was reduced to splinters, instantly killing the two passengers on board, a man and his wife.

"Mother fuck!" Kordt screamed. "What in the hell is happening?"

"All hell, that's what!"

They stood like statues at the window, transfixed by the fireballs at each end of the harbor and the frenetic activity of those below on the spacious waterfront. Instinctively, Kordt looked at his watch. It was seconds past 9:05 p.m. "Jesus Christ, Magnus, the time window! You've got to ring in."

The watchman moved as fast as he could, but before he could insert the bronze key and give it the required two turns, it was 9:06 p.m. One minute too late.

In the van, Volmer patiently waited for two minutes to pass, his eyes glued to the face of his watch. When he saw the second hand approach 9:08, he turned to Fuchs and Eriksson.

"Go, now! You have twelve minutes, not a second longer."

Fuchs and Eriksson jumped from the van and moved quickly to the small door at the rear of the Gade Collection. Fuchs reached the door first, and rang the bell three times. He paused and rang it again.

Kordt and Clausen responded immediately, asking each other as they hurried to the rear door how the police could have gotten there so quickly. Liam Kordt was the first to reach the rear door. He slid the panel to the right and found himself looking squarely into the face of uniformed Gunther Fuchs.

"Open the door!" Fuchs yelled. "Your building is at risk!"

Both watchmen knew from their training and years of experience that in the event of an extraordinary circumstance—and the dramatic explosions in the harbor certainly qualified as such—that they were to admit law officials, if ordered to do so.

Without hesitation, Kordt unlocked the door and stepped aside so the two policemen could enter. Kordt noticed that the other officer was carrying a large, black leather portfolio. Everything was happening so fast. Before he could even ask a question, Fuchs and Eriksson were pointing revolvers at the two men. "To the floor!" Fuchs demanded.

The watchmen did as directed. Within seconds, Eriksson was binding their wrists with duct tape. He then ordered them to place their wrists at their belt buckles. Quickly, he wrapped the tape around their arms and then their legs. They looked like wrapped rugs. Five-inch pieces of tape were then slapped over their mouths.

Satisfied the men were not going anywhere, Fuchs and Eriksson entered the collection. They were seeking four paintings, all modest in size. The largest was a Blue Period painting by Picasso, 24"wide x 30" in height. On the third floor Fuchs located one of the paintings designated by Volmer, a small but colorful Gauguin, one of the artist's last pictures. With box cutters, he carefully slit the canvas along the edges where it met the frame and then placed it in the portfolio. From another gallery, he removed a lovely Whistler nocturne. Eriksson took the final painting from the second floor, the Vermeer study of the girl with the earring.

With the targeted art works in their possession, they scarcely paid any attention to the two watchmen as they exited the back door. Fuchs glanced at his watch: 9:19 p.m. They had completed their assignment in just over eleven minutes. Within seconds, they were in the van.

Volmer sped away from the rear of the Gade Collection at 9:20 p.m. and headed for the train station, a five minute drive away. He knew that very soon all transportation into and out of Copenhagen would be halted. Bager and Eriksson had tickets for the 9:45 train to Hamburg. Hopefully, Bager was already on board. Eriksson, quickly changing his clothing in the van, would have ample time to get on the train. Barring a major problem, he and Bager would be out of Copenhagen before the authorities put a noose around the station.

Everything was going smoothly until Volmer turned a corner near the station and had to come to an abrupt halt. A woman pushing a baby carriage had dropped several hand held objects and was bending over with some difficulty to retrieve them. A man on the sidewalk had run to her aid, but after providing the needed help stood near the carriage talking with her.

Traffic behind the van was stacking up. Volmer made another check of the time. It was nearing 9:30 p.m. The train would be leaving in fifteen minutes. He had no patience with the situation and immediately blew his horn. The Good Samaritan glowered at Volmer and continued to chat with the woman. Volmer dismissed the man's response and steered into the oncoming lane, defying the driver of a tiny Fiat, and proceeded to the station. After depositing Eriksson at the main entrance of the terminal three minutes later, Volmer began looking for available parking spaces. The Buxtehude concert had attracted more than the normal number of cars. About fifty feet away, he spotted a "No Parking" area. It would suffice.

As he and Fuchs stepped from the vehicle, Volmer made one final check of the time. It was a few seconds before 9:41 p.m. *We have four minutes.* "I suggest we walk briskly," he said to Fuchs with surprising calmness, the portfolio in hand.

Moments later, as they were turning a corner, Ilyus Bager stepped down from the train to the platform. It was 9:44 p.m. He then depressed a red button on the remote control device, detonating the nearby van. Just after doing so, he dropped the electronic device in a nearby trash receptacle and returned to the train. Its engine hissed a huge plume of steam and the giant steel wheels began to turn at precisely 9:45 p.m.

Smiling at the sound of the explosion, Volmer turned to Fuchs as they continued down the darkened street. "There is absolutely no match for German efficiency."

In the aftermath of the final explosion, police were everywhere. Sirens wailed. About a block from the condo, Volmer and Fuchs had to step into an alley to avoid a throng of police at a distant corner where yet another barricade was erected to screen motorists. One sensed that the entire city of Copenhagen was under siege.

At the distant end of the alley, they found a relatively empty street, and reached the condo without further incident. Volmer immediately turned on the television while Fuchs grabbed two cold beers from the refrigerator.

"I'm tired of beer," Volmer remarked, making his way to the kitchen in search of a beverage more to his liking. He settled on a vintage burgundy and brought it, a corkscrew and a wineglass to the living room. Fuchs had turned on the television set. One of the local stations had already reached the harbor and the train station.

"What's happening?" Volmer asked.

Fuchs' eyes were glued to changing scenes of the city: images from the waterfront, the area just outside the station and the concert hall where hundreds of persons were running in all directions.

"They're calling it terrorism." Fuchs wore a huge grin on his face. "Was this a special night, or what?"

Volmer's response, in contrast, was almost stoic. As far as he was concerned, the operation went like clockwork, the result of his minute attention to detail. The one sour edge to it all was Jannik Eriksson. He had done his job, but his brooding manner and lack of appropriate respect had not gone down well. Volmer knew that one loose word from Eriksson's lips could be catastrophic. "Turn that off," he said to Fuchs. "We need to talk."

Fuchs did as directed and then turned in Volmer's direction. "Talk about what?" The smallest edge of irritability showed. He wasn't ready to leave the television coverage.

"Eriksson," Volmer snapped. "He's a risk now."

"So, what do we do about that?"

"We don't do anything," Volmer replied crisply. "You will."

"What are you thinking?"

"I'm thinking you might contact Jannik once you return to Munich and tell him you have the rest of his money. You might want to suggest that he meet you at the Botanical Gardens. The weather might be on the cold side, but perhaps the two of you could take a stroll in the warm Arboretum with only one of you coming out, if you get my drift."

Fuchs smiled. "I should be the person coming out, I assume?"

"I would hope so, yes."

Thursday, February 6
Munich, Germany

Two elderly women wearing enormous furs entered the Arboretum in the Botanical Gardens, each boasting of her healthy orchid collection. A few minutes later, they stopped before a huge mass of rhododendron plants, marveling at the size of the dark green leaves. The display was centered in a large area of mossy soil, damp from a recent watering.

One of the women noticed a large rock behind the pale brown rhododendron limbs. As they slowly walked around the exhibit, she saw a small, white shape emerging from beneath the rock. "My, whatever can that be? Might it be a patch of mushrooms?"

Her companion moved in just a bit for a better look. Two seconds later, she recoiled, as if bitten by a snake. Her hands immediately went to the top of her head. *"Das ist eine Hand!* That is a hand!" she screamed. *"die Hand eines Mannes!* A man's hand!"

The following morning, the *Sueddeutsche Zeitung* ran a front page article about the discovery of a man's body in the Arboretum. The name of the victim was being withheld, pending notification of next of kin. The article went on to suggest foul play.

That evening, Fuchs called Volmer and provided a brief account of the death of Jannik Eriksson.

Volmer's response was simple. "I will see to it that you get his share."

Fuchs hesitated momentarily and then replied, "Hmmm, I do like the sound of that."

CHAPTER SIXTEEN

Train to Izmir

Friday, February 7
Nashville, Tennessee

Largo first learned from a friend about the Copenhagen theft two nights earlier. Focused on her own academic tasks, she had not even thought about following television coverage.

On this rainy morning, she was thumbing through a travel guide on Poland while waiting for a faculty meeting to begin. A colleague seated next to her mentioned the robbery. "I can't believe what happened to that gallery in Copenhagen last week. Have you been following the story?"

"Not really. I heard about it a couple of nights ago, but I haven't had the television on for days. What's the latest news?"

"They're still puzzled about why the watchmen let the policemen enter the museum. Talk about crazy."

"I haven't heard the bit about the police."

"Yeah, two of them walked away with four paintings worth big bucks while boats were being blown up in the harbor. It was like a James Bond movie."

Dinner was a Lean Cuisine and a glass of Chardonnay. Topping it off, she took the glass to the bathroom where she treated herself to a long, hot bath. The aromatic steam and the warm glow of cinnamon-scented candles at each end of the tub provided a wonderful conclusion to what had been a long day.

As she sipped the cool wine, she allowed her fantasies to take flight. She was in Krakow, shopping with her great-grandmother in a neighborhood market, absorbing the sounds and smells of her new surroundings. From Poland, she darted to the intimacy of the Sistine Chapel where she craned her neck to watch Michelangelo apply the final brushstrokes to the powerful figure of Jeremiah. One adventure followed another. When the water began to lose its magic, she slipped into a peach-colored robe and brushed her teeth. It was nearly ten-thirty.

Curious about the robbery in Copenhagen, she started channel-surfing, hoping to find something about it. After enduring snippets of one sitcom after another, she clicked on a special CNN report in progress. A reporter with her back facing the Gade Collection was commenting on the daring theft.

"... and Danish police are still baffled by the events of February first. It seems clear that the two violent explosions in this harbor and the one near the rail station are linked to the robbery, but as yet there are no tangible clues." The scene shifted to the water. The camera made a slow pan of the area before returning to the reporter. "All we know at this time is that approximately twenty million dollars in valuable art was taken. There is speculation that the thieves had inside help, but this has yet to be confirmed. One thing does seem clear: everything seems to have been meticulously planned. We're taking a brief break at this time, but when we come back, our own Charles Niven in London will be with Nils Gade, the owner and director of the Gade Collection. For CNN News, this is Rebecca Laine reporting."

Largo took advantage of the upcoming commercials to change into her pajamas. Just before climbing into bed, she took the last sip of wine and watched the end of an inane commercial on the newest in hair removal for women. When CNN returned, Niven was sitting in the London studio with an obviously battered Nils Gade. He looked like he had not slept in days.

Niven began with characteristic affectation:

"I'm here this evening with Nils Gade whose Copenhagen collection of fine art was boldly robbed last Saturday." The camera framed Gade's face, revealing dark circles under his eyes. "Nils, I'd like to begin by going straight to the question on the minds of many who have been following this tragic event, and that is the possibility of inside help. Are you inclined to believe that is the case here?"

Gade cleared his throat before responding to the question. "I would have to say, no, Charles. In talking with our two night watchmen, both longtime and loyal employees, they said that the thieves—two men wearing police uniforms—bound them immediately on entering."

Niven's antennae were raised by Gade's disclosure of the two watchmen. "You referenced two watchmen. I find that surprising. I would have assumed a much larger after-hours staff, especially given the extraordinary value of your collection."

For Gade, the question triggered a mental flashback to 1986 and the evening he spent with Theo Volmer. He couldn't recall chapter and verse of their conversation about security—the consumption of alcohol contributing to that—but Volmer's questions were still ringing like a clarion bell in his mind: "Two men? Are you serious?" Ill-advisedly, he had given his guest detailed information about their security protocol. And, finally, there was Volmer's keen interest in the Vermeer study of the girl with the earring. He seemed fascinated with the picture. The thought then arrived like a silent arrow, the man died in a fire in his own home. Surely...

Niven pulled Gade from his reverie with a blunt question. "If not one of your own employees, then whom do you suspect, or do you even have suspicions at this time?"

"To be honest, we are completely baffled." He hesitated briefly. "I'm hesitant to say this, but the only person I can think of—and it absurd to even think along these lines because the man is dead—is a museum man, who died last year in a fire. I did talk at length with him in 1986 about our operations, but ... no, it's an absurd thought."

Niven was quick to spear the provocative comment. "Are you comfortable in sharing his name with our audience?"

Gade reacted just as quickly. "I think not, Charles. The last thing I want to do at this time is disrespect a deceased man. I spoke without fully thinking, and I apologize for that."

Niven had one final question for Gade. "One of the puzzling things to me about this whole thing is that the thieves took only four of your paintings. Why just four?"

Why just four? Gade struggled to conceal his irritation at Niven. *Those were four very precious pictures, you buffoon!* "Perhaps they were not greedy thieves," Gade replied, spitting out the words.

Largo listened to Gade in disbelief, for in her galloping thoughts Volmer had earlier scrolled across her mind. Gade might think he was dead and the world might believe accordingly, but she knew differently. Theo Volmer was very much alive. He might not have been involved

144

in this robbery, but he had to be somewhere. It made as much sense for him to be in Copenhagen as anywhere else.

She listened to the remainder of the interview and then turned off the television. The last thing she did before disappearing under the covers was to double-check the security panel to make sure it was armed.

Before she fell asleep, Blue called. It was a little before midnight. "I hope I'm not waking you," he said. "I just wanted to hear the sound of your voice. I've missed you."

"I'm awake. Missed you too." She hoped the words sounded sincere. "How's everything?"

"Okay, I suppose. I received a call from Damon Kirk. He's been in contact with Gladiator about their schedule and a million other things related to the book. It sounds like the wheels are turning, but so far I'm pretty much in the dark. About all I know is that I need to be lining up places close to home where I can begin making presentations."

"Sounds exciting."

The tone of her voice told him she was just trying to be supportive.

Largo wondered if he'd been following the news. "Have you heard about the Copenhagen art robbery?"

"A bit. They were talking about it at the library here."

She adjusted her position and then surprised him by saying, "I think I know who did it."

He laughed. "Well, of course you do! The robbery occurred in Copenhagen over a week ago, but with your awesome mental powers you have already solved the crime. Why is it I am not surprised to hear that?"

"Go ahead, laugh your butt off, Porter, but I know I'm right on this."

The thought of alienating her caused Blue to restate things. "Okay, you have my full attention. Who was the culprit?"

"Theo Volmer. I'm not saying he was actually there, but I'll bet you a dollar to a dime he was involved in some way."

A long moment of silence followed. In the darkness of the bedroom it felt heavy, like a layer of lead. The merest mention of Volmer's name gave her pause. Her fears had not truly abated since their return to the States; they lingered like foul odors from a landfill.

"So, your money is on Volmer?" he asked

"Yes. I watched a special CNN report tonight. An interview with Nils Gade, the man who owns the Gade Collection. He mentioned that he met a museum man—those were his exact words—in the late eighties who later died in a fire in his own home. He went on to say that he had shared operational information about his collection with this man. I found that very odd. Do you want me to stop there?"

Blue was unnerved by what he was hearing. "No."

"I know you never believed I saw Volmer leaving that hotel in Florence after his official death, but do you not think the coincidence here is weird? I mean, what doesn't fit?"

"Largo, I never said I didn't believe you. My position has always been that I find it hard to believe that he, of all persons living in Florence at the time, would appear in public in such a blatant way. If you are convinced he's still alive, that's enough justification to contact Gade and tell him your story."

"Contact Gade? Are you serious, Porter?"

"Absolutely. Tell him that you are convinced you saw Volmer last year near the train station in Florence after the fire. Tell him about the Memling."

The simple suggestion caught her completely off guard. It was the last thing she expected him to say. For a moment, she said nothing. "And just how would you suggest I do this? Contact Gade, I mean?"

"Just call him. Pick up the phone, dial his number and when he answers say something sexy. You'll get his attention."

She realized how empty the condo was without him. "I like the way you think. When are you coming home?"

"In a day, or so. I'll give you call. Sleep tight. I love you."

"Love you too."

After stewing about the Gade matter over breakfast, Largo obtained the international long distance code for Denmark and the telephone number of the Gade Collection. By her reckoning, it was early afternoon in Copenhagen. The office should be open. After three rings, she was greeted by a woman's voice. *"Goddag. Der er Gade Samilingen. De taler med Annelise Larsen.* Good day. This is the Gade Collection. You are speaking with Annelise Larsen."

"Hello Annelise, my name is Largo Kopacz. Do you speak English?"

"Yes, of course," came the polite reply.

"I am calling from the United States. I would like to speak with Director Gade about an important matter."

There was a pause before the woman replied. "May I ask the nature of your call?"

"I may have information of use to Mr. Gade. It is in regard to your recent theft."

"One moment, please."

Largo waited for about thirty seconds before the woman returned to the phone.

"I'm sorry, but Mr. Gade is busy at the moment. Perhaps you could call again."

"Please," Largo replied quickly. "Just tell him that Theo Volmer is still alive. When he hears that, I believe Mr. Gade will want to speak with me. Please, this is important."

Another pause followed. This time, a different voice greeted her, a much deeper one.

"Good afternoon, Ms. Kopacz, this is Nils Gade. How may I help you?" The response carried little in the way of cordiality.

"Good afternoon, sir. I was sorry to hear about the robbery at the Gade Collection. I recently saw your interview with Charles Niven on CNN."

"Yes?"

"When you mentioned the museum man who died in a fire, were you by chance referring to Theo Volmer, the former director of the Uffizi Gallery in Florence, Italy? If so, you should know he is very much alive. He did not die in the fire at his Fiesole home."

A protracted moment of silence followed. "Ms. Kopacz, is this some form of a joke?"

"No, sir, this is a fact." She went on to tell him about her time in Florence, the Memling that had been stolen by Volmer's father and her visits to Volmer's home in Fiesole. She told Gade about the Florentine police chief, how he had shielded Volmer and was ultimately arrested on corruption charges. When she mentioned her sighting of him in Florence days after the fire, Gade realized his caller was not some practical joker.

"How can you be certain the man you saw was Volmer?" her asked.

For a moment, Largo toyed with the idea of telling Gade that he sounded just like Porter, but wisely chose not to do so. "I'm absolutely certain, sir. The man I saw entering the car was Theo Volmer. I saw his eyes."

Gade immediately recalled the first time he saw Volmer's eyes. "Icy gray," he said. "They were very unusual, like those of a wolf."

"Yes, yes," Largo replied, her excitement reflected in the tone of the two words. "We are talking about the same man."

"Ms. Kopacz, I cannot thank you enough for placing your call. I will have to consult with my attorneys before approaching the police here, but I will do that promptly. Should they wish to talk with you, will you consent to that?"

"Of course, I will, sir. I want to do everything I can to help in the return of the stolen works." She then gave Gade her telephone number and the number of the Art Department at Vanderbilt.

Gade's mind was whirling in all directions. If what he was hearing from Largo Kopacz were true, he would have something the Danish authorities had been searching for—a suspect. But how to convince anyone that a legally dead man had masterminded the costly theft? What proof could he offer? And even if he could convince the authorities of Volmer's existence, where would one begin looking for him? Surely, he would be miles from Copenhagen at this time.

But at that very moment, Volmer was not miles from Copenhagen. He was, in fact, conferring with a yacht dealer near Nyhavn, not more than a kilometer from Gade. Volmer's business in Copenhagen had run its course, and it was time to relocate.

The dealer, a thin, dark man with rimless glasses, spoke with a decidedly Middle Eastern accent. As they talked, the man referenced the years he spent in Tripoli, before moving to Denmark.

The vessel under consideration was at the present time in Izmir, Turkey, bobbing gently in the warm water of the Aegean Sea. It was a MEDUSE, a sleek 198 feet in length. As the dealer explained, "It is meticulously crafted with the two DITA engines, capable of generating three thousand, four hundred twenty horse power." The seller continued, "The steel-constructed beauty comes with a helicopter pad and an exquisite pool."

"Its seaworthiness?" Volmer asked casually. He wanted—no, he needed—a vessel with the greatest possible command of vast distances of open sea.

"The best. It can take on the most hostile of storms."

Volmer's final question was asked with a frown. "And the cost?"

The dealer's smile faded. "The owner is Danish. He is asking only fifteen million Krone."

A casual conversation earlier in the morning with a French yacht owner had provided Volmer with an interesting nugget of information. The Danish owner of the vessel in question, a junior partner in one of Copenhagen's most prestigious law firms was about to be mired in a deep and costly divorce. According to the Frenchman, the owner was being forced to sell the yacht and other personal belongings in order to be able to buy a home in Cannes. The actual worth of his possessions was secondary to remediating the situation at hand.

"I would think so," Volmer replied condescendingly, "especially given his current predicament." Applying the current currency exchange, Volmer knew the asking price was nearly three million. Before the dealer could counter, he added, "I am prepared to offer at this moment one and a quarter million, but it comes with a condition attached."

"A condition?"

"Yes. I will give you fifteen minutes to confer with the owner. You might wish to inform him that I am considering several other vessels here in Izmir." He glanced at his watch. The time was 11:07 a.m. "Fifteen minutes will give me time to visit your lavatory. If I don't have his response by 11:22 a.m., I am walking out of this office. Understood?"

The yacht dealer had no intention of letting Volmer slip away. He saw the shortfall, but he would still walk away with a lot of money. "My client will accept your offer." With the utmost of courtesy, he added, "We can secure a transfer crew to deliver the craft to Copenhagen, if that pleases you."

"No, I think I'll go to Izmir myself. I'm due a little holiday. I've always wanted to visit Turkey. If you will contact the person there and take care of the financial arrangements, I'll take the train to Izmir."

"Very good, sir. Then let me at least make a recommendation. There is a man in Izmir, a friend of mine named Okur, Rasim Okur. I'll give you his name and contact information. He has a brother, a very experienced seaman who would be perfect for you, assuming he is available."

"I appreciate that."

"It is my pleasure, sir."

As Volmer was concluding his conversation with the man, he recalled his previous yacht *Parsifal* and the miles of red tape he had to go through getting it registered and inspected. "I know I'll be quite busy getting the craft registered and inspected before I can leave Izmir."

The dealer gave a nod. "Okur can handle all of that for you, sir. He is very thorough."

"That pleases me. I'll want to talk with him."

The following afternoon, Volmer called on the Copenhagen rental agency and paid them quite handsomely to terminate the lease on the condo. "Something has come up," he said amiably, as he chatted with the realtor, "that necessitates my immediate presence elsewhere. I trust you will be able to have it back on the market soon."

"You are not to worry about that, Mr. Thorssen. We are more than comfortable with the resolution of our business arrangement. Meeting the needs of our clients is our highest priority."

"What a laudable perspective," Volmer replied, wanting to leave behind no ill feelings. "How I wish other businesses showed such understanding."

That night, Ankiel Thorssen left by train for Izmir, Turkey.

Wednesday, February 19
Copenhagen, Denmark

Prior to leaving Copenhagen, Volmer contacted Dimitri Glaskov, a man in St. Petersburg through whom he had moved several forgeries during the seventies. He knew the man to be open to any kind of deal that would yield handsome profits. There was some risk involved in reaching out to the man, but Volmer knew the avaricious Russian would not cut his own throat by revealing to others that he was very much alive. Were he captured by authorities, it would not benefit Glaskov in any way. Moreover, Volmer wanted him within reach if, at some point in the future, he needed him again.

When Glaskov answered the phone, he could not have been more surprised. "Mother fuck!" he cried when he recognized the sound of Volmer's voice. "I thought your ass was dead."

Volmer couldn't resist paraphrasing a quote he remembered from a dark corner of his past: "It seems that word of my death has been somewhat exaggerated."

"I would say that's an understatement! Where are you?"

"Where I am is not important, but I will be in Monaco soon. Is there a chance you could meet me there? I have a lucrative business proposal to place before you."

"Only if you promise me two women in a Jacuzzi full of vodka." Glaskov laughed, a hearty, guttural Russian laugh. "I can be there when you like. When and where do you suggest we meet?"

Volmer thought for a moment. "How about the Shark Lagoon in the Oceanographic Museum? I've always had a soft spot for it."

"Ah, yes, the majestic predators. Why am I not surprised you would select it as the place for us to rendezvous. You sly devil, you!"

Volmer let the jocular comment pass. "I will be contacting you soon regarding the specific date."

The trip from Copenhagen to Izmir was broken by stops in Berlin and Leipzig on the Black Sea in the Ukraine. Volmer had not been to Berlin since the toppling of the Berlin Wall. Walking the streets of the city brought back some wonderful youthful memories, none more glorious than standing at his father's side as *der Führer* mesmerized an ocean of devoted Germans in front of the Brandenburg Gate. That had been in 1943. After the war, he followed with interest the shifting political climate in the Eastern Bloc countries that eventually led to unrest in East Berlin. The discontent manifested itself with the picking away at the wall by dissident Berliners until it was officially destroyed by the GDR. That action led to the reunification of Germany in October of 1990. Volmer, long a champion of one strong and unified Berlin, played the role of souvenir hunter by gathering a handful of pebbles at the crossing between what had been the two Berlins.

That evening, he ate a hearty meal at a neighborhood Wirtshaus. As the hour grew late and the beer flowed like an amber river, a party of elderly German men led the singing of *Deutschland, Deutschland, Uber Alles*. Seconds later, they were all raising their steins in salute, old men tearing, torn between the pain of guilt and the thought of what could have been. The thought arrived quickly. *I hear the wounded strings of their hearts.* The room looked like an underwater grotto through Volmer's misting eyes.

An hour later, he and a dancer named Greta shared a bottle and a half of wine in his hotel room. After which and much to his pleasure, she turned off the lights and started removing her clothing.

The only illumination came from a blinking red neon sign next to the window. As Greta pulled back the bed covers to welcome him, her splendid body became the color of blood. Volmer quickly shed his garments and inherited the seductive space. And then it happened again; his weapon deserted him. Arousal never came.

Greta was dressed and gone in a matter of minutes, but not before hurling a stinging jab at him. "Old men like you don't need to be playing this kind of game."

The stopover in Liepzig was different. The wine consumption from the night before, the humiliation of his sudden impotency and the long train ride from Berlin, found Volmer exhausted and depressed. He found a clean but inexpensive hotel near the train station and slept for nearly ten hours.

CHAPTER SEVENTEEN

A Beautiful Gypsy

Sunday, February 23
Izmir, Turkey

The sun was high in the sky when Volmer reached Izmir.

The yacht dealer in Nyhavn told him that his cousin who lived there had agreed to meet him at the base of the clock tower in Konak Square. The man, Rasim Okur, would be at the tower at 11:00 a.m., wearing a red fez. Okur would take Volmer to his brother Sadik.

Volmer found the clock tower without difficulty, arriving a few minutes before eleven. A stiff breeze floated in from the Aegean.

After waiting for a few minutes, he was approached by a middle-aged man in a crimson hat. He recognized Volmer by the description his cousin had provided.

"Good morning." His English was very precise. "May I assume you are Ankiel Thorssen from Copenhagen?"

"I am. You must be Rasim."

"Yes, yes. Welcome to Turkey!"

The two men talked briefly of the weather before Volmer asked to see his new purchase.

"Well, of course." Rasim's broad smile revealed a mouthful of teeth in need of attention. "It is only a short distance from here to the harbor. She is a beauty. I believe you will be well pleased."

The yacht carried the name *Clytemnestra* and was flying a Turkish flag. Volmer inwardly smiled at the appellation, recalling that in Greek legend Clytemnestra was accused of murdering her husband Agamemnon.

"A dramatic choice of names," he said, the inward smile now very much on the outside.

"Yes, I would agree," Rasim replied.

Volmer then raised the issue central to his being in Izmir. "I'm told

153

you can take me to your brother, Sadik."

"Yes, we can go there now, if you like."

"I would like that. I have some urgent business this afternoon for which I may need Sadik's services—assuming, he is interested in becoming my captain."

Rasim led Volmer through several narrow streets lined with food vendors. The blended aromas appealed to Volmer's olfactory senses. As they passed a darkened alley filled with cats, Volmer's nostrils caught a distinctive scent. "What is that delightful smell?"

"You are smelling *lokrna*," Rasim said with a smile. "Assorted fried pastries. They are absolutely delicious." He could tell from Volmer's comments and visual curiosity that he was intrigued with the densely populated section of Izmir. "We are on the fringe of the Kemeralti Bazaar. It is quite famous ... very low prices. We can stroll about for a few minutes, if you like."

"No thank you, Rasim. I don't have the time for the luxury of shopping. I need to find Sadik as soon as possible."

"I understand." Rasim sensed Volmer's urgency and the slight shift in his mood. "We are quite close now, just a few more minutes."

Rasim walked briskly and soon came to a small doorway draped with strings of colorful beads. He made an opening and gestured for Volmer to enter. Volmer was greeted by a thick blanket of cigarette smoke. It was a bar, he realized, staying close on Rasim's heels.

"We wait here," Rasim said cheerfully. "Sadik should be here soon. Would you care to join me in a cup of *Turk Kahvesi*? It is a coffee special to Izmir. We call it a drink of friendship."

Volmer would have preferred a *Dewar's*, but yielded to his host's suggestion. While they sat, waiting on Okur and enjoying the robust coffee, Volmer asked, "What can you tell me about your brother?"

"Oh, he is a legend here, a sailor without peer. He was born in Diyarbakir, north of the Syrian border and fought in the brief nineteen seventy-four Turkish invasion of Cyprus. He lost his left eye to a grenade, but he can still see more from his one good eye than most seamen can do with two. Sadik is as strong as a bull ... feared by most men." Rasim paused to take a deep sip of coffee. "Perhaps the most complimentary thing I can say about him is that he is remarkably loyal to those he trusts."

Rasim's description was cut short by the appearance of a giant of a man nearly six and a half feet tall. When Rasim saw him coming to their table, he immediately stood up and extended both arms. After they embraced, Rasim made the introductions.

Okur towered above Volmer. Rasim had told Volmer that his brother was in his forties, but his heavy, black beard, distinctively lobed brow and lone penetrating eye made him look older. In his left occipital socket, Okur had a glass eye that did not appear in synch with his right eye. It looked as if it had been selected for no good reason other than to fill the cavity.

When the two men shook hands, Volmer had the unsettling feeling he was exchanging greetings with a large bear. To his relief, Sadik Okur spoke acceptable English.

"I hear you look for an experienced captain." Okur's voice was deep, resonant. "I am that man."

"Yes, Volmer responded. "I need a captain and a crew to get my yacht back to Copenhagen. I was told you are as good as they come."

"For the right price, yes." The glass eye shifted slightly.

Rasim followed the conversation for a few minutes before finding a good opportunity to take his leave. "It has been a pleasure, Mr. Thorssen. I do hope things will work out well for you."

"Thank you, Rasim. You have been very helpful." He placed a few folded bills in the man's hand.

"You are too kind." Rasim bowed slightly before scurrying away.

Volmer waited until Rasim had disappeared and then asked Okur, "Perhaps you would like to see the boat. We can talk there in a much more private way."

Okur nodded, but offered no verbal response.

There were probably many unusual sights to be experienced that day in Izmir, but none more striking than the one of diminutive Theo Volmer walking alongside the colossus with the glass eye.

When they reached the boat, Okur stood silently for a few moments, absorbing the beauty of the shining black vessel.

Volmer was curious about his impression. "Do you approve?"

"She is like a beautiful gypsy."

Volmer took Okur's response as a positive one and ushered him aboard. He then essentially stepped back so that Okur could have full run of the ship.

After fifteen minutes of meticulous inspection, Okur returned to Volmer and said five words that summarized his reaction and position: "I go as your captain."

For the next few minutes, Okur said few words as he scratched out numerous notes on a small, pocket tablet, things that would need to be done before they could depart. When he had concluded his assessment of needs, he turned to Volmer. "We talk now."

As a student might listen to the words of a gifted teacher, Volmer absorbed Okur's words without interruption. "I need these things to do: One, the boat must be registered. I go to Istanbul for this. Two, we need a crew of seven: a chief engineer, four able seamen—AB's—a cook, a doctor. Three, I need to know days at sea. From Izmir, where to go? Four, provisions for journey." He looked at Volmer. "Where do we go?"

Volmer was not expecting the question in such a blunt fashion. He had already decided against returning to Copenhagen. In looking at a map of the French coastline earlier in the day, he initially thought of Charron, the last port in France before the border with Belgium. The downside to Charron was its small size. If he didn't want his new vessel anchored in the harbor at Nyhavn where it most certainly would attract attention, it would garner precisely that in Charron. Le Havre was ideal. It was a larger, busier port in which he would be less visible. He experienced a moment of uncertainty as to how Okur would respond to a man from Denmark selecting a French port as his final destination. "Our initial destination is Le Havre, but I first have business to take care of in Monaco. Are you good with that?"

Okur nodded without expression. "Yes, good." He worked for a few more minutes in his note pad and then added, "Monaco nine hundred nautical miles ... ten knots ... three to four days at sea. Monaco to Le Havre, eleven days at sea. From Monaco, we stop at Lisbon and Brest. Crew rest, repairs, provisions."

Volmer wanted to know the bookends. "From Izmir to Le Havre, how long will it take us?"

"If we keep ten to twelve knots, make stops and no bad weather we be there in three to four weeks. Four to five hundred sea hours. This a long trip."

Volmer was displeased. *I didn't realize it would take so long.*

"We be in some rough currents. The Strait of Gibraltar can be fucking bitch. Winds, layovers for crew rest ... three weeks ... could be longer."

"All right," Volmer conceded, not wanting to irritate the one man who at the present time held control over his life. Okur had been very thorough in checking and double-checking everything. From his own certificate of international competency to the vessel's radio license, the veteran captain had checked off a litany of necessary concerns prior to departure: liability insurance papers; immigration forms; crew selections including passports and vaccinations; proof of VAT, value added tax; registration papers through the Danish Consulate in Istanbul; clearance papers from Izmir.

Volmer knew only too well that the transfer of a boat from one owner to another was not a routine matter, especially given the fact that his passport and papers were bogus. By his calculations, it would be April before they could reach Le Havre. He faced the option of remaining in Izmir twiddling his thumbs while Okur completed his checklist, or spending the time in a more rewarding way. He opted for the latter.

"One last question, Okur. How long before we will be ready to leave Izmir?"

"Hard to say ... maybe ten days. Much to do."

Volmer had hoped to be away sooner. "Very good. There is something I want you to do before we sail from Izmir."

"Yes?"

"I want the name of the yacht changed to Largo. He withdrew a small piece of paper from his trouser pocket and gave it to Okur. "As you will see," he began in a slow, deliberate manner, "the new name is here and I would like the lettering to be a close as possible to the font used with the current name. Will you see to this?"

"I think it not a good idea to change name of boat, sir."

"And why not?" Volmer countered sharply. "I'm not happy with the existing name."

"Change of boat name bring bad luck."

At first, Volmer thought Okur might be joking, but the intense expression on his dark face suggested otherwise. The man was quite serious. "Well, let me say this about luck, Okur. I don't believe in luck ... good or bad."

Okur was openly disturbed, but his limited command of English prevented him from adequately explaining the time-honored protocol for approaching such an act. "The god of the sea ... we must ask Poseidon ..." Okur's huge arms began waving in the air like blades of a large windmill in a frantic effort to clarify what he was unable to do with words.

Two men were standing within earshot of their conversation, admiring the yacht. One of the men, thinking he might help the owner understand Okur's concerns, offered, "If I may be permitted to intrude, the seaman is referring to a widely held belief—legend, some would say—which calls for the purging of a boat's name from the Ledger of the Deep. He is trying to tell you there is a ceremony associated with the changing of a vessel's name."

Volmer shot him an angry glance. "I'm not the least bit interested in such ridiculous folklore." Turning back to Okur, he said, "I want this done before we leave. I will be in Naples for the next several days on business. When you have completed everything and are within two days of leaving, contact me at the Grand Hotel Vesuvio." He handed Okur a folded sheet of white paper with the contact information. "I can be back here within twenty-four hours." He paused for a moment. "Sadik, it is not my wish to offend you in this regard. If it will ease your unrest, we can talk about this ceremony once we are underway."

Okur looked at him without a hint of anything resembling thanks or appreciation. "It is best to do, sir."

"Of course," Volmer replied, bristling with irritation.

Before leaving Izmir, and on the recommendation of Rasim Okur, Volmer met with a Turkish doctor, who spoke passable German. His meds were gone and he needed a fresh supply. The subject of their conversation was not a comfortable one for Volmer.

"And you say this ... this sexual problem has happened before?" the doctor asked.

"Yes, a couple of times," Volmer replied, forcing the words out.

"If I may ask, what is your age and what medications are you taking?"

"I was on a statin and some pill for hypertension," Volmer replied.

"And your age, sir?"

"Fifty-seven," Volmer replied through a frown.

He studied Volmer's face carefully. "The drugs you referenced ... you were taking them, or you are taking them?"

"Was taking. I ran out of them two weeks ago."

The physician excused himself for a moment. When he returned to the examining room, he had two green plastic bottles in his hand, each with an identifying label in English.

The doctor took a moment to explain the dosage of each drug.

Volmer then realized that this man of medicine didn't write prescriptions. If one had the money, the good doctor had the pills.

Tuesday, February 25
Anghiari, Italy

A day had not passed since Astrid Borgmann learned of the Gade robbery that she didn't think of Gatti's comment while they were in Cortona: *If I were to come to you with a proposal to relieve the Louvre or the Prado of one of its most valuable paintings, would you consider joining me in the venture?* Had that been just playful talk, or did he already have the Gade Collection in his sights? And what about the hairbrush she took from his bathroom? If she could get it into the hands of the Danish authorities, would it aid them in making an arrest?

That evening The Verrocchio was busier than usual. Astrid went through her usual courtship of new customers, greeted her familiar patrons with hugs and, for the most part, put thoughts of Azzo Gatti aside.

About nine o'clock, the latter changed when she saw the police chief and his wife arrive. She knew the man as a diligent, fair, committed, and stubborn civil servant. Antonio Fleri had been keeping the residents and streets of Anghiari safe for over twenty years and if the word beloved could be applied to an officer of the law, Fleri was entitled to wear the badge.

She extended a warm welcome after they were seated, complimented Sophia Fleri on her dress and then asked Fleri if he would be able to see her on the following day. "It's probably nothing," she said, smiling at his wife Sophia," but I may have some information that could be of some value regarding the recent art theft in Copenhagen. I assume you are familiar with it."

In his richly textured voice, he replied evenly, "I am aware of it, yes." His deep brown eyes—eyes which always reminded Astrid of the actor Omar Shariff—studied her face for a moment. "My morning is open. Come at your pleasure."

"Then around nine?"

Fleri seemed more reserved than usual, somber almost. "I will be expecting you," he replied, picking up the menu and scanning it quickly. "As interested as I am in what you wish to share with me tomorrow, I am more curious about your specialties tonight. What are you recommending?"

"The veal scaloppini is beyond wonderful, but if I were joining the two of you for dinner tonight I would have the yellowfin corvina. It is simply delicious. The best we've had in months."

Fleri hinted at a smile. "Why do you always make it difficult, *signora*?"

Her smile was like a ray of sunshine. "So you will keep coming back!"

Fleri was surprisingly cheerful when she entered his office the following morning shortly before nine. "Have a seat, please. You will have to forgive my mood last evening, Astrid. I spent most of the day with grieving parents. Their only child had been struck by a car. The injuries were fatal."

"I'm so sorry. I sensed something last night. I can't imagine having to deal with such a tragedy."

Fleri didn't want to revisit yesterday. "So," he began, interlacing his large fingers and placing them across his chest, "what is this about Copenhagen? You said you had some information about the theft."

"A question first, Antonio. Did you meet Azzo Gatti during his brief time here?"

"Gatti, the short fellow? Yes, I met him. I passed him from time to time on the street. He seemed a bit remote, especially for an Italian." Fleri smiled and added, "Please don't take this the wrong way, Astrid, but the first time I met him I thought he was quite odd."

Astrid moved quickly to another topic. "I never told you this about my late husband Fritz. He once took part in a museum robbery. The Musee Mormottan Monet in Paris. He died before he would have been sent to prison."

Fleri knew she was taking the long way home. He also knew about the Mormottan. "1985, I believe."

She nodded, avoiding eye contact with him. "When I told Azzo about Fritz, he showed considerable interest in the robbery. One day, he asked me—in jest, I thought—if I would accompany him if he chose to rob a museum."

"How very interesting," Fleri replied, releasing his fingers in order to scratch an itching spot near his ankle. "How did you answer that question?"

She hesitated for a moment before replying. "I told him I would. Does that shock you?"

"Not in the least. Women in love sometimes say strange things."

"We were not in love, Antonio. We were just good friends."

"Yes, of course. And just what does your relationship with Azzo Gatti have to do with the Gade Collection? What am I missing?"

"Azzo left Anghiari around Christmastime without saying a word to me. Thinking he might have taken a bad fall, I went to his villa to make sure he was all right. He was not there. The place was in shambles. It was obvious he had departed very quickly. Just as I was leaving, I saw his hairbrush on the bathroom sink. I took it and left immediately."

"You took his hairbrush? Why? A souvenir, perhaps?"

"No, Antonio. I took it because of its possible DNA value."

Fleri sat upright in his chair. "Go on."

"Gatti was involved in the Gade theft, I just know it."

Fleri leveled his eyes on hers. "How can you be certain of this?"

"The hairbrush! It will prove it."

Fleri paused before he asked, "Do you still have it?"

"I do. I want you to take it." Astrid produced a small paper bag from her tote and handed it across the desk. "If Gatti was involved in the Gade robbery, it might be of value to the Danish police. Will you see that the police in Copenhagen get it?"

Fleri studied her face for a long moment before replying, "I will place a call there later today."

"Bravo! There ... I have said what I came to say." She got up to leave and then paused in front of his desk. "Did you have the veal scaloppini or the corvina?"

"The corvina. It was superb."

Two days later, as she was preparing to leave for her duties at The Verrocchio, Antonio Fleri called her. She could tell from the tone of his voice that the call was not just a social one.

"Astrid, I trust I am not catching you at a bad time."

"No, not at all. I'm wrapping up a few things before leaving for the restaurant. This is a good time, actually."

There was a brief pause before Fleri said, "I received a call earlier in the day from the Danish authorities in Copenhagen.

"Yes?" Astrid bit her lower lip, afraid to hear what Fleri was about to say.

"I'm sorry to have to tell you this, but the person I spoke with said it was virtually useless."

"Useless? How can that be?"

"A combination of things. The police were unable to retrieve any evidence with usable DNA from the crime scene. Even if they had Gatti's hairs, there was no way for them to establish a match. They appreciated your efforts, but ..."

Fighting back tears, she asked, "So, what now?"

"I believe you should keep it in a secure, dry place, should the day come when it can be of some use." He could imagine the disappointment etched on her face. "I'm sorry, Astrid."

"So am I."

CHAPTER EIGHTEEN

Shark Lagoon

Thursday, March 6
Naples, Italy

Sadik Okur reached Volmer at his hotel in Naples, shortly before noon. Eleven days had passed since Volmer left Izmir and he had become increasingly irritable. The call could not have been more welcomed. Volmer struggled to hide his feelings. Alienating Okur at this juncture was not a good idea. "It is time we go." Okur's voice was scratchy due to the connection. "I have delay in Instanbul, but everything now good."

"And the name change?"

There was a moment of silence before Okur said,"Yes, it is done."

"Good. I will be there by morning."

"Yes, tomorrow. We go then."

Volmer made a quick call to Glaskov while packing and half-listening to a news report on television. Thus far, there had apparently been no major developments in the Gade Collection case, or at least none that surfaced in the media. Interpol was involved, but he felt comfortable in knowing there were no links to him or his team. Fuchs had returned to his farm in Stuttgart to meet with a potential buyer and Jannik Eriksson no longer existed. As for Bager, they had talked a few times by phone since parting company. Volmer was quite pleased with his role in the operation and wanted to strengthen their relationship. There could well come a time when he would need the German again, and Bager had made it clear he could drop what he was doing at a moment's notice.

Once Volmer checked in at the Naples International Airport, he stopped at a kiosk for a paper and then at a coffee shop for a cappuchino and a biscotti in order to quell the rumbling in his stomach. While enjoying the few minutes before departure, he perused the paper. If there were any new developments with the Gade Collection case, the paper would carry them. In glancing at the headlines, he saw that Italy's plan for an eight-year schooling plan was drawing heavy fire from Islamists, and that the Italian government was clamping down on the flood of illegal immigrants from Albania, calling them "dangerous" and "undesirable." In a small block showing major news events on that date in history, he read that in 1945 Adolf Hitler issued his "Nero Decree," calling for the destruction of all German factories. He also noted that it was on this date in 1965 that Rembrandt's "Titus" sold for the then record 7,770,000 guilders. Volmer approximated the conversion in American dollars: a little over two million. Pocket change. It was on page three that his core received a seismic shock. The article was not lengthy, but a specific passage greatly disturbed him:

... doubt cast on former Uffici director's death ...

There is emerging speculation that Theo Volmer was sighted in Florence, just days after the fire that destroyed his home in nearby Fiesole on April 2, 1996. German authorities, as well as Scotland Yard, have confirmed that on April 6 a large number of artworks from Volmer's private collection were discovered in a Stuttgart storage facility. Included in this remarkable find were a number of stolen paintings that were traced back to Nazi thefts from Jewish collectors and museums in the late thirties. Also of comparable interest, a number of forged artworks were found in the storage facility, works from a highly orchestrated forgery ring now believed to have been masterminded by Volmer from the sixties to the early eighties.

Danish authorities are now looking into the very real possibility that Theo Volmer perpetrated the recent theft at the prestigious Gade Collection in Copenhagen. As additional information is made known to the *Berlingski Tidende*, we will share that with the public."

As upset as he was by the newspaper article, Volmer was still satisfied that he had left no damning evidence behind in the van, or in the Copenhagen condo following the heist. As far as his appearance, he had taken pains to alter it as much as possible. Ever the chameleon, the contact lenses had been altered, his hair was now in a ponytail and his bogus passports and papers had yet to raise the first question. He just had to keep moving, changing his colors. He knew that he would soon need to make a long-awaited trip to Nashville, but after that the *Largo* could disappear forever in South America, or any number of places on the Asian rim.

Several days before Volmer left Copenhagen for Izmir, he rented a car and took a flat cardboard box containing the Gade paintings to Gunther Fuchs in Stuttgart. "I will ask you to hold this for me until I contact you," In his mind, he was reliving his father's arrangement with Gunther's father in 1944.

Fuchs smiled. "I'm sorry to say it is no longer with us." He pointed to a large structure with a bright green roof. "During the heavy summer rains in 1972, it completely collapsed. I bulldozed that entire area and built the barn you see there. I have plenty of space inside. It's as dry as a bone."

"Keep it safe." Without saying another word, Volmer returned to the car with the empty portfolio.

Fuchs watched him drive away. *Something has pissed him off, big time.*

✒

Saturday, March 8
Nashville, Tennessee

Largo and Blue were enjoying the rarity of a few hours of extra morning sleep when the bedside telephone rang. Blue took the call, but when he heard the soft voice of a woman asking for Largo, he rolled over and handed her the phone. It was Nils Gade's secretary, calling from Copenhagen.

"I trust I am not calling too early, the woman said in perfect English. Mr. Gade will be leaving within the hour for Brussels and he wishes to speak with you briefly, if this is a convenient time."

"Yes, of course," Largo's voice was still laced with sleep. "This is a good time."

"I'll get coffee," Blue said softly, as Largo waited for Gade to pick up the phone.

She nodded.

Gade apologized for the early call, but wasted little time in getting to his reason for doing so. "Ms. Kopacz, you were kind enough to phone me recently with information about Theo Volmer, the former director of the Uffizi Gallery in Florence, Italy. I have since relayed that information to the police who are investigating the matter. My reason for calling today is that the editor of one of our major newspapers, the *Beriingske Tidende*, has been in Washington, D.C. for a meeting of international newspaper editors. He will be returning to Denmark next week. He would very much like to interview you before he leaves the States regarding your association with Volmer, especially your sighting of him in Florence days after the fire at his Fiesole home. I know this is very short notice and the last thing I want to do is intrude on your privacy, but would it be possible for you to meet with him on the eleventh or the twelfth? A follow-up article on this matter might help to move faster in arresting those responsible for this crime."

"I will be glad to assist, in any way I can, Mr. Gade. I am teaching two classes at Vanderbilt University, but I feel sure I can make some time available on Wednesday, the twelfth. My office is small, but it should provide adequate privacy. May I have his name please, so I will recognize him when he calls."

"His name is Christer Njord. The last name is spelled N-J-O-R-D. Again, the newspaper is the *Berlingske Tidende*. As with Njord's name, Gade spelled each of the two words. "I will contact him and tell him that you will be available on the twelfth. With your permission, I'll give him your telephone number, so a suitable time can be arranged."

"Yes, that's fine. I will be listening for his call."

"Thank you, Ms. Kopacz, for your assistance and cooperation."

"I'm happy to do so."

Largo handed Blue the telephone and repositioned herself in the bed so she could drink her coffee. "I don't know how much of that you were able to follow, but one of the Danish papers wants to interview me about Volmer."

"How do you feel about that?"

She took a delicate sip of the hot coffee. "I have mixed feelings, but I feel an obligation to help Nils Gade, if I can. It's the right thing to do."

"You're a nice lady," Blue replied from his position at the foot of the bed, a broad smile forming on his face. "I think I like you."

She returned it. "You say the nicest things."

Wednesday, March 12
Nashville, Tennessee

The editor of Copenhagen's *Berlingske Tidende*, Christer Njord, knocked loudly on the door of Largo's office shortly after one-thirty in the afternoon. She was in the midst of grading some exams, and before she could reach the door the knocking intensified. "I'm coming," she called out, her irritation subsiding when she remembered that she had agreed to meet the man that afternoon. "I'm coming."

The reporter took a step back when she opened the door and promptly introduced himself. "I am very grateful to you, Ms. Kopacz, for making this time available to me. I promise, I will not take long."

"That's fine, I'm happy to do this. Please come in, and do call me Largo." As she moved aside so he could enter, she added, "I'm just about to fix a cup of tea. I hope you'll join me."

"I will indeed, thank you."

She gestured to an empty chair next to her desk. "Then please make yourself comfortable. I won't be but a second."

For the next two or three minutes while Largo fixed their tea, he glanced about the office, making note of the books that filled a small bookcase. *Someone is a reader of fiction.* He studied two paintings that hung on either side of a window, deciding they were a bit too abstract for his taste. "Your office has a comfortable feel about it, cluttered, but comfortable."

Largo found herself smiling at Njord's candor. "We moved to Nashville recently. I would have invited you to come to our home, but things are still in boxes. It's a mess."

"This arrangement is fine. I rather like seeing where teachers work."

The man sitting across from her appeared to be in his fifties with sandy colored hair, graying slightly at the temples, nearly six feet tall. A shy smile dominated his face. His voice was low, husky even, and carried a decided Danish flavor. To her way of thinking, he looked more like a bank teller. "So, you wish to interview me about Theo Volmer?"

"Well, yes, and a few related issues, with your consent."

"Before you begin, Christer, I do want to ask a favor or, to put it more bluntly, establish a condition for this interview."

"A condition?"

"Yes, I do not want my name used in any way. My reasons are quite personal."

Njord nodded, appreciating the flavor of the tea. "We can work around that. Would you be comfortable if I said something like a person who wishes to remain anonymous, says thus and so?"

"Yes, I'm fine with that."

"He reached into one of the pockets in his jacket and withdrew a small recording device. "Do you have objections to my taping this interview, Largo?"

"No, not at all."

"Then let us begin. If, for any reason, you want or need to stop, just say so."

For the first minute or so of the interview, Njord provided a brief summary of Volmer's ascendancy to the position of director of the Uffizi Gallery in Florence, Italy. He then turned to Largo. "For the record, will you please tell me when you first met director Volmer and under what conditions?"

"I met him, as best I can recall, in mid-March of last year. I flew to Italy to spend some time with my fiancée Porter Blue in Florence. Porter had recently made Volmer's acquaintance, and he was anxious for me to meet him. Our initial meeting was in his Uffizi office."

"In general, how would you describe Theo Volmer?"

"Do you mean physically?"

"Yes, that, as well as his manner or personality."

She thought for a moment. "Well, I would begin by saying that he initially struck me as being quite charismatic—intelligent, cultured, very self-confident. Striking eyes, like those of a wolf."

"A wolf? How interesting. I take it he made a strong first impression."

"Yes, he did."

"As you came to know him, did that first impression change in any way?"

"Yes."

"Will you qualify that, please?"

"I grew uncomfortable in his presence. He was not—how shall I put it—respectful of personal boundaries."

Njord's face morphed into a frown. "Are you saying he was inappropriate with you at times?"

"Yes, that would be an accurate way of putting it."

Njord paused again. "Largo, I have tried to do my homework on you, and Volmer for that matter, so that my questions today could be as focused as possible. In doing so, I was made aware that you are of Jewish lineage. Is that correct?"

"Yes, that is true."

"And, by contrast," Njord continued, "Volmer's father served under Hermann Göring in Hitler's SS."

"Yes, that is my understanding," Largo replied, a bit uncomfortable with the path he was taking.

"I understand a detective from Scotland Yard found a painting once owned by your great-grandparents in a storage facility in Stuttgart, Germany, surrounded by scores of stolen artworks and forgeries, all from Volmer's personal collection."

"That's correct."

"Was that before or after the fire in his Fiesole home?"

"After the fire."

Njord's bombsight was now squarely above the target. "Largo, I was sent here by my paper to specifically question you about the assertion you recently shared with Mr. Nils Gade that Theo Volmer survived the fire in his home. As you may know, the official Florentine report clearly states that he perished in that fire and that his remains were cremated shortly thereafter. So that I may be absolutely certain of your position on this matter, let me ask you to state for the record the basis of your claim."

Largo took a slow, deep breath before replying. "I will give you two instances that will show the official police report to be erroneous: First, I saw Theo Volmer walk from a building near the station of Santa Maria Novella to a waiting car days after the fire. He was not more than twenty-five feet away. Just before he entered the vehicle, he looked my way—not at me specifically, but in my direction—and I saw his distinctive eyes. Secondly, on one of my final days in Florence, my fiancee and I were meeting with Interim Uffizi director Lucca Palma when a vase of flowers was delivered to his office." She handed Njord a small card. "This card was attached to the flowers. I will ask you to read the inscription."

Njord read it slowly and carefully.

Happy Birthday! Sorry about the little mishap on the way to Choggia. Had that pesky little dog not run in front of the car, we would be having cocktails about now on my yacht. I'll never be far from you.

When he returned the card to Largo, he said, "I don't wish to appear insensitive, but the note is not signed. How can you be certain it came from Theo Volmer?"

"While I was in Florence, I was abducted at gunpoint from a tour bus returning from Pisa and driven miles from Florence. I was held for several days by three criminals. On my last day in captivity, I was being taken to Choggia when the driver swerved to miss a little dog and slammed into the rear of the car in front of him. Fortunately, I was able to escape." It was her turn to pause. "Guess who owned a yacht at anchor in Choggia that day?"

"I am assuming it was Volmer," Njord said, easily reading between the lines. "Did Volmer's background pose any problems for you? In other words, did that contribute in any way to the inappropriateness you referenced a few moments ago?"

"I would like to answer that by showing you something." She reached behind her chair and picked up a large tan leather shoulder bag. From it she removed an object wrapped with a white pillow case. As she removed the protective material, she said "This painting was done by a fifteenth-century painter from the Netherlands by the name of Hans Memling. My great-grandparents in Krakow owned this painting until it was stolen by the Nazis in 1939. During my initial visit to Volmer's home last year, I found this painting hanging on a wall in a secluded part of the home. There's a long story here, but I think this should answer completely any questions about the inappropriateness of his actions."

Njord closed a small notebook and turned off the recording device. Looking at her, he said in a gentle and caring way, "You have been more than helpful, Largo. What you have shared with me today satisfies not only my questions, but those of my paper. I have every reason to believe this information, coupled with the recent article on our paper, will raise strong doubt about the death of Theo Volmer. Who knows, it might be the first step in revealing the truth about him and that, more than anything else, is my primary objective here. Thank you for your courtesy, courage and hospitality."

"You are more than welcome, Christer. It has been a pleasure meeting you."

As he stepped to the door, he reassured her that her name would not appear in any article the paper released.

"You have no idea how appreciative I am of that sensitivity. I will tell you honestly, I am frightened to death of that man."

"And understandably so."

CHAPTER NINETEEN

The Prince of Deceit

The news that Theo Volmer might be alive arrested the full attention of Lucca Palma, the current director of the Uffizi Gallery. Following Volmer's abrupt and unexpected abdication of his duties in late March of 1996, Palma was appointed interim director. Six months later, the term interim was removed.

During the twelve years that Palma had faithfully served Volmer, he endured countless times of embarrassment and humiliation at the hands of his superior. As they differed more than night and day in their work ethic and views on the role of a major museum, Volmer delighted in poking fun at Palma's old-fashioned ideas when the two were together at public gatherings and charity events.

From his end, Palma saw Volmer as a skilled showman, much more interested in being the center of attention than a dedicated public servant. The Uffizi, as Palma saw it, belonged to the people of Florence. In contrast, Volmer saw the vast collection as a backdrop for his own interests and ambitions, a stage on which he could trumpet his own achievements.

When Crister Njord's article in the *Berlingski Tidende* revealed that Volmer had orchestrated a twenty-year forgery ring under the umbrella of the Uffizi, Lucca Palma's years of frustration and anger rushed forward like a raging river over its banks. In an uncharacteristic fashion, he contacted every Italian newspaper and television station and told them it was time for the public to be fully aware of Volmer's dark and destructive hand.

Interviews followed by the dozens. Phrases like *the prince of deceit, abuser of the public trust, the conscience of a viper,* and the like, flowed from Palma's lips.

None of this was lost on Volmer. With so much of his time going to the scrutiny of European newspapers and media outlets for information relating to the status of the Gade Collection investigation, Palma's excoriations were known to him within hours of their release. *How dare this bean counter slander my genius!* He toyed with the idea of bottling his vitriol and sending it in the form of a letter to Palma, but wisely realized there was a much better way to vent his spleen. *Your day is coming, Lucca. Of that, you may be certain.*

For men like Theo Volmer, the ultimate goal in life was possession; wealth, power and women being the most enticing ends, though not always in that order. Such a driven person thrives on adventure and views risks as not only part of the process, but the essence of the hunt. Like a parachutist, it is the act of throwing oneself out of an airplane that is the opiate, not the planting of one's feet safely on the ground.

Consider Volmer's elaborate planning for and execution of the Gade Collection theft. The thrill of it all was the split-second timing, knowing as he parked the van near the train station that the slightest miscalculation could result in his demise. To walk away from the van and seconds later experience the vibrations of its destruction was orgasmic.

Through men like Glaskov, he had disposed of scores of forgeries and realized millions in return. He enjoyed having paintings on the walls of his home, but when he looked at them he saw the by-product of his ingenuity, not the magic that had come from and through the painter's brush. His goal was to possess his treasures, not enjoy, or learn, or be enlightened or fed by them. But all of this had come with a cost. Approaching the age of sixty, he was finding emptiness where there had been plenty. Until his devastating experiences with Dona and Greta, he had known every conceivable sensual pleasure with women, but never had he heard the whisper of love from them. Only Astrid had expressed such depth of feeling, but her words of endearment had the reverse effect: they made him feel trapped.

And now, the blistering words of Lucca Palma and Njord's exposé had Volmer confronting a black-cloaked adversary for the first time in his life: fear.

He made two telephone calls before leaving Izmir. He called Fuchs and directed him to deliver the package to a gallery dealer in Monaco. He provided all necessary details. "I will appreciate it, Gunther, if you do this right away." He then called Verne Bazinet, the asthmatic owner of a gallery in Monaco. Bazinet had fenced several paintings for him in earlier days. In his phone conversation with Bazinet, Volmer told him a package was being delivered to him at the gallery by a private courier. "You are not to open it," he said with bluntness. "Once I can get to Monaco, I will come to your gallery with a friend. We will have need of a private room to review its contents. If you will do as I request and keep your mouth shut, you will not be disappointed by your compensation."

Bazinet made a motion with his fingers across his mouth. "My mouth is zippered."

"Keep an eye out for the courier. I will contact you again when I get there."

<hr>

Monday, March 24
Izmir, Turkey

The *Largo* left for Monaco an hour after sunset in a light fog. "It poses no problem," Okur explained to Volmer as he followed the channel lights and eased away from the harbor. "It will clear."

From the tone of his voice, Volmer sensed that he was still upset about the name change. As the craft gradually moved further and further away from land, Okur turned to Volmer and said, "It is like this at times."

By nine o'clock, Okur's prophecy had proven true.

Overhead, an absolutely cloud-free night sky looked like something that might have come from the brushes of van Gogh; glittering stars for as far as the eye could see. Below the water's surface, thousands upon thousands of phosphorescent lights sparkled, as if in harmony with the stars. Volmer had called Galskov. They would meet in Monaco three days hence. The evening seemed cool, but for Volmer the operative word for the moment was gorgeous.

It was during the journey from Izmir to Monaco that Volmer first noticed it; the difference between a fair-skinned, blond-headed sailor and the other able-bodied seamen. What immediately arrested his attention was the boy's physique. Lean and muscular, approximately six feet tall with a slightly sloping forehead and firm jaw, he so closely resembled the young Aryan men that exemplified Hitler's vision of a master race that it was all Volmer could do not to stare. His striking looks evoked vivid recollections of torch-lit Nazi rallies, standing with his father and relishing the endless rows of German warriors, all girded for war and raising their strong arms in salute to Adolph Hitler. In this young man he saw that same sense of pride. Volmer found himself struggling to suppress his immediate physical attraction to the boy.

The sailor, Dieter Acker, spoke fluent Turkish with a command of grammar far exceeding that of his colleagues. Volmer would come to learn that the young man was equally fluent in English, German and French; a linguistic skill bank nearly comparable to his own.

Taken as a whole, the other seamen could have come from the same set of parents. They were all dark-skinned, physically assertive, profane and given to fighting at the slightest provocation, usually during or following a high-stakes poker game. Acker, by contrast, spent his free time either reading or drawing in a small sketchbook. He could match any man on the ship in tackling demanding tasks, but when he was off the clock he was a very private person.

On the second day out of Izmir, Volmer was enjoying a few minutes of reading near the bow of the ship. He was about midway through a passage in Hitler's *Mein Kampf* when he realized that two eyes were observing him intently. They belonged to Acker who was seated at the base of a flight of metal steps leading up to the bridge, his left hand deftly recording the strong contours of Volmer's face.

"Sorry," the young man said when he saw an expression of disapproval form on Volmer's face.

"Are you not supposed to be working?" Volmer barked.

"I'm on my break, sir. I was just having a smoke."

Volmer studied his golden hair in the light. He was indeed a handsome young man. "Let me see it ... the drawing you were making."

Acker surrendered the folded sketchbook showing the portrait.

For a few moments, Volmer examined it without speaking. He flipped several pages of the sketchbook, astonished at the level of graphic competency. In addition to studies of the crew, he had made meticulous drawings of rope knots and other features of the boat. Volmer was immediately reminded of the incisive markings of Leonardo da Vinci in his studies for a woman's womb or an armored tank. Acker showed the same economy of means, the ability to summarize a subject, or object, with laser-like accuracy. Some of his studies showed the slightest hint of shading which gave the image a stronger sense of three-dimensionality. When returning the sketchbook to the young man, Volmer realized another similarity with Leonardo; the young man was also left-handed.

"You draw quite well." Volmer's earlier show of disapproval was now gone. After turning a few more pages, he came to one filled with numerical symbols. "What are these?" he asked, focusing his eyes on Acker's own.

"*Das sind mathematische Vorstellungen.* They are mathematical notations," the young man replied in German. "*Mathe Ratzel, nichts besonderes.* Math puzzles, if you like. Nothing special."

"*Warum sprichst Du jetzt Deutsch?* Why did you shift to German?" Volmer asked with a blend of uncertainty and suspicion.

Acker replied in English, "I thought you might appreciate it, sir."

"Appreciate it?" Volmer snapped. "What do you mean?"

"You are German, as well, are you not?"

"I am a Dane." Volmer replied emphatically. "Whatever gave you the impression I am German?"

"Sorry, sir. I am obviously mistaken. It was something I picked up on when I first heard your voice. I offer my apologies."

Volmer evaded a direct response. If he was critical of the sailor's presumptousness, he was equally impressed with the size of his balls. "What is your name?"

"Acker, sir. Dieter Acker."

"Then tell me, Dieter," Volmer said in German with a coy smile, "*Wo bist Du aufgewachsen? In Suddutsclands?* Where did you grow up? In southern Germany?"

Acker looked surprised. "*Woher weist Du, das ich dort aufgewaschen bin?* How did you know I was raised there?"

Ich hore es am Dialekt. I hear it in the dialect."

For a moment, the young man felt trapped, as if he had entered a cage with no way out. "*Reutlingen, Herr Thorssen, in der Nahe von*

Tubingen. Reutlingen, Herr Thorssen, near Tubingen."

"Beautiful country," Volmer flashed a melancholy smile as he shifted to English. "I know it well." He was still pondering Acker's presence in Turkey. *Why is he here, of all places?* "One last question, Dieter: How is it that you wound up in Turkey?"

Acker smiled. "Two years ago I came here with a girlfriend. We traveled all over Europe, coming here for the sheer adventure of it all. When our money ran out, she split. I met Okur. We hit it off well. I needed work. That's about it."

For the remainder of the trip to Monaco, Volmer and Acker talked of many things, circumstances permitting, particularly the seaman's interest in and command of mathematics. It came as no surprise to Volmer to learn that Acker's knowledge base went far beyond the world of numbers. In just the short time since meeting Acker, Volmer was developing quite a liking for his young countryman.

"*Schön, dass wir Deutsch sprechen.* I like it when we speak German," Volmer said, "but we will do this only when we are alone. Is that understood?" Since fleeing Florence, he had carefully shielded his true identity. While speaking in German might not be that much of an issue in itself, he was constantly aware that any form of German connection could prove costly. It was a risk he was not prepared to take.

Acker nodded. "*Ja, mein Herr.*"

Sunday, March 30
The Principality of Monaco

The Largo arrived in the latter part of the afternoon and was promptly berthed in the harbor amidst other grand vessels. While Okur handled the arrangements with the harbormaster, Volmer called Bazinet. Fuchs had delivered the carton containing the stolen paintings. Everything was in place.

The following morning, Volmer enjoyed his breakfast on the aft deck of the *Largo*; a bowl of mixed fruits, two soft-boiled eggs, toast and a generous serving of salt mackerel. Following an initial cup of strong Turkish coffee, and despite his dependency on statins, he switched to grapefruit juice. He was about an hour away from his meeting with Glaskov.

Two clouds hovered above Volmer: the first being the article in the *Berlingski Tidende,* and the second a lingering bruise from Greta's mocking comment about old men and the games they play. The bitter taste was still in his mouth.

Sauntering along the spacious dock, he was aware of the blended smells and sounds that came from the opulent ships: the purr of inboard motors, the mingled aromas of gasoline and marijuana and the visual delight of so many young, topless women on the resplendent yachts, hungry for sun and sex. The words came back like angry bees, *Old men like you shouldn't try to play games like this.* "Fuck you!" he said aloud, "Fuck you, Greta!"

He was the first to arrive at the Shark Lagoon. Standing in front of over two inches of polished glass, he looked up at the top of the giant holding tank, marveling at the fact that the glass was capable of withstanding the pressure of nearly 120,000 gallons of seawater. Just as he turned away, he saw Glaskov approaching from the distant end of the facility.

The man had put on a few pounds since Volmer last saw him. Always heavyset, he now looked shorter, as if the added weight had somehow compressed his frame. His sanguine complexion had deepened and become splotchy in places. The jowly head still rocked from side to side as he walked, giving the impression it could roll off his shoulders at the slightest provocation. For Volmer, who religiously watched the food he ate and prided himself on still having the same waist size he had when he was thirty-five, Glaskov's girth was nothing short of obscene. And he was smoking like a factory. "I see you haven't given up your cigarettes," Volmer said when Glaskov was just a few feet away.

"I know. I'm trying to quit."

They talked for a few minutes about insignificant things before Volmer asked a leading question. "Do you still have your Asian clientele?"

Volmer watched a large silvery shark glide past him, its opaque eyes looking like charcoal agates.

"That depends on why you have asked me to meet you here."

Volmer appreciated the man's counter. "What if I told you that I have a few things which should have your customers running to the table and, in turn, adding substantially to your coffers?"

"How substantial?"

"Several million."

"You have my full attention."

"Then I suggest we take a taxi to a local gallery. I have something to show you."

"And the boat with the Jacuzzi? When do I see that?"

"All in due time."

Bazinet welcomed Volmer and Glaskov warmly when they entered the gallery. With evident pride, he showed them the current show, a series of small landscapes done in and around Monaco. Most were "touristy" in nature, prompting Volmer to say they made his stomach crawl.

"It's good to see you are your usual blunt self," Bazinet winked for the benefit of Glaskov. "A gallery owner has to pay the rent, you know."

"The package?" Volmer asked in a tone laced with sudden impatience.

"Of course." Bazinet quickly backed away from the two men. "If you will please follow me, it is in my office. I have the tools to open it." Once there, Bazinet picked up a pair of scissors and slit the tape at the ends of the box. "Please take all the time you want. I'll be in the gallery."

Volmer's dark mood shifted.

From the carton, he removed Picasso's canvas of a man and woman in an embrace, their blue-toned limbs resembling vines. The Gauguin and Whistler works followed. The contrast in colors was stunning. Gauguin had used a wide range of warm hues whereas Whistler's moody night scene was done almost entirely in velvety grays. He intentionally withheld the Vermeer study. He would keep that. "Nice, are they not?"

Glaskov nodded.

"Take a minute and look them over, Dimitri."

Glaskov studied the three pictures after Volmer stepped away, noting the cleanly cut edges of the canvases. "The Gade Collection. I'm impressed, Theo."

"Good for you! I see you're keeping up with the art world."

"They're impressive."

"Are you impressed enough to move them?"

"Possibly. The critical issue will be the price, especially the Picasso."

"Very well," Volmer began, let's start there. From what has been made public by the Gade Collection, it carried a value of twelve million."

"That sounds reasonable."

"I'm prepared to let you have it for six. You should be able to turn it for at least eight."

"And the Gauguin?"

"Three. Gade listed it at eight. The Whistler carries a tag of six."

Glaskov hesitated for a moment. "I'll give you thirteen for all three"

"Thirteen? They are worth far more than that."

"These are hot, Theo. I'll have to pick my investors carefully." He hesitated for a moment and then added, "If I'm successful in finding the backers I need, I'll likely want to receive the paintings from you in Paris."

"You are living in Paris now?"

"More or less. It's beautiful at this time of year."

Volmer smiled inwardly. His decision to use Le Havre for the next few months was well chosen. It was only a two to three hour drive from Paris. "Okay, thirteen it is. You let me know when you want them." He could have demanded more from Glaskov, but the money, per se, didn't interest him. His thrill had come from taking the paintings from Gade. That Glaskov wanted all three removed the problem of what to do with them.

Volmer returned the paintings to the crate and called for Bazinet to secure it.

"I will be sending someone to pick it up within the hour." He remembered. "While I am here, I want to pick up four of your heavy plastic sleeves ... no deeper than eighty centimeters. You still carry them, do you not?"

"Yes, of course. Do you want the ones open at the top, or those with the seal at the top?"

"Those with the seal, please."

While Bazinet was searching for the plastic sleeves, Volmer noticed a bin of assorted charcoal drawings by a member of the gallery's stable. They were not especially good—for the most part large portraits in an expressive style—but they were neatly matted and covered with clear acetate. The best thing about them was their size. If he removed the

CHAMELEON

mats, the drawings would fill the plastic sleeves. If some were too large in either direction, he would simply trim the drawing to the desired size.

Bazinet returned a minute later with the plastic covers.

"I want to add these," Volmer said, holding up four acetate-covered drawings. "And one other thing. You used to carry full sheets of Arches watercolor paper. Are you still doing that?"

"Yes."

"Then add four sheets to the sleeves and the drawings. Make sure everything is together when my man gets here."

Bazinet nodded. "And my compensation for looking over your package," he asked with hesitancy. "Have I not done as you requested?"

"Yes, my friend, you have done well. The man who will be coming for these items will bring your money in a sealed envelope. As I assured you earlier, you will not be disappointed."

Volmer and Glaskov soon found a nice bar where Volmer treated the dealer to a martini. Second martinis followed ten minutes later. After draining his glass, the contented Russian took his leave.

Volmer returned to the *Largo* and from a small wall safe in his stateroom removed cash to cover Bazinet's services and the materials he'd purchased. He placed the money in a plain brown envelope and sealed it. On a separate piece of paper, he provided detailed directions to Bazinet's gallery. That done, he went up top looking for Okur. The captain was examining a large map. "I need Dieter for a few minutes, if you can spare him. An important errand."

Okur had observed the developing association of Acker and his employer. He was not happy with it, but he knew his place and refrained from making any comment. He shrugged his huge shoulders. "I get him."

Volmer then spoke briefly with Acker and gave him the sealed envelope and the sheet of directions. "Go and return promptly. It is important that you not stop for anything."

"I understand."

Upon Acker's return with the carton and the other materials, Volmer tipped him handsomely and then repaired to the privacy of his quarters. He opened the carton and removed the Vermeer study. Carefully sliding it into one of the plastic sleeves, he then removed the mat on one of the charcoal drawings and trimmed the drawing until it fit snugly in the sleeve. He positioned it in front of the valuable canvas. Lastly, he cut a piece of the watercolor paper to size, and slid it behind the piece of canvas. So that he would be able to identify the sleeve containing the Vermeer from the others, he placed a small mark near the bottom on the drawing. To one looking at the sleeve, nothing would suggest that Vermeer's canvas was in between the matted drawing and the piece of stiff drawing paper. When he picked up the plastic sleeve, he was relieved to find that it did not seem inordinately heavy.

Satisfied, Volmer sealed the sleeve. He then repeated the procedure until all of the paintings were securely concealed. From this point until they reached Le Havre, they would be on board the ship. If asked by anyone what the sleeves contained—an inspector, or harbormaster, for example—he would say that he bought the sketches and was keeping them safely within the sleeves until he could have them framed, charcoal being extremely fragile.

It was highly unlikely anyone would ask to have the plastic sleeves opened. One could see the drawings perfectly well through the clear plastic. Add to that, he would have the receipt for the drawings. Even the most art-aware civil servant could tell at a glance that the drawings hardly merited the expenditure of valuable time needed to examine other, more pressing, inspection concerns. For the duration of his journey, the sleeves would be stored in the closet of his stateroom.

Early the following morning, the *Largo* left Monaco under worsening weather conditions. A storm front was expected to hit them before they reached Gibraltar. Volmer remained in his stateroom, following the news on television. He would be of little use on the bridge.

Two days later, the Strait of Gibraltar proved every bit as imposing as Okur had anticipated. With six-to eight-foot swells and winds in excess of 60 miles an hour, the *Largo* experienced her first test by fire. Throughout it all, Okur remained composed and calm, barking out commands to his six able seamen while conversing constantly with his chief engineer about navigational requisites. Eight hours after entering the narrow and perilous strait, the large, black yacht drew a sigh of relief as she reached the calmer waters of the Atlantic.

With Gibraltar behind them, they moved effortlessly and without incident around the southwestern tip of Portugal, past Lagos and Sines.

Okur's check of their fresh water, coupled with unexpectedly high winds that had made extra demands on their fuel, confirmed his belief they should make port in Lisbon. An added cause for the stop was the shifting mood of the crew. He'd been at sea long enough to spot the first signs of irritability. To a man, the crew needed rest, a couple of nights of hard drinking and the feel of women's legs wrapped around their waists. When he told Volmer that he felt it best to stop for a few days, he was relieved to find support from his boss.

"Hell," Volmer replied after Okur summarized the situation, the thought of Greta scorching his ego, "we all probably need a good fuck."

CHAPTER TWENTY

Find Him!

Friday, April 4
Florence, Italy

For most Florentines, the announcement put forth by the Uffizi Gallery that director Palma had called a special news conference for eleven o'clock in the morning could mean only one thing: the museum had consummated another prized acquisition.

Wrong. Lucca Palma wished to address another issue of major significance: Theo Volmer.

Palma, a bald, trim, gangly man with a high, sloping forehead and heavily-lidded brown eyes, was dressed in gray, corduroy slacks that looked in need of pressing. The cuffs of a white button-down dress shirt fell about three inches above his hairy wrists. He was an affable man, well-liked, but hardly the personification of a major museum director.

When he took the steps of the Palazzo Vecchio before a throng of approximately five hundred people and the cameras of the world, he began his remarks with a provocative sentence: "Today marks the beginning of the end for an evil man." A lengthy pause followed. A few voiced responses, but for the most part, the crowd was too stunned to think in terms of responding. If he was disappointed by the reaction to his announcement, Palma did not show it. "The Uffizi Gallery is one of this proud city's most cherished possessions," he began. "It was first opened to the public in seventeen sixty-five. For the past two hundred and thirty-two years it has enabled the citizens of the world to experience the talent of extraordinary artists like Botticelli, Giotto, Cimabue, Michelangelo, da Vinci and Raphael. All gave the world their inspired visions, visions that hang today inside these hallowed walls. We have endured floods, Nazi aggression, and a bombing: all to the end that we have persevered."

The content as well as the tone of Palma's remarks abruptly changed. "From nineteen sixty-eight until the early eighties — the reputation of this most respected house of art was tarnished by Theo Volmer. This immoral man, son of a Nazi SS officer, used the Uffizi's good name to conceal an evil empire that included art forgery, theft and murder. The Uffizi Gallery cannot and will not stand idly by and let these atrocities go unpunished."

This time, the response from the souls in the Piazza della Signoria was immediate. Cheers and shouts in mixed languages filled the iconic place.

Palma absorbed the voices of support impassively, but beneath his controlled facade, he was ecstatic. "Let us vow now to go from here and look under every stone, explore every dank hole, scour the dens of thieves, and let nothing stop us until we have this man in custody. Think of him as a virus that infected the lives of the decent, innocent people of the world. Think of him as a descendant of the plague-carrying rats that brought death to this city in the thirteen hundreds. Think of him as the Devil's son, a cancer that must be removed. Let Florence carry the banner! Let Florence lead the way! Find Volmer!"

The phrase erupted like the tongues of a wildfire, "Find Him! Find Him! Find Him!"

Watching the spectacle on television, Volmer seethed.

Four days later the *Largo* reached Lisbon.

Sunday, April 6
Lisbon, Portugal

It was during his first day in Lisbon that Volmer contacted Ilyus Bager by phone, the reliable German who had handled the intricate explosions in Copenhagen. "I need to know if you are available to do a little work for me."

"Yes, sir. I will make myself available. When do you need me?"

"Let me answer you this way. I am currently in Lisbon, traveling by boat to Le Havre. My best guess at this time is approximately two weeks from now ... the middle of the month. From here, we will make one last stop in Brest. What if I call you again from there? I'll have a much better idea then as to when we should reach Le Havre."

"That's fine."

"How long to you plan to remain in Bremen?"

"For another six months, or so."

"Then you could get over to Le Havre easily?"

"Of course."

"Very good. I will be back in touch soon."

"Thank you, Mr. Thorssen. I will listen out for your call."

Most of the crew had gone ashore for two days of leave. Acker and one of the AB's with a bad case of intestinal flu remained on board, as had Okur who was squirreled away in his cabin doing paperwork.

Volmer found these quiet moments most appealing. They gave him the opportunity to reflect on his long-term interests without noisy interruptions or distractions. The sand in the hourglass told him that he would soon be making the trip to Boston and, from there, to Nashville where he would consummate his grand plan. He had talked at length with Ernest Fromm about the preparations necessary to have his plane fueled and ready to go on a moment's notice. Fromm assured him that he need not give the matter additional thought. He would be ready whenever Volmer chose to pull the switch.

To his surprise and pleasure, he found Dieter Acker near the bow of the ship, totally absorbed in a thick book with a ragged cover. He was seated in a deck chair beneath a large blue umbrella. The day was already quite warm.

"A grand day for reading," Volmer said, approaching Acker.

The young man looked up, squinting against the reflections on the water. Seeing that the questioner was Volmer, he immediately jumped to his feet.

"No need for that. Please have a seat and continue your reading. I don't wish to intrude." He looked at the cover, trying unsuccessfully to make out the title. "A good story, I trust."

"Unfortunately, this is not that kind of book," Acker replied, placing a marker near the spine. "It is something I need to read."

"Oh?"

"William Shirer's definitive *Rise and Fall of the Third Reich*," Acker said. "I imagine you are familiar with it."

Volmer knew the book well. He remembered the pain that came

when he first read it in 1970, a decade or so after its release. Like Dieter Acker, he had felt the same compelling need to experience the book. His father had spoken on so many occasions about the key individuals in Hitler's inner circle, men like Goebbels and Göring and Speer whose personal diaries provided so much of the first-hand information about the Nazi world. He had followed the gut-wrenching Nuremburg Trials on the American Military radio. It had not been easy to look back at wartime Germany through Shirer's eyes. And yet, he had managed to complete the lengthy story, not once, but three times, each time with the same hope and expectation: that Shirer would reveal a different ending, one of triumphant German warriors. It never happened. He felt compelled to ask the question. "Dieter, did you have family members in the war?"

"Yes, sir, my grandfather. He was in the Luftwaffe. He died over London on seven September, nineteen forty."

"The Blitz," Volmer said solemnly. "That was the first of fifty-seven, consecutive nightly bombings of London. Are you aware of that, Dieter?"

"Yes, sir." Acker looked out over the water, forming the question he was about to ask Volmer. "I've often asked myself why the nightly bombings were not successful? Why didn't the British crumble?"

Before Volmer could respond, Acker continued, "I've read that three reasons are usually cited. The first is that Hitler had no overall strategy in mind when he began the operation. His choice of targets was too random to be effective. The second reason was that the Luftwaffe at the time had bombers of limited size. Had payloads been doubled in size, the ending might well have been different. Finally, the Germans were not prepared for the indomitable will of the British. Do you accept any of those reasons, sir?"

For a long and uncomfortable moment, Volmer was at a loss for words. He had not expected intimate questions of this kind from the seaman. A son might ask such things of a father, but he and Dieter were little more than strangers and from totally different stations in life. And yet, from the moment he first met the boy, Volmer found himself strangely drawn to him.

"No, I do not," he replied. "*Der Führer* planned everything very carefully. These assumptions are the work of revisionists, or those who wanted to find fault with our leader. Talk like this makes me angry."

Acker was silent for a moment. He knew Volmer was in denial. "I wish we had annihilated them," he said. The sadness in his eyes reflected his inner pain.

"So do I," replied Volmer in little more than a whisper. He turned and retreated to his stateroom without saying another word to Acker. The bright and sunny day had suddenly turned dark and sour.

PART THREE

"It is not love that should be depicted
as blind, but self-love."
—Voltaire

CHAPTER TWENTY-ONE

Tuscan Secret

Monday, April 7
Nashville, Tennessee

The telephone call came about ten minutes before Porter Blue was about to leave for his commute to the campus of Balfour College. His afternoon was open and he planned to spend most of it the library.

"Porter, this is Damon Kirk. Got a second?"

"Yeah. I'm about to head out the door for the college, but I've got a few minutes. What's up?"

"A couple of things. First of all, I've talked on a few occasions with Worth Manion. He's now fully engaged with your book. He and his minions are doing some heavy-duty planning with respect to promotional concerns. The other thing—the main reason for my call—is that I attended a function at the Whitney Museum of Art two nights ago and had the good fortune of sharing a few minutes with Lucrezia Wildenstein, the wife of Manion's producer friend. I told you about him, didn't I?"

"Manion mentioned him when I was in New York."

"Well, I took the liberty of telling her about your story. I told her you had placed the manuscript with Gladiator. She caught me by surprise by asking if she could read it. If you're okay about it, I'd like to get a copy to her. You never know what might happen."

"I don't have any problems with that. She's the one with family ties to the Pazzi, isn't she?"

"That's right. I'd forgotten that. Gotta run, pal. Keep me in the loop."

"I'll do that Damon and thanks for calling."

"You got it!"

CHAPTER TWENTY-TWO

The Ballgame is Over

Sunday, May 11
Le Harve, France

The port city of Le Havre sits on the right bank of the estuary of the Seine on the channel southwest of the Pays de Caux. It is the second largest port in France, after that of Marseilles. Founded in 1517 by King Francois I, the city and port endured centuries of religious wars, hostile engagements with England, epidemics and storms. It had been a favorite haunt of the French Impressionists, Monet chief among them. It was virtually rebuilt in 1944, following merciless German bombardments.

Due to her size, the *Largo* was anchored in the harbor. For the first time since leaving Izmir, Theo Volmer felt a sense of relief. Not only was the long and tiring trip behind him, but the teeming port afforded him a comforting mantle of anonymity. He should be able to blend in with the local color without difficulty.

If he thought, however, that his arrival would be a simple matter, he was mistaken. When Okur met with port authorities to process the normal protocol associated with establishing temporary residence in the harbor, he was informed that the *Largo* would have to undergo inspection.

An hour later, two men came aboard, a corpulent Frenchman with a black briefcase containing various forms and a younger man from Interpol. Volmer was not at all surprised by an inspection, but he had not counted on the Interpol agent.

The Frenchman and Okur talked for a few minutes before the man asked to see certain required documents, including registration papers, the International Load Line Certificate, the Certificate of Compliance, an International Tonnage Certificate and crew-related records, all routine points of inspection. He and Okur chatted amiably as these documents were examined. The inspector then moved on to issues of safety, marine environment, medical preparations, fuel and ballast operations, electrical and electronic equipment, and communication capabilities: a lengthy checklist that he processed with the utmost deliberation and thoroughness.

The Interpol agent went about his business without requesting any assistance from anyone. He began by examining all visible storage facilities on the vessel, from the bridge to the engine room. When he began his examination of the quarters of the crew, he asked Volmer to accompany him. The request actually pleased Volmer, for it would allow him to be at the agent's side. "My name is Lars Broden." He extended his hand to Volmer. He looked to be in his early forties, clean-shaven with a firm jaw and clear, almost pretty, green eyes.

"My pleasure. I am Ankiel Thorssen, owner of this boat."

Broden nodded. "You are Danish, I see. What part of Denmark?"

Volmer had anticipated the question, sooner or later. "I was born in Tisvilde, a tiny place near Helsinge. Do you know it?"

"No, I'm afraid I only know Copenhagen."

Volmer felt a small wave of relief. "And you? Swedish?"

"Yes, I'm from Yastd, just across the channel from Denmark. You could say we are neighbors. Less than a few kilometers separate us."

They made small talk for a couple of minutes before Broden shifted to the final aspect of his mission. "I would now like to check out your staterooms, if you please."

"Certainly." Volmer led the agent down a narrow hallway leading to the rooms.

"Very nice," Broden said on entering the bedroom. "This is larger than I thought."

"Yes," Volmer replied. "Its size was one of the factors that impressed me. I wanted only the best for my guests."

Brodan spent a few minutes in the room and then moved across to Volmer's stateroom. "I regret having to be so intrusive, but I will need to make a thorough examination of everything. I'll try to leave things as I find them."

Volmer flashed a smile. "Please don't worry about that. I fully understand the demands of your job and the reasons for them."

"I appreciate your attitude, Mr. Thorssen. You have no idea how many people view us with hostility." He looked around the room for a moment and then said, "I'd like to begin with your dresser, if that is agreeable with you, and then have a look in the closet."

Volmer nodded. "By all means."

Broden went about his task silently, knowing from past experience that social conversations often interfered with his ability to stay focused. He went from drawer to drawer, carefully removing and then re-positioning items. When he finished, he moved to the closet.

Volmer's clothing was arranged according to colors, everything meticulously positioned. Broden smiled at the sight of such order. "My wife wants me to keep such a closet, but unfortunately I find it difficult to meet her request. She would approve of yours, however."

His eyes then went to the floor. He noticed the four plastic sleeves. "Do you mind placing these on the bed?" he asked.

"Not at all," Volmer replied, positioning the sleeves with the drawings facing up.

Broden separated the sleeves and examined each of the charcoal drawings. "What are these?"

"Charcoal drawings. I purchased them recently in Monaco at a gallery. I was quite taken with their expressive quality. I'm embarrassed to say that I know little about the artist. With art, I'm something of an impulse buyer."

Broden, like all Interpol agents, was well aware of the Gade robbery some three months earlier. He did not undertake an inspection without realizing that none of the stolen Gade paintings had been recovered. He picked up one of the sleeves and turned it over, assuming that he was looking at the reverse side of the drawing through the clear backside. He also noticed the sealed top. "You mentioned a moment ago that you recently purchased these drawings. Do you have the receipt, by chance?"

"Yes, of course." Volmer removed his wallet and withdrew the receipt, handing it to Broden. "Ah, here it is. The name of the artist is Conrad Aubin," Volmer offered. "It is there on the receipt."

"Why, yes, so it is," Broden responded, carefully scrutinizing the receipt before making a few notations in a small tablet. He picked up one of the sleeves by the top and moved it slowly up and down a few times.

For a moment, Volmer was taken aback by the inspector's interest in the sleeve. Until he had finished placing the drawing and paper in the sleeve with the Vermeer study, it had not occurred to him that the concealed canvas added slightly to the weight of the sleeve. He wondered if Broden was contemplating the issue of weight. "Yes, the gallery owner recommended the thicker plastic. He said it would be slightly heavier, but with charcoal being so fragile, he felt these sleeves would afford better protection." He paused for a moment and then added a risk-laden comment, "If you need to examine the drawings, I'll be more than happy to remove them from the sleeves."

Broden had other inspections to make over the course of the next few hours. The boat owner had been more than cooperative, so he saw no need to prolong things. Taking one final look at the sleeves, he said, "No, I don't believe that will be necessary. That could smudge the charcoal. Your receipt is more than satisfactory."

Volmer was now enjoying himself. It seemed apparent that Broden was satisfied with what he had seen. "Tell me, agent Broden, to the extent that you know, how are things progressing with the Gade Collection theft? We Danes are deeply saddened by the loss of the paintings."

Broden seemed surprised by the question. "I'm not at liberty to discuss the specifics of that case, Mr. Thorssen, but we feel we are making headway. I feel comfortable in saying it is only a matter of time before we will have the thieves in custody."

Volmer's expression was stoic. "That's reassuring."

Just before Broden left Volmer's stateroom, he noticed Pieter Bajek's copy of the Memling hanging near the bed and walked over to examine it. "Is this an original?"

Volmer laughed. "How I wish it were! No, it's a copy of an old painting. I've had it for a few months now and I amuse myself, at times, by pretending it is the real thing."

"And the original is where?" The question arrived like a bird to a limb.

"Oh, it's in a private collection, or a museum, I would imagine." He saw the slight crease form above Broden's eyebrows. "I have the receipt for this, as well, if you care to see it."

"No, I was just curious." He walked closer to the painting. "It is remarkably well done."

"Yes, I was quite taken with its quality."

Agent Broden concluded his examination, while the Frenchman did likewise with Okur. An hour and a half after coming aboard the *Largo*, they left.

Volmer turned to Okur and said, "I believe we have earned a drink, my friend. What is your pleasure?"

Three days later, Volmer called Ilyus Bager in Bremen, Germany. "I am now in Le Havre. As I mentioned to you earlier, I have job for you, if you are interested. It will pay handsomely."

"I am always at your service, sir."

"Well then, is it possible for you to be here on Monday? That's the nineteenth."

"That should be no problem, sir."

Volmer provided him with directions to the *Largo*. "Then I will see you in a few days."

"Yes, sir."

～

Monday, May 19
Le Havre

It was shortly before noon on Sunday when Bager arrived. Volmer insisted that they have lunch before they talked business. Thirty minutes later, the umbrella-covered table was cleared and Volmer got straight to the point. "For the next three weeks, I need you in Florence, Italy. Does your schedule permit that?"

"Yes," Bager replied, taking a quick sip of his brandy. "I am available."

"Good. I need you to shadow a man who lives there, a man by the name of Lucca Palma." Volmer gave Bager a recent newspaper picture of Palma, one which clearly revealed his facial features. "This is what he looks like."

Bager studied the picture for several moments without speaking. He has a long face, like that of a horse. "What does this man do, this Palma?"

"He is the current director of the Uffizi Gallery. I want you to track him from the time he gets up in the morning until he retires for the night."

Bager nodded.

"I want to know how he gets to work," Volmer continued, "when he gets there, when, and where he goes during the day. If you notice reoccurring patterns, those are of special importance. You must be careful that he not see or notice you, do you understand."

"Yes, sir."

"Fine. We understand each other." Volmer reached in his pocket and removed a white envelope.

"Ilyus, this contains enough money to cover your expenses during this time, and then some. In addition, I will reward you well after you have completed your assignment. Do you have any questions?"

"Only one, sir. How do you want me to report his movements? By phone?"

"No, make no telephone connections. Keep a journal, or notes of some kind, and then summarize them at the end for me in written form. I will expect these references to be very detailed." He looked at his watch. "Today is the nineteenth. On June third, I want you to call me at the number I have given you. When I answer the phone, all you need to say is that the ball game is over. On the following day, I will expect you here to submit your written report. Is that clear?"

"Yes, sir, I understand perfectly."

Volmer smiled. "It is a pleasure doing business with you, Ilyus. Would you care for another brandy?"

"Perhaps one more."

Wednesday, May 21
Florence, Italy

Bager reached the terminal of Firenze Santa Maria Novella a few minutes before eleven a.m., traveling overnight from Le Havre. He walked a short distance from the station to the two-star Faenza Hotel. When he registered, he gave his German passport to the desk clerk who was quick to ask a question.

"How long will you be with us, Herr Bager?"

"Two or three weeks," Bager replied simply.

"Wonderful! We'll try to make your stay as pleasant and comfortable as possible. Do you have a floor preference?"

"Anything but street level."

The clerk checked the accommodation options and gave him a key to room 215. "Please let us know if you need anything."

After a shower and a shave, Bager donned tan slacks and a short-sleeved white shirt, placing a small notepad and a ballpoint pen in the pocket. He left the hotel and walked to the Piazza della Signoria.

The sunny day found scores of persons milling about the piazza; the ever-present Japanese with their necks ringed with cameras, lovers with their arms around each other and the expected assortment of vo-cal, and at times abusive, American tourists.

He selected a table at one of the outside restaurants and within min-utes a waiter appeared and took his order for a small margherita pizza and a Peroni. To combat the glaring sun, he put on expensive Italian sunglasses he'd purchased on his walk from the train station. For the next few minutes while waiting for his pizza, he simply watched the passing parade of humanity, enjoying what for him was the first day of a paid vacation.

After finishing his meal, he walked the short distance to the Uffizi Gallery. He entered, purchased a ticket and made his way up the long flight of stairs to the upper level galleries, scanning as he did so, a floor plan of the extraordinary museum. He took special note of the offices. Three hours later, he was waiting outside the Uffizi for Lucca Palma to appear.

A few minutes after five, Palma exited the museum and walked to the Guibbe Rosse, one of the oldest and most respected watering holes in Florence. Bager followed a discrete distance behind.

The man who liked to blow up things was now officially on the clock.

Monday, May 26
Le Havre

Theo Volmer was contacted by Dimitri Glaskov. The Russian was in an ebullient mood. "I have my customers! I'll take the goodies as soon as you can get them to me."

"How about tomorrow?" Volmer was anxious to get the stolen paintings off the boat, and enjoy a few days on solid ground. He'd had his fill of bobbing up and down. "I can rent a car and be there for lunch."

"Excellent! I'm at the Hotel Le Meurice, two-twenty-eight Rue de Rivoli."

Volmer knew the five-star hotel with nightly rates over a thousand dollars. It was one of the finest in Paris. "I see you've parked at one of the priciest places in town, Dimitri. Can't wait to spend all that money, is that it?"

"Something along those lines. I'll look for you."

Volmer spent the rest of the day in his quarters. Unexpected showers had blown in during late morning and the forecast was for more of the same until evening. During a mid-afternoon break in the weather, he went topside and saw Dieter Acker removing excess water on the deck with a squeegee. He had a question for the young man. "Step over here for a minute, Dieter. I have something to ask you."

Acker ambled over to the chair in which Volmer was seated. "A question, sir?"

"Yes, when we talked recently about the war, I don't recall you mentioning anything about your military service. Did you serve?"

"No, sir. I had chronic asthma as a child. When I was called for my physical exam, I failed to meet minimum standards." He hesitated for a few seconds before adding, "I carry the shame of having not been able to serve my country."

"Don't be so hard on yourself. In today's army, conditions like yours are more commonplace than not." Volmer shifted lanes unexpectedly. "You mentioned your grandfather's military service, but what about your father? I don't recall your mention of him. Did he serve?"

A distant expression formed on the handsome young German's face. "He was an abusive drunk. He beat me regularly until I reached sixteen. One day when he attacked me, I responded by breaking his nose and his left arm. I would have killed him, but my mother pleaded for me to stop. I left home the next day."

"Where did you go? How did you support yourself?"

"Odd jobs for the most part."

"That must have been a difficult time for you."

"Not really. Women were easy targets. I'd satisfy their needs and they would pay me well. I was—how do you put it?—a pretty good fuck-boy."

"I understand," Volmer replied with a peculiar smile. "So, you liked women?"

"I used women," Acker replied simply. Acker sensed Volmer's mounting interest in his past. Continuing, he said, "When I was nineteen I bought my first rifle. I joined a gun club and was soon the best shot in the group. I loved shooting. Had I been able to get in the army, I would have tried to be a sniper."

Volmer's ears perked up. "Is that so? You were that good with a rifle?"

"Yes, sir, I was damned good."

A thought flashed in Volmer's mind and he salted it away, one of those rainy day thoughts. "Then one day you and I will have to go to a range. I like shooting as well, although from the sound of it I am probably far below your class."

Acker smiled. "I would like to do that, sir."

"Then we will make it happen."

The following morning, Volmer dressed and collected the three sleeves of charcoal drawings that concealed the paintings Glaskov wanted: the Picasso, the Gauguin, and the Whistler. He asked Okur to call a cab that could get him to a car rental agency. Before leaving the ship, he said to his captain, "I may be in Paris for a few days. I'll check in with you tomorrow."

Okur nodded, but said nothing.

Volmer sensed his tension. "I think you need to get over the changing of my boat's name. This Voodoo shit ill becomes you."

Before leaving for Paris, Volmer removed the faux Memling from the wall and picked up the plastic sleeve concealing the Vermeer sketch. Best not to leave these on board, he thought. From now on, they'll be close to my side.

Volmer returned to the *Largo* from Paris with thirteen million dollars in his pocket.

Okur greeted him in a testy way, but Volmer let him have his moment of petulance. He was more interested in Bager's report than

Okur's moody ways. He was ready to make his move. Ever since the first words from Palma's mouth were sent across the planet by the media, Volmer had developed an insatiable loathing for the man he remembered as a museum nothing.

✒

Tuesday, June 3
Le Havre, France

A few minutes after Volmer finished breakfast, Bager called. "The ball game is over." The simple declaration was made in a clipped, military manner.

"Then, I will expect you tomorrow."

"I understand."

"I'm quite anxious to receive your report. Thank you."

Bager was well received when he reached the *Largo* the following day. His verbal report exceeded Volmer's expectations. "Each day has been fully documented," Bager began when he and Volmer sat in private. "Palma has done nothing or gone anywhere that I have not observed." Bager summarized all the details.

When he had concluded his report, Volmer was clearly pleased. "You have done extremely well, Ilyus. You are to be commended for such attention to detail."

As they talked, Volmer asked Bager to comment on anything that stood out as particularly unusual regarding Palma's patterns.

"A very colorless person," Bager replied. "His daily routine quickly became predictable, especially in one regard."

"Really? How so?"

"Each morning, regardless of the day, the weather or any other circumstance, he entered The Basilica of Santa Croce exactly at ten o'clock in the morning. He sat in front of the Machiavelli's tomb, as in prayer, for four or five minutes. I could hear him speaking softly, but I could not make out the words."

"How odd," Volmer replied, recalling the interior of the church and the tombs of Machiavelli, Galileo and Michelangelo. *Why Machiavelli?*

"After observing this for a few days," Bager continued, "I ventured to the area and sat a few pews away. He never took notice of me, or anyone else, for that matter. It seemed to me that during that time period—ten minutes at the most—he was in another world. Then, abruptly it seemed, he would arise and leave the church promptly without ever lighting a candle or placing alms in the basins."

"Is there anything else I should know about?"

"I can't think of anything, sir. As far as I could tell, he went to work and at the end of the day he went home."

"No mistress?"

"Not that I could detect, sir."

Volmer wanted to be certain. "And these visits to the basilica, they were always at the same time?"

"To the minute, sir. Ten o'clock ... every day."

Volmer nodded, well satisfied with the work of the former submariner. "You were very thorough, Ilyus. I will want to review your written report, but from what you have told me I am well pleased." He handed the muscular man an envelope and shook his hand. "If you have any problems with the contents of this, please let me know."

Bager flashed a rare smile. "I have no doubt it will be more than satisfactory."

"Then I will bid you safe travels back to Germany. Please kiss the soil for me."

"It will be done, sir. *Heil Hitler!*"

How strange it sounded after all these years. Yet, in some respects, it was yesterday all over again; the sea of swastikas, the hard claps of boots on pavement and, above all, the towering father with the gleaming medals on his broad chest. How he missed it all. Volmer's right arm instantly morphed into a spear. *"Heil Hitler!"*

CHAPTER TWENTY-THREE

Mason Creed

Saturday, June 7
Nashville, Tennessee

Having decided not to remain at Vanderbilt past the semester, Largo's sights were now set on Krakow, some two short months ahead. For days she'd been making a list of the things she would need to address before leaving the states, uppermost among them to finalize things with the Atlanta High Museum. If she wanted to go through with the gifting of the Memling, then she needed to put things in motion. By the time she blinked twice, it would be August.

Her call to Geller went through without delay.

"It's good to hear from you again," he said. "I trust your world is looking good today."

"I'm fine, thank you. I'm calling to begin the formal transfer of the Memling to the museum. I'll be leaving the country soon for an extended period of time, and would like to know what's involved."

"It's fairly simple, Largo. If you like, we can send someone to Nashville to pick up the painting. There are a few papers that will need your signature, but for the most part it will call for little effort on your part. You've already indicated to me your wish that at some point in the future you would like to see the painting placed on loan to a museum of your choice in Krakow. That poses no problem at all. I will, of course, initiate contact with the person there and both parties can iron out the details." He hesitated for a moment. "I want to do everything I can to make this happen in accordance with your wishes."

"I appreciate that. Although my plans are not yet finalized, I'll be leaving for Poland in early August."

"Then let me make this as easy on you as I can. I'm more than happy to fly to Nashville at a time of your choosing and we can wrap this up quite easily."

Largo was both pleased and relieved. "Thank you. That sounds fine to me. I'll be in touch."

Had it not been for the interior decorating tastes of a London woman, there might well have been no Memling for Largo to give to the Atlanta High Museum.

Everything started when the woman directed her husband Willister Coleman, an investment banker, to take an original Giacometti painting in for reframing. They had purchased it from a Frankfurt dealer in the early eighties. The provenance indicated that the work was completed by Giacometti in March of 1919 and framed a few weeks thereafter. The painting, Coleman had been told at the time of purchase, was in its original frame. That meant little to Mrs. Coleman who wanted it placed in a much simpler frame, preferably silver or bronze.

After the framer had selected a frame to match his customer's wishes, he began transferring the oil on canvas to the new frame. In removing the backing, he noticed a small part of an adhesive bandage, apparently overlooked by the first framer. "It looks like an old Band-Aid," the framer said to the banker who was watching him finish the job. "I find all kinds of things on the back of paintings, everything from love notes to grocery lists. This is a first, however, for bandages." On impulse, the framer looked at the rear of the frame which had contained the Giacometti. He noticed a small label at the base of the frame. It read simply:

Oil painting by Alberto Giacometti in the original frame: 1919

"Are you sure your wife wants to get rid of this frame?" the framer asked.

"Better let me take it with me, just in case," Coleman replied. "She can be sentimental at times." As he was returning home, his curiosity about the bandage fragment intensified. Something seemed odd.

Once home, he went to his computer and searched for "Band-Aids." The protective covering was invented in 1920. He then went to his library where he kept all his important papers. After a few moments of searching, he found the provenance that came with the purchase of the painting. He read what he already knew: it clearly stated that Giacometti completed the painting in 1919 and had it framed within the year. How, the man asked himself, could a Band-Aid be affixed to the painting in 1919 if it had not even been invented? Even so, the early bandages would not have been the flesh-colred plastic of the fragment.

That realization prompted him to take the painting and the initial frame to the Tate Gallery in London for verification of its authenticity. He was not surprised to receive the verdict from the curators: the work was a fake, a bogus Giacometti. Scotland Yard was promptly notified.

Such a simple situation set in motion a chain of events that brought veteran Scotland Yard detective Mason Creed to Florence on March 26, 1996. It was at the conclusion of a program at the Uffizi two days later that Creed first met Largo and Porter Blue. They exchanged small talk for a few minutes. It was during this time that Creed referenced the reason he was in Florence. Largo was immediately fascinated by his account of the Giacometti forgery.

"Inspector Creed," she asked, "have you ever been involved with the recovery of artworks stolen by the Nazis during WWII?"

Behind Largo's question was the Memling painting that had been stolen in 1939 from her Polish great-grandparents Levi and Zohara Nowak in Krakow, the painting she had seen at Theo Volmer's home shortly after she arrived in Florence.

Largo and Porter Blue came to know and trust Creed. He eventually found the Memling in a storage facility in Stuttgart, Germany, and from that moment on she carried special feelings for him in her heart.

For Scotland Yard Inspector Mason Creed, excitement came in the form of an occasional night at the theatre, a quiet Sunday walk in Hyde Park, and a visit to his favorite pub after a soccer match. After most days at the office, he fixed something resembling dinner, watched the evening news, and then settled in with a good book. At forty-three, he was trim and fit. Although he would be the last to recognize it, he was an attractive man. His thick, always neatly trimmed black moustache and steady, trustworthy eyes did not go unnoticed by women. He sometimes lamented his solitary life, though for the most part he was a contented bachelor.

When he thought about the women in his life, four usually came to mind: Patricia Bentley, his college sweetheart who died tragically in an automobile accident in Cardiff, Wales in 1977; the love of his life, Molly Caulfield, who left him standing at the altar in 1982; Gracie Sheffield with whom he spent three stressful years of marriage before she left him for a pipefitter in 1987 and Largo Kopacz whom he'd met in Florence, Italy, just the year before.

He had been intimate with the first three, but his relationship with Largo could best be described as that of good friends. At the time, she was committed to Porter Blue, and he never thought of crossing that line. He had helped find her missing Memling, and her expression of gratitude still warmed him. If there had been no Porter Blue ... well, there was a Porter Blue. But when Creed went to bed at night, there were times when he would drag a pillow to his chest, hug it and let random thoughts about a woman like Largo flow like a clear mountain stream.

On this day, he was attempting to organize the surface of his desk when the phone rang. "Hello," The response was mechanical. "Mason Creed, Scotland Yard."

"Uncle Mason, this is Ashley! How is my favorite uncle?"

Ashley Creed was his niece, his brother's daughter, a vibrant young woman in the world of law. She was the closest thing he had to a daughter and when occasions permitted he relished her company. At twenty-five, she was the epitome of the beautiful, career-driven woman.

"I'm my usual fine." He easily pictured her lovely smile. "To what do I owe this marvelous surprise?"

"I'm getting married, Uncle Mason! I wanted you to be among the first to know."

"My goodness," he replied, sounding, he felt sure, like an old man. "You don't mean it."

"I do, I do, and you two are going to hit it off famously, I just know it."

"When is the big day? What does he do, this prince charming of yours?"

"His name is Jacques. He's a wonderful French architect. We met last summer in Liverpool. The wedding is scheduled for early September. We haven't picked the date."

"Where's the wedding?" He blinked repeatedly in hopes of removing an eyelash.

"Rouen, France. His family is from there. I do hope you will come." She paused, waiting on him to offer a response. "I know it's short notice, but we don't want to wait until Christmas. Oh, please tell me, Uncle Mason, that you will be there ... please ... please do come."

He glanced at his desk calendar. September showed no major roadblocks. "I wouldn't miss this for the world. As soon as you can, call me with the details."

"I will, I will!"

Following the brief conversation with his niece, Creed gave thought to the matter and then decided to take the occasion of his niece's wedding to schedule a real vacation. Most years he never used any of his leave time, but this year would be different. He'd never seen Normandy and the beaches on which so many British and American soldiers had died. Every year he told himself to make it a priority, but every year he found an excuse to postpone it. Neither had he seen much of Europe. This would provide a perfect time to visit Paris and Nice, perhaps even enjoy another taste of Italy. There was no good reason not to go. He could make the crossing from Dover to Calais or Le Havre, rent a car and tour the area before driving to Rouen. He could even make impromptu stops along the way. After examining the logistical concerns associated with the trip, he made his final travel plans. He would leave England a few days before the wedding.

After that, he would decide on other places. He could simply let the wind take him. He could have fun, like other tourists did. Who knows, he might even meet an attractive woman in a smoky bar. *Hell's Bells! I've got weeks of leave time just sitting in the bank. I may as well use it.*

Mason Creed did not know it, but a major change in his life was just around the corner.

CHAPTER TWENTY-FOUR

The Exchange

Thursday, July 3
Le Havre, France

For Volmer, the month of June passed like a slow moving weather front. He used the time to put the final wraps on his plan to fly to Boston and from there to his ultimate destination of Nashville. He had waited a long time to put this critical plan in motion and now the time had come to play his trump card.

In his relentless tracking of Porter Blue's book-related adventures, Volmer had seen a live interview with the writer in Washington, D.C. When asked about his plans, Blue casually mentioned that both he and Largo would be vacationing for a week in Cabo San Lucas following a big book-signing event in Aspen, Colorado. Volmer had written down the dates cited by Blue: July 10th through the 20th. Of even more interest, Blue referenced in the interview that Largo would be leaving in early August for Krakow, Poland to continue her studies in the field of art history. What bounty that half hour program yielded.

Earlier in the month, he had contacted his personal pilot Ernst Fromm and instructed him to have the Learjet serviced and ready to go when he reached the Kastrup airport in Copenhagen on Tuesday, July 8th. Only two tasks remained before he packed his bags: he needed to make contact with Arnar Bjorn and tell him that his airline tickets to and from Nashville, plus travel expenses, would be waiting for him at Kastrup. Secondly, he needed to carefully pack Pieter Bajek's splendid copy of the Memling.

As for the remaining treasure from the Gade Collection, the exquisite Vermeer study, he would remove it from the plastic sleeve and place it in a smaller container that would fit within a locker at the airport. It was too risky to leave it aboard the *Largo*. Okur could abandon ship at the slightest provocation. The painting could easily be collected after his return from the States. He had other plans for the Memling.

Hardly a day passed that Volmer didn't see something in the papers that referenced Lucca Palma's crusade, or the efforts of Interpol to find him. To be sure, he had become more circumspect in his daily life, but an undeniable adrenalin rush came from playing this cat and mouse game. His physical appearance was so changed from what it was when he left Florence that he felt confident he could go almost anywhere he wanted without being spotted. Ankiel Thorssen had blossomed into a convincing reality.

Friday, July 11
Boston, Massachusetts

The sky was overcast when the taxi arrived at the Beacon Hill home of Zoa Carrin-Mellan to take Volmer to Logan airport for his noon flight to Nashville. His time with her had been quite pleasant, since arriving from Copenhagen on the eighth. As delicious as her scented body was, he was more than ready to leave Boston and consummate his long-awaited plan.

He was met in the Barclay's VIP lounge by his personal pilot Ernst Fromm. For several minutes they discussed the upcoming flight, scheduled to depart around noon. Fromm, as always, had been meticulous in his preparations. "Everything has been cleared for our departure."

"Excellent! I'm anxious to be underway."

Arnar Bjorn had already reached Nashville from Copenhagen. He was in the bar when Volmer, that is to say, Thorssen, arrived. After their brief discussion, they joined Fromm for the short drive to downtown Nashville. Little was said by Volmer to Bjorn about their shared interests during the ride into the city. What conversation there was centered on the unsettled weather and the numerous cedar trees that dotted the landscape surrounding Donelson. Fromm, respectful of his position as an employee, said nothing.

Once the three men checked into the Renaissance Nashville Hotel, Volmer and Bjorn went to the bar to fine tune the operation that would come with the following morning. Fromm happily settled for room service and unlimited free movies.

Saturday, July 12
Nashville, Tennessee

Volmer, Bjorn, and Fromm entered the parking lot of the Renaissance Nashville Hotel from the lobby shortly after eight-thirty a.m. Volmer was carrying a large black briefcase with a five-inch base and a clear plastic bag containing two white jumpsuits. Bjorn's visible luggage, small by comparison, was a tan leather pouch about the size of a loaf of bread. They were met by a parking lot attendant who ushered them to a waiting white cargo van, leased for one-day usage. The van carried no signage.

Once the attendant left, Volmer removed the jumpsuits and directed Bjorn to join him in donning one. He then placed his briefcase on the floor behind the driver's seat before joining Bjorn in the back seat. Their destination was the condo of Porter Blue, just a few blocks away.

As Fromm pulled out from the underground garage, rain was falling in sheets. Deep, rolling thunder was followed by brilliant lightning flashes. The sky looked like rolled lead. The scene resembled something from an apocalyptic movie.

Volmer had no problems with the weather. If anything, it would mean fewer people were likely to see or pay attention to them once they reached their destination. He turned to Bjorn. "Your return ticket to Copenhagen this evening cannot be changed, so it is imperative you make the flight. I've checked the schedule again, and there are no changes. It leaves Nashville at 4:02 p.m., connecting in Atlanta for New York, and Delta's 8:05 p.m. flight to Copenhagen. We should be back to the hotel well before noon, so you should have plenty of time to shower and dress before leaving for the airport."

He handed the Dane a sealed white envelope containing the balance of their financial arrangement. "Do you have any questions about any of this?"

Bjorn frowned. "How many times do you need to tell me this? You mentioned this shit yesterday at the airport. Everything is clear. I know the time of my return flight," he replied, fingering the envelope for a moment before stuffing it in his trouser pocket.

Volmer looked at him through a wintry smile. He was surprised at not remembering the earlier converation with Bjorn about the flight back to Copenhagen. It unnerved him that the unpleasant Dane had been so insensitive in reminding him of the memory lapse. "You're not even going to count it?" he said, evident irritation showing.

"I will do that later."

"Of course," Volmer replied, far from pleased with his attitude.

As lightning lit the dark, morning sky, Fromm negotiated the elements and found the condo with little difficulty. Volmer had earlier gleaned the address from one of the hotel bellhops familiar with the area surrounding The Grand Ole Opry. "I was in the service with the guy who lives there," Volmer told the bellhop. "I want this to be something of a surprise." The hotel employee had been able to fashion a simplified map.

Fromm parked the van in one of the street side parking spaces from which Volmer could see the door of Blue's condo. As he did so, he looked at Bjorn. "I want you to walk slowly to the front door and after gaining entry deactivate the security system. Once that has been done, return to the door so that I can see you. I will then join you."

Bjorn knew nothing about Volmer's need to enter the home. He had his suspicions—a theft of some kind—but he couldn't care less. He would soon be getting his money, and that was all he cared about. Volmer had been very clear on this when they first met. "I will be paying you handsomely for a few minutes of your time. For all you know, I need to go to a friend's condo and feed his fish."

Twenty-two seconds after reaching the front door, Bjorn was soaked. Muttering to himself, he picked the lock and entered the home.

For a few anxious moments, Volmer's eyes alternated between the front door and what he could see of the sidewalk and street through the rear mirror. Thus far, no one had appeared. The storm was minimizing movements on the streets. Then to his relief, Bjorn reappeared. He raised his right thumb and fashioned a saccharin smile, vacillating between annoyance at having being asked to perform such a simple task in such miserable weather and thoughts of pleasure surrounding what he was going to do with the all the money he was being paid.

In rehearsing his plan, Volmer felt he and Bjorn had to be in and out of the house within ten minutes, fifteen at the most. Any extended stay risked discovery by a neighbor. When he entered the dwelling in near darkness, he saw a straight-backed chair in the foyer, next to a small table. "Sit here until I return."

Although handicapped by the lack of light, he soon found the bedroom where, true to what he had read from interviews Blue had given in promoting of his book, the Memling hung next to the right side of the bed, Largo's side. Using the knuckle of his left index finger, Volmer flipped the light switch inside the bedroom door.

The abrupt illumination of her space caused a ripple of emotions, foremost among them a heightened sense of eroticism. On a deeper level, the thrill came from knowing that, in time, he would possess the desirable, young Jewish woman. When that time came, he would humiliate her, as the Nazis had done at Auschwitz and the other camps with Jewish women they desired. He would enjoy the ample pleasures of Largo's body and then discard her like the trash she was. Make no mistake; she would pay the price for refusing him.

Volmer worked quickly. After removing the Memling from the wall, he placed it on Largo's pillow, but not before burying his face in its softness. Her scent was so overwhelming that he quickly became aroused. From his briefcase, he took out Bajek's splendid replica and positioned it on the empty hanger. After making minor adjustments, Volmer was satisfied that it looked just like the original, even down to the frame.

Unzipping his trousers, he then raced to the nearby closet and snatched a pair of Largo's crimson lace panties from the dirty clothes hamper. Within seconds he ejaculated on it. When his breathing returned to normal, he stuffed it back in the hamper.

Volmer glanced at his watch; nearly seven minutes had passed since he entered the bedroom. He then removed three additional items from the bedroom dresser: a bright red scarf, a black brassiere and a lavender pair of panties, quickly placing them in his briefcase. He looked again at his watch; he was now into the ninth minute. He made one final look around the room to make sure he was leaving nothing behind and made a final adjustment with Bajek's painting. The light flickered for a moment in the wake of a violent clap of thunder, and then everything went dark. As Volmer walked through the door of the bedroom, he had the presence of mind to flip the light switch to off. He then closed the door behind him.

Bjorn arose from the chair when he saw Volmer approaching. He was more than ready to leave.

Volmer caught the aroma of tobacco before he saw the cigarette dangling from Bjorn's mouth. "You idiot!" He waved a hand, as if to make the easily identifiable odor vanish, "They will know someone has been here. Are you not thinking?"

"Fuck them!" Bjorn was irritated at being treated like a child. "And fuck you too. I'll smoke where and when I damned well please!"

"Let's go!" Volmer declared, not wanting to provoke the man. Any additional time spent in Blue's condo could have negative consequences. "Toss the cigarette outside."

Bjorn took a deep, final drag from the cigarette as he passed through the doorway of the house, flicking the butt into a boxwood at the left of the stoop. He was in no mood for additional discussion of the subject.

Notwithstanding his displeasure with Bjorn, Volmer felt waves of relief as Fromm moved the van down the street. There was no one on the sidewalk, few cars on the street. As for the residual smell of tobacco, perhaps it would dissipate before Blue and Largo returned. After all, he and Bjorn had only been in the condo for a matter of minutes.

What Volmer did not know was that the smoker had left a tiny deposit of white ashes on the polished floor near the base of the chair on which he had been sitting.

Volmer and Fromm left Nashville a few minutes ahead of Bjorn's return to Denmark. Once in the air, Volmer allowed himself to relax for the first time in days. As he drifted to sleep, he relished the success of his mission. He now had the Memling. Largo Kopacz would return home to a remarkable deception.

CHAPTER TWENTY-FIVE

Ashes

Sunday, July 20
Nashville, Tennessee

The central part of Tennessee is comprised of forty counties that extend from the Cumberland Plateau in the east to Henderson County in the western part of the region. This part of the state is commonly referred to as the Central Basin, so named because it takes on the appearance of a massive bowl. Almost in the center lies Nashville. This unique geographic area is ideal for farming, but does carry one significant summer problem; exceptional humidity. During the months of summer, Nashville usually swelters.

On this day, as Largo and Porter arrived from Cabo San Lucas, a slight drizzle created a veritable steam bath outside the air-conditioned terminal at the Nashville International Airport. At ninety-three degrees Fahrenheit, it felt like one hundred and three. Little was said between them as they retrieved their car from one of the long term lots and returned to their condo. Blue was the first to speak, negotiating heavy traffic into the city. "The big day is almost here, sweetheart. Are you excited about finally getting to Poland?"

"Yes, and a bit scared, if you want to know the truth. This is a big step for me."

"A big one for both of us."

She nodded. "Yes, I suppose it is."

Her eyes followed the changing landscape of Davidson County. She couldn't help but wonder about the changes Poland would bring about in her life, in their lives. The trip, she knew, represented a significant gamble. Of late, he had voiced support for her doctoral pursuit, but did he really mean it? The way she saw it, it was all right to be a little scared.

Within minutes of reaching the condo, Blue unlocked the front door and quickly disarmed the security. The interior seemed stuffy, stale. *It figures. It's been closed for ten days.* Largo entered behind him and immediately experienced similar sensations. Stuffy, yes, but also the faintest trace of a specific odor in the small foyer that seemed foreign.

While Porter was bringing up the last of their luggage, she noticed something else that seemed odd. The door to their bedroom was closed. She always left it open. Returning to the foyer to open the door for him, she saw the tiny deposit of ashes near the rear leg of the chair. *I'm smelling tobacco!* "Porter, someone was in here while we were gone!" she exclaimed. "I just know it."

He placed the bags on the floor and wiped his brow with his forearm. "What are you saying?"

"Look." She pointed to the ashes. "Can't you smell it? Someone has been in here." Before he could fashion a sensible response, her thoughts raced to the Memling. "Oh, my God! No! No!" She raced to the bedroom, opened the door and stopped, as if her feet were frozen to the floor. The small painting was positioned where it had always been, the men still at prayer.

"There could have been a problem in the building while we were gone." Blue wanted to believe that might explain the cigarette ashes. "I'll check with the building manager tomorrow. There has to be some explanation."

Largo didn't hear a word he said. She was already removing the Memling from the wall. A huge wave of relief came when she saw the backside. There, as they had been all along since her great-grandparents had the painting framed in 1931, she saw the partial label of the framer and the telltale orange sticker carrying the numerals 7002. The painting was safe.

As she went about unpacking her suitcase and returning clean garments to the appropriate drawers, she found the drawer where she kept her panties and bras in surprising disarray. The usual order was not there. *Strange,* she thought, *I don't remember leaving it this way.* While putting away a few things in the closet, she saw a black fountain pen with a gold band lying on the carpeted floor near the bedroom closet. She picked it up and moments later placed it on her bed side table. Porter must have dropped it before they left on their trip.

Throughout the remainder of the day and into the evening they took care of those things which accompany a return home after a lengthy time away: Porter going through the accumulated mail and placing due bills in a pile while she returned toiletries to the bathroom and put away clean clothes. Deep within her bones, she felt an unaccustomed sense of anxiety. In the darkest channels of her gut, one name kept surfacing: *Volmer.* She poured herself a glass of Chardonnay and before she realized it she was refilling the glass.

"You seem fidgety tonight." Blue said as he finished his labors. He was uncomfortable with the tension that surrounded them.

"I'm still disturbed by the cigarette ashes," she replied. "You will check with the management tomorrow?"

"Yes, first thing. I promise."

She returned to the bedroom. After a visit to the bathroom, she saw the fountain pen on the bed side table. She picked it up and returned to Porter in the living room, sitting down next to him on the sofa. "Here, you must have dropped this before we left. It was in my closet, near the hamper."

Blue took the black Cross pen from her, a puzzled expression forming on his face.

She saw it. "It is yours, isn't it?" she asked with a measure of hesitancy.

He looked at the shiny pen for a long moment. "I've never owned a Cross pen in my life, Largo. This isn't mine."

The following morning after breakfast, Blue spoke with the manager of True Opry, a rail thin man by the name of Ben Thompson. "Ben, we've been gone for about two weeks," he said by way of a preamble. "When we returned last evening, Largo noticed some cigarette ashes on the floor in our foyer. As neither of us smoke, I'm wondering if there was some problem while we were gone, some reason why housekeeping had to enter our unit."

"Not that I'm aware of," Thompson replied.

"What about your security cameras? Would they show anyone coming or going from our place while we were gone?"

"We began upgrading all of our cameras just after you left. We weren't operational until two days before you returned."

Blue felt a cold rush of fear. Thanks, Ben."

Might you have had a visitor before you left, a smoker, perhaps?"

CHAMELEON

"No, I'm quite sure we didn't." Just as he was about to walk away, Blue asked Thompson, "Has anyone reported seeing an unauthorized person, or persons, in our area of the complex during the time we were away?"

"No, sir. No one has reported anything out of the ordinary."

Blue turned away without saying another word. He returned to their condo, dreading to have to tell Largo that management had no explanation for the ashes. *Someone was in our condo. She's right about that, but how did they get in?* And then the more vexing question: *Why didn't they take something?*

While Blue was concluding his business with Thompson, Largo was emptying their suitcases and making a pile of dirty clothes. Remembering that the clothes hamper was nearly full when they left, she began adding its contents to her pile. *At least two loads,* she thought. It was then that her nostrils picked up a sickly sweet scent from the hamper. When she removed a handful of soiled undergarments she saw its source; her cimson panties. Volmer's aromatic ejaculate was now a hardened patch of chalky matter, and when she held it closer to her nose the distinctive odor was nearly overwhelming. Her first thought was that of the ashes near the front door. *The intruder deposited both!* The he in this case had a name, as far as Largo was concerned: it had to be Volmer.

When Blue returned to the condo, Largo met him at the door with the soiled panties in a zip-lock bag. "Volmer was here, Porter! There's no doubt in my mind." She held up the unsavory souvenir. "His cum is all over my panties! Porter, the son of a bitch jacked off in our bedroom!"

❦

Wednesday, July 23
Nashville, Tennessee.

Their homecoming prompted Largo to move quickly in contacting the Atlanta High Museum. With each passing day, she feared the intruder might return. As for the soiled panties, she wedged the plastic bag between a stack of clean bath towels and the interior wall of the closet. It was now imperative she place the painting with the museum as soon as possible. The last thing she wanted to do was to leave for

217

Krakow with it hanging on her bedroom wall. Something unexpected must have happened that prevented him from taking the Memling.

The following morning, she called Geller and told him she was about to leave the country. "I believe it will work best if Porter and I deliver the painting. That way, we can save you the trouble of driving to Nashville. It will give us a nice opportunity to have a little outing before I head to Poland. What day would work for you?"

He seemed only too happy to know he would be receiving it sooner, rather than later. He quickly checked his calendar and replied, "I can meet you and Porter tomorrow or Monday, the twenty-eighth. I'll have the paperwork ready for you. This will not be a complicated process, I assure you."

"Fine, let's shoot for Monday. We'll try to get away early. We should be there by noon."

"Yes, it's a straight shot around Chattanooga. It's an easy drive, about four hours, as I recall. I'm looking forward to meeting your fiancee. I understand he's just written a wonderful book. My wife Claryce can't wait to read it."

The precious Memling was carefully secured in bubble wrap and placed in a slightly larger cardboard box before she and Porter left Nashville on Monday.

Geller greeted them warmly at his office when they arrived. "It's good to see you again, Largo. Hope your trip down was a pleasant one."

"Yes, very nice, thank you."

Before she could introduce Blue, Geller turned to him and said, "You must be Porter," he said affably. "Congratulations on your new book."

"Thank you. It's keeping me pretty busy these days."

"I can imagine." He smiled at Largo, the small box in her hands. "I take it your baby is inside that package."

"Yes." She handed him her treasured painting. "I'm sure I didn't wrap it the way a museum would, but I was primarily concerned with its safety."

Geller took the proffered box and quickly invited them into his spacious office and its commanding view of downtown Atlanta. "Can I get the two of you anything? Coffee?"

Blue nodded a yes. Largo declined.

As Geller removed the Memling, his face reflected his pleasure. "It is quite beautiful. The colors are even more vibrant than I had imagined."

Largo smiled. "It was the pride and joy of my great-grandparents."

A small furrow appeared above Geller's thick eyebrows. "Yes, they were in Krakow when the Nazis took it from their home, as I recall."

"In 1939," Largo replied, puzzled by Geller's expression. "There's something of a story about the painting, but I won't get into all that right now." She said nothing about the recent condo incident.

"Perhaps another time." Geller's eyes lingered on the surface of the painting. He hesitated for a moment and then added, "Well then, I suppose all that remains is for you to sign a few papers. As I told you, this is not complicated."

"And you did say that you will make contact with the museum I select in Krakow about a loan?"

"Certainly. You have to but give me a call when you are ready to move on that."

"Thank you. I'll be leaving the States in four days. If for any reason you need to get in touch with me after I leave, Porter will be at home when he's not gallivanting across the country promoting his book. He can always reach me." She left their number with Geller.

He made a gesture with both hands, not unlike a priest officiating at a Eucharist. "Ah, to be young and enjoy the gift of travel. I envy you that." After a few minutes of small talk, Largo signed three documents and they were on their way back to Nashville.

The museum director sat for a long time at his desk, looking at the Memling in front of him. He arose from his chair and removed a small watercolor from the wall across from his desk. He then positioned the painting on the hanger. He returned to his desk and for the next few minutes studied the painting intently. He then picked up his phone and dialed the three digit number of his senior European curator, Percy Harland.

"If you have a second, Percy, I'd like to see you for a few minutes. I have something that should interest you."

CHAPTER TWENTY-SIX

To Krakow

Friday, August 1
Nashville, Tennessee

The morning was a difficult one for Largo, hardly what she'd envisioned when she first decided to go to Krakow. Porter Blue had been gone for the past three days pushing his book and she had made the necessary arrangements to leave without benefit of a send-off. She had known he would not be there to say goodbye, but still she missed his presence. She tried to look ahead at the attractiveness of the upcoming adventure, but it felt like there was a gaping hole in her heart. To make matters worse, he had not called to say goodbye or even wished her a safe trip. In trying to pinpoint her specific emotional mood, she was not sure whether it reflected her anger at him, or fears that had suddenly become full blown. Perhaps both.

It felt odd—empty was a better word—to see the vacant spot on the bedroom wall where she had positioned the Memling. If there was a silver lining to its absence, it was the comforting assurance that it was in safe hands. She wished she could delay leaving long enough to see it on display at the museum, but she would do that when she returned. Thoughts of the cigarette ashes in the foyer continued to disturb her.

As the hours slowly ticked away, she repacked her suitcase for the fourth time. Waiting to leave was the worst part of it. She wished Porter would call. At a little past two in the afternoon, she heard the horn of the cab. It was time to go to Poland.

At that very moment, Porter Blue was returning to Nashville from a talk he'd given in Knoxville. Realizing that his fuel gauge was at the one-quarter mark, he pulled into a service station near Cookeville. After filling up, he called Largo to wish her safe travels to Krakow and to ask that she call him as soon as possible after arriving.

Please be there, he thought as the first ring was registered. He listened as four more rings followed. And then, the dreaded recording:

"You've reached the home of Porter Blue and Largo Kopacz. Neither of us can come to the phone at the moment, but if you'll leave your name, number and a brief message, we'll get back with you as soon as we can."

He'd missed her. By now, she must have left for the airport. As he returned the phone to the cradle, he chastised himself. *Why didn't I try to call earlier? Stupid! Stupid! Stupid!* Within minutes, he was back on I-40.

After entering the condo at True Opry, he saw the blinking red light on the phone in the bedroom. The second he activated phone, he heard her voice.

"I imagine you were too busy to call before I had to leave for Atlanta. I'll call again after I get there. Know that I love you."

After taking a long, hot shower, he stretched out on the sofa, still punishing himself for not having contacted Largo before she had to leave. He was soon asleep. Minutes before four p.m., he was awakened by the phone. His spirits soared. *She's calling from Atlanta!*

The call was from Atlanta, but it wasn't Largo's voice that greeted him.

"Porter, this is Norman Geller at the Atlanta High Museum."

It took Blue a moment to adjust to Geller's voice, so certain was he that the call was from Largo. "Good to hear from you, Norman. I trust you are doing well."

"Thank you, I'm just fine." A lengthy pause followed. "I don't quite know how to say this, Porter," Geller began with hesitancy, "but there is a problem associated with Largo's gift of the Memling, a big problem."

"What kind of problem?"

"We have just discovered that the painting is a fraudulent one. It is a forgery, I'm sad to say."

"That can't be. This painting came to Largo from her family." Grasping for another straw, Blue added, "Even the Uffizi Gallery in Florence verified the authenticity of this picture."

There was another moment of silence from Geller's end of the phone. "Please understand, Porter, I wouldn't be making this assertion had I not received compelling evidence to support it. Our curators have run several conclusive tests. There is no doubt in our minds that the painting was completed recently, perhaps even during the past year, or so."

"How can you be sure of this?"

Geller sympathized with Blue's reaction. He could easily imagine the thoughts that were whirling about in his head, not the least of which was that of notifying Largo. How would he tell her? "To begin with, Porter, the paint is still technically wet. It is dry to the touch, of course, but near the surface of the panel it has not completely cured. For another, at least three of the colors used were not in existence until the early part of the nineteenth century. I'm afraid there is no doubt that the work was completed by an artist other that Hans Memling. I'm very sorry." Not receiving a response from Blue, Geller continued, "There is one other thing."

"What?" Blue asked, almost rudely.

"In the lower left hand portion of the panel, behind the row of men at prayer, there are four holy men wearing vestments with stoles. Three of the faces resembled men of the period, but one face seems very much out of character. This may not be the case, but it appears to us that the artist used his own facial features."

Blue was incredulous. "He painted his self-portrait?"

"We can't be totally sure." Geller paused briefly. "But when you look at the heads of the other priests, the one priest looks much younger."

Blue felt deflated. His thoughts quickly centered on the ashes. *Someone must have swapped the paintings while we were in Cabo.*

Geller continued, "Rest assured, there is no urgency about coming for the picture. I know that Largo won't be returning soon, so I will keep it in my office until it's convenient for you ... or her ... to pick it up. Again, I am so sorry to be the bearer of such sad news."

Blue thanked Geller for calling and hung up the phone in complete disbelief. He needed to notify Largo, but until she contacted him he was powerless to do anything.

Wheelchairs

Friday, August 1, 1997
Copenhagen, Denmark

The first day of August carried special meaning in Denmark. It marked the six month anniversary of the Gade Collection robbery. The Danish government, as well as Nils Gade and art-conscious citizens throughout country, were growing increasingly critical of the inability of the police to apprehend those responsible for the theft. Not one substantial lead had been registered.

In all fairness to the local constabulary, they had been dealt a very thin hand. One of the thieves, Jannik Eriksson, was dead. Ilyus Bager was living a mole-like existence in Bremen and Gunther Fuchs was squirreled away in his Stuttgart farm. Both Fuchs and Bager were sitting on their money, avoiding anything approaching lavish lifestyles. Dimitri Glaskov had long since sold the paintings Volmer placed with him, all going to his Asian collectors. He was enjoying the high life in Paris.

Under such intensifying pressure, the police were directed to establish a series of checkpoints throughout Denmark. The press and related media were asked to slow roll things, to refrain from advertising these measures, in hopes of catching the perpetrators by surprise. There were random searches of all vehicles, boats and airliners leaving Denmark. Rumors abounded that the stolen works were still within Danish borders.

In Poland, Largo was struggling to establish her equilibrium. Aside from the cramped seating in the middle of the aircraft, the flight over had not been that bad.

Her troubles began when she deplaned and began the labyrinth-like process of Customs. She soon realized that Polish signage was virtually undecipherable. All of the hours she'd spent trying to memorize simple directions meant nothing. She found that the only thing she could do was follow the current of fellow travelers that she recognized from the plane. She would take her chances that at some point along the way she would either realize where she needed to go, or find someone who could help her find her way.

She'd gone only a few additional paces when she spotted a young woman she had seen in the Atlanta terminal before departure, a student she supposed. She had passed the woman in conversation with another passenger before boarding, and while she couldn't be sure of it, she thought they were speaking in English. She latched onto the walking woman like a heat-seeking missile, trying to keep pace with her hurried footsteps. The woman soon stopped at one of the restrooms, but by the time Largo reached it the woman was gone.

"You appear to be lost."

The male voice came from behind her. The spoken English sounded strange, almost foreign. "Perhaps I might be of help."

She turned and found herself looking at an attractive young man with dark, neatly cut hair and a warm smile. He looked to be in his early thirties. The thought formed quickly. *A university student.*

"I assume you are not Polish," he said.

"No," replied Largo defensively. "but my roots are Polish."

"English?"

"American." Largo blushed with irritation and embarrassment.

He was about her height, perhaps an inch or so taller. Lean and muscular, he looked like an athlete. *Soccer*, she assumed.

"If I can be of any assistance, I will be only so happy to do so."

"I'm trying to make my way to Immigration and then to Customs, but obviously I don't know where anything is."

"Let me show you the way. That's where I'm going. Once we get there, I will have to use one lane and you another, but we will meet just beyond the officials."

"Thank you. I appreciate your help."

Once Largo had passed through Customs, she found him waiting on the other side of a bank of glass doors. The question was polite. "May I be of any additional help?"

"Yes, as a matter of fact you can. I need to find the place where buses take passengers to town. Can you direct me there?"

"I can do better than that. I'm driving into the city as soon as I get out of here. You are welcome to join me, if you like. What part of Krakow?"

For a moment, Largo froze with hesitation. Thoughts of Jasper Beane peppered her mind like strobe lights. She knew absolutely nothing about the young man.

He spoke before she could fashion a response. "My name is Adam Czarnecki. I know what you are thinking, and I would probably think the same thing were the situation reversed. I am a student at The Jagiellonian. I am not a criminal or a rapist, nor am I a Communist. I do like the music of Metallica, and I am a big fan of American baseball. I'll give you my hat size, if you would like to have that."

Largo could not help producing a relieved smile. "I'm Largo Kopacz and I'll take you up on your offer. Thank you. I've rented an apartment in Rynek Glo ... Glowny," she said, feeling that she had just butchered the Polish language.

Czarnecki smiled as they reached his car. "We call it The Rynek to make it easy."

As he weaved in and out of traffic leaving the airport, he continued, "The heart of Krakow is Stare Miasto, or the Northern Old Town. That's where the Rynek is located. In 1995, the city districts were redefined. Stare Miasto is one of eighteen districts. Each has distinct characteristics."

"And the Jagiellonian is located in the Northern Old Town," she said, more as a question.

"Correct. Where is your apartment? What street?"

Largo pulled a city map from her purse, folded to show the Northern Old Town.

"It's on Bracka, eight thirty-four Bracka." She hesitated for a moment. "My great-grandparents lived on Bracka during the twenties and thirties. Following Hitler's rise to power, they were herded away to Auschwitz where they died. I thought it would be special to live on their street. My place is supposed to be just a few buildings down from where they once lived."

Czarnecki thought for a moment about trying to say something that might make her feel better, but settled for, "That's a good location, close to the university." When he approached the trendy area, he started looking for available parking spots. "We will have to park outside the Rynek," Czarnecki said. "The area, itself, is now strictly pedestrian."

"I like that concept." Largo was feeling at ease with the young man. "I wish more American cities would follow that practice in downtown sections."

"What was street number again?" he asked, as he snaked his small and well-traveled car, a 1990 Polish Fiat, into an open parking space.

"Eight thirty-four. I understand it is above a meat market." She looked at him quickly. "You said a few minutes ago that you were a student at The Jagiellonian?"

"Yes, I'm doing advanced studies in political theory."

"How interesting. I'll be attending the university. My field is art history."

Czarnecki nodded before helping her from the car and removing her suitcase. "Would you like any help in getting your things to your flat?"

"No thank you, Adam. I just have my purse and the small suitcase. It has wheels."

"Very well. Perhaps we'll see each other on campus. Looking deeply into her eyes, he added, "I would like to show you some of Krakow's nicest places. We have a beautiful city."

"That would be nice. I would like that."

With some hesitancy he asked, "Will you be offended if I offer you my phone number? In case you need me later for anything."

"How thoughtful. That's very nice of you."

He scribbled the number on the back of a receipt from his pocket. Smiling, he said, "I'm usually available during the evenings."

"There is one other thing," Largo said with some hesitation. "What?"

"Have you ever been to Auschwitz-Birkenau?"

"Yes, several times. Some of my relatives died there."

"You are Jewish, then?"

"Yes, but I'm not always good with the cooking. I like pork too much to be kosher all the time. I suppose that makes me a part-time Jew." He pointed to Bracka Street. "There you are. You are near the market area, right in the heart of the Rynek."

Largo thanked him for his assistance and then walked the short distance to her apartment. The information she had received about the meat market was correct. The front window was filled with strings of fat, greasy pork sausages. *I'll not be having any of those.* She knocked on a thick wooden door with peeling dark green paint. She was finally in Poland and she had never felt more alone.

Sunday, August 3,
Le Havre, France

The thought first formed in Volmer's dark mind shortly after his conversation with Dieter Acker regarding Germany's crushing defeat in the war. The young man had struck a buried chord within him, one that rekindled his nationalistic pride and the pain of his absent father. Thoughts that had been dormant for years suddenly flared like a brush fire, images of the uniform that once so stirred his boyhood dreams and his unabashed devotion to Adolf Hitler. With Acker, he could recreate those halcyon days.

Volmer chose breakfast as the time to talk with Okur. In an uncharacteristic move, he invited the captain to join him for the morning meal. Okur never shared a meal with his employer, nor was he comfortable in changing that practice. He respectfully declined.

"Come on, Sadik," Volmer said in less than a cheerful way, "let me treat you, for a change. It won't hurt you to enjoy a few of my favorite specialties. Who knows, you might actually enjoy them." With reluctance, the man consented. Over poached eggs in champagne, fish roe and assorted fruits and cheeses, Volmer presented his thoughts to Okur: "I would like for you to find a replacement for Acker."

"Acker? Why him? He do good job."

"This is not about his job performance, Sadik. I need him for a special assignment. In fact, I plan to make use of his talents in other ways in the future. Surely, it will not be difficult to find a qualified replacement here in Le Havre."

"I do what you say." Okur replied, gradually pushing his chair back from the table. "I thank you for the meal."

Volmer looked at his plate. The roe had not been touched. "I'm sorry, the breakfast did not appeal to you?"

Okur showed his embarrassment. "I not a fish eater."

"You've got to be kidding," Volmer replied before breaking into laughter. "A sailor who doesn't like fish? That's a new one for me." The laughter disappeared quickly. He speared a wedge of brie and without looking at Okur said, "Send Acker to me ... now."

Dieter Acker arrived at Volmer's table within minutes. "You wish to see me, sir?"

Okur's dishes had already been cleared.

"Yes, pull up a chair." Volmer did not rise to greet the handsome German. "I'm about to have a Bloody Mary. Will you join me?"

"I have work to—" Acker began before being interrupted by Volmer.

"I wish to offer you a new job, Dieter, one that doubles your current salary. Does the Bloody Mary now have any appeal?"

"Ja, mein Herr. Danke. Yes, sir. Thank you."

"Schön, dass wir Deutsch sprechen. I like it when we speak German," Volmer said, finishing off the roe. He paused for a long moment as he wiped his mouth with a freshly laundered napkin. In English, he continued, "Dieter, are you proud of your heritage?"

The question caught the young man by surprise, but he fashioned a quick response. "I have always been proud to be a German."

Volmer's eyes fell on the copy of *Mein Kampf* he had been reading moments earlier. "Hitler would have liked you." He searched the depth of Acker's clear blue eyes.

Acker replied softly, reverently. "I wish I had known him."

"Yes, you would have been his idea of a good soldier." He paused while a server positioned the two drinks on the table. When the man retreated, Volmer looked at Acker and continued. "I have asked for you in order that you and I can carry out a very important assignment. It is one that would have pleased our *Führer*, had this occurred during wartime."

Acker smiled, but remained silent.

Volmer appreciated the deference. Most men in Acker's position would have asked about the job, especially if it meant more money. "Before I ask if you would like the job, I have a question for you."

"Sir?"

"If this were a time of war and you were serving under my command, is there any directive I might give you that would cause you to pause?"

"No, sir. Were I as soldier, I would do anything asked of me."

"Anything?"

"Yes, sir."

"Do you mean to say that if we were walking down a street in occupied Paris and I asked you to shoot a small child waving a French flag, that you would do so without questioning the order?"

"Without any hesitation, sir."

"Would the same devotion apply if the person was a Jew simply going about his business?"

"Of course, sir."

Volmer was not expecting such a total absence of equivocation. "Another question, if I may."

"Certainly, sir."

"Are you a Christian, Dieter?"

"I am, sir. Lutheran."

"Do you attend Sunday services here in Le Havre?"

"I do, sir, when circumstances permit."

Volmer shifted lanes. "And what about conscience? How would you reconcile the shooting of the little French child, or a Jew, given God's commandment to do no murder?"

"Under the conditions you set, sir—that it was a time of war—I would not consider either death to be murder. I would only be doing a soldier's duty."

Volmer smiled. "I'm quite impressed with your responses, Dieter. I believe we will make a fine team." He withdrew a small piece of paper from his pocket and placed it before Acker on the table. "Before I tell you about the new job, I am going to ask you to do a few things for me." He pushed the paper across to him. "Please read this aloud."

Acker studied the paper for a moment and then referenced the contents in the order given: "Three white dress shirts—short sleeves permitted. Three pair of white linen trousers, cuffed. Several pair of white socks and appropriate underwear. Black belt—conservative. Black shoes—conservative. Three black ties. Go to a good salon and have your hair nicely styled. Do not have much taken from the length.

Do this before Tuesday, August fifth."

When he completed his recitation, the young German found Volmer's eyes locked squarely on his. Volmer was the first to speak. "Are there any questions?"

"None, sir."

"I presume you have a suitcase?"

"I do, sir."

"Good! We're about to do a little traveling."

Acker's eyes sparkled. "Traveling?"

"Wir fahren nach Florenz. We are driving to Florence. Now let me tell you about our mission."

After dismissing Acker a few minutes later, Volmer opened his briefcase and removed a large brown envelope. It contained months of correspondence and transactions with the Swiss and Caribbean banks in which he had placed most of his fortune before leaving Anghiari. For some time he had worried about the security of these papers. The most sensitive information in the packet related to his two coded accounts in Zurich and the Grand Caymans, respectively. Each carried a password.

A second concern had been festering in his mind for the past two or three months: occasional forgetfulness. His mental acuity had never posed problems or concerns, but of late these momentary voids had visited him; the placement of things like keys or glasses somewhere and then not remembering where, or going from one room to the next to get something only to realize in transit that he had forgotten the purpose of his actions. Earlier in the year he completely blanked on the name of a man he'd known for over thirty years. And then there was the uncomfortable exchange with Bjorn in the Nashville airport. While these situations were little more than inconveniences, what if he was experiencing the early stages of dementia? After all, dementia of some kind accompanied his mother's death in 1956. He could have a genetic predisposition.

Two questions faced Volmer, both related to the numbered accounts: if he asked his attorney Mario Drago to position the brown envelope in a safety deposit box in the Deutsche Bank in Florence—an easy enough solution—would he be able to remember the numerical codes and passwords at a later date? The second question was even more basic: where to hide the valuable data if he sent the envelope to Drago? After considering several locations, the idea arrived like the first robin: in *Mein Kampf*, of course. What better place to conceal the critical information about the two banks in which he held the bulk of his fortune? Each carried a five-digit code. *Mein Kampf* was with him virtually every minute of the day; what better place to conceal things of importance than in its aged pages?

From the moment he first read volumes I and II, two chapters resonated most strongly: Chapter Eleven from Volume One, "Nation and Race," and the eighth chapter of volume II, "The Strong Man is Mightiest Alone." When he would reread for inspiration, he always started with these two chapters.

Opening his worn copy of *Mein Kampf*, he quickly turned to "Nation and Race" on page 147. To the left of the numeral one, he penned the number four neatly in black ink, so close in size and character to the printed number it could easily pass unnoticed. After the numeral seven, he added the number nine in a similar fashion. He now had the five-digit number of his account in Zurich: 41479. On line seventeen of the page he placed a small black dot above the word, *immer*, always, the password for the account. He then turned to "The Strong Man is Mightiest Alone" which began on page 307 of volume two. He altered the page number to read 13075, the code for his account in the Grand Caymans. The selected password on line seven of that page was *nie*, never. There was no way he would forget those pages. The only remaining thing for him to do was conceal the names of the two banks Turning to the backside of the last page, near the spine, he formed two anagrams that looked like pure gibberish: Nolecadian and Seditsucrie, the scrambled names of the two banks where his fortune was stored; the Caledonian in the Grand Caymans and the Credit Suisse in Zurich, respectively. He smiled at the thought: *Breaking my code might be a chip shot for a master code breaker, but no such person will ever lay his hands on this book.*

His final task of the day took him to the Le Havre telephone directory. He quickly scanned the alphabetical listings from back to front: ...I, H, G, pausing at F. His slender finger moved down the column until he found the desired subject: *fauteuils roulants*. Wheelchairs.

CHAPTER TWENTY-EIGHT

Poor Man

Tuesday, August 5
Krakow, Poland

While waiting for the phone line in her apartment to be installed, Largo called Blue from a public phone in the train station. As she computed the time difference, it was mid-morning in the States. She dialed the number, waiting excitedly for the sound of his voice. She couldn't remember when they were last together. She missed him. The phone rang several times. The next ring would surely trigger the recording. Just as she was about to resign herself to that, he picked up the phone. He sounded out of breath.

"Porter Blue here."

"Hi, sweetheart, it's me. I'm glad I caught you at home. How are you?"

It took Blue a moment to connect the dots. "Largo! What a surprise! I've been waiting for your call. How are you?"

"Better now. It's been crazy here. Just getting a phone installed has been an adventure from hell."

"I can imagine."

"I'm still far from settled, but I'm getting there. I'll be doing my first serious shopping today. There's a nice market just a block away. Tons of vegetables."

Like a bump in the night, his thoughts went immediately to the Memling, to Geller's call. He'd been dreading how to tell her, but now the wait was over. She needed to know.

"Largo, there's something I need to tell you. I wish I were there ..."

"What is it Porter? What's wrong?"

"It's about your painting, the Memling. I received a call yesterday or the day before from Geller."

"And?"

232

Blue paused as long as he could, before replying. "The museum believes it is a recent forgery." The word forgery seemed to hang in space. He could almost see it.

"What are you saying ... a forgery? No,no,no!" she screamed.

"Sweetheart, listen to me. Calm down and take a deep breath. I know this is coming as a shock, but Geller said they have run conclusive tests. They—"

"They are mistaken! They have to be!"

"Listen to me," he said. "There is no doubt in their minds."

Deafening silence.

"But how? When?" she asked. "It's been with me since it was sent from Florence."

He could hear the sobbing. And then he remembered the holy men. "You took some photographs of the Memling before I left on my last trip. Do you have any of those with you?"

"Yes, I brought one with me. Why?"

"You took several pictures as well after it was returned to you from Florence, as I recall."

"Yes, Porter, why are you concerned with the photographs?"

"Can you get to them now?"

"They're in my purse. Just a second."

Blue wanted Geller to be wrong about the holy men, but in his gut he knew the man would not have made the accusation without compelling proof.

"I have them in my hand," Largo said, her sobbing slowly subsiding. "What are you concerned about? They look identical."

"Look at the lower left hand part of the most recent photograph. Do you see four men wearing vestments near the praying men?"

"Yes." Her voice now sounded like brittle vellum. "They are in both photos. What about them?"

"In your most recent photograph, does one priest look much younger than the others, even with the beard?"

Her eyes raked the surface of the photograph, before stopping at the image of a young, handsome man. She had never noticed him before. She quickly scanned the older photograph. She saw the difference. "I don't understand," she said. "I've never noticed the difference."

"Geller believes the forger painted his self-portrait on the figure in your last photograph, his signature, of sorts."

For Largo, it was like experiencing a horrible dream. Blue didn't sound real. The preposterous notion that someone, somehow, had fabricated a copy … that didn't seem real. *When could someone have done it?* How could it have taken the place of the painting hanging next to their bed? And then it came to her like a violent clap of thunder: *The cigarette ashes! The panties!*

⟶

Tuesday, August 5
Le Havre, France

The Le Havre Granville train station was packed with tourists and French commuters during the busy morning hour. When a young man in white trousers and a matching shirt pushed a wheelchair past a long queue of ticket buyers, many of them crossed themselves. The object of their concern was the man in the wheelchair, a Catholic priest.

In spite of the warm day, the man's legs were covered with a small gray blanket. Above the black shirt and white, round collar, he looked vacantly ahead through rimless glasses. One hand clutched the end of the armrest, as if he might fall out at the slightest bounce. The other hand cradled a thin black briefcase in his lap; the only item inside was his dog-eared copy of *Mein Kampf.*

"*Pauvre homme.* Poor man," said a profusely sweating woman of fifty, looking as if she would relish a few minutes in the wheelchair.

Acker negotiated the swarming mass with ease, eventually bringing the wheelchair to a stop from which he could scan a constantly changing overhead sign showing arrivals and departures. After a few moments of observation, he saw the desired train and track number. It showed a departure time of 17:05 hours. Destination: Firenze, Italy. He checked his wristwatch: 16:35. Twenty minutes, or so, before boarding. He quickly wheeled the priest to the track number. The lengthy train was waiting. Steam hissed from openings near the platform.

"May I get you something cool to drink?" Acker asked. "We still have a few minutes before departure.

Volmer nodded. "Water would be nice. With gas, please."

Acker departed quickly for the carbonated water, finding a kiosk nearby from which he could maintain eye contact with the priest. Just as the vendor was about to give him two bottles of water, Acker saw a man in black trousers approaching his employer. A second later, he realized the man was wearing a round white collar and appeared to be asking a question, or saying something. He hurriedly paid for the water and scurried back to the two men.

The standing priest showed signs of impatience at having to wait for a response. The blank stare he was receiving from his confined colleague only added to his restive manner.

Acker moved quickly. *"Excusez moi, Pere,* Excuse me, Father," he said, handing Volmer a bottle of the water. Continuing in French, he said, "Father Contaldo is recuperating from throat cancer. Sadly, he is still unable to verbally communicate. If you were asking a question, perhaps I can provide the answer."

The demeanor of the standing priest changed quickly when he realized the fragile condition of the man whose legs were covered. "I should apologize," he said. "I had no idea ..."

"It is my fault, Father," Acker interrupted with an apology of his own. "I should have been here."

"I was only asking a liturgical question, one which hardly merits repeating," the man replied. "You know how it is with us, always eager to talk a little shop."

"I will convey your feelings of concern," Acker said. "Are you, by chance, headed for Firenze?"

"No, no, I'm just killing some time. My train doesn't leave for another hour. I'm going to Brussels."

After the priest walked away, Volmer looked up at Acker. "You handled that quite well."

"I was only trying to follow your instructions, sir. The bit about the throat cancer was most ingenious on your part."

Volmer smiled. "One has to be prepared for the unexpected at all times, my young friend. It's an important lesson to learn."

Eleven minutes later, the long train headed south. As it eased its way out of Le Havre, Volmer looked at the sky with delight. Streaks of a velvety salmon color laced the pale cerulean dome. By his reckoning, they should reach Florence in the early morning, just in time for breakfast. It had been a long year since he had enjoyed the city's ambience. This time he was coming with a big surprise in his pocket. What fun!

Another person was embarking on a journey to Florence that day: Astrid Borgmann. The past few months had been difficult ones for her. Business had been good, but she was in sore need of a respite. Following the sudden departure of the man she knew as Azzo Gatti, she had reeled about for a while until regaining her balance. With the help of her devoted friend Sofia Abate, she had purged the vile toxins that accompanied her breakup with Gatti.

While she thought she had initially handled his exit well, it had taken a good two months before she was able to completely put the heartbreak behind her. Sophia's love and attention had helped considerably. It was she who first suggested they get away from Anghiari during the hot month of August.

Sophia was enthusiastic. "I say we go to Florence for *Ferragosto*. It is one of the biggest religious holidays in Italy, the time of the year when bean counters to bakers shed their work clothes and head for the beaches or the mountains. We'll eat and drink like tourists and maybe even find a man to play with in bed!"

"Just one man?" Astrid asked before laughing.

"Make that two men," Sofia corrected.

That had been in June.

During the trip, Astrid told Sofia almost everything about Azzo Gatti, including his commanding personality and bedroom skills. She had even shared with her the day in Cortona when he asked her if she would join him in a museum or gallery robbery.

"He sounds like a royal shit, if you ask me," Sophia replied, absentmindedly rolling a few strands of her hair on her right index finger. "All they want to do is fuck us."

"And you would complain about that if some Florentine Romeo took you to his room while we're there?" Astrid asked, a wide smile forming on her attractive face.

"Well, perhaps I would make an exception if he looked like the golfer Seve Ballesteros."

"Ballesteros is Spanish and young enough to be your son, Sofia."

"Well, who is to say that a little incest is a totally bad thing. Anyway, he looks Italian."

Wednesday, August 6
Nashville, Tennessee

After concluding his painful conversation with Largo the day before, Blue paced around their condo like a caged animal for hours, trying to comprehend the magnitude of her distress. In his mind, he could imagine her crying like a small child in the dark, unable to quell the unthinkable truth. If only he could be with her. If only he could place his arms around her and provide some comfort. He had gone to bed wrestling with the problem. Fretful sleep followed. Sometime in the middle of the night, he awoke abruptly, the name of Mason Creed on his lips.

Following breakfast, Blue called the office of Scotland Yard in London. Creed should be in the middle of his work day. After working through a maze of zealous employees, he was eventually able to make contact. The connection was quite good.

"Mason, this is Porter Blue. I trust you remember me?"

"Porter, most certainly!" Creed shifted his position in his desk chair. "What a pleasant surprise. How are you and Largo?"

"We are fine, thank you." He went on to say that Largo was in Krakow and he was trotting about the country with his new book. After covering these bases, he said with a shift in tone, "We've just run into a problem, Mason, a big time problem."

"Oh, what might that be?"

"It's a long story, but the essence is this: we recently had a break-in at our home. The intruder took Largo's treasured Memling and replaced it with a very convincing copy."

Creed's mind danced with memories of Largo, his encounter with Theo Volmer and his discovery of the real Memling in Stuttgart. "A copy, you say?"

"Yes, but that's not all of it. Prior to departing for Krakow, Largo met with a museum director in Atlanta at which time she formally gave her treasured Memling to them. Just a few days ago, the gentleman called to say that the painting was a forgery, a recent one in his opinion."

"Did you say she is presently in Krakow?" Creed was surprised that she was in Europe.

"Yes, she left on the first of August to begin a doctoral program at the Jagiellonian University."

"Does she know of the forgery?"

"Yes, I spoke with her recently, but she did not take the news well."

Creed's organized mind quickly processed Blue's call. "You've notified local authorities, I assume?"

"Yes, but they have little to go on. They've been to our condo, taken fingerprints and all that, but they're not optimistic about finding the thief. My guess is that whoever took it has already left the area, perhaps even the country." Blue paused for a moment. "This may sound preposterous, but Largo and I suspect Theo Volmer of having something to do with this."

"I see." Creed had been one of the few to suspect that Volmer had not perished in the fire at his Fiesole home, but it was best to let Blue do the talking.

"Her classes begin in early October. I have her phone number in Krakow. Would you mind calling her and giving her your perspective? I know she would appreciate hearing from you"

The image of Volmer returned to the screen in Creed's mind. He remembered the cold, gray eyes and his detached manner. For a passing second, he wondered why Blue was calling him. *Is he wanting me to make contact with Largo, is that it?*

"Yes, of course. I will be happy to do that. I can only imagine her distress."

"I would really appreciate that, Mason. I have no idea what, if anything, she can do about this from Poland, but perhaps you could give her some advice. I know this is imposing on you, but—"

"No, it's no imposition at all. I'm glad you called me. I'll do everything I can to be of assistance, you know that."

"Then let me give you her address and telephone number," Blue continued. "Give me a second."

While Blue was looking for the note pad on which he'd written Largo's contact information, Creed pondered the situation. There was no good reason why he couldn't get to Krakow following the wedding. He would have ample time between now and the wedding to check into a few things.

"Here it is," Blue said, obviously a bit winded. "Eight thirty-four Bracka Street, or whatever a street is called in Polish." He provided the telephone number. "As I said, her apartment is quite close to the Jagiellonian." A brief pause followed before he added, "It's been good talking with you, Mason. Thanks for offering to help us."

"You're quite welcome, Porter. I'm sorry to hear about her painting, but I'll do what I can to help in its recovery."

"Thanks. I know you will."

Having a day to think about Blue's call, Creed poured himself a dark beer and called Largo shortly before dusk. As he heard the phone ring, he took a deep swallow of the warm, amber brew.

"Hello," came the soft reply. "This is Largo."

"Largo, this is Mason Creed." He hesitated momentarily before adding, "Porter gave me your telephone number. Do you remember me?"

"Mason! I do, indeed. What a pleasant surprise."

"Porter tells me you've just received some disturbing news from a museum in Atlanta. I'm so sorry."

"Oh, Mason, how sweet of you to call. Yes, it is simply dreadful. I still can't believe it."

"Someone broke into your home and took the original. Is that it?"

"It was Volmer, Mason, I just know it was him."

She sounded so close. He could feel the depth of her despair. "I plan to be in Rouen, France, soon for a wedding," he began, not knowing exactly what to say. "I don't know that I can be of any help, officially speaking, but it would be no trouble at all for me to drive down to Krakow afterwards. I have some vacation time. I was just thinking that—"

"Mason, I can't tell you how much a visit from you would do for me right now. I'll soon be starting classes at the Jagiellonian, but right now I'm basically moving in circles. I don't know anyone here. I'm terribly disoriented, and the theft of the Memling is ... well, it's simply incomprehensible."

"Then let me try to be of some help. I'll do what I can to garner some information before I leave for France, and we can look at this more rationally once I'm in Krakow. It's important that you try to stay focused, Largo, that you hang in there, as you Americans so aptly put it. We'll get to the bottom of this."

After another brief pause, he said, "I want to give you my telephone number. Call me at any hour of the day or night. Do you understand?"

"Yes, thank you. I will if I need to." Tears of relief were forming in her eyes. She knew if she didn't step away from the phone in the next few moments she would start crying. The sound of his voice had been like a soothing balm. He was counting on her to be strong. The last thing she wanted to do was falter now. If she was hurting, she was not going to show it, not at this moment. "Thank you, Mason, for calling. I needed to hear the strength of your voice. I will look forward to seeing you soon."

"Good night, Largo. I'll be in touch."

CHAPTER TWENTY-NINE

Santa Croce

Wednesday, August 6
Florence, Italy

After arriving in Florence on the fifth, Astrid and Sofia wasted no
time in hopscotching all over the charming city by the Arno: the
Boboli Gardens, the Pitti Palace, the huge flea market near San Lorenzo, even the long, killing climb up Giotto's majestic Campanile.
And, as might be expected, each stop was followed by gelati and several glasses of chilled white wine.

On this spectacular day—not one cloud to mar a vivid cobalt sky—
a spur of the moment decision was about to collide with a carefully
orchestrated plan.

Astrid and Sofia had just finished a delightful breakfast and were
walking to morning mass in the Basilica of Santa Croce. The motiva-
tion to attend the ten o'clock service was not to confess their respective sins but to experience a service in the Gothic church that first
opened its doors in 1294. The Basilica is home to the remains of five
distinguished Florentines: Galileo; Lorenzo Ghiberti, creator of the
majestic doors of the Baptisty in 1401; Niccolo Machiavelli; the great
Humanist Leonardo Bruni and, arguably, the most famous Florentine
of them all, Michelangelo Buonarroti. The walls of the hallowed place
showcased frescoes by such masters as Giotto and Masaccio and the
architecture reflects as well as any the precision of the Renaissance.

On this day, relatively few people were in the sanctuary, and those
were near the altar where the priest and his acolytes were engaged with
the service. With the censers disseminating the perfume of guilt, the
Latin chants of the priest reverberated in the high rafters of the church.
A few tourists and pilgrims discretely strolled about in the chapels surrounding the sanctuary, whispering when talk was necessary.

Astrid and Sofia took seats on the left side of the sanctuary, between the tomb of Lorenzo Ghiberti and the altar. From her seat, Astrid glanced back and saw a young man wheeling in an elderly looking man with a briefcase in his lap. After seating the man near the rear of the church, the younger man walked halfway up the nave and took a seat directly behind a solitary worshipper seated in front of Machiavelli's tomb on the right. She didn't think much of what she was observing, other than the fact that the elderly man—a priest, as she could now determine from the white collar—was seated at the rear of the church. *It'd odd they are not sitting together.* Her attention drifted back to the front of the sanctuary.

As Dieter Acker took his seat behind the worshipper, he glanced across the rows of empty pews, relieved that there was no one in the immediate vicinity. What few people there were in the sanctuary were seated near the altar. He then removed a syringe from a folded white envelope. Kneeling behind the man for a moment, he quickly slid his strong right hand over the man's mouth to secure him. Seated as they were near the right end of the pews, no one observed Acker's sudden movements.

Instinctively, the man turned his head slightly to the right in order to see who was responsible for the entrapment. In doing so, he fully exposed the left side of his neck and his carotid artery. It looked like a rope beneath his skin. Before the victim could fully comprehend what was happening, the tip of the syringe was beneath the skin and into the artery. Knowing the man might register some physical reaction to his situation, Acker tightened his grip. In a matter of seconds, Acker felt the man grow limp. He then calmly removed the syringe and pulled himself up from the kneeling bench and returned to his seat. By this time, the worshipper had slumped over in his seat, looking as if he had fallen asleep. Acker waited for a few additional moments and then returned to Volmer at the rear of the church.

Just as Acker began to turn the wheelchair and make his move to the large doors of the church, something, perhaps a sound of some kind, compelled Astrid Borgman to look behind her. This time she had a much clearer side view of the priest as he was being wheeled to the massive doorway. She couldn't believe her eyes. The man in the wheelchair looked exactly like Azzo Gatti.

She turned to Sofia and whispered, "I think I've just seen him!"

"Seen whom?"

"Azzo Gatti. I'm almost certain it was him. He was in a wheelchair."

"Do you want to leave? Do you want to make sure?"

"Yes, I must!"

By the time the two women exited the church, there was no sign of Acker and Volmer.

"Maybe you were mistaken, Astrid," Sofia offered gently. "I don't see a wheelchair anywhere in the piazza."

Astrid was adamant. "Damn it, I know it was him!"

Just then, a woman came running out of the church, her hands to her face. *"Un uomo e' morto in chiesa!* A man is dead in the church!" she screamed. She was followed by a dozen distraught persons, all fleeing the church like rats from a sinking ship.

Volmer and Acker were already in the shadows behind Santa Croce. They took the Borgo Allegri up to Via Ghibellina where they turned left and continued to the Bargello on the Via del Proconsolo. They could hear sirens from the vicinity of the church. Eleven minutes later, they were taking seats in one of the outdoor restaurants in the Piazza della Signoria.

"My goodness," Volmer said as he eased into a comfortable chair near a well-trimmed hedge. "Whatever in the world is happening?"

It did not take long before word of the man's death was all over Florence. It would have been tragic enough if the man had been a simple man wanting only the forgiveness of Christ. But the dead man was not a simple sinner. The man was Lucca Palma, the Director of the Uffizi Gallery.

Volmer had waited a long time for this moment of satisfaction and he was in no hurry to leave Florence. He wanted to savor the kill. That night in their hotel room, he and Acker watched assorted news coverage of the event. It was the lead story on almost all of the major news networks.

As John Caine of CNN put it at the end of his story,

"...and by all outward appearances, the well-liked museum director suffered a heart attack and died quickly."

243

Dieter Acker watched the telecast with a Peroni in his hands. Volmer held a glass of his preferred *Dewar's* on the rocks. "They don't have a fucking clue!" Acker said, turning to Volmer. "Did we do good, or what?"

"You performed admirably, Dieter." Volmer's eyes misted with satisfaction, not only at the death of Palma but at the good fortune that had enabled him to find the perfect means of mimicking a heart attack. It was during a casual discussion with a pharmacist in Bangkok several years earlier that he learned of the potency of the Northern Phillipine Cobra. A vial of the poison was bought on the black market, to be saved for a time of need. As the pharmacist told Volmer at the time, "An injection of the venom results in instant death and is virtually undetectable in an autopsy. Only a skilled coroner who knows to look can find it."

Buried beneath Volmer's respect for the boy's skill in carrying out his assignment, was an undeniable blossoming of affection. The actions of the handsome young man that day could not have made him prouder. Standing and raising his glass he said, "I propose a toast, my young friend: to the Fatherland and Adolf Hitler. The obligatory salute followed: *"Heil Hitler!"*

"Heil Hitler!" Acker countered, grinning from ear to ear.

It was not until the following afternoon that the cause of Palma's death was officially announced. In a hurriedly called press conference, a spokesperson for the Ospedale Saint Maria Nuova announced that Palma had died of heart failure. In the words of the spokesperson, "Death was almost immediate."

If the medical and police authorities of Florence were satisfied that the Uffizi director's death was due to natural causes, at least one person in the city refused to accept the announcement: Palma's wife Alba.

"Lucca was as strong as an ox," she declared when interviewed by the Florentine press. "To my knowledge, he never had problems of any kind with his heart. Why just yesterday, we enjoyed a lengthy hike together in Fiesole. He was in robust health."

Volmer was more than pleased with the eradication of Palma. Instead of returning to Le Havre and thus eliminating any chances of being discovered in Florence, he decided to remain for another day and enjoy a few victory laps. He was playing his own game of Russian roulette. It was a decision that almost proved catastrophic.

Volmer spent the following morning in the Church of San Lorenzo, once the private church of the Medici. He was most anxious for Acker to see the four funerary carvings made by Michelangelo that symbolized *Night, Day, Dawn,* and *Dusk.* The emotionally charged works exuded a profound sense of melancholy that reflected the artist's own love and affection for the Medici family. After all, it was Lorenzo de'Medici who nurtured his young passion for art. Volmer's thoughts drifted to Porter Blue and the novel he began after arriving in Florence.

"Dieter, if you are to accompany me in my travels," Volmer began, gently stroking the knee of Dawn, "then it is important that you be properly educated. I will show you some of the greatest art ever made by man, but it is vital that you comprehend the significance and power of these works."

Acker nodded, as if to signify that he understood.

"Make no mistake here, Dieter. This has less to do with appreciating Michelangelo's genius than positioning yourself to use art to your advantage. Knowledge is the cornerstone of power, never forget that. I have great plans for you and I don't want to be disappointed."

San Lorenzo was followed by lunch near one of the major markets in Florence. Acker deftly wheeled Volmer—still in the garb of a priest—to a small table under a huge red and blue striped canopy. A gentle breeze stirred the sticky air.

As was Volmer's self-protective habit in restaurants, he visually scanned the tables, making sure his surroundings were safe before he seated himself with a wall to his back. In doing so, he noticed two women sitting about five tables away. They were chatting and laughing a bit louder than he preferred. He then shifted his attention to the menu and made his selections. After Acker had done the same, Volmer ordered a bottle of the restaurant's finest chilled Pinot Grigio.

"I think a little celebration is in order, my dear friend. Yesterday, you demonstrated admirable allegiance to our cause. You have proven yourself to be the perfect soldier."

Acker delivered a modest smile, less with regard to Volmer's delusional blathering than the realization that his life was in the process of changing for the better.

A short while after Volmer and Acker raised their glasses, the two women settled their bill and, with some difficulty, raised themselves from their chairs. They, too, had enjoyed wine with their meal and were showing its effects. As they wobbled past adjacent tables for the exit, Volmer recognized Astrid Borgmann walking behind her companion. *Just keep walking, Astrid.* He let his weight sag in the seat of the wheelchair, hoping to minimize his visibility. *Don't look back this way.*

But look back she did, just before passing the last table. She grabbed Sofia by the shoulder, prompting her friend to turn at the sudden pressure.

"What is it, Astrid? What's the matter?"

"Azzo Gatti is seated behind me, a few tables away! He's near the corner. I told you I saw him in the church." Both women looked back in Volmer's direction.

"What do you want to do, Astrid?" Sofia asked, knowing the severity of her friend's injured feelings.

"I want to confront him!"

Before Sofia could dissuade her from taking such invasive action, Astrid added, "I want him to know he did not destroy me, that I am stronger now than ever." She bolted away from Sofia's side and walked with surprising quickness towards the confined priest.

Volmer saw her and quickly countered. "Dieter, I know the woman who is coming in our direction. She is from Anghiari and was institutionalized for psychiatric observation shortly before I left there. She had been implicated in the death of a child. I want you to cover for me, just as you did in the Le Havre station. Do you understand?"

"Quite well, sir."

Astrid Borgmann leveled her first volley when she neared Volmer's table. "Well, well, Azzo Gatti, what does the coward have to say for himself? Did you think you could dismiss me so easily?"

Nearby diners witnessed the situation with expressions of wonder and curiosity.

Acker stepped between Volmer and the now noticeably disturbed woman. "With all due respect, *signora*, I believe you are confused. The man in the wheelchair is Father Ankiel Thorssen from Copenhagen. He has recently undergone serious surgery for throat cancer and cannot respond to your questions. I beg you to turn around and leave before you create an embarrassing incident."

"I'll do no such thing," Astrid struggled to get around Acker. "I have a score to settle with this piece of trash."

By this time, word of the woman's emotional behavior had reached the *maître d'*. He wasted no time in moving rapidly to the scene, determined to prevent the situation from escalating.

"I'm telling you, I know this man!" Astrid bellowed, looking around at fellow diners. "He is no priest! Ask him about the Gade Collection robbery."

Before she could complete her accusations, the *maître d'* arrived and placed his two large hands on her shoulders. "*Signora, venga con me per favore*. Please come with me, madam," he said in a firm voice. "*Non mi faccia chiamare la polizia*. Don't make me call the police."

"Call the police! Do that!" Astrid thundered, pointing to Volmer's seat at the table. "I want you to call them. Let them test his wineglass. You'll see!"

After the *maître d'* escorted Astrid Borgmann away from the table, Dieter Acker quickly wheeled Volmer to the entrance to the restaurant. More than one restaurant patron bowed in respect as the stoic priest passed. Within minutes, Volmer was a safe distance from the restaurant. There was no sign of the woman or her companion.

Volmer repositioned himself in the seat and said to Acker, "I think it is time for us to say farewell to Florence, Dieter." He glanced at his watch. "Our train to Le Havre leaves shortly."

The *maître d'* encountered such difficulty in getting Astrid Borgmann to the front of the restaurant, he did call the police. Her explosive behavior could present serious problems for the establishment.

The police responded promptly and whisked both women from the restaurant. While one of the men talked with Astrid, she returned to the wineglass. "I told the *maître d'* to get the wineglass for you. The DNA would prove that the priest was Azzo Gatti." She paused for a moment. "Are you unaware of the Gade Collection robbery in Copenhagen?"

One of the officers responded quickly. "Of course we are aware of it. It is a major unsolved crime. Why are you mentioning it?"

"Because I know Azzo Gatti is responsible for that robbery!" she screamed. "You fool! Don't you understand what I am trying to tell you? Get his wineglass! His fingerprints!"

The officer hesitated for a brief moment and then dispatched his junior partner back to the restaurant for the wineglass and any other utensils that had been touched by the priest. "Hurry!"

When the policeman reached the restaurant, he conveyed his need to the *maître d'*. They moved like the wind in returning to Volmer's table, but everything had been removed. A waitress was in the process of positioning a clean tabletop and new place settings.

"Where are the plates and utensils from the previous party?" the *maître d'* asked. He knew the answer.

"They are being cleaned, sir."

"And the tablecloth?"

"The same, sir. We are asked to be prompt in clearing empty tables."

"Yes, I know," he muttered as he and the officer turned and walked away.

The senior officer was not at all happy to receive the news a few moments later. Before he could set in motion a plan for finding the priest and his young assistant, Volmer and Dieter Acker were on a train pulling out of Statzione Santa Maria Novella for their overnight return to Le Havre.

Just before the train disengaged from the many rail arteries coming into and leaving the large station, Volmer turned to Acker with a stern expression on his face.

"Dieter, you disappointed me today."

"Sir?"

"Back there when you were trying to shield me from that woman, you told her my name was Father Ankiel Thorssen, not Father Contaldo. Why did you do that?"

Acker's embarrassment showed.

"And you mentioned Copenhagen," Volmer added. "Were you not thinking?"

Acker's face was flushed. "It happened so fast, I could not remember the name Contaldo. I'm sorry. It won't happen again."

Volmer frowned. "A mistake like that could bring serious consequences. Never let that happen again, do you understand?"

"Yes, sir, I understand perfectly."

As for Astrid Borgmann, she was detained and questioned by Florentine police for three hours and then released.

Somewhere in Switzerland:

Little in the way of conversation passed between Volmer and Acker as the train rumbled through northern Italy and Switzerland on its way to the French border. A steward came by to make their beds.

Volmer suggested they go to the club car while the change was made. He was not yet ready to let go of Acker's mistake. From everything he had been following on the news, the death of Lucca Palma had ignited growing assumptions by the police that he had survived the fire in his Fiesole home. It was as if Theo Volmer had come back from the grave. All eyes were now looking for him.

It was approximately three a.m. when Dieter Acker quietly pulled back the covers on his bed and stepped to the floor. In the ever-changing light of the sleeper, he could see Volmer lying on his side, his face turned to the wall of the chamber. *Perfect*, he thought as he untied the string of his pajama bottoms. They fell silently to the floor. Without making a sound, he moved to Volmer's bed.

For a moment he stood motionless above his sleeping employer, swaying gracefully with the rhythm of the train. As it passed outside lights, Acker's naked and muscular body glistened.

Volmer made a slight moaning sound as he shifted his position. It was not until Acker's hand slithered beneath his covers and caressed his genitals that Volmer became aware of the presence of the night visitor. He tried to turn, but Acker's warm body was pressed against his backside.

"What...?" Volmer muttered in that half-awake state that follows arousal from a deep sleep.

"Shhh," Acker whispered close to his ear. "Let me play. Let me atone for my errors in Florence."

Volmer was now awake, all vestiges of sleep and the dreams that came with it erased. "Dieter?" he said, "what in the hell are...?"

Acker's tongue gently raked Volmer's left ear. "Be still, savor this moment. Let me treat you, my lord."

For Volmer, the moment was charged with conflict. As a young boy, he had been taught by his father that homosexuality was not only morally wrong for the individual, but a threat to public values, more specifically the cornerstones of Nazi ideology. Any show of such deviant behavior needed to be suppressed. As he grew older, he continued to view homosexuality with criticism, but beneath that façade, he carried secret curiosity. It was his very father, after all, who came to his bed in the night and fondled his boyhood weapon. His relationship with Sarto Carpaccio had been fueled by precisely the same dark fascination

Now in the darkness of night, Acker's warm hand was leading him to a new sexual threshold. To his surprise he succumbed to the seductive whisper without any appreciable resistance. His arousal was immediate.

His instincts and reflexes were focused like lasers. He rolled over and faced Acker, his right hand now enjoying the elegant, hard contours of the young German's body. As it moved across Acker's bare chest and down to his pelvis, Volmer shuddered at the tactile splendor of his companion's body. "Jesus Christ!" he said with hoarseness to his voice. "You are sublime."

Minutes ticked away as Volmer was carried to and then dropped from dizzying heights. Lying in Acker's strong arms, he clung like a baby to his seducer.

"You are pleased, Herr Thorssen?"

"Pleased, yes! Pleased beyond measure, my son."

"Am I forgiven?"

"Yes, of course." Volmer intentionally waited a long moment before saying, "Dieter, I have a request to make."

"What is it?"

"I think you would look handsome in a goatee. Will you grow one for me?"

Acker laughed, a deep guttural laugh, as he lit a cigarette. "You are serious?"

"Quite." A moment passed before Volmer responded to the cigarette. "Smoking is a nasty habit, Dieter. One day these will kill you."

Acker leaned over and kissed him, not in the least concerned that the second hand smoke was enveloping Volmer like morning fog.

The train emitted a long, shrill whistle that penetrated the opaque parchment of the night. They were approaching Dijon, France.

CHAPTER THIRTY

Fela

Monday, August 11
Krakow, Poland

The poster was one of many plastered on a kiosk in the Rynek. Had Largo's eyes not picked up on it in passing, it is highly unlikely that she would have never known the event was scheduled. Dr. Shelby Atkinson, noted American professor of psychology, was delivering a three-day program on Expressive Arts in Lugano, Switzerland, from the fourteenth of August through the sixteenth.

Largo was familiar with the innovative program Atkinson created at the University of Kentucky in the late 80s, a workshop format designed to enable participants to reach their inner creative being. The professor had presented at Vanderbilt the previous year, but circumstances had prevented her from participating. From everything she heard about the program, it was simply wonderful.

Fall classes at the Jagiellonian were scheduled to begin on September 15th. She would have time to attend the program and be back well in advance of the start of the term. From her perspective, it would do her good to take a little unscheduled holiday. The disturbing news from Blue had cast quite a shadow on her mood and enthusiasm. The defeatist side of her contemplated a return to the States, but the stubborn and determined side pleaded for her to remain in Krakow.

She examined the rail schedule from Krakow to Lugano and saw that it was a lengthy journey. The cost was reasonable, however, and the experience could be invaluable. She jotted down the contact information, with the intention of phoning for details on the following day. She was excited.

When Largo called the contact number for information the following morning, she was told that Atkinson had leased living, dining, and classroom facilities from Jefferson College for the program. She was surprised to learn that Jefferson was a private American university in Lugano, the Italian canton of Switzerland. Jefferson's fall term did not officially begin until September 15th.

She tried to call Blue to tell him of her travel plans, but when she received the recording that he would not be returning until the following day, she hung up the phone, trying to decide if she was angry or disappointed.

Thursday, August 14
Lugano, Switzerland

Largo's first view of Lugano was spectacular. When the train pulled into the station around noon, she looked out on a huge lake with a high, mountainous backdrop. Palm trees were growing next to massive rhododendron bushes. The thought formed quickly, *The lambs are lying with the wolves.* She stepped carefully from the train. It was as if she had been dropped into a fairyland. She caught a taxi and within minutes was deposited at Jefferson's administration building. A member of the staff quickly processed her application and gave her a packet containing everything she needed to know about the coming three days; her lodging assignment, directions to the dining room and the location of the classroom.

"You have been assigned Suite C in *Adagio,*" the woman said in perfect English. As you will see, the dormitories Dr. Atkinson has leased are actually small residential units, each capable of housing four to six students. In your case, you will be sharing a unit with three women. We trust you will be comfortable."

"I'm sure I will." Largo admired the woman's unusual earrings.

"Well then," continued the woman behind the desk, "nothing is scheduled before the opening reception at five this afternoon and the dinner following. If you are a walker, you might want to walk down to the town's center." She pointed to the right. "Just follow the paved walkway. It will take you there."

Largo unpacked her things, met one of the two women with whom she would be quartered for the workshop—a delightful college student from Geneva by the name of Michelle—and then decided to treat herself to the walk down to town center. When she returned around four o'clock, she showered and dressed for the reception and dinner.

The third roommate arrived while Largo was dressing; a young teacher from Milan. By the time they were ready for the short walk to the reception, the three of them were talking and laughing like long-lost friends. Largo's spirits were buoyed. *I'm really glad I came.* The fragrant late afternoon air caressed her. *I needed a break like this.*

Not long after she arrived at the reception and processed the first awkward introductions, she found herself in a small pod of animated women who had come to Lugano to worship at the feet of Dr. Atkinson. One member of the group seemed more reserved, more distant, and said little. She was a petite but attractive young woman with soft, auburn hair.

Largo sensed her nervousness and made it her business to offer something of a welcome. "Hi," she said, careful not to slosh her glass of Chardonnay as she moved closer to the young woman. "I'm Largo."

"Fela Bejek." The young woman's voice was soft, little more than a whisper. "It's so nice to meet you."

Feeling the need to add fuel to the fire, Largo continued, "Are you an artist?"

Fela registered a hesitant smile. "Not really, not any more. I'm more of a full-time caregiver. I used to paint, but I only do it infrequently now. How about you?"

Largo paused for a moment before fashioning a reply. "I'm an art historian, but I've always been interested in—intrigued would be a better way of putting it—the creative side of art, the making of paintings and drawings." She glanced quickly around the room at the number of persons in attendance and added, "If there had been expressive arts classes when I was in college, who knows, I might have become an artist." She caught the far-away look in Fela's eyes. She sensed the weight of something on her shoulders. "Are you from Switzerland?" She hoped the question would bring Fela out of her shell and become more engaged.

"No, I live in Ravenna, Italy, at the present time, but I was born in Krakow."

"How interesting is that!" Largo sent a broad smile Fela's way. "I just arrived in Krakow a few days ago. I'll be working on my doctorate at the Jagiellonian."

"Then you are not from here, either?"

"No, I'm an American, but my family—my great-grandparents, that is—came from Krakow. They were Jewish." An additional sentence seemed merited. "They perished at Auschwitz."

Before they could carry their conversation further, someone near the administrative part of campus rang a bell. It was the signal for everyone to assemble for dinner. As they turned in that direction, Fela surprised Largo with a question. "I wonder if you and I might share a table."

"I would love to do that," Largo replied, relieved that the woman was finally relaxing. "I'd like to hear more about your interest in art, your background, and that sort of thing."

"It's too bad my husband is not here," Fela replied. "He is an exceptional artist. He could bring more to the conversation than I."

Largo sensed that she was concealing more than she was revealing. "Oh, you are both artists?"

A faint smile came to Fela's lips. "That's a nice way of putting it. I phoned Pieter after arriving ... felt like I needed to check on him."

"How sweet." Her thoughts raced to Porter. It seemed like ages since last they talked. *He has obviously not felt the need to check on me.*

Fela sighed and took a sip of wine. "Pieter is confined to a wheelchair. He is paralyzed from the neck down."

For a moment, Largo couldn't speak. She felt her eyes misting. "I'm so sorry," she said with some effort. "I had no idea when I asked about his ..."

"It's okay," Fela interrupted, "You had no way of knowing." She then summarized for Largo the path they had been following since his accident; the long months of hospitalization and therapy, the struggle they faced with everyday things, not to mention their financial insecurity and Pieter's occasional bouts with depression.

She then added, "This is one of the first times I've been able to get away for a few days. In talking recently with Pieter's sister about this workshop—she lives near Ravenna now—she insisted that I attend. She said her schedule was quite flexible and she would love to come for a visit with him. She's very familiar with his needs."

"How thoughtful."

"Yes, she's been a big help to me in a lot of ways."

The dinner that followed the reception was nice, but a bit bland. Dr. Atkinson came to the podium, welcomed everyone and registered a few remarks. The program ended shortly before nine-thirty. A few of the participants lingered to chat, but most headed for the door, eager to enjoy something of the Lugano night life.

"I'm not much of a party animal," Largo admitted after they worked their way outside to a large, walled patio, "but I have a nice bottle of Chianti in my room. Would you care to join me? I have a thing about drinking alone."

"I would enjoy that."

As they began walking, Largo said, "I'm in *Adagio*. Where did they put you?"

"*Andante*. I believe it's just next door to you."

When they reached *Adagio*, Fela said she needed to stop at her unit for a minute.

"Take your time. I'll be uncorking the bottle."

When Fela returned a few minutes later, Largo greeted her at the door and suggested they shift to a more secluded place on the patio. The evening breeze from the water was exquisite. "I don't want this lovely evening to go to waste."

"I was thinking the same thing." Largo returned to something Fela had said before the reception. "You were saying earlier in the evening that your husband is an artist. I take that to mean he is still painting in spite of his disability."

"Yes, almost every day, if you can believe it. Painting has been his salvation. Every stroke of paint is applied by a tool he holds his mouth. All in all, we've managed pretty well." She looked away for a moment and then added, "You know, this might sound very bizarre, but for all the difficulties we've faced, one of our most stressful situations concerns a very sizeable commission that Pieter received from a customer last December. One would think that a bundle of money would be seen as a blessing, but, I promise you, it has had the reverse effect on our lives."

"Oh, in what way?"

"Pieter was so thrilled by the patron's generosity, so flattered by his words of praise for his artistic talents, that he viewed the commission as a way of solving our financial problems. I told him that the whole arrangement with the man was wrong, but he couldn't see beyond the glittering coins. As far as he was concerned, the man had come to rescue us. He was, in Pieter's eyes, a benevolent benefactor."

She hesitated for a moment. "Yes, the money made it possible for me to come here, but that's a two-edged sword; one side of me appreciates the opportunity to be here, but the money has left me with a bad taste in my mouth."

Largo didn't have to raise any more questions. It was obvious to her that Fela needed to purge her toxins. She needed to talk. Largo noticed that her glass was nearly empty. She topped it off and hers, as well.

"I probably put that the wrong way, the bundle of money and all that," Fela continued. "What I'm trying to say is that the man was deceptive. He came into our lives and poisoned Pieter. I have seen evil men in my life, but none to match this man."

Largo felt like she was a priest in a confession booth, but she was having trouble connecting with the words that were coming from Fela's mouth. She was soft-pedalling something. Largo probed gently. "This man ... the man who commissioned your husband ... what was it about him that caused you to think he was evil?"

"Several things," Fela replied without hesitation. "For one, he offered Pieter far too much money for the picture. For another, I'm convinced he lied to us when he requested the painting. He said it was for his dying aunt in Florence. He wanted the painting for some other reason, though. I just know it."

She paused for a moment. "And there was another reason I grew uncomfortable in his presence. I had the feeling he was undressing me, that he thought I must be craving physical pleasures because of Pieter's condition." She saw the expression change on Largo's face. "We still have sex, I don't mean that, but it has become ... what's the best word ... more mechanical than spontaneous. Catheters and bed pans aren't exactly turn-ons, if you know what I mean. Anyway, this man seemed to think that I was attracted to him. Can you believe such a thing?"

Largo's thoughts had already left the *Adagio*. She was in Fiesole, standing mere inches away from Theo Volmer, inhaling the unusual scent of his body. "I've known men like that."

On impulse, she asked Fela, "Tell me, what was his name, this man who frightened you?"

"Azzo Gatti." Fela wore a puzzled expression on her face. "Why do you ask?"

Largo sidestepped the question. In her mind, visual fragments were morphing, as if she were looking into a kaleidoscope. The image of the man was forming. "What do you remember about his eyes?"

"His eyes? Gatti's eyes?"

"Yes."

"I don't recall them in any particular way," she said. "Brown perhaps, maybe hazel."

Largo shifted gears, setting in motion a flow of questions. "His size? Was he tall?"

"No, quite the contrary. He was only slightly taller than I."

"The painting he commissioned? Was it a portrait, a landscape?"

"No, it was a small picture of holy men, perhaps a famous masterpiece, or something. I didn't recognize the artist." She hesitated for a moment. "About all I remember about the painting was that the men looked like they were praying."

Largo felt her throat constrict. Her worst fears were quickly surrounding her. "The painting," she began with a slight quiver to her voice, "Was it a small, vertical painting on a wooden panel? Luminous colors?"

"Why, yes. Do you know the work?"

Largo nodded affirmatively. "The men at prayer?" she asked, controlling her emotions. "Did each man have his hands together just below the chin, four or five men in all?"

Fela's demeanor changed abruptly. "Largo, you're scaring me. How do you know these things about the painting?"

Largo's tone was even. "Because I've been living with this painting for the last month."

Fela Bajek looked at her with an expression of astonishment. "I can't begin to understand what you are saying. How could you ...?"

Largo paused and opened her purse. A moment later, she withdrew a small photograph of the Memling. It was the one Blue had asked about, the most recent photo of the painting. She handed it to Fela.

"Is this Pieter's painting?"

Fela's eyes went immediately to the row of priests and the likeness of her husband. "Yes! Yes!" Her small hands flew to her mouth. "Where did you get this photograph?"

"I took it on the morning before I left the States. The original Memling, the one that once belonged to my great-grandparents, had been hanging in my bedroom since our return from Florence last year. Obviously, I thought I was photographing it."

Largo reached in her purse and removed the earlier photograph of the Memling. "Look at the same face," she said, pointing to an elderly robed man. "Do you see the difference?"

Fela said nothing for a moment. Her eyes kept going from one photograph to the other. "My God, I do!"

"In July of this year," Largo continued, "Porter and I made a trip out west. When we returned on the twentieth, we realized someone had entered our condo while we were away. My first thought was that the painting had been stolen, but it was right where we left it, on the wall in our bedroom, or so I thought. Nothing caused me to think it was a copy. From what you have just told me, however, it's clear that the person, or persons, who entered our home swapped your husband's copy for the original."

Fela's eyes returned to the two photographs. She zeroed in on the four holy men near the bottom of both pictures. "Look at this," she said, pointing to the much younger looking priest in the copy. "This is Pieter's face. Until right now, I didn't know why he did this. Now I think I understand." Suddenly, the world got considerably smaller for Fela Bajek. "Then Pieter's painting, the one you photographed before coming to Krakow ... it was swapped for the original. Is that what you are saying?"

"Yes." Largo looked into Fela's eyes and saw the pain. "Fela, I know the man who commissioned your husband, and his name is Theo Volmer. Gatti is a phantom, an alias."

Fela nodded. "Pieter and I had a long discussion about his faith when he was making this painting. He didn't feel that his spiritual core merited God's blessing. I believe he imposed his own image so that he would appear to be comparable in devotion to the other priests.

Largo's mind was now racing at the speed of light. Clearly, the

Memling photograph she took before leaving for the airport was Pieter Bajek's copy. As Volmer had to be the person who approached Fela and her husband with the commission, then Volmer had to have been involved in the swapping of the paintings.

"I trust you will not hold bad feelings about Pieter," Fela said. "Had he only known about—"

"Fela, I don't blame Pieter for anything. He did nothing wrong, as far as I'm concerned." Largo had one final question that begged an answer.

"This man who entered your life—the man I believe was Volmer—where did he live, do you know?"

"No. I know he was not from Ravenna, but near the end of his arrangement with Pieter, he did write a brief note saying that he could be reached at a restaurant in Anghiari. Perhaps he was living there."

"Do you recall the name of the restaurant?"

"It was the name of an artist, as I recall, a Renaissance artist maybe, or around that time period."

Largo quickly raced through her mental inventory of early through late Renaissance artists. "Was it Raphael? Giorgione? Titian? Michelangelo?"

"No, I would have remembered them. I seem to recall it beginning with the letter V. I have the letter at home."

Largo dug deeper. "Veronese, Verrocchio?"

"Yes, Verrocchio!" Fela cried. "I'm certain of it. His letter said he could be reached there. He even provided the telephone number."

Largo made a mental note of the restaurant. So, Volmer was staying in Anghiari, a veritable stone's throw from Florence.

The hour was late and Fela Bajek looked exhausted. Over the course of the past two hours, they had drained the bottle of chianti. Both needed some sleep. Largo set the wheels in motion. "Let's call it a night, Fela. Are you good with that?"

"You'll get no argument from me. I'm ready for bed."

They embraced at the door to Largo's unit. "I feel like I've known you forever, Fela. I know the subject of our discussion tonight was difficult for both of us, but speaking for myself I needed to know the things you shared with me."

"I feel the same way. Sleep well."

Around sunrise, Largo awakened from an upsetting dream in which she was a college student again. It was exam time, and she had not been to class for several weeks. To make matters worse, she didn't know where the final exam was being held: an anxiety dream, she realized on waking.

Shortly after breakfast and before the morning session of the workshop, Largo placed a call to Blue. She knew it would be in the middle of the night in Nashville, but she felt such a sense of urgency in contacting him, she decided to let him grumble.

He answered the phone in a less than pleasant manner. "Who in the hell is calling at such a God-awful hour?"

"Hi, sweetheart, it's me. Sorry if I woke you."

For a second or two, *me* carried no meaning at all for Blue. Slowly, he put the voice with the face. "Largo, what's wrong?"

"Nothing's wrong, Porter. I just need to talk with you for a second."

In his half-awake, half-asleep stage, he was trying to remember why she was not with him. "Where are you, babe?"

She had but a split-second to decide on the best answer to his question. If she said she was in Lugano, Switzerland, she'd have to spend the next five minutes explaining why she was there. "I'm in Krakow, Porter. You know that."

"Krakow, right."

"Listen, sweetheart, I only have a couple of minutes left on this card. I don't want to waste them on a sleeping man. Are you awake now?"

Blue yawned. "I'm getting there. What's up?"

She had intended to tell Blue that she met Fela Bajek in Krakow and from that conversation confirmed her thoughts about the Memling, but this was clearly not the time to try and explain all that. She would have to do it later. "Nothing, really. I just wanted to hear the sound of your voice. I miss you."

"I miss you, too."

They talked for another minute before she said, "I have to go, sweetie. I love you."

"Love you. Call me when you can."

Throughout the course of the workshop, Fela and Largo took advantage of every break to return to the man who haunted both of them. They attended the sessions, did the acrostic poetry, the "blind" self-portraits, and the other creatively inspired exercises in Atkinson's bag, but neither woman was really focused. Both knew they had been thrown together in order for their paths to cross. Largo would say it was serendipity; Fela would describe it as pre-destined. Whatever it was, it would prove pivotal.

CHAPTER THIRTY-ONE

Auschwitz-Birkenau

Sunday, August 17
Krakow, Poland

Following Largo's return from Lugano, she was surprised to find a letter from Mason Creed in her mailbox. A smile formed on her lips as she opened it. The letter was brief and, given Creed's manner, a bit formal. After extending greetings and inquiring about recent weather patterns, he addressed his primary reason for writing: the upcoming wedding of his niece in Rouen, France, and his wish to meet with her afterwards regarding the theft of the Memling.

> *My plans have finally been set. The wedding is on Monday, September 1. I'll be leaving London on Friday, August 15th for a week's vacation in Normandy before driving to Rouen. My intention at this time is to leave for Krakow on Tuesday, September 2nd. I trust this is still convenient with you. Between now and then, I'll get back in touch with you regarding a more specific timetable.*

> *Most sincerely, Mason*

Largo reread the letter before returning it to the envelope. She wished he were leaving sooner, for after her weekend with Fela Bajek she had so much to tell him. She resisted the thought, but it forced its way in anyway. *I am so anxious to see him again.*

Taped to her small and never cold enough refrigerator, was a short punch list of things Largo wanted to do before having to devote all of her time to her studies. She wanted to become fully familiar with Krakow. She wanted to know where she would be safe, especially at night. She needed to visit Auschwitz-Birkenau. It wasn't a *wanting* to see the death camp where her great-grandparents had died as much as it was a *needing* to go there. It was all a part of finding closure. Now, more than ever, she needed to explain to them what had happened to their precious Memling and she wanted to find someone—and it mattered not whether the person was a man or a woman—with whom she could just talk, or go to a movie, or share an occasional dinner. She was not looking for romance, she kept telling herself.

To that list, she added three items: clean her apartment thoroughly and pick up some nice French wine before Creed arrived; purchase a good map of central Europe, a package of red push pins and a spool of heavy red thread; and finally, make a quick trip to Anghiari, Italy. After what Fela told her about Azzo Gatti, she now had business with someone at The Verrocchio.

Monday, August 18
Krakow, Poland

The time spent with Fela Bajek had been the perfect tonic for Largo. For her, their talks had a surprisingly cathartic effect. She had called Fela on two occasions after returning from Lugano. Both calls had been warmly received. Fela told her how much their blossoming friendship meant to her.

Largo moved quickly. "Then let's nurture it. I want to know how you and Pieter are doing. I want to meet him one day."

"I'd like that. I've told him all about you."

Over the weekend, she was able to put two of most the troublesome aspects of her life in perspective. First, the infrequency of calls from Porter probably said more about his hectic schedule than any loss of affection. To be fair, how many times had she initiated calls to him? Secondly, there was nothing she could do at the present time about the theft of the Memling. For the first time since hearing Porter's account of the discovery by the Atlanta High Museum, she was thinking and reacting unemotionally.

Creed's upcoming visit had some bearing on this, but something was changing within herself and she was unsure what it was, or why. All she knew was that she was not the same person who left the United States on the first of August. Most significant of all, a decision of considerable magnitude was forming in her mind.

The late summer day was absolutely gorgeous. Not a cloud in the sky. Largo decided to use the occasion to explore the Rynek, and her new neighborhood. From everything she had read and heard, it was one of Krakow's most exciting and progressive gathering spots. The night life was highly rated. It might be a nice place to bring Creed. She needed the exercise and what could be safer than exploring her new haunts during the middle of the day?

Dressed in comfortable black slacks and a peach blouse, she put her long, dark hair in a ponytail. Porter had cautioned her about taking a recognizeable American ball cap to Europe—she would have taken her Atlanta Braves cap—so she decided to forego a cap of any kind.

She looked in the mirror and smiled. Ever since deciding on the pursuit of her doctorate in Krakow, she had strong feelings about seeing Bracka Street where her great-grandparents lived and Auschwitz-Birkenau, where they died. Only by the best of good fortune, had she been able to find the empty apartment on Bracka. Each time she left the building, she played the game of running into Levi and Zohara Nowak. With classes about to get underway and Creed's visit not far off, she knew that now was the best time for her to bond with the street she had longed to see.

After strolling about like a tourist—but not wanting to look like one—she stopped at Coffee Heaven, Poland's version of Starbucks, and ordered a cappuccino. In looking over the menu, she spotted cheesecake, *sernik* in Polish.

When her server arrived with the coffee, she asked in her best Polish for a slice. The server smiled and replied, "*Diekuje*. Thank you." Largo beamed with pleasure. The first of the language hurdles had been accomplished. *I can learn to speak this stuff!*

"I thought that was you."

The speaker's voice was familiar. It was coming from the table right behind her. When she turned, she found herself looking at Adam Czarnecki, the young man who had driven her from the airport to Krakow.

"Well, good morning, Adam. What a pleasant surprise." After a moment of hesitation, "Would you care to join me?"

He did so immediately, carefully moving the things on his table to hers. "If I may ask, what brings you to the Rynek this morning?"

"I'm exploring today. It's too nice a day to waste inside."

"Yes, days like today are to be spent wisely. Do you have any particular places in mind?"

She told him more about her great-grandparents, their home on Bracka Street, and their demise at Auschwitz-Birkenau.

"If you like, I will be happy to take you there. I am not a guide, or anything, but I know the layout and most of the most important aspects of the place."

"That would be wonderful. How long does it take to go and return?"

Czarnecki thought for a moment. "Most of a day. We could go tomorrow, if you like."

"I didn't bring many of my nicer clothes with me. I wouldn't want to be disrespectful."

"You look fine, as you are. Casual dress is not unusual, especially in warm weather like this."

"Then I say, yes. I would like to go, if you are sure your schedule is flexible."

He grinned. "I don't have a schedule until school starts."

They met at Coffee Heaven the next morning for a quick breakfast then walked out of the Rynek in order to reach his car. Czarnecki chatted away. "From here, we'll be going to the town of Oswiecim. It's about sixty-five kilometers away, about forty miles in your country."

"I know about kilometers," Largo giggled. "I'm not your typical American tourist, you know."

"I'm sorry, I didn't mean to offend you." He enjoyed the moment of levity. "Anyway, Auschwitz-Birkenau is located a short distance from the town. What do you know of it?"

"Only what I've read. It was built around the turn of the century as some kind of labor exchange facility. I don't know a lot of specifics. At some point before the war it was converted to a concentration camp."

"Yes, more particularly a death camp," Czarnecki replied softly, hesitating briefly. "You will see foundations of several buildings, long since torn down. The mass killings began in the early forties at Birkenau. The two facilities were known as Auschwitz I and Auschwitz II. Jews by the thousands were shipped in by trains from all over Poland."

Minutes later, Czarnecki's car was motoring along the road to Oswiecim. With her eyes fixed on the beautiful Polish countryside, Largo wondered what it must have been like for her great-grandparents to make the journey from Bracka Street to their death. What thoughts must have filled their heads as they saw the same landscape pass? The thought followed, *The boxcar didn't even have windows!* "Do you think my great-grandparents knew what was about to happen to them as they made the short trip from Krakow to Auschwitz?"

Czarnecki had pondered the same thought hundreds of times with reference to his own blood line. It was a difficult question to answer with a simple yes or no. "My own belief is that the Jews who died there, or most of them anyway, thought they were taking part in a massive re-location program. They were told to hurriedly pack one suitcase with their most cherished belongings. I want to think they believed they were going to a better place, as strange as that may sound."

"How could they not know what was about to happen to them?"

"Because no one could imagine the depths of Nazi depravity." The tone of Czarnecki's voice turned colder. "Let me put it this way; when the Nazis took their first steps in trying to eradicate Jews in order to grow their Aryan world—*Krystallnacht* in November of 1938, for ex-ample, when they vandalized Jewish businesses and then imposed a boycott—Jews said, 'this is bad, but surely it won't get worse.' Every time, the Nazis followed with something that was worse. Jews contin-ued to say, 'But surely, it can't get worse than this.' But it did get worse, every single time, right up until the gassing."

When they reached Auschwitz, Czarnecki and Largo walked into the main building, passing a bookstore and a snack bar before reach-ing a window where they obtained their entry cards. They received a packet of information before continuing through a turnstile. Czar-necki said they could stop and see a movie about life in the camp, but Largo wanted to move ahead.

Continuing on the path, they reached brick barracks at the back of the camp. Inside, they found the museum displays of the his-tory—maps showing where the prisoners came from and how many were killed. Upstairs, they found the display rooms, large rooms with glassed spaces filled with poignant reminders of the final steps of life for millions of Jews. Largo stopped in her tracks at the sight of a room filled with human hair, all gray now, looking like rolls of some lethal growth. She looked in silence and thought of her great-grandmother Zohara. Then, softly, almost imperceptibly, she asked, "Is your lovely hair part of this tangled mass?"

She and Czarnecki passed a room filled with a small display of the steel gray cans of Zyklon-B, the gas used in the frenzied killings. In other rooms they saw similar display cases containing painful reminders of those times: spoons, eyeglasses and spectacles of assorted sizes and designs, shawls, shaving brushes and razors, prostheses and the disturbing display of shoes. When they came upon a room stuffed with suitcases, she paused. "What became of my great-grandparents' suitcases after they were ... after they were separated?"

"Suitcases were rifled for anything of value to the Reich ... gold, silver, candlesticks. The Germans kept what they wanted and then disposed of most of the luggage. We're looking at hundreds of suitcases here, but these constitute only a fraction of the whole. You will note that each suitcase carries the family name and a Star of David emblem. The Jews had been told to make the mark before leaving for Auschwitz. In my view, this display is one of the most haunting in the entire museum. I don't see these suitcases without thinking of the lives that were packed inside."

The display was a seemingly endless parade of rooms that reflected their final steps and seconds. And the painful journey didn't get any easier.

They went into the next building and saw how the inmates toileted; open spaces with no privacy. Along the walls were displayed photographs of the prisoners, the date they arrived and the date they died. Most died within six months of arrival, some less than a month. In the next building they were shown how people slept and lived. Largo was feeling nauseous, claustrophobic, struggling for air.

"Are you okay?" Czarnecki saw that her face was as pale as candle wax. "We can step outside, if you like."

She nodded. "No, I need to see this. I need to see and experience every sickening aspect of this place. Only then will I be able to say that I walked in my great-grandparents' footsteps. I want to continue." When her nausea subsided, they moved on, soon coming to a large barracks.

"This place is known as Black #11, the killing barracks." Czarnecki spoke softly, knowing that Largo was witnessing something far beyond anything she had ever imagined. "Most everything took place in the cellar. There were four standing cells here," he continued, "where thirty people would be placed in a cell with no room to sit down."

"What would happen to them?" she asked, trying to imagine such cramped conditions.

"They would die standing."

Largo inhaled deeply, fighting the urge to cry.

After leaving the killing barracks, Czarnecki pointed out a replica of the Black Wall, the place where Jews who had violated some rule were taken and shot. He reached down to the ground and removed two small stones. "Later, we'll place these stones on the smaller monuments as a tribute to those who lost their lives here. Flowers would just die and blow away. The stones resist the wind."

"What is that house over there?" Largo asked, pointing to a wood framed structure that seemed out of place. It appeared to be about seventy yards from the remains of a disintegrating crematorium chimney.

"That was the commandant's home," he said bitterly. "Rudolf Hoess and his wife and five children lived there. Hoess was the first and longest serving commandant at Auschwitz. He was there from 1940 until November of 1943 and again from May 1944 to January 1945."

"How old were the children?" Largo tried to imagine innocent children just a stone's throw from the belching chimneys. They had to smell the burning bodies. They had to see the horrors.

"Young," Czarnecki replied with little expression. "He played games with them like Kill the Jew, right behind the fence."

"I can't imagine."

"But surely it can't get worse than this," Czarnecki said in a taunting manner. He paused for a moment and followed with, "I'm sorry, I didn't mean to direct that at you. It's just that the Jews would see just such a thing and think that nothing could become worse, but it always did. Human nature, I suppose."

Largo walked a few paces. "What happened to Hoess after the war?"

Czarnecki frowned as he pointed to a nearby gallows, left after the camp was dismantled. It was now part of the museum. "He was hanged there, on the gallows. Just think," he added tersely, "if the children were still behind the fence they could see their daddy hanging like a monstrous bag of potatoes."

"Perhaps they could have made up a game about that," Largo replied in a far-away, brittle voice.

Czarnecki nodded, his dark mood still quite evident. "I carry a deep regret about the execution of Hoess."

"A regret? What could that possibly be?" she asked, finding it hard to believe that Czarnecki, a Jewish Pole, could have such any feelings of regret, given the scope of the man's brutal role at Auschwitz.

"That he could die only one time. How fitting it would have been for him to be hanged a million times. That might constitute appropriate justice."

"That many Jews died here?"

"Yes," he replied softly, "more than a million."

They paused near an open area and Czarnecki pointed to a large structure quite a distance away. "It used to be a chemical factory. It was called Buna. Technically speaking, it was a subcamp of Auschwitz III." He paused to pick up another stone. "Interesting footnote on the place. They needed labor, the cheaper the better. The SS met their needs with young, fit inmates. The factory paid the SS a pittance for each inmate and guess what ... the SS took the money and gave themselves bonuses. A win-win situation for the factory and the SS, a lose-lose situation for the Jews."

Czarnecki and Largo returned to his car and made the short, two-kilometer drive to Birkenau. When they arrived at Birkenau, they saw the iconic sign, *Arbeit Macht Frei*. Work Makes You Free.

"So, what likely happened the day my relatives climbed down from the train?" Largo asked, not wanting to hear the answer, but knowing she needed to ask the question.

He knew how important the visit was for Largo. He could not sugarcoat his response. "A question first. How old were they at the time, your great-grandparents?"

Largo thought for a moment before replying, "Probably in their mid-sixties."

"Well," Czarnecki began, "When the Jews were ordered out of the trains, they assembled on long platforms. Some referred to this area as the *chute*." With transparent bitterness, he added, "The end of life as Jews knew it. The men were screened in order to determine their fitness for work. Younger men who could work and handle the strain of labor were sent to one location, while men like your great-grandfather—"

"Men of no value," Largo interrupted.

Czarnecki nodded. "That's a sad way of putting it. Blunt but correct. Yes, the older men met the same fate as the women. Your great-grandmother and other women her age were most likely directed to one of the crematoria that used to be here. They were likely herded into a basement and told to disrobe. Most thought they were going to have a shower and then be disinfected. When the door was closed, the gas pellets were released and ... everyone inside died in a matter of minutes." He looked at her to see if she was in control of her emotions. "The bodies were taken by elevator upstairs to the ovens. This part of the death camp is what most people think of when they think of Birkenau. You can imagine the rest."

Largo had seen pictures of the track where it abruptly ended in a large open area in front of a broad building with a tall, raised center. The structure reminded her of a big warehouse or office building. For her, the area where the platforms had been was beyond surreal. Overhead, a postcard blue sky resembled a giant umbrella.

Czarnecki read her thoughts. He paused for a moment and added, "Before we leave here, I want you to see the International Monument. It was erected in 1967."

When she reached the monument, she stood in silence for a few moments, stunned by the brutal power of the design. Her initial reaction was to draw a parallel with the works of British sculptor, Henry Moore, similar massive, brooding forms that sat heavy on the earth. The austerity of the geometric monument contrasted sharply with the backdrop of tall Linden trees, trees that appeared to be standing at attention out of respect for the victims of Nazi savagery. The thought came to her like an unexpected sound, *those trees weren't even here when these atrocities happened.* She then read the inscription on a plaque. In sixteen different languages, the tribute made the case that what happened at Auschwitz must never happen again. When they turned to leave, Largo asked Czarnecki, "And what was the other thing you wanted me to see?"

"The ash pond," Czarnecki replied softly. "It is where the ashes of the dead were dumped. For many Jews, viewing this pond is one of the most uncomfortable experiences associated with Auschwitz. Many stand and say silent prayers."

"May we take the time for me to do that?" Largo asked.

"Of course."

Ten minutes later, Largo's personal tribute to her great-grandparents had been completed. As they returned to Krakow, she was drained of feelings, numb. "May I ask you a question, Adam? It's rather personal."

"Certainly."

"Was this day as difficult for you as it was for me?"

The question caught him by surprise. "Probably not. Coming here always makes me sad, but my relatives who died here ... we were not all that close. You had great-grandparents; mine were two uncles and a distant cousin. I grieved at first like you, but grief turned to bitterness and anger the more I came here. I don't feel pain now as much as acute hatred for the animals that did this. I simply despise the Germans. I'll always hate them. It's that simple."

Largo had made the difficult pilgrimage. At that very moment, no problem or condition of difficulty that she faced came even close to matching the horrors she had just witnessed. She would outlast Volmer, she knew that. She would make her life one of purpose and resolve. She knew that, as well. And she would make her great-grandparents proud.

It was late afternoon before they reached the Rynek. As Czarnecki walked her to her apartment, he asked her, "Would you care to have a beer with me? I know a wonderful place. This is the best time of day to people-watch."

Largo was carrying the weight of Auschwitz-Birkenau. The experience of actually being there was much more stressful than she had expected. Standing on the same patch of earth where her great-grandparents spent the final minutes of their lives had been beyond difficult. The idea of now sitting down and enjoying a beer while watching people strut about seemed obscene. "I would like to do that with you, Adam, but can we do this some other time? I don't believe I would be good company right now."

"I understand. I felt much the same way after my first visit."

Largo gave him a hug and walked away without saying anything else. She cried again as she made her way back to her flat.

PART FOUR

"It takes many sheep to
satisfy one wolf."

—Nenia Campbell

CHAPTER THIRTY-TWO

The Largo

Thursday, August 28
Le Havre, France

Creed arrived in Le Havre from Dover, England, around midday on August twentieth. After doing business with a car rental agency, he set his sails for Normandy. Over the course of the next eight days, he saw Omaha Beach and its sacred grounds. He did, indeed, play the role of tourist, enjoying those little things that people do on holidays before backtracking to Le Havre. He found a nice hotel near the harbor and spent most of the morning on the waterfront, enjoying the scenery and a strong Danish beer, topped off by a delicious plate of mussels.

As he ambled along the harbor's edge, in front of quaint, seaside structures, he noticed a long, sleek boat at anchor, black in color, bobbing gently some fifty to seventy-five feet away. Taking a small pair of binoculars from the pocket of his jacket, Creed studied the craft's elegant lines. Near the stern of the vessel, he noticed a seaman descending a small ladder to a dinghy secured to the ladder. Far from being a boat connoisseur, he pondered for a moment how much money a man would need to maintain and operate such a treasure. It was then he noticed the name of the boat. Emblazoned in gold on a field of black: *Largo.*

For the next few moments, Creed felt frozen in space. His methodically organized mind whisked him back to the previous summer and the abduction of Largo Kopacz on the way back to Florence from Pisa. How well he recalled every detail; the difficulties of establishing any cooperation with the Florentine authorities, the anguish of Porter Blue and his own sense of distress.

More recently, Scotland Yard learned of the robbery at the Gade Collection and he had read Crister Njord's article in the *Berlingski Tidende*. He'd heard the talk that Volmer was still alive, it coming as no surprise. Even before he returned to London from Florence last year, he had strong reason to believe Volmer had not perished in the fire. Blue's call about Largo's Memling had only strengthened that assumption. Mesmerized by the cursive gold lettering, he wondered if there could be a connection.

Moments later, the seaman neared the dock on which Creed was standing. As he maneuvered the dinghy into a vacant slip, he waved a friendly greeting, to which Creed replied with a wave of his own and then asked the seaman, "Can you give me a minute?"

The young man came promptly to Creed's side of the boat. "What can I do for you?" The question was asked in English.

"This boat. Can you tell me who owns it?"

The young man studied Creed. "Why are you asking?"

"I'm just curious. I've been looking for a boat like this and I wonder if it might be for sale? I might like to get in touch with the owner."

"He's from Copenhgen," the young man replied. "That's all I know."

Creed understood his hesitancy in providing specifics. If he valued his job, he was not about to reveal the owner's name. "Is the owner on board, by chance?"

"No, sir, he is out of town."

"Do you have any idea when he might be returning?"

"Later this evening or tomorrow, perhaps. He didn't say, exactly."

Creed smiled pleasantly. "You've been most helpful."

He removed a small notepad from his pocket and quickly jotted down a description of the boat and the information provided by the young man. He would make a call later at the harbormaster's office. He could obtain any other specific information he needed.

The following morning, he found the *Largo* still in the harbor. After a hasty breakfast, he went to the harbormaster's office. A heavily bearded man was sitting behind the desk. He looked up when Creed entered.

"Oui?" the man asked with indifference.

The French language was not one of Creed's strong cards. He knew enough to know that oui meant "yes," but he was not prepared to go beyond that. He removed his Scotland Yard badge and placed it on the desk in front of the man, just beyond a name plate that read, A. Duchamps.

"Do you speak English?" Creed knew the general tendency of the French to show disdain for anyone who cannot, or will not, speak the native tongue.

Duchamps' response, if not cordial, was pleasant enough. "Some English, yes."

"I would like some information on one of the boats in the harbor."

The harbormaster nodded up and down.

Creed then asked about the owner of the sleek, black yacht, the *Largo*. "Do you have his name?"

The man looked in a large book and after a moment replied, "Ankiel Thorssen." He confirmed that Thorssen paid all taxes and fees before putting his boat at anchor.

"Did you personally meet Thorssen?" Creed asked, eager to know if Duchamps' physical description of Thorssen would fit that of Theo Volmer.

"No, sir," he replied before stumbling through the fact that he was on vacation at the time. "My assistant did the registration."

"I see." He hesitated for a moment and then stated, "I would like your assistant's name."

"Luc Aydelotte," the harbormaster replied.

Creed pressed gently. "Did Thorssen pay by check, credit card, or cash? Do your records show that?"

The man referred to his book again before removing his glasses. "He paid in cash."

"One final question. Is Aydelotte working today?"

"No, sir. He is off this week."

Creed thanked him for his time and gave him his card. "I will be leaving Le Havre tomorrow, but I may be calling you at some later date. Do you understand?"

"Yes, I understand. I give Aydelotte your name and number."

After leaving the harbormaster's office, Creed found an empty bench near the edge of the water and claimed it. He had ample time before leaving for Rouen. Perhaps Thorssen had returned and would show himself soon, or arrive while he was waiting. The thought crossed his mind that he might remain in Le Havre until he could talk with Aydelotte, but then realized he was not there on official business. A wedding beckoned him.

The better part of an hour passed. Creed saw the same seaman he had seem earlier approaching the boat and arose to meet him. "I've been hoping to have a chat with Mr. Thorssen. Are you expecting him today?"

"No, sir, not today. He telephoned me last night from Helsinki ... said he would not be returning for another week, or two ... something about a business complication."

Creed noticed the glittering surface of the water near the center of the harbor. The ripples looked like tiny shards of glass. "Too bad, perhaps I can catch up with him later. I presume he plans to have his boat here for a while."

"That's my understanding, sir. Would you like to leave your card?"

"No, I don't think that's necessary," Creed replied pleasantly. "My name would mean absolutely nothing to him."

On his drive to Rouen, Creed thought of little else but Volmer and Largo. It had been nearly a year since he helped her retain the cherished Memling painting. He had the strong feeling that the sooner he could get to Krakow, the better. He needed to tell her of the yacht he'd just seen.

Saturday, August 30
Krakow, Poland

With Creed's visit now just days away, Largo looked again at her punch list of things to do before his arrival. She had made the difficult trip to Auchwitz-Birkenau. Now she needed to follow up on the information Fela had given her, the Verrocchio and the man Fela knew as Azzo Gatti. She decided to make a quick trip to Anghiari, but after looking at the map she realized the distance was far greater than she had assumed. By train—and renting a car and driving would mean an overnight in unfamiliar territory—it was a lengthy journey, almost twenty-four hours. But what if she had to change trains? She decided to postpone everything until Creed reached Krakow. Depending on his schedule, maybe they could make the trip together. The more she thought about it, the better she felt about not trying to do it alone.

Given that decision, she decided to return to Bracka Street. She remembered her mother once saying that her great-grandparents lived on the second floor in a building near the Goethe Institute. Most of the buildings looked as if they were built ages ago, but the storefronts were very upscale in character, with a number of highly-rated hotels and boutiques. Quite the place to be today. A far cry from what her great-grandparents knew. Families had come and gone, but the solid foundations of the buildings had enabled contractors to make cosmetic enhancements to reflect contemporary architectual priorities.

She found the street number without much difficulty, noticing that at the distant end of the street she could see a portion of the Goethe Institute. Largo tried to imagine the night in September of 1939 when the Nazis forced their way inside, the night they took the Memling. As she walked up and down the street, it was not hard to hear the sound of heavy German boots on the cobblestones. After standing silently for a few minutes, she lowered her head and whispered aloud, "I pray that both of you are in God's hand, removed from all pain and suffering. Rest in peace, sweet people."

Another checkmark was registered on the punch list.

Tuesday, September 2
Rouen, France

With the wedding behind him, Creed shifted his thoughts to Largo. Time and distance being what they were, he decided against driving from Rouen to Krakow. It would take at least two days of driving. By plane from Paris, he could be there in about three hours. It might cost him a few extra pounds to fly, but he could maximize his time with Largo and be spared the punishing round trip drive. He called Lufthansa about a last minute seat on the 11:10 morning flight and was told that two seats were available. He would reach Krakow in the early afternoon, hopefully finding Largo's schedule flexible enough for them to have ample time to discuss her troubling concerns.

She had suggested they meet in the Rynek at a bar called the Shisha Club. It should be easy enough for Creed to take a local train from the airport, thus sparing her the need to make arrangements to meet him when he deplaned.

After the aircraft reached its cruising altitude, Creed read for a while and then ordered a gin and tonic. He allowed himself the luxury of looking down on the changing landscape through open patches in the cloudy mattress sky. It was not long before he was visualizing what those very landscape vignettes looked like in August of 1944 as Allied Forces forced Hitler's Army back to Berlin. Where rich farmlands stretched below him on this day, the same hills and valleys were covered with ash and smoke fifty-three years ago. Bodies dotted the fertile fields like black-eyed Susans.

Gradually, his thoughts shifted to Largo. The mental pictures he had carried for the past year were not completely in focus. Time had blurred them. Were her eyes as dark as he remembered? And what was he to do with his feelings for her, those most private of emotions that he'd been careful to keep in the corked bottle. Would she sense the radiant images of her that came with his pillow thoughts of her?

With the help of a few English-speaking travelers in the Krakow airport, Creed was able to find the train that would take him to city center. From there it was just a short walk to his rendezvous point. Would she be there?

Largo reached the Shisha Club well in advance of Creed's arrival. She was nursing a warm glass of Tyskie beer, thinking to herself that Europeans need to know that a properly chilled beer makes all the difference in the world. She saw Creed enter the busy watering hole, dressed as she expected him to be in his conservative, British way—the ubiquitous pipe in his mouth and pulling a small brown suitcase on wheels. She smiled as he walked closer, wondering if she should jump up and run to him, or wait for his trained eyes to spot her. She decided it would be more fun to do the former.

She almost caught him completely by surprise. At the very last second, he turned her way and caught the flashing smile. Before he could react to her sudden presence, her arms were wrapped tightly around him. "Mason, Mason, is it really you?"

"I'm afraid so," he replied in a self-deprecating way. "It is so good to see you, Largo."

She kissed him on the cheek, feeling the sandpapery surface of his face. At that moment, she was beside herself with joy. She didn't want to let go. "I can't believe you're really here." She took a step back so that she could look into his eyes. *He hasn't changed a bit.* She remembered how they had embraced in Florence that day he arrived at their rented villa with her Memling. That he had found the painting in a Stuttgart storage facility still seemed like a miracle.

"You're looking well," he said, inwardly wincing at his choice of words. It's what old people say.

"I'm just getting the hang of this place," she confessed. "Everything is so new, so different." She could tell he felt somewhat awkward, standing there with his suitcase and briefcase. "Let's find a table. I can't wait to find out what you've been doing."

A waiter guided them to a small, out-of-the-way table and took their drink orders. Largo chose a chilled white wine, while Creed settled for a scotch and water. It was a good five minutes into their conversation before Creed addressed the matter he knew was weighing heavily on her mind, the bogus Memling. "When Porter called me with the news, I was heartsick for you. It must have come as quite a shock."

Largo's face twisted into a peculiar smile. "I just lost it when Porter called to tell me that the museum had made the discovery. I simply couldn't believe it."

When her lips formed Blue's name, Creed shifted into cautious gear. "And how is Porter?" The question was asked out of courtesy.

"He's fine," Largo replied, looking away for a moment. "He's into the publishing of his book and all that goes with it. I haven't heard from him lately."

Creed detected just a hint of resentment. "I'm excited about reading it. Is it available?"

Her reply was registered flatly. "Yes, in the near future."

"How wonderful! The two of you must be very happy at such good fortune."

Largo said nothing and for a few seconds a cloud of discomfort seemed to hover above the table. Creed picked up on it and quickly shifted to another subject. "I'm eager to hear about your decision to come to Krakow for your doctorate. I don't suppose that was an easy call."

"No, it wasn't. Porter was not exactly thrilled, as you might expect." She failed to mention that classes at the Jagiellonion had not begun. She would be getting to that soon.

Creed knew better than to put an oar in the water. He thought for a passing second before saying, "Separations can be difficult for both sides."

Largo chose not to respond to his remark. She was in another place now. "I have some extraordinary news to share with you. It's about the Memling."

"And what might that be?" Creed noticed how her lips glistened in the light, how vibrant she seemed.

"It's a long story and I'll tell you everything in time, but the essence of it is that I now have absolute proof that Volmer was behind the swap."

Creed removed a curve-stemmed pipe from a pocket in his jacket. He gently tapped it on an ashtray to remove the now cold, dark tobacco chards. He allowed his fingers to fondle it for a few seconds before replying, "And what is that proof, if I may ask?"

"Last week at a workshop in Lugano, I met the wife of the artist who painted the copy."

He was visibly surprised. "You don't mean it."

"Yes. She said her husband was commissioned by a man to paint the picture. When I showed her a photograph I made of the painting just before leaving the States—and I'm thinking at the time that the painting in my bedroom was the same one you found in Stuttgart—she pointed out her husband's face in the lower left hand corner of the painting. She said the man who commissioned the painting was Azzo Gatti, but I now know that was an alias. The man was Volmer. And there's something else," she added, not wanting to yield the floor. "She said this man Gatti sent her husband a note saying that when the painting was finished he could be reached at a restaurant in Anghiari. When Volmer left Florence last year, it appears he went there."

"And picked up the new name," Creed mused. As he refilled his pipe, he added, "I too have some news that should interest you.

"What is it?"

"On my way here, I passed through Le Havre, France. By the best of good fortune, I happened to pass a splendid yacht in the harbor, velvety black. Would you like to venture a guess as to its name?" Creed smiled infrequently, but at that moment he looked like the proverbial Cheshire cat.

She shifted from her serious manner. "Tell me!"

"It was a beautiful name," he replied teasingly: "*Largo*. And guess what?"

"Mason!"

"In talking with a seaman, I learned that the vessel was owned by a Dane, Ankiel Thorssen. It looks like *signor* Gatti may have adopted a new appellation. Our man is on the move, or so it would appear." They had been talking nonstop for nearly an hour. To his embarrassment, Creed heard the rumble of his stomach. He could tell from the expression that formed on her face that she'd also heard it. "Are you hungry?"

Smiling, she replied, "I am famished, if you really want to know the truth. I've been living on crackers and cheese."

He stole a quick glance at his watch. It was mid-afternoon and he had not eaten since breakfast, and then only a bowl of cereal and a glass of juice. "Then why don't you suggest a place where can we get something special? It's been awhile since I've eaten, as well."

Largo thought for a moment before recommending an eatery known to the locals as the Grey House. "It's on the way to my flat."

"Wonderful. I'm ready if you are."

He settled their bar tab and then sent his suitcase in motion, carefully steering past young legs and feet. They walked out into the sunshine. Creed was pleasantly surprised when Largo took his free hand. "I'll play the role of tour guide," she said playfully, relishing the feel of his warm, moist hand.

"You're an expert by now, I suppose," Creed tried to project a humorous side. "You must already know Krakow like the back of your hand."

"Hardly an expert, but I'm getting comfortable in my little neighborhood. Everything is so new and confusing." She looked at him. "God, it is so good to see you again!" As they walked to the restaurant, she asked, "Where are you staying, Mason? In the Rynek, I mean."

"I've made reservations at the Hotel Stary near here," He said. "I'm told it is close to the university."

"It is. It is quite close and nice."

"Yes, I recall my first days in London," Creed said, as if Largo had asked a question. "It's exhilarating, isn't it, to discover a new world?"

She was not quite sure what he meant by the remark, but she squeezed his hand as they neared the restaurant. "I hope you like this place. I've not been there yet, but everyone speaks highly of it, so the food can't be too bad."

After they were seated and a young waiter had gone through the specials of the day, Largo wasted no time in mentioning the cigarette ashes she found in their condo after their mini-vacation in Cabo San Lucas.

Creed listened intently.

"I still find it hard to believe Volmer broke into my home, but if he did, why did he risk being caught by coming to the States and taking the Memling? I just don't understand."

"So, you are assuming he was the smoker? Do you have anything else, evidence of any kind that places him in your home while you and Porter were away?"

"The ashes. We don't smoke. It had to be him."

"That's not enough," countered the seasoned Scotland Yard investigator. "That hardly qualifies as a smoking gun, as you Americans are fond of putting it."

Largo looked away, appearing to be checking out the new surroundings, but not liking the fact that Creed failed to give the cigarette ashes greater weight. "I haven't mentioned this to Porter," she said, her eyes now back to Creed, "but I'm missing a few personal things from my closet."

"Go on," he pressed gently.

"I'm pretty OCD about my clothes and jewelry," she continued, projecting a blush of self-consciousness. "Everything has a place and there's a place for everything, if you know what I mean."

Creed nodded with something resembling a smile. "That sounds very British."

"Well, I'm missing a red scarf, the only comfortable black bra I own and a pair of lavender panties. I've turned my closet upside down, and they are nowhere to be seen. I know they were there when we left, for I almost took the bra. How could these things simply disappear?"

"If Volmer took the Memling, then he was emulating his father," Creed replied. "His father stole the painting from your Jewish great-grandparents. Now he steals the very same painting from you. He is trying to relive his father's role, to become his father, in so many words." He paused long enough to relight his pipe. "The very fact that the museum in Atlanta spotted the forgery so quickly makes me wonder if he did not intend for that to happen."

"Why would he do that?"

"To humiliate you. This man, as I've come to know him, is not care-less, not by any stretch of the imagination." Creed reflected on what he just said and concluded by adding, "As for the clothes and jewelry, one could say they were souvenirs, but on some deeper level they probably satisfied some sexual need. I've seen this kind of thing before."

"This may surprise you, Mason, but my reaction to the theft of the painting pales in comparison to the sense of violation I've experienced. It's like he had been watching me, almost like he had been peering in the windows of our home for a long time, just waiting on us to leave. It makes my skin crawl."

"He is a predator, Largo. He is an evil man," Creed said, "Your feel-ings are perfectly appropriate," he replied, hoping to keep his focus on her best interests.

"So, where is this going?" Largo asked. "Do I just accept the fact that one of these days he will appear in front of me? Is that what I'm looking at? Is it just a matter of time?"

"It pains me to say this, but the likelihood is that one day he will reappear." He again hesitated. "He will do this, however, only when he is ready."

Her reaction could not have been more spontaneous. "What are you saying, Mason? What do you mean, only when he is ready?"

"I don't mean to frighten you, Largo. What I am trying to say is that Theo Volmer—wherever he is and by whatever name tag he is wear-ing—has an agenda and its centerpiece is you. From what you've told me, he was behind your abduction near Pisa last spring. We both know he sent you those flowers when you and Porter were in Lucca Palma's office. It would not surprise me if he had been watching for you and Porter to come out of the Uffizi that day. For whatever the reason, he has become increasingly obsessive. Our best hope of finding him lies in the possibility that he will misstep somewhere along the way, that he will do or say something that will allow us to expose him." Creed puffed his pipe before saying, "There are two other quite interesting things to add to what I told you about the yacht."

Her dark eyes blazed. "What?"

"One of my closest colleagues at the Yard was recently in Florence for a few days. Before he left London, I asked him to talk with the police chief there. You may or may not know this, but the chief in charge at the time of Volmer's presumed death in the fire, a man by the name of Comidas, was arrested on corruption charges not long after Volmer disappeared. The ex-chief was offered reduced prison time in exchange for confessing to the particulars of Volmer's death. He admitted that neither of the bodies in the Fiesole fire was Volmer. He had been paid royally to stage the cover-up so that Volmer could flee Florence."

"And what was the second thing?" she asked.

"It pertains to the Gade Collection robbery in Copenhagen. I assume you know about that?"

"I do. I've even talked by phone with Nils Gade, the owner. What about the robbery?"

"Scotland Yard received a call from our Danish counterparts several weeks ago about hairs that had been forwarded to them by a police official in Anghiari, Italy. The Italian officer wanted it examined for possible DNA."

"That's genetic coding, isn't it?"

"Yes," Creed replied. "It's a fairly new process, but I'm told it will be a revolutionary means of identifying criminals, much more reliable that fingerprints. Anyway, an Anghiari resident, a woman, had given a hairbrush to the police there. They had sent it on to authorities in Copenhagen. She apparently had been involved with this man, Gatti, and was adamant that he had orchestrated the Copenhagen theft."

Largo's thoughts immediately soared to Fela Bajek. "The young woman I mentioned a few moments ago, the one I met in Lugano, told me that her husband Pieter received a letter from Gatti in which he indicated that he could be contacted at a restaurant in Anghiari when he was finished with the painting."

"Did he mention the name of the restaurant?"

"Yes! It was The Verrocchio."

"Well, this gets better all the time," Creed replied. "This same woman was involved just last month in an altercation with a priest in a Florentine restaurant. According to my colleague, she kept screaming for someone to take his wineglass and test it for prints and DNA."

"So, Volmer was in Florence at the time of Palma's murder?" Largo asked, remembering the late director with fondness.

"Yes, it would appear so."

She had been carrying the thought for the past several days, but she'd not mentioned it to Blue on the few occasions they had talked by phone. "You said something a moment ago about Volmer finding me when he is ready to do so, or words to that effect."

"Yes?"

"Well, what if I find him first?"

Creed frowned. "I'm not sure I'm following you."

"Look," she began tentatively, "for the last year, or more, I've lived in total dread of him. My coming here was simple. I wanted to get my doctorate. Porter has tried to shield me from Volmer, but lodged deep in my gut is the constant worry that one day our paths will cross."

"Go on," he replied softly, emptying his pipe in an ashtray.

"I'm tired of living in fear, Mason."

Before he could reply, Largo dropped her bomb. "I have canceled my fall term classes at the Jagiellonian. As of this moment, I am going to change roles. I am no longer going to play the part of the terrified victim. I am going to become the hunter. I want to see him arrested."

Creed was not expecting her disclosure, and for a moment was at a loss for words. She could have said she planned to grow wings and fly back to America and he would not have been more surprised. "Do you know what you are saying?" Creed finally asked. "You would be fresh bait."

"Yes, I've thought of that."

"If you want my honest opinion, Largo, I'm not convinced this is a good idea. What you are suggesting is far too dangerous. It could cost you your life."

"Fuck it!" she said without hesitation. "If he finds me first, he will kill me. What's the big difference?"

"I can understand that, but—"

"What if you helped me, Mason? We could do it. We could find the rock under which he is hiding. We could eliminate him from decent society."

"Are you forgetting that I am still with Scotland Yard? One of these days, sooner than I like, I must return to London."

"Could you not request a leave of absence and stay longer?" Before he could respond, she added with a crushing smile, "We can do this together, Mason. I know we can."

As Creed considered Largo's suggestion, he had to admit it had some merit. True, it was extremely risky, but sooner or later Volmer would find her and then the situation would be reversed; he would be in the driver's seat. If she—if they—could corner him first, catch him by his blindside, it might work. A trailing thought followed, *and then what? Would she return to the United States and Porter?*

"So?" she asked like a little girl wanting to know if he could come to a sleep-over. "Can we make this happen?"

Creed had ample vacation time stored away, so that was not a problem. The larger question was that of getting leave on such short notice. It wasn't like Scotland Yard was sitting around waiting for a crime of some magnitude to be committed. "Do I have to give you my answer this moment?" Creed asked, as the smallest of smiles formed under his moustache. "May I at least be permitted to make a call to the home office?"

She stood and leaned over to give him a big hug. "I can live with that, but only if we can have dinner together tonight."

Creed tried to think of a clever saying that fitted moments like this, but came up empty. Realizing he had not registered a reply to her suggestion, he draped his strong arms around her shoulders and replied, "What a wonderful idea!"

She kissed him hard on the mouth. "Oops!" she said playfully, putting her slender hand to her mouth. "I suppose I got carried away."

"I rather enjoyed that," Creed replied, as only a Brit could do, emotions held well in check.

After they talked for a while, defusing the obvious awkwardness of the situation with focus on the weather, he said, "I think it is time for me to find my hotel. It has been a rather long day."

Largo did not want to appear too forward. "I bought a bottle of Drambuie just for you. Why don't I walk you back to your hotel and we'll have a tiny glass? We will call it a celebration."

The smile was a broad one. "And just what are we celebrating?"

"You! The fact that you are here."

"Well, perhaps a small glass, but I do need to make a couple of calls tonight."

She registered the slightest hint of a pretend frown. "Is there someone special waiting for a call?"

"No, no, it's not that. I want to talk with a colleague about Le Havre and the yacht I saw there with your name emblazoned across its bow. I want him to follow up on that."

Largo left Creed's hotel room a little past ten o'clock. She was cleaning up the kitchen when the phone rang. The unaccustomed sound of the telephone startled her at first, but then she thought it must be Creed. Perhaps he left something behind. "Are you calling to ask if I would like another Drambuie?"

A pause followed before she heard Porter clear his throat. "Largo?"

She recovered quickly. "Hi! What a surprise!"

"I wasn't sure I had the right number. What was that about Drambuie? Am I missing a party, or something?"

Largo wrestled with her nerves. "No, no, I thought you were the girl who lives on the floor above me. She was just here. We had enjoyed a glass of Drambuie, her first ever, and I had offered her a refill, but she passed on it. I thought she was calling to say she'd changed her mind."

"So, how is everything with my girl? I haven't heard from you in a while."

"I'm fine, I really am. Just busy."

"Yeah, I suppose you're getting excited about starting classes."

"A little bit," she replied, struggling with a blanket of guilt. "You know how that is." She quickly redirected the conversation. "Are you calling from home, or are you on the road?"

"I'm home. I just returned yesterday from a nine-day stint in Florida and Louisiana. I'll be here for a week, or so, and then I'm back on the road again." A pause followed. "I miss you, baby."

"I miss you too."

"You sound tired. I hope I'm not calling too late."

"No, I'm still up. I'm glad you called."

"Speaking of calling, has Mason Creed called you?"

She felt the tiny hairs on her neck stand at full attention. "Mason, yes, he called sometime back. He mentioned that the two of you had spoken."

"I'm just curious. What were his thoughts on the situation with the Memling?"

It was a struggle now to simply talk. She wanted to hang up the receiver, but she knew she couldn't do that. "Nothing specific. He said he would look into things from London ... urged me to keep the faith and all that stuff. I appreciated the call, his thoughtfulness."

"He's a good man," Blue said, the words pummeling her like cudgels.

"Yes, I'll forever be indebted to him."

"Are you sure you're all right? You sound a little stressed."

"A little, I guess. Everything is so new, so different here."

"Well, I won't keep you. Will you call me in a day, or so? I do worry about you, you know."

"I know."

"I love you. Be safe."

Before she could reply, she heard the click on the line. She waited for a long moment before placing her phone on the cradle. She cupped her face with her hands and cried like a baby.

❧

Wednesday, September 3
Krakow, Poland

Creed was able to secure a three-week leave of absence and that only because of his long and unblemished record with the Yard. They had twenty-one days to catch the biggest of fish in the water and the hook had not yet been baited. He would have to place calls throughout Europe, collecting markers from friends and colleagues. Almost everyone owed him. He wanted to know what they were hearing about the Gade Collection robbery and the death of Palma. Had Interpol been able to make any significant advances? Had Theo Volmer been spotted anywhere? It would be a slow and agonizing process, but that was what police work was all about. If he had learned anything from his long years of service, it was patience. With only a month to work with, the P in patience had to be lower case.

Around noon, he walked out into the crisp morning air and covered the short distance to Largo's flat, still harboring some troubling thoughts about her decision to become the aggressor, to take on the dangerous pursuit of Volmer. "What about your studies" he asked, starting with one of the more obvious hurdles in front of Largo. "Did I understand you to say that you are not planning to attend classes?"

"Yes. I went through the necessary steps with the Jagiellonian to

290

cancel my classes without prejudice. Even though it was a lie through and through, I told university officials that I'd received sad news from home that my mother had just been seriously injured in an automobile accident. It looked highly likely that I would have to return to the United States and assume primary care duties with my family until her recovery. The university was exceptionally understanding."

"What about your lease?"

"I'm stuck with it for now, but I see that as more positive than negative. We'll have a base of operations."

The choice of pronouns hit Creed like a blast of hot air. We will, instead of I will. "Before we begin this," he said, "there is one point on which I must be insistent."

Largo forced the smile to stay down. Creed of all people being insistent. "What is it?"

"That if, or when, we discover anything of significance, we pass it on to local authorities. This cannot be a Scotland Yard investigation, nor should we try to apprehend Volmer on our own. I must insist on this."

"I love it when you insist, Mason." The smile was not about to be contained. It burst forth like a ray of golden sunshine.

Creed tried to remain serious. He was used to having to make on-the-spot decisions, so notwithstanding all of the swirling emotions that were screaming for attention he said as calmly as a priest might lead a congregation in prayer, "I think our first stop should be Anghiari and lunch at The Verrocchio. Are you game?"

"Italian food is my favorite!"

Following dinner and a nightcap with Largo, Creed returned to his hotel. He needed to look at the train schedule and connections, if any, between Krakow and Anghiari. On a larger scale, he wanted to map out a few things they could and couldn't do before he would have to return to London. The coming three weeks carried a strong sense of anticipation.

Her first item of business after parting with Creed was to tape all four corners of her map of Europe to a bare spot on her bedroom wall. For good measure, she ran a long piece of tape across the top of the map.

She then took one of the red push pins and positioned it over the

L in Florence, applying enough pressure to drive it into the wall. A second red pin was pushed into the wall just below Anghiari. Recalling Creed's description of the yacht at Le Harve, she positioned a third pin there. A final red pin was positioned about an inch from the one she'd earlier placed over Florence. Pins in place, she secured a long piece of red thread to the first pin. Moving the thread to the right she looped it twice over Anghiari and then moved it up to Le Havre, repeating the looping. With the remainder of the length of thread, she lowered it to Florence and secured it to the second red pin. She now had a visual tracking of Volmer's whereabouts since he left Florence last July through August of 1997. The big question begging an answer: Where is he now? As they uncovered more information about him, additional red thread and pins would show his movements.

She stepped back and admired her handiwork. Every part of her, with one exception, felt energized by the decision she had reached. She was especially happy that Creed had agreed to join her. The lone exception was Blue. She had to tell him that things had changed. Just how much of that change she would divulge was the sticky part.

CHAPTER THIRTY-THREE

Crossing The Line

Thursday, September 4
Krakow, Poland

A steady rain was falling when Largo and Creed arrived by taxi at the main railway station in Krakow. They had tickets for the 10:07 a.m. train to Florence with major stops in Vienna, Salzburg and Venice. Largo had packed assorted eatables and Creed had selected two bottles of a red table wine on the recommendation of his hotel bellhop. Once in Florence, they would rent a car for the short drive to Anghiari.

The lengthy journey gave them ample time to discuss a myriad of topics, some related to Anghiari, most running the gamut from their respective careers to personal issues and concerns. Creed described his life as a bachelor and Largo delicately skirted around the recent bumps in her relationship with Blue. It was a comfortable sharing, made all the more enjoyable by the delicacies that Largo had packed and Creed's two bottles of wine. By the time they reached Florence, each felt like they had known the other for a long time.

Creed spent little time locating a car rental agency, and within an hour of arriving in Florence they were motoring along the narrow, winding roads of mountainous Tuscany. Each small village afforded its own charm and on more than one occasion one or the other would say they wanted to return and savor the place.

Both found Anghiari steeped in charm and uniqueness. Their objective was to locate The Verrocchio, but as they strolled about the charming network of narrow streets they found themselves fascinated by the many small shops and decidedly different feel of their surroundings.

"I'm so glad we came the way we did," Largo said "I really enjoyed having the opportunity to see something of the Tuscan countryside. When Porter and I were in Florence last ..." she broke off, realizing she might have upset or offended Creed.

"I totally agree," he replied, giving no indication the reference to Blue had bothered him. He was feeling as if he had been swept up in some marvelous fantasy adventure, and he was content to let the slip of the tongue pass.

The Verrocchio was found without difficulty.

"I believe our timing is perfect." Creed patted his firm stomach. "I am more than hungry."

"You'll get no argument from me," Largo's eyes checked out the tastefully decorated restaurant.

Within minutes, Astrid Borgmann appeared at their table and extended her personal welcome, complete with the offer of complimentary glasses of wine. "So, this is your first time here," she said with a broad smile. "A honeymoon, perhaps?"

Creed was the first to respond. "No, no, we are just good friends," he said, reflecting an evident shade of embarrassment.

Largo seemed more than a little amused by his fumbling manner. "I've always dreamed of a honeymoon, but I'm not so sure a special occasion like that would be in the cards for a father and his daughter."

"I say there!" Creed shot back, not recognizing the intended humor in Largo's reply. His expression was a blend of astonishment and offense.

"I'm only teasing, Mason." She looked quickly at Astrid and added, "One has to be so careful when in the presence of a Brit. They take everything so seriously."

Astrid Borgmann laughed, as did Creed after an awkward moment.

"Your server today will be Raquel," she said. "I trust you will enjoy your meal."

Before she could leave the table, Creed asked, "Might we speak with you after our meal? We're hopeful you, or someone from The Verrocchio, can help us with some essential information."

"I'll be glad to if I can," Astrid replied. "I am the owner of this place. If I may inquire about the nature of your information request, then I will be in a much better position to talk with you later."

"Certainly. It concerns a man who frequented your establishment in the recent past. From what we understand, he must have been a regular here. His name is Azzo Gatti."

The color drained from Astrid Borgmann's face. For a moment, her composure seemed shaken. "Are you with Interpol?" she asked.

"No," Creed replied quickly. "I am an inspector with Scotland Yard, but this is not an official visit. I am on official leave, accompanying Ms. Kopacz in her effort to find a stolen painting. We have reason to believe *signor* Gatti might be involved in that case."

With her emotions in check, Astrid looked first at Largo and then Creed before saying, "Let me suggest that you enjoy your meal first. I need a few minutes to talk with my manager and then let me treat you to an espresso and dessert. We can find a more private place to chat. I too, have an interest in Gatti."

Largo and Creed placed their order for a seafood antipasto. Within minutes, the waiter returned to the table with a bottle of Chianti and a plate of assorted cheeses and breads.

"Compliments of the management." he said, placing the opened bottle next to Creed.

As he walked away, Largo asked, "What do you make of all that ... Astrid's interest in Gatti, or Volmer, or whoever the hell he is?"

Creed delicately wiped his mouth. "A good question. By the way, the cheese is extraordinary. Would you care to try one?"

"I think not. Cheese and I do not exactly get along."

"A question? Do I really look that much older than you?"

Largo laughed so spontaneously that she had difficulty keeping a peeled shrimp in her mouth. "You are one sexy man, Mason Creed. I was only teasing."

During their dinner, Creed was struck by Largo's beauty. Her dark brown eyes and long, raven hair were riveting. Her porcelain skin and just a touch of pale pink lipstick transformed her face so that it appeared to glow, as if lighted by some mysterious inner candle.

After the meal, they were escorted by Astrid Borgmann to a small, charming room overlooking a broad courtyard. A waiter followed with three cups of espresso and an equal number of servings of cheesecake topped with raspberries. Once everyone was seated, Creed took the initiative. "Will you begin by telling us how and when you met this man, Azzo Gatti?"

Astrid provided a detailed answer. She concluded by saying, "It is my personal belief that Azzo was directly involved in the recent Gade robbery in Copenhagen."

"And why do you say that?" Largo asked.

"Because he talked of his fascination with the idea of perpetrating just such a crime. He even asked me if I would join him in such a theft, were he to ever launch such a thing."

"This was before the Gade robbery?" Creed asked for clarification.

"Yes."

"Tell me, Astrid," Creed continued, "did he ever speak with you about commissioning an artist to paint a detailed copy of an existing masterwork?"

"You are talking about the artist in Ravenna," she replied evenly, catching Largo and Creed by surprise. "No, he never shared the details with me about that, but I do recall him making a trip to Ravenna shortly before he left Anghiari to pick up a painting he had commissioned."

As the afternoon brought long shadows across the courtyard, Astrid Borgmann released her pent up anger at Gatti. She told Creed and Largo about her confrontation with Gatti in Florence, that she had seen him in the Church of Santa Croce on the very day Lucca Palma died.

She spoke in detail about local police Chief Antonio Fleri and their efforts to get the Florentine police to obtain a sample of Gatti's DNA. "Had they only been able to do that," she continued with heavy words, "he might now be in custody. No one in Florence would listen to me. They treated me like I was the criminal. It was just awful."

Midway through the cheesecake, she slapped her hand on the table and said, "I almost forgot this! When I confronted Azzo in the restaurant, seated as he was in a wheelchair and wearing the clothes of a priest, his companion got between us and tried to convince me that I was confused. He said that the man I was accusing of such awful things was not Gatti, but rather a man from Copenhagen by the name of Ankel Thornton, or something like that. It was a Danish name, and I'm not sure of the correct spelling. But one thing I do know is that the man in the wheelchair was Gatti, the last man on earth I would consider a priest. The Azzo Gatti I knew was and is an evil man, that's all I can say."

Creed never missed anything. He recalled his brief conversation with the seaman in Le Havre. He had written down the correct spelling of the name. After a moment of flipping through his small pocket notepad, he found it. "The name is Thorssen. Ankiel Thorssen. And this young man with Gatti," he continued, "what can you tell me about him?"

"He was young, quite attractive." Astrid continued, "I would guess German, or Scandinavian. In his twenties. Blond. Blue Eyes. What struck me as odd was his clothing. It looked like he was wearing a uniform of some kind ... a white shirt and trousers, black shoes. My first thought was that he might have been a hospital orderly." She hesitated for a moment and then added, "There is one other thing I should tell you." For the next few minutes she told Largo and Creed about the hairbrush and her disappointment on learning that it carried little value to the Danish police. "It seems they couldn't come up with a DNA match."

For Largo, it was as if her head was suddenly filled with the ringing of bells.

She looked quickly at Creed and then back at Astrid. "The hairbrush? Do you still have it?"

"I do, sadly. The Danish police returned it as they had no evidence with which to provide a match."

Largo's eyes, now ablaze with excitement, looked back at Creed. "I believe I can produce that match."

Creed looked at her, astonishment covering his face like a mask. "What are you saying?"

"I told you about returning home with Porter and finding ashes in our foyer?"

"Yes, but I don't get the connection." Creed offered.

Largo's eyes returned to Astrid. "Someone broke into our condo while we were away—I'm convinced it was Volmer, the man you knew as Azzo Gatti—and while he was there he masturbated all over a pair of my red panties. There's your match! I placed them in a small plastic bag, hoping the day would come when my underwear could be used to catch him, but never believing something like this would actually happen." She glanced back at Creed. "What do you think?"

"If this were evidence in an active case, we'd send it to a company called Cellmark, but it's not." Creed passed a hand over his forehead. "Even so, it could take weeks or months to get the results back."

The women looked at each other, and Largo said, "So, what's the point?"

"The good news is that the students at Leicester will test anything you send them." Creed smiled, the excitement of the possibilities taking hold. "That's where they developed the process they're calling 'DNA fingerprinting' about a dozen years ago. I believe some young research assistants will jump at the chance to examine the hairs in that brush and your panties." He turned to Astrid and asked, "Would you permit us to take the hairbrush and see what happens?"

"Of course," she replied quickly. "It's of no value at all in my closet."

Largo was eager to be alone with Creed so they could discuss the best way to proceed in making the DNA connection. They thanked Astrid for her candor and determination to bring Gatti to justice. Largo warmly embraced her. "You have been extremely helpful. We'll put the hairbrush with my panties and make this man pay for his crimes." She hesitated for a moment. "And the meal was to die for!"

It had been a long day, tiring but quite beneficial. Largo thought about her red push pins. She could now place Volmer in Copenhagen before returning to Florence. It was nearing ten p.m. by the time she and Creed left The Verrocchio. Both were tired, but pleased with the day's effort.

"I suppose we should find a hotel for the night," Creed said, feeling less than comfortable with the sound of the words coming from his mouth. He'd known that sooner, or later, they would be crossing this bridge, but he had not expected to be crossing it at such a late hour.

Largo took his arm. "Well, I'm not about to spend the night in the train station. Let's do it."

Creed remembered a hotel they had passed on their way to The Verrocchio. They retraced their steps and found La Meridiana with little difficulty. When they entered the lobby, a desk clerk gave them a broad smile. He assumed they were husband and wife. After hospitable greetings, he asked how he might be of service.

"We need a room for the night," Creed hoped his awkwardness wouldn't show.

"Very good, sir," the clerk replied. "Almost all of our rooms are booked for tonight's concert, but we do have two left—one with twin beds and the other a nice queen size."

Creed looked at Largo, hoping she would make the call. She just returned his quizzical expression, trying to look as if she had no idea what to do. Inwardly, she was smiling. He turned to her. "Do you have a preference?"

"No, dear, I'm fine with either room."

"We'll take the twin beds," Creed said with something of a hollow voice. He dared not look back at Largo. His world was moving at warp speed and it was all he could do to just hang on. The line was crossed a few minutes past two in the morning.

"Mason, are you asleep?" The voice came from the darkened side of the room.

"No. I may have dozed off, but I'm awake now. You?"

Largo laughed. "No, Mason, I'm not sleeping, either."

"Yes, of course."

"Do you like your little single bed?" A playful tone accompanied the question.

"Not especially."

"I don't particularly care for mine, either."

A lengthy pause.

"Perhaps we should have taken the room with the queen-sized bed," he said, turning to face her and seeing only a dark shape.

"Yes, perhaps we should have done that. I don't like sleeping alone."

"Nor do I," Creed replied, realizing as he did so that he'd spent most of his life sleeping alone. "I mean I would prefer not to sleep alone."

"Mason?"

"Yes?"

"Would you like to bring your little pillow to my bed?"

"What a splendid suggestion. I would like that very much."

Largo was thoroughly enjoying her little tease. He was such the gentleman, but she knew that beneath his British façade, he wanted to lie next to her. The image of Porter Blue appeared like a summer shower, but she gently pushed it aside, out of sight, out of mind. She waited.

"Largo?"

"Yes, Mason?"

"What about Porter?"

"This isn't about Porter, Mason. This is about us."

The silhouette of a man in his shorts carrying a pillow walked across the carpeted floor, tip-toeing, as if not to make a sound.

The following morning as they were checking out of La Meridiana,

Largo locked her arm in his and asked, "Did you sleep well last night, dear?"

Creed smiled. He liked the feeling of her arm next to his. He liked everything about her.

"Yes, once I got settled."

"Me, too."

Saturday, September 6
Le Havre, France

Upon their return from Volmer's successful hunting expedition to Florence, he engaged Acker in several "research" tasks that kept him busy in the city of Le Havre, a comfortable distance from Okur and the other men.

Acker would return at the end of the day, submit his materials to Volmer, and then try to be as inconspicuous as possible. It was only after Okur and the crew had retired to their bunks that Acker's silent feet moved in the direction of Volmer's stateroom, and then only when invited to do so.

Okur appeared to be none the wiser.

It was clear to Volmer that Okur held some resentment of the special treatment the young German was receiving, but to his credit he had kept such feelings to himself. Outwardly, at least, Okur appeared to be content with maintaining the status quo. When he and Volmer talked, however, the one subject that Okur kept raising was that of travel. How long were they going to remain at Le Havre? The men were growing listless.

Volmer had played his cards carefully. Just prior to leaving with Acker for Florence, Volmer discovered a delicious tidbit from a televised program on emerging American writers, one that would have strong and immediate bearings on his plans for travel. Featured on the program was Porter Blue whose soon to be published novel, *Tuscan Secret*, was receiving rave reviews.

"It has to be exciting to find such a positive response to your story," chirped the show's host Jan Stauffer, a social leader and a decent writer in her own right.

"Yes, it is deeply gratifying, especially since I never expected to find a publisher courageous enough to take on a complete unknown such as me."

"You're being far too modest Porter. Someone in high places must be quite fond of the story."

Volmer had made a careful mental note of Blue's disclosure. He knew that his own days in Le Havre were numbered, but he had no intention of divulging any details to Okur, not at this time, anyway. A second realization followed quickly, one sparked by his fascination with the thought of a resurrected Nazi vision. *How foolish of me to see Largo Kopacz as anything more than a filthy Jew. My* Führer *will be pleased if I do away with her like he did with all the others, the sooner the better.*

It was not enough to say that the Acker had opened a whole new world to Volmer; he was experiencing a seismic shift in the management of feelings that went far beyond mere sexual pleasures. He had known legions of women in his life, but none of them had awakened such depth of feelings as had Acker. If a night passed without being in his presence, Volmer felt cheated, empty. As he tried to structure these new horizons—and Volmer was the consummate planner and organizer—he realized that for the first time in his life, he was experiencing the intoxicating nectar of love.

But his feelings went far beyond love. Through Acker, the perfect specimen of Aryan supremacy—the superman—Volmer was rekindling the same fires he had known as a boy, the exhilarating flames of nationalism; the spectacle of a sea of swastikas yielding to the throbbing strains of *Tannhauser* and, soaring above it all, the magnetism of Adolf Hitler. Where he had once ached over the collapse of *der Führer*'s world view, he could experience the fragrance again with Acker at his side. It was a feeling of invincibility, that nothing could now exceed his grasp, that everything in his life up to this very moment had been prelude.

From the innermost reaches of his mind, came a memory fragment from his youth, a wisp of a long forgotten yesterday. Though he had no way of knowing it, he was with his father for the last time. Within days, his father, the grand soldier, would die at the hands of Hermann Göring. His father was home on leave and the family had gathered in the parlor of their home in Munich. Volmer was seated on his father's lap, his mother in a nearby chair.

"You are too young now, Theo, to the fully appreciate this," his father said, holding up a school photograph of Adolf Hitler, his most prized possession. "One day your mother will repeat what I have shared with her about this photograph. I never want you to forget it."

Seven years later when Theo was about the age of Hitler in the photograph, his mother sat down with him to register her late husband's wishes. Holding the photograph so her son could see it, she said, "In this photograph, the teacher is seated in the middle of the second row. To his left is the top student in the class and to the teacher's right is the student who finished second. The most gifted students are seated on the first two rows. From the second row to the top, students are seated in terms of their academic accomplishments." She paused to make sure she had her son's full attention.

"Where is Hitler in the photograph," he asked.

"He is at the far right on the top row," she said, studying her son's eyes. "Were your father here, he would ask you for the lesson to be learned from this photograph. How would you answer that?"

The boy examined the photograph for a moment and replied, "Hitler was not smart."

It pained the mother to continue with the issue, for her views on Nazi ideology were far removed from those of her late husband. But as she had promised him before he died, she felt obligated to echo his words. "No, Theo, the lesson your father would want you to learn is far more important than that. Your father would want you to know that this little school boy who never finished gymnasium rose to become the most powerful man in Germany. He was able to do this because of his indomitable will. Your father would want you to know that you should never, ever let your dreams and ambitions be thwarted by others. Do you understand that?"

"Yes, Mama." Thoughts of his father's fingers returned.

But the euphoria such as Volmer was now experiencing came with a price. Problems loomed ahead, major concerns that threatened his course. Just as Azzo Gatti had to perish in order for Ankiel Thorssen to emerge, it was time once again for a changing of hues, time to become someone else. The footsteps behind him were growing closer. He and Acker had to vanish in order to reappear a safe distance away from those who would do them harm.

Tuesday, September 9
Le Havre, France

It was midday on the *Largo*.
On the pretense of needing to inform Acker of an upcoming conference in Bern, Switzerland, Volmer asked Okur to send the young man
to his stateroom. Acker arrived within minutes.

Volmer spoke with an absence of expression. "Dieter, we will be
leaving Le Havre in a few days. Before we do so, I need to ask you to
do something for me."

"I will gladly do anything,"

"I have a small, old painting in my possession that must be protected. I will wrap the painting, after which I want you to construct a
shallow wooden box with a lid sufficient to house it. After making the
box, I want you to fashion a cavity in the wall behind the headboard of
my bed where I can store it."

"That poses no problem."

"Good."

"Where are we going?"

"You and I will make a quick trip to Stuttgart and do a little shopping. I want to buy you some pretty, new things."

Acker's eyes sparkled. "And after Stuttgart?" he asked impishly.

"I will tell you later. Now, do as I say. Prepare the box and the storage compartment." The tone of Volmer's voice left little doubt in Acker's mind that his employer felt no need to explain anything.

CHAPTER THIRTY-FOUR

So Edible

Wednesday, September 10
Le Havre, France

Volmer needed the expertise of Ilyus Bager regarding a matter of considerable importance. As he placed the call to the efficient German, he thought back to the spectacular explosions in the harbor at Nyhavn, how the night sky had glowed.

Bager picked up on the second ring. *"Ja, Bager."*

"Ilyus, my friend, this is Ankiel Thornssen. I trust you are well?"

"Sehr gut, mein Herr! Very good, sir. *Und Sie?* And you?"

"I'm fine, thank you. If you have a moment, I would like your opinion on something."

"Yes, I am free at the moment. How may I serve you?"

"Sniper rifles. I need a good one."

"Yes, of course, I believe I can help you. May I ask a question?"

"Certainly."

"My question is this: Your target ... what is the approximate distance from the shooter?"

Volmer was surprised by the question. "About two hundred meters."

Bager paused for a moment. "I would recommend a Blaser 93r Tactical. It came out in nineteen ninety-three and has been used most effectively by German and Dutch police. Very accurate from the distance you referenced."

"It comes with a telescopic sight, I presume?"

"Of course and a five-round magazine. It should meet your needs. My guess is that an experienced marksman could hit the center of an egg from two hundred meters."

"Are you that experienced, Ilyus?"

"I am, sir. Do you require my services?"

"Let me think about it."

"Very good, sir."

"Where could I get such a rifle? I will need it soon."

"I have some contacts," Bager obliged. "Most of them are in Germany and Holland."

"Any in Italy? Any close to Florence?" Volmer doodled an image of a man hanging from the end of a rope.

"I have a reliable contact in Milan and another in Murano."

"Nothing closer?"

"No, sir. I'm sorry."

Volmer had been to Murano. A short distance from Venice, it was known for its remarkable blown glassworks. "I'm familiar with Murano."

Bager's voice was firm. "Give me a day, or so, to line things up. I'll be back in touch soon."

Volmer thought for a moment about the travel required to obtain the rifle. Every mile on the road heightened the chances of being identified. Still, he had planned everything so carefully. The rifle was central to its success. "Fine. Murano will work."

"Do you wish to know the price on it?" Bager knew the question was unnecessary, but he asked it out of courtesy.

"No, my friend. Price is never an issue."

"Very well," Bager concluded. "I will call you back at this number in two days. I should have the information you need."

"I'm very impressed with your professionalism, Ilyus. I knew I could count on you. I will be placing a token of my appreciation in the mail tomorrow."

"Thank you, sir, but that is not necessary."

Volmer registered a slight chuckle. "But I insist."

"Very good, sir. Thank you."

Volmer hung up the phone thinking, *They don't make them like Bager anymore.*

He read a few chapters in *Mein Kampf* before calling Okur and asking that Acker come to his quarters. When the young man arrived and took a seat near Volmer, he saw the copy of *Mein Kampf* positioned next to the phone. *It's always with him.*

Volmer settled back in his chair. "Dieter, you once told me that had you been in the German military, you would have preferred the army. You wanted to be a sniper, as I recall."

"Yes, I did say that, sir."

"How extensive is your knowledge of sniper rifles?"

"I'm reasonably well versed," the blond German replied with a trace of a frown. "Why do you ask?"

"Don't be testy with me, Dieter."

"Sorry."

"The Blaser 93r Tactical. Do you know it?"

"Yes sir, it's a killer rifle. It's a favorite of the Australian military."

"I like the sound of that," Volmer countered. "That's all I need to know."

Acker seemed relieved. "Before I return to my duties, may I ask you a question?"

"A question about what?" Volmer replied, bemused by his straight-forwardness.

"The book there, Hitler's book, *Mein Kampf*."

"What about it?"

"I see you frequently reading it. May I see it?"

Volmer's body language suddenly changed. One would have had to be observant to notice it, a slight flinching in the shoulders.

"I will see to it that you have your own copy. Please do not be offended, Dieter, but I never allow this copy to be handled by others. It may seem rude, I suppose, but it's one ideosyncrasy I have never been able to put aside. My apologies, if I have offended you."

"No, that's fine, I was just curious."

When Acker returned to his work, thoughts of the book were uppermost in his mind. *There is something special about that book.*

The following morning, Volmer informed Okur that he wanted him to prepare for sailing. "Please have things ready for the *Largo* to leave Le Havre immediately. Business interests in Venice dictate that Dieter and I leave on the fifteenth. We won't be returning to the *Largo* until October first."

"The destination, sir?" Okur asked dryly.

"Livorno, near Pisa."

Okur was curious about the abruptness of it all. "As you wish, sir."

"Then gather your provisions and make ready."

"And from Livorno?" Okur asked.

Volmer hesitated for a moment and then replied, "We will be making a very long trip. I will give you the details soon."

From Okur's end of the line a lengthy pause. "Very good, sir."

Saturday, September 13
Le Havre, France

Acker promptly satisfied Volmer's request for the wooden box and the storage cavity behind his bed. "Lock the compartment when you're finished and then join me," Volmer said. With the Memling carefully sealed away, he felt comfortable. "It's time we leave for the train to Stuttgart."

"I'll need to get my things and visit the head," Acker said. "I'll be right with you."

"Make it quick," Volmer barked.

Enroute to his quarters, Acker slipped into Volmer's stateroom and with the key unlocked the small storage area and quickly removed the box. He removed the Memling and placed it on Volmer's bed while he returned the empty box to the cavity. He quickly locked it and then went straight to his bunk with the small painting under his shirt. Once in the privacy of his own quarters, he placed the Memling in a small gray shoulder bag. Within minutes, he was back at Volmer's side. "Here's the key," he said respectfully.

Volmer nodded and pocketed the shiny, brass key. "It took you long enough." He had made reservations on the 8:17 train, one of three faster trains between Le Havre and Stuttgart. Without delays, the trip required just a little over seven hours. The slower trains made stops along the route. Volmer hoped to take care of several matters in the city before checking into the Arcotel Camino Stuttgart, one of the city's finer hotels. In making those reservations by phone, he cited his name as Dr. Wilhelm Schroeder, and that of Acker as Werner Dietz. As he told a woman at the other end of the line, he was currently associated with the Goethe Institute and Dietz was his administrative assistant.

The woman caught him completely by surprise with a question.

"I've lived here for most of my life, but I am not all that familiar with the Institute. What is its principle mission?"

The hours of homework had not been in vain. "Our primary goal is to promote the study of the German language through the exchange of films, music, theatre and literature," Volmer said. "We've been doing this for more than sixty years."

"How wonderful! We will look forward to your arrival."

Okur watched Volmer and Acker as they left the yacht and stepped into a waiting taxi. *Something not right.*

One pressing matter of business in Stuttgart was the preparation of new identities for the two of them. Media reports were suggesting that the net for Volmer was growing tighter. Working through a supplier in Berlin, he had been able to obain false passports before leaving Stuttgar for Venice. He was once again changing his hues. "Before we can pick up our new passports," Volmer said to Acker as they rode to the station by taxi, "we will need to visit a hair salon in Stuttgart. I think it is time for both of us to ... how shall I put it ... change our feathers."

"Like what?"

"I'm seeing you with black hair. By the way, I like the goatee. I told you it would be an enhancement. You will be even more striking with the change in color."

It was evident from his expression that Acker was not eager to say goodbye to his golden, curly locks.

Volmer did not want a war to suddenly take place. "You will like the new you, I promise."

"And what about you?" Acker's question was asked in a peevish way.

Volmer pulled a folded advertisement from a GQ magazine and handed it to his young delight. "What do you think?" The image was that of a man with close-cropped russet hair, a moustache, a beret and wearing round, silver eyeglasses.

Acker pondered the image for a moment, wanting to laugh. He then tossed the advertisement on the seat of the cab. "You will resemble a chauffeur."

Volmer swallowed his disappointment. "You'll get used to it." Volmer allowed his hand to slide between Acker's muscular thighs.

Acker flashed a seductive smile as he directed the path of the visiting hand. "You are such a dirty little man."

Volmer had stayed at the five-star hotel in Stuttgart on two previous occasions. He liked the simplicity—some would say severity—of the place; the impeccably designed furnishings and the interplay between stone and the resonant, dark wood. Because Volmer had contacts there, it was a place where a man could easily hide.

The desk clerk was the model of German precision; every gesture, every action that of polished efficiency. "And how long do you and your associate plan to be with us, Dr. Schroeder?" he asked in crisp German, carefully examining their respective passports.

"Several days at least," Volmer replied. "I have been looking forward to this visit."

The desk clerk seemed quite satisfied. "*Sehr gut!* We will do everything we can to make your stay an enjoyable one."

"*Danke, schön,*" Volmer replied. Just before leaving the glistening desk, he asked, "Would it be possible to have a bottle of your best vodka delivered to my room within the next few minutes?"

"I will see to it, sir. With ice, I presume?"

"Yes, ice would be fine."

With the vodka came an unexpected announcement from Volmer. "It is time for us to celebrate something, Dieter. I intended to wait a bit to share this with you, but I can think of no better time than now to do so." He handed a glass of chilled vodka to Acker before continuing, "You and I will be returning to Florence soon to perform one final mission for *der Führer.*"

Acker was familiar with the *Führer* game, but this time Volmer's voice took on a different tone, one laced with melancholy, or perhaps a better word would be finality. Acker could see it in Volmer's eyes. He sounded and looked like a man who had just received orders from Adolf Hitler. It was as if the game had morphed into reality for Volmer.

Acker resisted a smile. "And just what are our orders, my general?"

Volmer answered him obliquely, ignoring the facetious reference to his rank. "Do you remember our talk the other day about your youthful dreams of becoming a sniper?"

"Yes, I did say that."

"Well, my dear friend, you are going to have your chance to become that sniper."

Acker's facial expression was an easy read; he could not imagine what Volmer was about to say.

"I want you to have the honor of eliminating a dangerous Jew. Her name is Largo Kopacz."

The thought formed quickly in Acker's mind. *The yacht. She is the source of its name.* "I don't understand. I don't even know her."

Volmer looked at him sternly. "Have you forgotten what you told me that day when we talked of a soldier's duty? Do you remember the little French girl with the flag?"

Acker tried to remember the conversation. He could grasp only fragments.

"Let me make it easy for you, sweet Dieter. I asked you what you would do if I, your commanding officer, ordered you to kill the girl. Do you now recall it?"

"Yes, I said I would do that, if ordered to do so."

"And then I raised the ugly issue of conscience. Remember?"

"I said that if we were at war I would only be doing my duty, or words to that effect." He was now growing irritated. "That it would not bother my fucking conscience, something like that."

"Ah, you do remember!"

Acker nodded with a frown. "But we are not at war."

Volmer's eyes blazed. "Not at war? Let me remind you we are very much at war!"

Acker looked at him in silence. He knew when not to press his buttons.

Volmer rubbed both hands as if they were cold. "Now I must now make a quick trip to a friend's home. I want you to remain here, until I return." He withdrew a roll of German currency from his pocket and peeled off several large bills for Acker. "Get what you need to eat, but otherwise remain in the room. I will return in several hours."

For Acker, a vestige of distaste surfaced at not having been invited to tag along. "What then?" He noticed the black briefcase next to the chair in which Volmer had been sitting.

"We will go shopping. I cannot wait to see you in extraordinary apparel."

Just as Volmer was about to walk out of the hotel room he realized it would be wise to visit the toilet before departing. A few moments later, he retuned to the living room and gave Acker a loving hug. "I'll be back soon. Please don't be mad at me."

"I'm not mad. I know you are a busy man."

Acker followed him to the door, positioning himself between Volmer and the briefcase. A moment later, Volmer disappeared down the stairs. Acker went to the other end of the room and looked down at the hotel entrance, three floors below. A little over a minute passed before he saw Volmer walk out into the sunshine. *He's forgotten the briefcase!* He continued to watch Volmer until he disappeared in a taxi. Acker remained by the window for another five minutes, wanting to make sure Volmer didn't return. When he was satisfied that Volmer would not be returning any time soon, he returned to the briefcase and removed Volmer's prized book.

The content of *Mein Kampf* mattered little to Acker. He was looking for something else. Page-by-page, his sharp eyes scanned the yellowed paper, looking for anything that might have been placed between pages, anything that might explain Volmer's possessiveness. There was some good reason why Volmer kept the copy so close to his vest, and he would find it. With Volmer gone for several hours, he had plenty of time to do that.

When he reached page 147, his number-sensitive eyes went to the bottom center of the page. To the left and right of the three numerals, he saw the two added numerals, the four and the nine. Acker's eyes then explored the text on the page. On line seventeen, he found the small black dot above the word, *immer*, always. On a scrap piece of paper, he scribbled down the word and the numerals, and continued his page-by-page examination. A few moments later, he found the second adjusted page number: 307 had been altered to read 13075. On that page, near the top of the text, he saw the second word above which there was the tiny dot: *nie*, never. He continued page by page until the end of the book, finding no other selected words, or altered page numbers.

"Always and never," he said aloud. He had two key words, two five-digit numbers and a burning question: *What did it all mean? I will eventually find it.*

Just before returning the copy of *Mein Kampf* to the briefcase, satisfied that he had repositioned it next to the chair correctly, Acker then
went to the kitchen and removed a warm beer from the countertop.
Sitting on one of the kitchen chairs, he studied the information he had
harvested. Suddenly, he stepped away from the table and went to the
door, from which he could see the briefcase. His eyes went straight to
the handle. Something was amiss. The handle had flopped to the front
and was facing the door. *That's not right. It needs to face the chair, I'm
certain of it.* He walked over to the briefcase and made the adjustment
with the handle.

Fuchs was waiting for Volmer when he arrived at his Stuttgart home
forty-five minutes later. They drank beer and ate assorted cheeses and
breads while Volmer outlined his reason for coming. As he did so, it
dawned on him that he had not brought the briefcase with him.

"In a matter of days, I will be leaving Europe for an indefinite period
of time," Volmer began, suppressing the roiling anger he was experiencing as a result of his negligence. "I have one final favor to ask of you."

"Name it," Fuchs replied.

Volmer handed his friend a white, sealed envelope. Fuchs could tell
it contained something small and hard.

"This is a key to a locker in the Kastrup Airport in Copenhagen.
Inside, you will find a small, wrapped package. It is the Vermeer study
from the Gade Collection. I want you to bring it back here and place
it in a secure place. I will contact you when I am ready to come for it."

"Just like old times, isn't it?" Fuchs was referencing the time his father had stored stolen paintings belonging to Volmer's father.

"Yes, something like that." Volmer's mind was still on the briefcase
and his forgetfulness in not taking it with him. He needed to stay more
focused. Had Acker been curious about it? He was positively nauseous
at the thought that Acker might have perused his copy of *Mein Kampf.*
But even if he had done so, what could he find?

Volmer removed a second envelope from his pocket and handed it
to Fuchs. "This should cover your time and inconvenience."

Fuchs took the envelope. ""When do want this done?"

"As soon as your schedule permits." Volmer hesitated for a moment before adding, "I am trusting you to tell no one about this. Is

that understood?"

"Yes, of course."

Fuchs was curious about the disposal of the other three stolen works from the Gade Collection. "The other three paintings we took from Gade, where are they?"

Volmer responded with irritation, most of it at himself. "That is none of your business, Gunther. I'm only asking you to remove the small Vermeer."

"Are they with the Russian?" Fuchs pressed, with a nod of his head. "Shapko, I believe?"

"Who in the hell are you talking about?" Volmer shot back angrily.

"Dimitri Shapko. You mentioned him some time back. You said he was the one who moved many of the forgeries."

"I never mentioned his name to you!"

Fuchs fully recalled Volmer's earlier reference to the Russian, but he could see Volmer's mounting anger. He quickly retreated. "I'm sorry I asked that question. I was out of line."

"Very much so."

Volmer left Fuchs' home abruptly and without additional conversation passing between them. He had no need to linger and talk, for a more pressing matter was central to his thoughts: Dieter Acker. He would be waiting in their hotel room. Again the thought surfaced, *Did he tamper with the briefcase?* He would know the second he saw it, for when he placed it near the chair he noticed that the handle flopped backwards.

Upon returning to his room, Volmer saw the briefcase right where he left it and breathed a deep sigh of relief. The handle was still facing the chair. It looked as if it had not been touched. He then found the now dark-haired Acker spread across the bed, naked except for a bright red scarf he'd draped over his loins—Largo's scarf. Pleased with Acker's look and putting thoughts of the briefcase behind him, he smiled broadly. "My, my, you remind me of Michelangelo's male nudes in the Sistine Chapel ceiling frescoes. The color becomes you." He promptly prepared two vodka martinis and said to Acker, "Before we play, I need to explain to you what we are about to do."

Acker smiled, but beneath the fabricated show of pleasure, thoughts of *Mein Kampf* burned. "I think I know what we are about to do."

After enjoying the pleasure of Acker's body and knocking off a second martini, Volmer outlined for the nude Adonis a simple and direct plan. "We will do our shopping in the morning and then travel by train to Venice in the afternoon, seated separately."

"When? For how long?"

"We will stay there until it is time to go to Florence." After the earlier restaurant incident there with Astrid Borgmann, Volmer did not want the two of them seen together, unless necessary. The dark alleys and waterways of Venice would provide a more protective cover.

The shopping blitz exceeded Acker's expectations. Volmer did, indeed, spare nothing in outfitting both of them. He was especially thrilled by the changes that came with Acker's new things. For Volmer, it was like dressing a mannequin. Every new shirt or pair of slacks fit him perfectly.

Volmer looked at his reflection in a full-length mirror, well pleased with the fit of a dark blue suit. "Both of us must dress appropriately. Soon I will become Doctor Wilhelm Schroeder and you, dear Dieter, will be traveling as my research assistant, Werner Deitz. We will be on special assignment in Venice." He glanced at his new passport photograph which showed him clean-shaven, except for a well-trimmed moustache just beneath his nose, russet in color like his now cropped hair. New contacts had given him dark eyes. The new look was completed by round, silver-rimmed glasses. His final purchase during their shopping spree was a striking maroon beret. With the excitement of a child, he placed it on his head. It was perfect. He tilted his head in a rakish way. "I'm rather fond of this. Does it make me look distinguished?"

"Something like that," Acker replied coldly.

"Why are you so unkind, so rude, Dieter? Could you not say it flatters me, or something of a positive nature?"

"Sorry," Acker replied with indifference, studying the condition of his own nails. "It makes you look so edible."

Volmer was less interested in what Acker said than in pondering his upcoming rendezvous with Largo Kopacz and Porter Blue. He recalled a specific televised response from Blue to a question from a reporter.

CHAMELEON

"I have been invited to attend a gala in Florence on October first. It is my hope that my fiancée Largo Kopacz will be able to join me there during this special time."

Volmer recalled how at first he had been so jealous of Blue's relationship with Largo.

But that had been then. Now, he saw Largo like the millions of Jews sent by Hitler to their deaths in places like Dachau, Treblinka and Auschwitz. How wise *der Führer* had been in planning their elimination, to wipe all Jews from the face of Europe.

"I'm ready to play some more, to repay you for your kindness," Acker replied before a yawn. "I've been a naughty boy, haven't I?"

"Oh, what have you done, sweet boy?" He wondered for a moment if he was referencing the briefcase.

"I shouldn't have said what I did about the beret. It's actually quite becoming."

Sunday, September 14
Stuttgart, Germany

Volmer left Stuttgart the following afternoon, bound for Venice. Acker, traveling under the name of Werner Dietz, made his departure an hour later. Their plan was to meet for dinner at the luxurious Ristorante da Ivo, not far from the Doge's Palace. The following morning he and Acker would pick up the rifle in Murano at a shop designated by Bager.

The ambience of the decaying city was sublime at dusk; the sounds and smells that floated in from the Adriatic melded with the soft strains of violins. As evening came to the magical city, candlelit white tablecloths looked like pale diamonds on the dark salmon and gray stones that formed the uneven floor of San Marco square.

Volmer greeted Acker with a decorous handshake when he arrived. They had drinks in the bar and tried to act as if they were there on a strictly business basis. Both were impeccably dressed. Volmer leaned in close, totally transfixed by his companion's stunning appearance. In such a brief span of time, his very core had been turned upside down by Dieter Acker. Five words came from his mouth, the final three he'd never used, except in the company of his father. "I think I love you."

Acker smiled at him, an enigmatic smile that lingered on his lips for several seconds before disappearing like small ripples in a pond. "You say the nicest things."

Emotional pain had been a stranger in Volmer's life, but now it raised its head with a vengeance. There was no, 'I love you, too' in return, no sign at all that Acker carried such depth of feeling for him. It was the first time in his memory that he had allowed himself to be so vulnerable. In a millisecond, his heartfelt feelings had been totally devalued by Acker's cold indifference. "You can be a horrible person, Dieter! Do you have no feelings for me? None at all?"

Acker glanced about the darkened room, noting only a few couples in deep conversation. He arose from his chair and   walked slowly over to the side of Volmer's chair. Looking down at the man who had spent a lifetime possessing anything, or anyone he desired, he kissed Volmer on the mouth, a long, lingering wet kiss. "There, are you happy now? Does that show feeling?"

Volmer's mind was whirling in a sea of confusion. He was torn between wanting to slit Acker's throat with a razor and wanting to return the kiss. His passion for the gorgeous German had blinded him to everything; all he could think about was spending the rest of his life with him. Never had he felt so helpless, never had he been so afraid of being discarded like an empty can or a pistachio shell.

Acker could read the pain etched on Volmer's face. "I am sorry. I spoke without thinking. Will you forgive me?"

"You always speak without thinking!" Volmer cried.

Acker laughed, walked a few paces away and stopped. "Tell me all about Venice. I can't wait to see everything!"

CHAPTER THIRTY-FIVE

Tears

Monday, September 15, 1997
Krakow, Poland

Following their return from Anghiari and bolstered by their talk with Astrid Borgmann, Creed suggested that Largo call Blue and ask him to send the soiled panties to Scotland Yard as soon as possible. He gave her the mailing address and the name of a colleague in the home office.

"What if he asks me how I happen to know this man?" Largo asked, feeling the prickly needles of discomfort.

"Tell him you called me for the information. He still believes I'm in London, does he not?"

Largo was able to reach Blue the following day and urged him not to delay in getting the package away. "It's the link we need to connect Volmer with the theft of the Memling." She reminded him that she had placed the zip lock bag containing her panties next to the folded towels in the linen closet. She also relayed a suggestion Creed had made that the package be mailed in the most secure fashion possible. Cost was not to be a consideration.

Blue had been surprisingly calm about everything in receiving her request. "I'll get on it right away." There was a brief pause before he added, "Are you okay? Is everything all right at your end?"

"I'm fine, just a bit anxious at this moment."

"Then you take care. I love you."

"I know. Same here."

Largo and Creed continued to enjoy each other, taking their new relationship to levels of intimacy neither could have imagined a month earlier. They talked frequently about how they should approach their newly discovered awareness of each other. As might be expected,

317

Creed was more content to listen that speak.

"I can say in all honesty," began Largo, "that I did not come to Krakow with intentions of meeting someone and starting an affair. What happened with us ... well, it did happen and I am not sorry." She looked at him. "Are you?"

"Sorry, no," Creed responded. "I find every moment with you to be beyond my wildest expectations. Never in a million years, did I—"

"Mason, I need to know something."

"What?" His uncertainty showed in the tone of his voice.

"How do we do this? Do you keep your hotel room, or are you comfortable staying here with me? I don't care how you answer that question, but I have to ask it." She didn't tell him that Blue had recently called.

Creed seemed frozen in his tracks.

"Mason? I need to know."

"Perhaps I should keep my hotel room," he said, much to her surprise. "I want you to have your privacy and ... well, we will see each other every day," he added awkwardly.

In some ways, his response pleased her. It was probably best this way. She smiled. "I should tell you, I am not much of a cook, but I make a great breakfast."

The smile Creed returned was one of relief. "Breakfast is my favorite meal."

She locked her arms around his waist. "You are a very shy man, do you know that?" She began unbuttoning his shirt. "That is one of the reasons I'm attracted to you." Other buttons went the way of the first button.

He was still sleeping when she gently removed herself from the bed. She donned a thin bathrobe and walked silently to her small living room, turning on a light only after she was a considerable distance from the bedroom. She went to her map, studied it for a moment, and then picked up a pair of scissors and removed a small length of red thread from the spool. She took a push pin and positioned it just above Copenhagen. To the push pin, she attached the thread. She stepped back from the map and studied it for a moment before turning off the light and returning to bed. Slipping out of the robe, she climbed beneath the covers and placed her arm across Creed's chest who continued sleeping, in spite of the warm touch of her body.

Tuesday, September 16
Krakow, Poland

They both slept late.

It was nearly 8:45 a.m. before Creed slipped out of bed without waking her, dressed quickly and went to the living room to prepare a few notes in advance of calling the home office. He'd realized when he went to bed with her the previous evening that his extended leave would expire over the weekend and he would be expected back in the office on Monday, the twenty-second. They talked about it in the dark. She had not handled it well.

While they had not yet found Volmer, he felt he and Largo were in possession of some significant material relating to his recent travels, and he could certainly follow up on these leads once back in London. He wanted his colleagues to do the same, for if Volmer was to be apprehended it would take a team effort. For one, he wanted someone to visit Le Havre and see if the *Largo* was still in port. He did not harbor optimistic thoughts in this regard. For another, he wanted all his Scotland Yard colleagues and the police in Copenhagen to know that Volmer was likely using the name Ankiel Thorssen.

Largo had said she would prepare breakfast, but he was already hungry. Why not surprise her with a breakfast tray on their final Saturday together? For the next few minutes, he busied himself with things available; a few boiled potatoes that he could convert to hash browns, half a package of bacon that either had to be eaten that morning or thrown out and five eggs that could be fried in the grease. Coffee, of course. He was moving ahead with things when she appeared in a long, white terrycloth robe, yawning. "That was supposed to be my job. Is the coffee ready?"

"Almost." He looked at her and smiled. "Sleep well?"

"Quite well. It must be the company."

"I'll take that as a compliment."

"I meant it that way. And if I may add, you look sexy in the apron."

"Thank you."

He was about to say something when the telephone surprised both of them.

She took a few steps in the direction of the phone. "Who can be calling at this hour?" In a less than warm or personal manner, she replied, "Hello."

"Largo, it's me. Am I calling too early?"

She instinctively turned to the side, away from Creed. "No, Porter, I'm up."

"I know it's early, but I have some wonderful news. I was at a gathering tonight at Gretchen Michaux's home. You remember her?"

"Of course. The one with the nice tits. Why are you calling right now?"

Blue sounded as if he'd had more than a few drinks. If he picked up on the tone of her remarks, he let it pass.

"We were celebrating. Vanguard Films is throwing a big party in Florence on the first of October. They are opening their new European studios there. Why I don't know, but Manion has invited me to come over, expenses paid. I thought I would schedule my flight into and out of Krakow. I'll be coming over in late September, a few days before the festivities begin. I know you'll be getting ready for classes, but you could show me your new haunts during your free time and when it's time, we could take the train to Florence. I'm hoping you can get away from your classes for a week, or so, for that. This can be tons of fun, sweetheart."

Largo was momentarily too stunned to speak. She looked back at Creed and tried to show by her expression that she was sorry for the interruption.

He took the expression to mean that she desired a few moments of privacy, so he made a quick exit from the kitchen, but not before removing the eggs from the gas eyelet.

"I'll have to see. Things are pretty busy here right now."

"I thought you'd jump at the chance to get back to Florence."

"It's not that, Porter. You know how much I love Florence and—"

"How excited you are that I'll be coming over. I get it."

"Porter, don't be this way. I would love to see you, you know that. It's just the timing. You call before I'm fully awake and want me to commit to dropping everything and go to Florence with you. I can't do that until I've had a chance to work out some things. Is that being too unrealistic?"

His response was subdued. "No, I had just hoped you'd be more excited, that's all. Why don't you think about it. I've made hotel reservations at the Relais in Florence for the night of September thirtieth through October second. It's on Via Ghibellina, a short distance from the Piazza della Signoria. Will you think about it? Okay?"

She paused for a moment and added, "Are you all right, Porter? You sound a bit ... well, you don't sound like yourself."

"I'm fine, Largo. To be accurate, I'm a bit drunk and pissed off, if you really want to know the truth. Goodnight."

The phone went dead in her hand. She stood there like a statue for a moment before returning the phone to its cradle. She looked back for Creed, but the kitchen was empty. *Great!* She thought. *Now he'll be all pissed off, too.*

Creed returned to the kitchen with the now hard, cold scrambled eggs. The question was asked with little affect. "So, how is Porter?"

"Drunk at the moment."

"Oh?"

"Yes, he informed me that he'll be coming over soon, some big gala in Florence on October first."

"How nice. He must be terribly excited."

"I get that impression." She tried to imagine what Creed must be thinking.

He surveyed the breakfast damage and then said, "Why don't we have breakfast out today? Will that suit your highness?"

She forced a laugh. "Her highness is fine with that, as long as she can be with you."

"That's good enough for me."

As they walked towards the Rynek, Creed brought up the combined subject of his leaving and Blue's upcoming arrival. "It's probably best that I will be returning to London. It would be awkward for me to be here when Porter arrives."

Her thoughts were elsewhere. "What are you saying?"

"My leaving. We talked about this last night."

"But ... but you can't leave now. We're getting close. You told me that."

"Largo, I don't have any choice. My superiors made that very clear."

She stopped on the pavement and looked at him. "Mason ..." Tears began to form in her eyes.

"No, no, none of that, girl. These past few weeks with you have been simply grand. We both knew this day would come. Let's not be sad about it. The way I see it, after Porter leaves here you will have to decide which man holds the key to your heart. And you will have to make that choice, out of fairness to both Porter and me. If it should be me, and I must say I want that more than I can tell you, then I will be back to Krakow in a fortnight. If you chose Porter, then I will take some solace in knowing he is a good man, a man who, very likely, loves you as much as I do."

Largo was abruptly whirled back to one of her final conversations with Blue before leaving for Krakow. He had referenced something that Vincent van Gogh had allegedly said. She couldn't remember it completely, but the metaphor seemed to fit the situation surrounding her decision to go to Poland.

"The way I see it, sweetheart," Blue had said, "both of us are looking at challenging unknowns right now. For you, it's the call to Poland—and for all the right reasons. I do understand that. For me, it's pushing this damned book, doing the grunt work that comes with the territory. I've given it a lot of thought, and it seems to me that neither of us will be happy with ourselves or each other unless we follow our bliss at this particular point in time. I don't doubt that your feelings are very real and deserving, mine perhaps a bit questionable, certainly a bit selfish. But, it is what it is. I will feel much better about sending you off to the European unknown if we can enjoy this quality time together."

He paused for a moment. "I'd like to read you a passage from one of Vincent van Gogh's letters to his brother. I ran across it the other day and it made me feel guilty." He felt the lump forming in his throat and the last thing he wanted was for her to see it. "It's about a caged bird."

"Guilty?" she asked.

"Yes, for wanting to keep you here, for initially not encouraging you to go to Poland and study."

"Porter, I don't believe—"

"No, humor me here. I think this is a beautiful statement and when

I read it I felt badly about not having given you more support."

He cleared his throat before adding, "I don't know when Vincent wrote this, but that doesn't matter." He put on his reading glasses and began, "A caged bird in spring knows perfectly well that there is some way in which he should be able to serve. He is well aware that there is something to be done, but he is unable to do it. What is it? He cannot quite remember, and then he bangs his head against the bars of the cage. But the cage does not give way and the bird is maddened by pain."

Blue stopped in his reading and said, "I should have probably been substituting she for he."

Largo smiled but said nothing.

He continued. "But then the season of the great migration arrives, an attack of melancholy. She has everything she needs, say the children who tend her in the cage—but she looks out at the heavy, thundering sky and in her heart of hearts she rebels against her fate. I am caged, I am caged, and you say I need nothing, you idiots! Oh! Please give me the freedom to be a bird like other birds."

Blue removed the glasses and for a long moment he was silent. "The last thing I want is to try and cage you, Largo. Please know that." He hesitated again and then asked her, "What do you think about Vincent's words? I find them terribly poignant."

"I think it's a beautiful sentiment." She walked over to him and embraced him tightly. "If this little bird is allowed to be like other birds, you need to know something, my sweet man."

"What's that?"

"That this little bird knows the way home, and you should never worry about that."

Creed squeezed her hand tightly, sensing her conflicted feelings. A chilling breeze had come out of nowhere.

Thursday, September 18
Krakow, Poland

In the wee hours of the morning, Largo sleeping soundly, Creed exited the bed and walked to the living room where he had placed his luggage the previous evening while she was removing her make-up. He had already written her a brief note. He dressed quickly and left her quarters, leaving the note on the kitchen stove. Within a matter of minutes, he was moving through the dark streets of the Rynek. He was returning to London earlier than he had planned with a heavy heart.

When Largo awakened, she reached for him. The other half of the bed was empty. She called out his name.

Silence.

She pulled something on quickly and scurried to the living room. There was no sign of him. Her eyes happened to fall on the stove in the adjacent kitchen. The folded piece of paper contained the following words:

> *When you read this, I will be on my way back home. Be brave and safe. I have given a great deal of thought to the situation that confronts us and I have reached the conclusion that we must go our separate ways, sweet lady. I must return to London and continue to chase the bad guys—men like Volmer—and you must follow your star. If that should be Porter, know that I can and will be happy for both of you. One day, who knows, our paths may again cross but one thing is absolutely certain: you will always be in the center of my heart. I love you. —Mason*

For the better part of an hour, Largo sat at her small kitchen table, unable to fully comprehend Creed's abrupt departure. She fixed a cup of coffee, but it grew cold on the table. She looked out the window next to the table at a slate gray sky and the ironic, if not mocking, whirling about of colorful leaves. She cried, dried her eyes, and cried some more. Empty. She felt totally empty. He was gone, not just from Krakow but from her life. Tears continued to fall.

CHAPTER THIRTY-SIX

A Short Film

Tuesday, September 23
Venice, Italy

Everything has bookends; something begins and something ends. Nothing is forever.

For Theo Volmer, whose world had been rocking along without a serious misstep since leaving Florence in July of 1996, an event occurred that caught the attention of every police agency from England to Italy, if not beyond.

While on holiday in Florence on Wednesday, August 6th, George Kiroki of Yokohama inadvertently filmed the death of Lucca Palma, the director of the Uffizi Museum. Koroki was an unassuming man. One of a group of sixteen Japanese-Americans from San Francisco, he was in the shadows on the far left side of the sanctuary in the Church of Santa Croce when Dieter Acker stuck the tip of the syringe into Palma's neck. His camcorder had, moments earlier, filmed the tombs of Michelangelo, Galileo and Bernini. He had just positioned himself directly across from the tomb of Machiavelli, about to complete his task. No one in the church, certainly not Volmer or Acker, saw the man. For all intents and purposes, Koroki had been invisible.

In his own way, he was doing exactly the same thing Abraham Zapruder had done in Dallas, Texas, on November 22, 1963, when he focused his home movie camera on the motorcade carrying John F. Kennedy, his wife Jackie and Texas Governor and Mrs. John Connally. Koroki was filming an assassination without realizing he was doing so. He was about to capture history.

On this day, thirty-five days after the death of Palma, a package arrived at the police station in Florence, Italy. It bore American franking and contained a small spool of film and a note. The note read:

I shot this film on August 6, 1997, in the Church of Santa Croce. Only after I returned to San Francisco and had the film developed did I realize its significance to police efforts in apprehending the killer responsible for the death of Uffizi director Lucca Palma. — *George Karoki*

By nightfall, copies of the nine minute film were on their way to selected police stations throughout Europe and to the central office of Interpol in Lyon, France. For the first time, law enforcement officials had a face to go along with Lucca Palma's death or, more correctly stated, his assassination.

Volmer, as he did almost every evening, was watching CCN in hopes of keeping up with the investigation of the Gade robbery and, of equal concern, the ascendancy of Porter Blue and his new novel, *Tuscan Secret*, which had been recently released. Dieter Acker was at his side.

When the news anchor dropped the Karoki bombshell and the screen was filled with a clear profile of the killer, both men were numbed. There for the world to see was Dieter Acker placing his right hand across the mouth of Lucca Palma just before jabbing the syringe into the man's neck. If the pictures gave them serious pause, the running commentary by the BBC reporter only added to their discomfort.

"...and authorities are now looking for this man. Every indication suggests the death of Lucca Palma, initially believed to be a heart attack, was carefully planned. While the identity of the young man in the white shirt is still unknown, Interpol agents have indicated that it is only a matter of time before it will be determined. Of equal interest to investigators is the question of complicity. Was the planning carried out by this young man, or perhaps by another person who had close ties to the former Uffizi director? Authorities are hesitant to voice their suspicions in a formal way, but those close to Palma feel strongly that someone known to the director might be involved. A reward posted by Palma, shortly before his death, for the arrest of former Uffizi director Theo Volmer—long thought dead—could provide strong motive for his untimely death. Interpol is orchestrating an aggressive pursuit of the killer. It is believed this man is, or was, traveling in the company of an older companion, a priest confined to a wheelchair.

Authorities do caution the public that both men might be armed and should be considered dangerous. Reporting for the BBC, this is Hector B. Gaines."

A long moment passed before Volmer or Acker could speak.

"They have me," Acker's voice was thin, unsteady. "They have it on film!"

"But you no longer look anything like that young man," Volmer countered, trying to quell the churning bile in his own gut, but moreover to calm Acker. "We will leave tomorrow for Venice. We will be safe there until we complete our triumphant finale in Florence."

"Florence? Our triumphant finale? Are you crazy?" Acker was beyond upset.

"Listen to me, Dieter. Calm down and control yourself. This is not the time to panic."

"You and your fucking Jew bitch! This war fantasy shit of yours will get us both caught."

Volmer knew he had to demonstrate command. Everything could unravel in a heartbeat if he couldn't control him. "Fine!" he said with a tone that left no doubt he was fed up with Acker's theatrics. "You want to run? You want to find some little dark hole into which you can crawl? Go ahead. See how long you can last outside of my protection. You have no money, no contacts. You have nothing. Your ass will be behind bars within hours. Is that what you think best? Is that your smart way of dealing with this?"

Acker looked at him incredulously. "What else can we do? Our photographs are now all over Europe."

"Your photograph is now all over Europe, Dieter. Have I missed something? Was mine on the telecast? I don't recall seeing it."

"But I only ... you told me to eliminate Palma. I was only following orders."

"Orders? Whatever are you talking about?"

"You know perfectly well what I am talking about. You said we were at war, that we—"

"Dieter, I trust you will never share that with anyone. They will think you are the crazy one and you will be put away, for certain. You really need to pull yourself together. This kind of childish behavior ill becomes you."

"But I am scared, Ankiel! Can't you see that?"

"Well, of course you are, my son. So am I. The issue is not whether we are experiencing a momentary feeling of anxiety. The larger issue is how we will avoid capture. Don't you agree?"

Acker said nothing.

"Dieter, I have been traveling this road for a long time. You must trust me on this. No one knows where we are. In a few days, we will be on our way to New Zealand. I have the money to buy us all the protection we will ever need. Just a few more days, and we will be free of this noxious cloud." Inwardly, Volmer was feeling the vise tighten. His thoughts centered on the telecast; if everyone in the CNN world had seen the images of Acker in the Church of Santa Croce, then it was only a matter of time before Okur and his men would see them. The agonizing question that followed begged an answer: How would Okur and the men respond to the news? Would Okur be waiting for them in Livorno, or would he turn and run straight to the police?

One thing was crystal clear in Volmer's mind: he and Acker now had to be extremely circumspect in everything they did. But even this sobering thought failed to dampen his mounting excitement over his endgame, now so clearly in reach. The probability of being caught before his moment of glory simply never entered his mind.

Once Largo and Blue were eliminated, it would be only a matter of days before they would be enjoying the balmy South Pacific and their new life together. Acker would come around. He knew better than to walk away from all he stood to gain. The question needled him: *Why does life have to be so fucking complicated?*

～✐

Wednesday, September 24
Stuttgart, Germany

Necessary arrangements were made by Fuchs for his absence while in Copenhagen. In talking with his two employees, he said he should be back in two days, three at the most. "If anyone makes inquiries about me, just tell them I am on a fishing trip."

After a hearty breakfast, he left the farm. He knew he had a full day of driving in front of him—eleven hours, or more. He would spend the night in Hamburg, and then make the short crossing to Denmark. Once the Vermeer painting was in his possession, he would return to Stuttgart without stopping, except for food, gas, and toilet needs.

Fuchs arrived at the Kastrup airport shortly before 9:00 o'clock the following morning. He found the locker with little difficulty. Inside lay the Vermeer painting, carefully wrapped. As he walked out of the airport, he tossed the locker key in a trash container. It would not be needed again.

Traffic out of Kastrup had intensified during the short while he was in the terminal. To his surprise, he found both lanes moving slowly. Frequent starts and stops. He looked at his watch. It was now 10:15 a.m. At this pace, it would be a long drive back to Stuttgart.

Up ahead, he saw the first revolving lights on a police vehicle. Must be a wreck, he thought. As he inched closer to the police vehicle and saw other police vehicles positioned on both sides of the highway, he revised his thinking. *Must be a bad one.*

The vehicle in front of him stopped a few moments later. This time, Fuchs saw a manually controlled gate lower from a vertical position. Two officers stood next to the door on the driver's side, one of whom was speaking to the driver. He couldn't hear the exact words. The police appeared to be satisfied with what they had heard, for they stepped back from the car and the gate swing upright. It closed immediately after the car sped away.

Fuchs moved his vehicle to the gate and stopped. He rolled down his window as the two officers approached. "What is the problem, officers?" he asked pleasantly.

"Your identification, please," one of the offers asked.

Fuchs removed his wallet and pulled his I.D. from behind a piece of clouded plastic. He gave it to the larger of the two officers, a man with thick glasses. The officer studied the card. The other officer looked into the rear seat of Fuchs' car. "Please step from the car, sir," said the officer with the glasses.

"Why? I have done nothing wrong."

The officer placed his gloved hand on the butt end of the revolver at his side. "Step from your car now, sir."

Fuchs released his seat belt and exited the vehicle, bumping his head on the frame of the car as he did so.

"Open the trunk, please," the shorter officer said in a surprisingly deep voice.

"The trunk?" Fuchs suddenly remembered that the Vermeer belonging to Volmer was inside.

"Yes, sir. Now."

Fuchs walked to the rear of the car and unlocked the trunk, raising the lid reluctantly.

Both officers looked at the small package. "What is this?" they asked in unison.

"I picked it up at the airport at a friend's request. The package is not mine."

"Open it."

"Is this really necessary?" Fuchs asked. "This is not my property."

The officer with the glasses reached in the trunk and removed the parcel. "If you do not open this package now, I will do so."

"Yes, sir," Fuchs replied lamely. When the wrapper was removed and the box opened, Fuchs removed the Vermeer study for *The Girl with the Pearl Earring* and handed it to the officer.

The shorter of the two officers, studied the painting, checking as he did so a laminated sheet of paper with photographs of each work taken from the Gade Collection. The Vermeer was positioned alongside the Picasso, the Whistler and the Gauguin. He walked a few paces to his car and called headquarters. "We have just stopped a man by the name of Gunther Fuchs. German plates. HDZN32. He has in his possession one of the paintings taken from the Gade Collection."

"Which picture?" the person asked.

"The missing Vermeer."

"Bring him in, and be careful with the painting, very careful."

"We will."

The car belonging to Fuchs was moved to the side of the highway. The keys were retained by the police. Within minutes, the man from Stuttgart was on his way to the police headquarters in Copenhagen.

An hour later, the news broke about the recovery of the Vermeer. Another domino had fallen.

Thursday, September 25
Copenhagen Denmark

True to Volmer's darkest fears, Gunther Fuchs sang like the prover-bial canary when pressure was applied. Less than three hours after being taken into custody, Fuchs was seated across a bare table from one of the senior investigators of the Copenhagen police, an exmili-tary officer known simply by the name of Rask. For hours, he grilled Fuchs about the Vermeer found in the trunk of his car. Initially, Fuchs persisted in claiming that the painting belonged to someone else, that he was simply the messenger, but Rask was tenacious. "Then give us names, Fuchs. Who owns the painting found in your vehicle, the one stolen from the Gade Collection last February?"

"I don't know his name," Fuchs argued. "I met him in a bar. He paid me a thousand dollars to bring him the painting."

"Do you take me for a fool?" Rask's ruddy face showed the strain of the long hunt for the stolen paintings. "Either you provide me with the names we need, or you take the fall for this all by yourself. I'm tired, goddammit. I've heard enough of your bullshit."

Fuchs knew that the man on the opposite side of the table had reached his limit of patience. He was damned if he was the only one going down. "I want a deal. I'll give you names, but I want something in return."

"Give me the manes of those who assisted you in the Gade robbery and I'll put in a good word for you."

"That's not enough," Fuchs said, knowing that he might not get anything more tangible.

"What if we reduce the charges for you?" Rask asked. "You'll draw some time, but nothing like you'll do if you continue to stall us. Two minutes. Think about it. If you don't tell me what we need to hear in two minutes, your ass is toast. No more bullshitting. I will walk away from this table, understand?"

Fuchs knew his string had run out. "The Copenhagen heist was the work of Theo Volmer. He was—"

"Are you saying that Volmer did this?" Rask's astonishment showed. "I thought he was dead, that he died in a fire at his home."

"He is in excellent physical condition," Fuchs responded. "He is very much alive."

"Who else?" hammered Rask.

"One has died since the operation, Jannik Ericksson."

"Go on!"

"Ilyus Bager. He's a German. I'm not sure where he is."

"So, it was Volmer, you, a dead guy and a man named Bager?" asked Rask. "Is that everyone?"

Fuchs hesitated for a moment and then said, "And a Russian art dealer, Dimitri Shapko."

Rask wiped his face with a clean handkerchief. "Where does this Shapko live?"

"I'm not sure. Maybe St. Petersburg."

"What's Volmer's connection with this dealer?" Rask pressed.

"Years ago, he moved several forged works in Volmer's possession."

Rask's patience was growing thin. "I need specifics!"

"Back in the eighties when Volmer was orchestrating his forgery ring," Fuchs chirped, "Shapko was his go to guy."

Rask was silent for a few moments, scribbling away in a small notebook. Without saying another word, he left the room, leaving Fuchs to contemplate his future. Within the hour, the names of Theo Volmer and Ilyus Bager were broadcast all over Europe. Investigative eyes also began looking for Dimitri Shapko, the Russian.

Sunday, September 28
Somewhere in northern Italy

Rifle in hand, though broken down into numerous parts and concealed in a slim, silver carrying case, Volmer and Acker made their way from Venice to Livorno by car. Aware that the Autostrada might be dotted with checkpoints, Volmer crafted a route through Lombardy and the northern tip of Tuscany, small roads that took them through sparsely populated areas. Were it not for the gravity surrounding the situation, the charm of rural Italy would have been a traveler's delight.

For the most part, Acker had little to say. From a purely objective position, he knew that Volmer's decision to go to New Zealand was smart. If he chose to break away and hopefully avoid arrest, his limited means would not take him far. New Zealand, on the other hand, was a galaxy away. He would be safe there for as long as he was with Volmer. Perhaps the best solution was to bide his time in the southern hemisphere until he could find a way to get back to Germany. As he saw it, there had to be any number of lonely rich women in New Zealand, ripe for the picking. He would find a way back home when the time came.

Volmer's mood was upbeat. He had spoken with Okur the night before by phone and was told that the *Largo* was in port. It reached Livorno on the 23rd. During their brief conversation, Volmer told him to make preparations for New Zealand. Okur had seemed pleased and said nothing to suggest any problems with hot news topics.

As Volmer processed the call, he felt the less said about the death of Lucca Palma, the better. He was concerned about Okur's reaction—and that of the crew—when he and Acker stepped aboard the *Largo* wearing their new looks. "We will be boarding the *Largo* late on Wednesday, October first. You are to sail immediately." He was paying Okur quite well, and if his captain valued his job he would not stir the pot.

Volmer negotiated a series of switchbacks that took them alongside a river flanked by the colors of autumn. "You are unusually quiet this morning, Dieter. Is anything bothering you?"

"I'm just thinking about the rifle."

"What about it?"

"The beauty of its design and efficiency. I knew there were such weapons, but until I held it in my hands I had never fully appreciated such fine craftsmanship."

Volmer smiled, pleased by the change in attitude. "I'm glad that you find favor in it. I'm sure you will please me even more with your upcoming performance."

Acker surprised him with a question: "Just what is the nature of my performance? I presume it has something to do with this rifle."

Volmer had been intentionally waiting for the best time to share with Acker the objective of their mission. He had not wanted to divulge specifics earlier, lest Acker defect. If this was not the best moment to address the matter, he had no qualms about delineating his finely crafted plan. It was important that his protégé know what was expected of him.

"It will happen this way," Volmer said, his hands clutching the steering wheel. "Largo and her lover Porter Blue will be attending a lavish reception and dinner in the Palazzo Vecchio two nights hence. When the affair ends, I will be outside the banquet hall in the shadows and you will be on a rooftop across the piazza."

Acker responded quickly. "You are placing us in the midst of a high profile function in Florence? Is not that the height of risk?"

"I have full confidence in our ability to slip into and out of Florence undetected in a matter of minutes." A smile formed on Volmer's face. "In fact, what better place to be at that time than in Florence? It would be the last place authorities would be looking for us." He continued. "As I was saying, Porter Blue, Largo's whatever—writer, teacher, lover—will likely be with her. Just before they leave the Palazzo Vecchio, I will be near the life-size replica of Michelangelo's *David*. You know the work?"

"My, yes." Acker's tongue moistened his upper and lower lips until they glistened. "Who doesn't know that peach of a man?"

Volmer's eyes were now sparkling. "It is important that she sees me when she exits the building. You will be wearing latex gloves and positioned on a roof top across the piazza with the best sniper rifle one can buy. At street level, the building houses one of Florence's most popular restaurants, the Caffe Rivoire. When Largo and Porter Blue pass in full view right next to me, not obstructed by others, I will say something to arrest her attention. At that precise moment, when you see her head turn in my direction, you will wait for three seconds and then split Blue's head in half with a bullet."

"Blue?"

"Yes, it is essential that you take him out first. That way she will have to deal with the compounded issue of his instant death and my immediate presence. Dieter, it is absolutely important that you pause again for at least another ten seconds before bringing her down. I want her to experience this interval of time, to fully know her lover has been killed and that I am there, to take her, if I like. She must experience the full dimension of reality, the complete range of fears before you kill her. I want my smiling face to be the last image in her mind before it is splashed across the cobblestones of the piazza."

"You have planned this very carefully, down to the millisecond, have you not?"

"I am a planner, Dieter, the best in the land. If we are to rid the world of this Jew bitch and consummate *der Führer's* dream, we cannot go into this on a haphazard basis."

"Is Blue, the man with her, a Jew, as well?"

"No. He is little more than an irritant."

"And then what?"

"You will leave the rifle on the rooftop and go by foot to a waiting gray limousine that will be parked on the north side of the Duomo. Its running lights will be clearly visible. I will arrive right behind you. Once we are inside, the driver will take us to Livorno. Okur and the *Largo* will be waiting for us. I have already paid the limo driver handsomely for his dependability and discretion."

Acker was silent.

Volmer sensed his hesitancy. "We are wanted men, Dieter. If we remain in Europe, it will only be a matter of time before we are caught. Surely, you can appreciate the importance of relocating."

"I do know that. I just—"

"Are you forgetting all I have done for you, Dieter? I have lifted you from the trough of mediocrity. Once we set sail for the south Pacific, I will be able to lavish upon you all manner of delicacies, treats you would not be able to enjoy if we both remain on the continent."

Acker played his next card carefully.

"It all sounds wonderful. I apologize for appearing to be ungrateful."

By mid-afternoon, the assassins passed Pisa. Livorno was just a few kilometers away. Volmer had read of Fuchs' arrest while having a cup of espresso at a small sidewalk café at the edge of the Ligurian Sea. The Vermeer had been found. Nothing else was mentioned in the news release. Volmer viewed the situation surrounding Fuchs with deepening concern, for under the kind of interrogation he might expect at the hands of Copenhagen authorities, he felt certain that Fuchs had sold him out. Every man and everything had a price. Still, Volmer was surprisingly content. Only five days remained before they would leave for Florence. The hour glass was about to empty.

They stopped just shy of Livorno for food. After being served, Volmer flagged his waiter and casually asked if he knew of any vacant stretches of land near Livorno. He positioned a large Italian note on the table so it would be seen by the waiter. Hopefully, it would stimulate his memory. "I'm giving serious consideration to building a plastics extrusion facility in this area," Volmer said. "I'll need a fair amount of land to accommodate everything. Anything like that available here?"

"The only place I know that might work for you is about ten kilometers south of Livorno. A large foundry was started a few years ago, but the financing fell through. The developer left everything and skipped town. The area is nothing but weeds now."

"That sounds perfect," Volmer replied, asking for an espresso refill. "I'll certainly look it over." He pushed the money closer to the edge of the table and watched it vanish.

The area in question matched up exactly with what Volmer wanted. Acker could bond with his new toy with the assurance that it would not arouse any suspicions. The desolate acres of asphalt provided an ideal place for target practice. Only an occasional car passed on the narrow beach road bordering the property. The rear of the architectural shell faced several acres of scruffy plant life. He parked the car under a stand of trees near the construction site, pleased that it seemed to disappear in the shadows.

Together, they entered and went to the rear of the aborted foundry, eventually establishing a position near the roof top that paralleled the elevation Acker would be experiencing in the Piazza della Signoria. "You get situated here," Volmer said. "I'll take our remaining cantaloupe from the car and position it a distance similar to that where you will be setting your sights on Largo."

A few moments later, Volmer positioned the small melon atop a discarded crate, making his way back to Acker through the tangled growth. He quickly reached Acker's position. From that distance he could not even see the cantaloupe. "Now show me your skills."

Acker had already assembled the rifle. He fashioned a makeshift support, comparable to what he was expecting to find in Florence, and took a kneeling position. After making a few adjustments with his body, he positioned the rifle and looked into the scope. The melon seemed mere inches away.

The first shot was considerably off the mark, finding a rotting wooden crate far to the right of the cantaloupe.

Volmer said nothing.

"The trigger is much more sensitive than I expected," Acker offered.

"Try again," Volmer said. "You will get it."

Acker's next shot hit the ground ten yards in front of the melon, ricocheting into a stand of dark, gnarly, trees. He made a quick adjustment with the sight. He could see the green indentation at one end of the cantaloupe where it had been separated from the vine. He now had the target perfectly positioned.

Volmer was focused on the cantaloupe through binoculars. "Imagine you are in position, Dieter. Start counting backwards from ten and when you get to zero, pull the trigger."

He took two or three deep breaths before placing his right index finger on the trigger. Following Volmer's instructions, he began his countdown: 10. 9, 8... This time, his movements were unhurried. When his count reached zero, he lovingly squeezed the trigger. To both his and Volmer's relief, the cantaloupe exploded.

"Wonderful!" Volmer screamed, delighted by the successful test. "You are every bit as good as I expected."

As they reached their hotel in Livorno, Volmer projected his thoughts about the upcoming finale. "There is a high probability that the station at Santa Maria Novella will be swarming with police, so we will go to Florence by car. We will ditch it in the industrialized outskirts and in separate cabs continue to our respective locations." He looked at Acker before adding, "I'm counting on you."

"I'll be ready," he replied.

A few moments passed before Volmer tested his protégé. "What is the landmark restaurant you will be looking for as you enter the Piazza della Signoria?"

"The Caffe Riviore. It's directly across from the Palazzo Vecchio."

"And what do you do immediately after taking out Largo and her escort, Porter Blue?"

"I leave the rifle on the rooftop and go straight to the Duomo where a limo will be waiting for us."

"What about the latex gloves?"

"I don't take them off until I'm in the limo."

"Very good!!"

Volmer knew the risk that was being taken by returning to Florence.

He had been careful during his exile, but no one knew better than he that they were walking a tight wire without a net, where the most insignificant misstep could prove catastrophic. Everything depended on Acker maintaining control of his emotions. If they could get through the next 48 hours, all of this would be behind them.

Paris, France

It happened quickly, catching Dimitri Shapko completely by surprise. He and an attractive woman from the Russian Embassy had just taken their seats at a five-star restaurant in Montmartre when three young men appeared, seemingly out of nowhere, and flanked their table. Before he could verbally protest the intrusion, the oldest of the men stated that he was under arrest for selling stolen property, the said property being three valuable paintings from the Gade Collection in Copenhagen, Denmark. Shapko was forcibly removed from the table and taken away in a black van.

The following morning brought disturbing news for the Russian. From the moment Gunther Fuchs had divulged Shapko's name, the three Asian buyers were quickly located and placed under arrest. Of critical support to the police in this respect were numerous recordings Shapko had made on his private phone between Hadaki Sansumoto, a Japanese financier; an Indonesian physician by the name of Cinta, and Kun Hong, a businessman from China.

Shapko's calls specifically urged each of his customers to remain calm. He reminded each man that he had been afforded an extraordinary art opportunity, and until things blew over he would be wise to do nothing that called attention to his purchase. Predictably, all three claimed they knew nothing about stolen art. When offered a better deal by Interpol, they quickly submitted the stolen paintings. Shapko's ass was left hanging in the sling.

CHAPTER THIRTY-SEVEN

Blue

Sunday, September 28
Krakow, Poland

When Largo went to bed shortly before eleven, she did so knowing that on the other side of the Atlantic Ocean Porter Blue was probably waiting in the Atlanta airport for his flight to Krakow. In a matter of hours she would have to face him. It was going to be difficult enough to tell him she was not attending classes at the Jagiellonian. The more troubling issue was Creed. One side of her felt Blue deserved the truth, however raw. The other side was lobbying hard to say nothing about the man from Scotland Yard who had shared her bed.

She climbed out from beneath the covers a little past seven, dressed, picked up the apartment, and stripped the sheets. Her eyes were peeled, looking for anything that Creed might have inadvertently left behind. A wave of panic followed when she detected the odor from his pipe. It had been a constant during his time with her. Notwithstanding the cool morning air, she opened all of the windows in an attempt to lure the aroma to the outside. An hour later, shivering, she closed them, telling herself she had eradicated most of the telltale scent, his scent. In some ways, she wanted what was left of it to remain.

It was now inching towards 9:00 a.m. Largo had the next five or six hours to make final preparations for Blue's arrival. They had talked of perhaps meeting somewhere in the Rynek, but it would likely be dark, posing unnecessary problems for him. She planned to take a cab to the airport and meet his plane. Afterwards they could have dinner in the Rynek, somewhere other than the places where she and Creed had frequented. A sense of uneasiness was steadily morphing into panic.

She reached the airport around five-thirty, reaching Gate 24 just minutes before the plane taxied to its position next to a dark green extension of the boarding ramp. Within minutes, the first of the 179 passengers entered the ramp's mouth, now secured to the aircraft.

From her position next to a large bank of windows, she watched for him, waiting nervously, wanting to turn and run. He was the eleventh person to exit the plane, right behind a young couple with an irate baby.

When their eyes met, he waved, triggering a broad grin that framed his face. She returned the smile and moved in his direction. He looked different. His hair was longer. He was still trim, but he walked with more of a slouch than she remembered. He's got to be tired. When he reached her, he dropped his luggage and gave her a firm squeeze. Their lips met and for a long moment they remained frozen.

"My God!" he exclaimed, "Can this really be you? It seems like you've been gone for months." Another kiss followed.

She brushed her dark hair from her face, enjoying the depths of his soft eyes. "It has been a while. You look very writerly."

"I suppose that's a good thing." He paused long enough to look her over from head to toe. "I've missed you, sweetheart."

"My sentiments, exactly," She fought to keep her mixed emotions in check. "How was your flight?" Images of Mason Creed popped up in her mind and then retreated into secure shadows.

"Long and tiring. My legs feel like they've been tied in a bundle." A moment of awkwardness followed before he continued, "I'm happy you're here. The last time we talked, I thought we were meeting somewhere in your neighborhood." No sooner than he realized she might take the remark the wrong way, he added, "Don't misunderstand. I'm delighted you're here."

"I thought a little surprise might be in order."

He kissed her again, but this time it felt like she was holding something back. Something seemed missing. "So? Where do we go from here? What's the plan?" He studied her face as the questions rolled from his lips.

"I thought we might find a nice restaurant, enjoy ourselves, and then head back to my place." She pondered a thought for a moment and then asked, "You didn't make hotel reservations, did you?"

"No." There was a slight edge to the small word. "Should I have done so?"

"No, no, I didn't mean it that way. You're staying with me, if you can manage a small place not much larger than our living room at True Opry."

"I'll be happy if it's just a single bed." He reached down, picked up his luggage and said, "Just lead the way, student. Rest assured, this professor is not letting you out of his sight."

Dinner was enjoyable. They talked for hours about what had happened to each of them since her departure on the first of August, Largo wanting a chapter and verse account of *Tuscan Secret* and the progress being made to promote the book.

"It didn't seem real after you left," he began. "It's true, I was on the road a lot, but when I returned to Nashville our place always seemed empty and cold."

Largo said little, preferring to listen to him. Her demons watched from the crevices of her mind.

Blue was trying to package a summary of what had transpired, but he was much more focused on the sight of Largo on the other side of the table. He still had to pinch himself that they were finally back together. "Everything has been crazy. Gladiator is spending more money in launching the damned project than I thought they would. It didn't take me long to realize that all I needed to do was stay out of the way."

"Tell me about this big event in Florence," she said. "It sounds exciting."

"Does that mean you'll go with me?"

"Yes, if you still want me to."

"It's pure Hollywood," he said with a relieved laugh. "Vanguard Films is opening a big complex in Florence. A lot of horn tooting and booze. I'm told there will be about two hundred V.I.P.'s from the industry and the two of us." He flashed a weary smile.

She was surprised at how quickly her feelings for Blue were changing since his arrival. Prior to Creed's sudden and unexpected departure, she'd allowed herself to transfer a lot of her frustrations to Blue; trying to convince herself that he was back in the States enjoying the celebrity role and that when she next saw him that he would not be the man she had once loved. That had made it considerably easier to welcome and lavish her affections on Creed. What she was experiencing now, however, was just the reverse. Blue was still the same man she left behind. All the folderol surrounding the book had not changed him. "I don't mean this the wrong way, but why are you—why are we being invited?"

"Quite honestly, I have no idea. I've asked both Damon Kirk and Worth Manion about it, but neither of them seems to know why our names were put on the invite list. The way I look at it, the invitation has gotten me here, and that's all that matters."

Around eleven they began walking to her flat. Blue was beyond tired. He kept telling himself that he could make it to Bracka Street, but to be perfectly honest, he didn't know if he had the energy to do so. He kept feeling his feet drag along the pavement. "I can't wait to tell you some of the more interesting particulars, but right now, all I can think about is going to bed ... with you."

"You're tired, I know it. I can wait for the juicy details."

"I've been doing all the talking," he said. "You haven't told me much about school.

Have classes started yet?"

She laced her arm in his as they turned onto Bracka Street. "Can we talk about school tomorrow? I think I'm on the tired side, too."

"Have you missed me?" The question caught her by surprise.

"Of course, I've missed you, silly. You know that."

"I just wondered."

After a very brief tour of Largo's apartment, both made ready for bed. When Largo pulled back the clean sheets, she began sobbing.

"What's the matter?" he asked, placing his arms around her bare shoulders, thinking it was something he'd said or done.

"I don't know," she lied. "I'm just a little emotional at the moment."

After the lights were turned off, Blue rolled over to face her. His left hand felt the curvature of her hips. "I've missed you so much," he whispered in her ear.

She placed her hand over his. "Will you just let me hold you for a minute?"

"I'd love for you to hold me for a minute, two minutes even." He thought the remark might solicit needed comic relief, but Largo said nothing, as a lone tear crept onto her pillow. They had only been apart for a little over a month, but it seemed longer. Perhaps this is not a good time.

He felt the waves of weariness wash across him. Just as he was about to succumb to the messengers of sleep, his nostrils picked up the unique scent. The question penetrated the darkness of the room: "What am I smelling?"

Silence was the reply.

Monday, September 29

He was still sleeping when Largo slipped out of the bed and walked soundlessly to the small kitchen to make coffee. Twelve minutes later, she heard deep groaning coming from the bedroom. She walked to the door and looked at him, his feet spread from one side of the bed to the other. For a brief moment, she felt like laughing. "Would the esteemed writer like his coffee in bed?" Her voice was on the hoarse side.

"Only if you will join me."

"Give me a minute. I have the Polish version of scones. Would you like one?"

"Sounds good."

During the few minutes it took her to heat the sweet cake and prepare the two cups of coffee, she decided to tell him outright about the Jagiellonian. He was bound to return to the subject, and the sooner she could jettison that weight, the better. Creed was another matter. She was not quite ready to cross that bridge. She placed his cup and the small, round cake of the bedside table. "There's something you need to know, Porter."

"That sounds ominous." He repositioned his pillows so he could assume a more upright position. "What is it?"

She made herself comfortable next to him and then said in a level voice, "I'm not attending classes at the Jagiellonian."

For a moment, Blue said nothing as he took the first tentative sip of coffee. "Do you want to tell me about it?"

"It's complicated."

"What isn't?"

She wasn't sure what he meant by the remark, but she began by telling him about her trip to Lugano and, more importantly, her chance

343

meeting with Fela Bajek. When she was concluding her account of their time together—her surprise at learning that Fela had known Volmer as Azzo Gatti and the fact that her husband had painted the Memling copy that the Atlanta High Museum rejected—she continued, "That painting by Fela's husband was in our bedroom, Porter! Don't you see, Volmer had to have been there while we were away. He made the swap. I decided then and there to take the offensive with Volmer. I'm tired of living in fear of him. Surely, you can understand that, you of all people."

"Just what are you saying, Largo? What do mean by 'taking the offensive?'"

"I've been tracking him, that's what I'm saying. I've committed myself to finding and exposing him."

"You'll have to help me here. You're saying that all the while you've been here you've been playing the role of detective?"

She didn't like his choice of words and the not so subtle hint of sarcasm, but added, "Yes, if you want to put it that way. That's exactly what I've been doing."

"And what have you learned, or discovered?"

"I know he spent some time in Anghiari, Italy, after he left Florence; I know, or rather strongly believe, he masterminded the theft of the Gade Collection in Copenhagen last February and that he purchased an expensive yacht in Copenhagen and named it the *Largo*."

Blue couldn't resist a slight chuckle. "You sound like Nancy Drew. How did you find out about all of this?"

Largo's irritation flashed like a sword. In that moment she lost her grip on control. "Laugh at me, if you like, but we've made several significant discoveries, thank you."

"*We've* made discoveries?" Blue asked. "Who are you talking about? Who is the other part of we?"

She couldn't have done a better job of revealing her involvement with Creed. She'd let her anger jeopardize her judgment. "Mason Creed," she replied testily. "He was a big help after he got here."

Blue recalled his long telephone conversation with Creed after learning about the faux Memling. At his own request, Creed had indicated he would be glad to contact Largo and offer what advice he could. He never imagined that Creed would come to Krakow. "So,

Creed came here?"

"Yes, but just for a short time. We made the trip together to Anghiari. That's where we discovered so much about Volmer's recent activi-
ties, though the person we spoke with there knew him as Azzo Gatti."

Blue was silent for a moment. He had little interest at that moment
in Anghiari. "It's a special Dunhill blend, the tobacco smell."

"What?"

"I remember it from Florence, from our time with Mason." He
paused for a moment to take a deep breath. "During the short while he
was here, where did Mason stay?"

Largo felt as if she had been struck by lightning. For an agonizing
few seconds, she was unable to speak.

He answered his own question. "The two of you were sleeping together, is that it?"

"It's over now," she said weakly. He's back in London." A long pause
followed. "I'm sorry, Porter."

Blue peeled back the covers and left the warmth of the bed. He
moved to the other side of the room and began dressing.

Her eyes followed him. "What are you doing?"

"I'm going for a walk, a long one."

"Porter, please don't do this to me. Be angry if you must, but talk
with me. I'm not asking for an on-the-spot forgiveness. I don't even
know if you can find it in your heart to forgive me, but please let me try
to explain how this happened. It's not what you think?"

"Oh? And just what am I thinking? Do you want to tell me that,
as well?" A moment later, the front door slammed shut behind him.

Largo sat numbly at her kitchen table, trying to process the consequences of her affair with Creed, her feeling of emptiness and awareness of the depth of Blue's pain and anger. Would he return and, if so,
how could she begin to make things right? Her state of displacement
was shattered by the ringing of the doorbell. When she opened the
door, she found a postman holding a small white envelope.

"I have a registered letter for Largo Kopacz," he said. "It requires
your signature."

Largo quickly signed her name and took the letter from the postman's hand. As he walked away from the door, she looked at the printed return address in the upper left-hand corner. It had come from Scot-

land Yard. She opened it and removed a small, type-written note. For a moment she felt cheated. It seemed cold, distant.

> *Largo:*
> *I just received a call from my friend at Leicester. They*
> *have matched the hairs from the brush with your knickers.*
> *I wanted you to know.*
> *Mason*

It was late in the afternoon before Blue returned to the apartment on Bracka Street. Largo was in the kitchen, peeling potatoes. Her colander was filled to overflowing with them, yet truth be known she had no idea why she was so intent on such a mundane domestic task. The thought of food was the furthest thing from her mind. She turned in his direction when he entered the kitchen. He seemed composed.

He spoke first. "Will you come out here for a minute? I have something to share with you."

She dried her hands and turned off the kitchen light, letting the rinsed potatoes dry themselves.

He patted the space next to him on the sofa. "Sit here, next to me, please."

She did so, not saying a word.

He cleared his throat. "About Mason Creed, I—"

Largo didn't let him finish what he wanted to say. "Porter, I'm so sorry. I was wrong. I don't know what words I can use to express my regrets."

He took her hands and kissed them. "Let me finish, sweetheart. I was about to say that I don't blame you or Mason for what happened. I won't deny that I initially felt as if I had been stabbed in the back, but during my walk around town I realized I had no grounds for holding such feelings."

She was ready to speak. The thought had mercifully formed while he was talking. "Porter, when I made the decision to come to Poland I wrestled with my feelings, my feelings for you, my feelings for us. I asked the same question I'd asked myself after we returned from Italy last year; were we really in love with each other, or had we just experienced an intense infatuation? The way I reasoned it, I could only answer that question by putting some space between us. We weren't married; we had not made any binding commitments to each other, or any of that stuff. I wanted to believe you held some of the same questions and reservations. Perhaps I was mistaken."

He shifted slightly in his chair. "We both know that I wasn't initially supportive of your wish to study in Poland. To be blunt about it, I feared you would meet some man, some man like Mason, and be swept off your feet. I guess my gut was right about that."

Largo said nothing.

"Well the short of it is that while I was being wined and dined during one of my book tours, I had my own sexual indiscretion."

"Who was she?"

"A woman in Charlottesville I met at a party. I was lonely, unsure of things. A situation presented itself and I simply couldn't walk away from it."

"And when were you going to tell me about this woman?" There was a sharpness to her words.

"While I was here."

"Was she pretty?"

Blue was taken aback by the question. Why is she asking that, of all things? "Yes, she was very pretty." He looked at her and smiled. "But it meant nothing."

As a woman, the last thing she wanted to hear was that Blue had found the grass greener on the other side of the fence. "Did you break it off, or did she?"

"Break it off? It was a one-night affair, for God's sake. Since you put the question to me, let me ask, did you break up with Creed, or did he do the breaking?"

Now the shoe was on the other foot.

"He was in Krakow on a brief extended leave. When the time came for him to return to London, he left." She chose not to divulge the fact that he had left her a letter or that a flow of tears followed her realization that he was gone.

Blue pressed, "And what would have happened if he had still been here when I arrived?"

"Do we have to go there?"

He placed a finger on her soft lips, and whispered, "No, we don't." When he removed the finger his lips took its place. He kissed her deeply and lovingly. "What we have experienced—our respective adventures, if I may call them that—can be viewed in two ways. We can each say that we've been hurt too much to even think in terms of building a life together, or we can view those indiscretions as a painful but necessary means of confirming our love for each other. I won't try to speak for you, but I know this, Largo: I want to spend the rest of my life with you. I love you."

She looked into his eyes, knowing that his back pages were filled with painful memories and disappointments; a father who walked out on him when he was just a boy, and a baby dying at childbirth. He was a man of such goodness and decency. How could she not want to be with him?

"I'm not asking for any long-term commitment now," he continued, "but when I think about my future—our future—I do want to know the joy of a family." He leaned over and kissed her again.

She returned the kiss as her eyes blinked at the return of tears. "Porter, I have loved you since you entered my life. These past few months have been difficult and confusing for me. I won't try to pretend otherwise, but I am happy we are together again." She paused for an uncomfortable moment. "Unlike your relationship with the woman in Charlottesville, you need to know that I cared for Mason—I have always cared for him and I probably always will—but I love you with my whole heart."

Largo took a deep breath as she looked into Blue's eyes. "There is something I want to show you," she said, placing Creed's folded note in his hand. "This came today."

Blue took the piece of paper and read the short message. Without speaking, he returned it to her.

"I know this is difficult for you," she began, "but it confirms what I have long believed. He was in our condo, Porter."

"Yes, he was. Apparently, he is very much alive." He placed his arms around her and drew her close. Words were no longer necessary.

London, England

If asked, Mason Creed would have said it was a hunch. It was one of those gut calls that could not be rationally defended.

During his time with Largo, he learned that Volmer had been using the name of Azzo Gatti and, more recently, that of Ankiel Thorssen. The latter name meant little when he had first seen the *Largo* at berth in Le Havre. But now it did. Coupled with the big Vanguard gala planned for tomorrow evening in Florence and his knowledge that both Largo and Porter Blue planned to be in attendance—it carried considerable importance. If the *Largo* was still in Le Havre, he could breathe a bit easier. If it was no longer there, however, the situation would be dramatically different.

He phoned the Le Havre harbormaster, the bearded August Duchamps. The man quickly recognized Creed's voice and his earlier visit. "And just what can I do for you, inspector?" Duchamps asked, fingering his impressive facial hair.

"Hopefully, provide some additional information. The yacht *Largo,* is she still in Le Havre?"

"No," Duchamps' reply came quickly. "She sailed from here weeks ago. I can tell you her destination, if you like?"

Yes, I would appreciate that."

Duchamps opened his ledger to a specific page and moved his index finger down to mid-page "It seems she was bound for Livorno, Italy. That would be south of Pisa on the Ligurian Sea," he added for Creed's information. "A handsome boat, she is."

"I can agree with you on that," Creed replied. Livorno is close to Florence! "Thank you for your assistance."

"You are welcome, Inspector."

Creed immediately called a trusted colleague with Interpol, Jason Keyes. The two of them had worked together at Scotland Yard before Keyes opted for Interpol. Over the years they had maintained contact with each other. They spent a few minutes catching up before Creed addressed the reason for his call. "This call is somewhat urgent, Jason."

"In what way?"

Creed summarized his past experiences with Volmer, his discovery of the *Largo*, and the theft of the Memling from Largo's home in Nashville. "Not long ago, I discovered a yacht in Le Harve that belongs to Volmer, though it is registered to Ankiel Thorssen, a fictitious Dane. I've had my eye on it for a while, but I've just learned that it recently sailed for Livorno, Italy. It is very important that I know if it has reached there."

"That's easy enough. We've got two men in Pisa as we speak. I can get them to jog over to the coast and check it out."

"Let me share something with you." Creed continued, feeling a knot form in his stomach. "If I'm right on this, Volmer has positioned the *Largo* there for one reason. He's planning something for tomorrow night during, or after, a big event in Florence. Two of my American friends will be at that party, one of whom is terrified of Volmer. I don't know what tomorrow evening holds, but it is vitally important that the *Largo* be prevented from leaving Livorno any time soon. Is there any way Interpol can stop the boat long enough for a search?"

"Rest easy, friend. If that boat is in Livorno, I'll find a way to keep it in quarantine."

"Good," Creed replied. "While you're searching it, I'd like you to be on the lookout for a fifteenth-century painting that might be in Volmer's possession. It's relatively small. My guess is that he has it concealed somewhere on the boat."

"If it's on that boat, we will find it."

"Will you get back with me after you've completed your search?"

"You've got it."

CHAPTER THIRTY-EIGHT

The Gala

Wednesday, October 1
Florence, Italy

For days, event planners, lighting equipment engineers, cameramen, florists, caterers and furniture deliverymen descended on the Palazzo Vecchio and its majestic Hall of the Five Hundred. All focused on one thing, insuring that the venerated chamber would be magically transformed and ready for Vanguard Films' gala that evening. By conservative estimates, over a thousand Florentines and tourists were expected to gather on the Piazza della Signoria to catch a glimpse of the rich and famous as they arrived at and exited from the distinctive entrance. From first light, Florentine police were busy blocking off certain accesses to the piazza, making certain that security positions were adequate for the occasion.

8:42 a.m.

Ninety kilometers away in a drab hotel in Livorno, Theo Volmer was rereading "The Strongest Man is Mightiest Alone."

Dieter Acker was disassembling and reassembling the rifle in preparation for his role in the upcoming event. Both would be sitting down together in eighteen minutes to go over for the umpteenth time the precise details of their mission. Volmer's reading of *Mein Kampf* was not lost on Acker.

11:30 a.m.

Following their arrival in Florence the day before, Largo and Blue were spending a leisurely morning, revisiting some of the places they had so enjoyed a year earlier. These first days together had been more difficult than either had expected. Fragile would have been a fitting word. It was going to take some time to sort through the complications and fractured feelings facing them.

As they walked, hand in hand, to the Piazza della Repubblica, Largo's thoughts returned to Sarto Carpaccio and the ill-fated excursion they made to Pisa. "I really liked Sarto. I still can't believe that Volmer killed him."

Blue recalled Carpaccio well. The garrulous and effeminate man had been of enormous help to him during the early stages of his research in Florence. "His writing on Savonarola provided me with details I would have never found anywhere. I think it's fair to say that I couldn't have completed that part of my book without his help."

She squeezed his hand. It felt like she was walking on eggshells. "I am enjoying every minute of this, Porter. Are you?"

"Yes, indeed, especially the part about being with you again. I'm less sure about tonight, though."

"Butterflies?"

"It's not that, exactly, but something doesn't seem ... what ... right about the whole thing. Call it a feeling, I don't know. Somehow, it seems more like I am a part of a circus that has come to town. I don't have good feelings about this evening's festivities."

"Everything will be fine, sweetheart." She repressed the scented memory of recently using the same term of endearment with Creed. "You will look distinguished in your new threads." She paused for just a moment and then added, "I am so proud of you."

11:48 a.m.

Creed was just leaving his office for lunch when his phone rang. He was tempted to leave it ringing, but then he remembered Keyes could be calling. "Mason Creed," he said evenly.

It was Keyes. "I've got some news for you. Your hunch was a good one. The *Largo* is in the harbor at Livorno. A lot of activity going on. My guys tell me that it is scheduled to leave port later tonight. Your timing was spot on."

"And you can keep her there for a few days?"

"Consider it done."

"I owe you, Jason."

"Buy me a Guiness the next time our paths cross."

"That I can do."

"I'll get back with you."

3:32 p.m.

The light was beginning to change appreciably. Darkness would begin to make its presence known in a few hours.

Volmer stood watching small waves lap Livorno's shoreline. In his state of reverie, he found himself back at the Uffizi, enjoying the feeling of immense power. All of that was gone now. He felt older than his years, the swagger he once commanded now gone. The one thing he did have—the only thing he had—was wealth, but it meant nothing more than a means to an end. His life now was totally centered on Acker and that realization gave him considerable pause. *What if he leaves me?* He turned and went to the kitchen to fix a drink, careful not to make any sudden noise that would awaken Acker from his nap. He wanted the boy to be fresh and focused, for in a few hours he would be asked to deliver the victory.

Those twenty or thirty seconds were going to be exhilarating, matching—perhaps even exceeding—the torch lit assemblies of his beloved jack-booted Nazis, the mania that excited every fiber of his young being, the thrill of listening to Hitler and his father speak of the thousand year Reich; everything was now coalescing into one glorious finale. As Volmer sat alone, fanning the flames of resentment, anger and hate, Largo and Porter Blue were making love.

Ying and yang.

7:15 p.m.

The time had come. Volmer and Acker left Livorno in a used car Volmer purchased the day before, a non-descript green Fiat with a less than well-repaired dent on the right front fender. Volmer carried his briefcase, Acker his gray shoulder bag holding the Memling. Volmer estimated the driving time to be a little more than an hour. The early evening was clear but cold.

Volmer was dressed in taupe trousers and a black turtleneck sweater, topped with a black leather jacket. He would be that much harder to see in the shadows outside the Palazzo Vecchio. The maroon beret that Acker had earlier disparaged was pulled snugly over his head, almost touching the round, silver glasses.

Acker, for his part, wore khaki pants and high topped brown hiking boots. He, too, wore a dark sweater, covered by an old, tan bomber jacket. His hair was topped with a dark brown cap that caused the black curls just above his ears to stick out like soft wings. In his right hand, he clutched the carrying case and its lethal contents.

Neither man said much of anything as they drove away from Livorno. Volmer broke the silence a few minutes later. "Dieter, I want you to assure me that you are ready to perform your duties tonight. Are you good with the details?"

"I'm good with everything. I'm ready."

"Then, I believe tonight will go exactly as I have planned."

Acker listened intently, but said nothing. His eyes were directed to the outside where there was still enough light to see the particulars of the passing landscape. A broad smile formed on his lips as he envisioned the adjusted numerals in *Mein Kampf*. It had been relatively easy for him to break both Volmer's codes and the anagrams. "You know I will, sweet man," He replied softly, turning back and facing Volmer. "You are the father I never had. You know that, don't you?"

"I would prefer that you think of me as your lover." A hesitant question followed: "Do you love me, Dieter?"

"You know I do."

"Can you at least say it?" Volmer shot back with surprising abruptness.

"I love you. I love you. I thought you knew that by now. Let's not act like an angry pussy about this." Acker's thoughts were on the task that awaited him.

The road leading into Florence carried light traffic. Volmer was in no hurry to reach their destination, thinking that the less time they were there the better. Their anonymity would be enhanced by the anticipated crowd. The affair was to begin around seven o'clock.

Both he and Acker would have ample time to get positioned before the grand exit of Largo and Blue from the Palazzo Vecchio. All he had to do was to continue to remain patient. *Nothing foolish. Nothing to arouse any questions or suspicions.*

An hour later, the Fiat reached the industrialized outskirts of Florence. Volmer pulled over at a small trattoria, parking the car around the corner in an unlighted space near a dumpster. They entered the sparsely populated establishment, ordered pasta dishes and coffee, and talked in hushed tones for the next thirty minutes. After using the toilet, Acker left the trattoria with a cigarette in his mouth, his tote bag and the rifle case under his arm. Volmer settled the bill.

Once outside, Acker waited for a few minutes before a cab appeared. It soon disappeared into the night with him inside. Volmer followed suit a few minutes later. By the time they would see each other again at the limo, Blue and Largo would be dead.

As for Porter Blue and Largo, they arrived at the gala shortly before seven. Once inside they were immediately treated to complimentary drinks and extraordinary *hors d'oeuvres*, all courtesy of Vanguard Films. With difficulty, but with Largo on his arm, Blue tried to mingle. Fortuitously, it was she who initiated the awkward introductions. Blue gradually became comfortable, or a version of comfortable.

Spotting the two of them, Damon Kirk, accompanied by his wife Katherine, hurried over and threw his arms around Blue from behind. "Goddammit, it's about time you lovers got here. The place has seemed empty without you. The georgeous woman with me is my better half, Katherine." He turned to her with a broad smile, "These are the two wonder kids I've been telling you about, Largo Kopacz and Porter Blue." He leaned in and kissed Largo on the cheek. "It's good to have both of you here."

Katherine followed with a warm hug. "I've been dying to meet you. Damon said you were pretty, but I think he understated things."

Largo smiled. "You're too kind."

"Well, Dr. Blue, What do you make of all this?" Kirk asked with a chuckle, sensing a reserve in Largo he'd not experienced before. "Is this not big time, or what?"

Blue scanned the gigantic hall as Kirk continued to chatter. Every time he had been in the celebrated space, the marble floors and ultra-high ceiling gave him the feeling he was walking into a elegant warehouse. Tonight, everything looked different. Vanguard had spared no expense in creating an absolutely delightful ambience. Hundreds of white candles illuminated the area, creating the illusion of living chiaroscuro. "It's quite impressive. I'm still wondering why we were on the guest list."

"That's an easy question to answer," Kirk replied with a jocular tone, "I told Worth and Bernie I wouldn't come if they didn't invite you and Largo."

"Of course," Blue countered with a straight face. "Why didn't I think of that?"

By this time, the Hall of the Five Hundred had filled with distinguished guests. Most were glancing about for tables with name tags, while trying not to spill their drinks.

Gladiator's Worth Manion made his presence known, expressing regrets that his wife could not make the gala. "The doctor says it's a stomach virus, but I expect her to be back in form in a day or so." He glanced at the place settings and smiled. "I see that Bernie has put us together," he chirped, pointing to a round table with eight place settings just below the dais. Three chairs were filled with guests. "We and those three other people must be important," he added before draining his glass. "What say we claim our seats and meet our new friends?"

Italian actress Sabrina Mancini and her husband Amedeo were chatting away with a German filmmaker seated next to them. Manion orchestrated the introductions and everyone, including Blue, began trying to make cross-table conversation.

All table talk abruptly ended moments later when Vanguard's Bernie Wildenstein came to the podium and welcomed everyone, giving extra attention to Florentine officials and celebrities from the Italian film industry. Wildenstein was a fleshy man, virtually bald with thick, dark lips. In movie circles, he was considered something of a maverick. Screen writers loved him because he seldom tried to tell them how to write. If he didn't like a passage, he would air his opinions, but for the most part he gave his crew a lot of freedom to do what was necessary to craft a quality film.

"I want to express my appreciation to the mayor and other Florentine officials for permitting us to stage this kickoff dinner in Florence," he began, smiling at his wife Lucretia, "This city is one of our very favorite places in the world and we—the whole Vanguard family—are immensely pleased that we will soon be opening a major film complex here."

For the next ten minutes, Wildenstein tooted his own horn, outlining with more specificity than was necessary Vanguard's expectations for the new venture. Polite applause followed at intervals, as if scripted. He ended his remarks with something of a teaser. "At the conclusion of our dinner, I will be returning to this podium to make a surprise announcement, but for now enjoy yourselves and the exquisite meal that has been provided. *Buon Appetit!*"

Wildenstein had engaged one of the best caterers in all of Florence and the meal was extraordinary. While enjoying aperitifs and Proseco, guests were treated to assorted antipasti: *Frittura Melanzane,* fried eggplant; *Seppie Ripiene,* stuffed squid; *Asparagi con Prosciutto,* asparagus with prosciutto and *Saisiccie di Cinghiale in Crosta,* wild boar sausages wrapped in a pastry. The main dish was *Bistecca Alla Florentine,* steak Florentine. A fountain of robust Chianti flowed to such an extent that glasses were continually topped off.

Forty-five minutes later as dessert was being served, Wildenstein returned as promised to the podium. After extending compliments to the chef and his army of servers, he began unwrapping his surprise. "Ladies and gentlemen, it has always been Vanguard's mission to make films of distinction. For twenty-five years we have set the highest standards in the industry and, as most of you know, our films have garnered numerous awards and accolades."

Blue leaned in towards Manion and whispered, "Where is he going with this, do you know?"

Manion shook his head. "Your guess is as good as mine."

Wildenstein continued. "You are looking at the most fortunate man in the world. Tonight marks a very important anniversary." He turned and looked at his wife Lucrezia. "Thirty-two years ago tonight, my lovely wife Lucrezia and I were married in this charming city. In considering a fitting anniversary gift, I asked her what would please her the most. At this time, I would like for her to join me at this podium and share with you her reply which is the surprise I earlier referenced.

Lucrezia Wildenstein, dressed in a glittering white gown that accentuated her coal black hair, approached her husband with a radiant smile. She gave the impression she was floating in the direction of the podium.

When she reached her husband's side, he kissed her and placed his arm around her bare shoulders. "Not only does this beautiful woman provide the center for my life, but as many of you know she is a descendant of one of Florence's most distinguished families, the Pazzi. Through her, I have been able to touch the essence of the Italian Renaissance."

Blue absorbed Wildenstein's words with more than casual interest as he remembered first learning about the family connection. He tried to imagine Lucrezia's innermost feelings about the rivalry that once existed between her family and the Medici. How could she not feel a tinge of guilt over the cataclysmic confrontation in the Duomo that resulted in Guiliano de' Medici's death?

"For most of my life," she began, "I have fiercely defended my family's name, wanting to believe that the tragic clash with the Medici family in fourteen seventy-eight was not rooted in greed or avarice on our part.

"Growing up as a girl, I was told that Lorenzo de' Medici was the villain, that the position of my family had been one of self-protection. I wanted to hold to that belief, but recently I read a new book that helped me gain a different and more realistic perspective on this matter. Although fictional, it is a story about young Michelangelo Buonarotti and his boyhood romance with Contessina de' Medici, the youngest of Lorenzo's children."

Hearing these words, Largo placed her hand on Blue's and gave it a loving squeeze. Blue's eyes were riveted on Lucrezia Wildenstein's mouth.

"This book," she continued, "enabled me to view the Medici in a much more charitable light and where there had been hardness in my heart towards the family it has been replaced by understanding, even affection. After reading this book, *Tuscan Secret*, I told Bernie that it should be the basis for the first film we make here in Florence, not simply because it helped to heal my injured and negative feelings but because these two young people—Michelangelo and Contessina— personify the romantic essence of this city."

For the first time during her remarks, her eyes fell to the table below the dais. "It is my pleasure at this time to ask our good friend Worth Manion, head of Gladiator Press in the United States, to come up here and introduce the author of this wonderful book." A milk-white hand reached out in the direction of Manion.

As Manion pushed his chair away from the table, Blue shot him a disturbed glance. "You knew about this?"

"Sorry, pal, I was sworn to secrecy. The details have to be ironed out and rest assured you will be a major player in those discussions. For the moment, go with the flow. I'll explain everything later."

Largo tightened her grip on Blue's hand and whispered, "I'm so happy for you, so very happy! Please don't create a scene."

Blue was so shocked and confused that he was unable to fashion anything resembling a coherent counter.

Manion provided a brief summary of the relationship he formed with Blue during the gestation of the book, saying that he and Blue had worked exceptionally well together. Clapping came in bursts, as Manion deftly maneuvered his role in the affair. "And now, ladies and gentlemen, I would like for the author, Porter Blue, to stand and be recognized. He is here tonight with his lovely fiancée Largo Kopacz. In fact, why don't both of you stand up so we can salute you!"

Blue and Largo rose from their seats to a loud ovation and waited awkwardly for it to subside. Periodically, he looked over at her for reassurance. Each time he did so, his eyes were met by a radiant smile.

Wildenstein returned to the podium to join his wife, clearly reflecting the effects of one glass of grappa too many. "My friends," he began with a slight slur to his words, "tonight has been a special one for Lucrezia and me." He rambled on for a few minutes before thanking everyone for coming. "Please know that the bar will remain open until the last reveler leaves. *Saluti!*"

It was now 9:47 p.m.

Minutes earlier, after reaching the Piazza della Croce, Acker moved quickly up the crowded Borgo De Greci in the direction of the Piazza della Signoria. When he reached the piazza, it was a veritable sea of humanity. Hundreds had come to stake out promising positions from which to observe the festivities. As he worked his way through the crowd, he could see the top of the building straight ahead from which he would soon carry out his responsibility. Crossing the spacious piazza, he kept his eyes on the middle of the building where the signage of the famous restaurant and bar, Caffe Rivoire, was clearly visible. Once there, he would go to the rear entrance on Via della Condotta. Volmer had told him that a stout man would be waiting for him at the rear of the building. Acker was relieved to find him waiting. He was led quickly to a metal door that opened onto the roof. Before Acker could take two steps towards the side of the building facing the Palazzo Vecchio, he heard the door close. He continued to the spot from where he would carry out his duty. He sat down on the cold rooftop and lit a cigarette. His wait began. In a few minutes, he would take his position.

Volmer could hear the applause from within the Hall of the Five Hundred and assumed correctly that the affair was about to come to an end. Following his arrival, he had worked his way through the gathering crowd before walking over to a roped-off section near the life-sized replica of Michelangelo's *David* to begin his watch. He was relieved to see that the viewing area where he was standing was not overly crowded. A few moments later, he took his final position in a desirable location closer to the rope. Volmer was grateful for the fact that most of the exterior lighting was focused on the grand entrance, cloaking him with shadows. He glanced up at the protruding balcony above the entrance, remembering that one of the Pazzi conspirators was hanged from the very spot. Turning his head, he looked high above the Caffe Riviore for signs of Acker. His keen eyes spotted Acker's head and shoulders above the Riviore. He was now getting into position.

When the first guests exited through the entrance to a sea of klieg lights, Volmer began watching for Largo. The multitude in the piazza began clapping and shouting, intensifying the ovation until it sounded like a monstrous roar.

Acker was now on his knees, making final body adjustments before placing the rifle on the sturdy, raised edge of the building. Through the telescopic sight, he could see the distinguishing facial features of those in the building walking towards the exit of the Palazzo Vecchio. He moved the rifle an inch, or so, to the left and picked up Volmer standing behind a peculiar smile. He returned the rifle to its initial position, framing the open entrance. He could now see the guests passing through the exit, eager to enjoy the rush of the cool evening air. All were smiling, all enjoying the last minutes of the festive occasion, none expecting what was to come. It was now 9:48 p.m.

From his position, Volmer was experiencing the first signs of impatience. He had anticipated that some, if not many, of the guests would want to enjoy a moment with Porter Blue, but he had expected to see him by now, accompanied by Largo. He glanced up again at the roof top over the Riviore. He could see the small shape that was Acker. *Come on, Largo! Come on!*

9:53 p.m.

The faces of Largo and Blue finally appeared in the center of Acker's cylindrical sight, just behind a corpulent man in a tuxedo with a red cummerbund. His companion, a once attractive woman now laden with cosmetics, walked unsteadily at his side, clutching his meaty arm as she neared the first step. Acker made a final adjustment with his body, his breathing now becoming deep and slow. His trigger finger itched.

Blue and Largo were now clearly visible a few feet from the entrance. Acker was struck by her beauty, aware for the first time that his targets were just moments away from Volmer. She was quite attractive. A stylish black jacket covered her shoulders, revealing just a pale slice of her body in the revealing black dress. The thought arrived like the first strains of a melody. *Moments now.* Just when Acker was expecting them to take their first step down, Blue paused to respond to a question or comment from one of the guests. Other guests stepped past them. Volmer was seeing the same thing from his position.

A few moments later, Blue and Largo reached the bottom step and then the ancient cobblestones of the piazza. They were now just a few feet from him.

Volmer made one last glance at the rooftop, just in time to catch a quick glint of light from the face of the telescopic sight. *He is ready!* Volmer's mind was in overdrive, his heart racing. *Start your count, Dieter. Start it now!* The moment he had waited for was now at hand, his victory seconds away. *Surely, Acker is counting.*

He then pressed against the rope and called out to Largo who was less than ten feet away. "Good evening, Largo, and the same to you Porter Blue. It has been a long time."

Surprised by the unexpected sound of their names, they turned in cadence towards him. Largo felt no fear at his unexpected presence. If anything, she welcomed the confrontation. She had been searching for him, afraid for her life, and now, in the most unlikely place, he was standing before her, looking small and frail. She was the first to speak. "Theo Volmer! My, what a surprise! Have you been hiding there for long?" Her reaction surprised him. Before he could fashion a fitting counter, she laughed. "What a funny costume, Theo! Are you going to a party?"

Volmer did not hear a word. Her voice was little more than a background sound, of no more significance than the humming of a motor. *Now, Dieter! Do it now!* He instinctively turned to face the Riviore, as if to prod Acker into action. His head was spinning.

Acker positioned the crosshairs of the scope on the center of his target's forehead. He took one final, deep breath as he felt his left index finger make contact with the cool trigger. A second later, it began its slow and lethal movement. After what seemed like an interminable period of time, the crack of the rifle followed.

The bullet struck Volmer in the right eye, taking out a large portion of the back of his head. Blood spattered across the assembled crowd as the beret spiraled away like a Frisbee. Fortunately, the bullet smashed harmlessly into the stone façade of the Palazzo Vecchio.

For a few seconds, the man who had continued to believe in the return of Nazi supremacy remained standing with his mouth wide open, his lone eye vacantly searching the depths of the dark sky. Then, like a doomed tree in the forest, he fell in a heap below the rope, his blood creating tiny rivulets in the crevices between the ancient cobblestones.

From where Volmer's still warm body lay on the stones, it was less than fifty paces to the spot on the covered Loggia de Orcagna where he had stood just a year and a half earlier. It was there, blending in with tourists from the Balkans that he waited for Largo Kopacz and Porter Blue to leave the Uffizi following their meeting with Lucca Palma, watching for a sign that she had been shaken to her core by the flowers. That day had been a joyous one for him.

Less than a minute after Volmer's death, Dieter Acker fled the rooftop, but not before dismantling the rifle and returning it to the silver carrying case. *I'm not leaving this beauty behind.* Taking off the latex gloves and stuffing them in his trouser pocket, he smiled and said aloud, "Your days of ordering me around are over!"

Once outside, he was met by surging pedestrian traffic, all headed in the direction of the Palazzo Vecchio. Sirens could be heard nearby. Struggling, he made his way to the Duomo where he found the waiting limousine. When he climbed into the rear seat, the driver turned and looked at him, the puzzled expression obvious. "Where is the other man?"

"He won't be coming. He told me to go on, that he wanted to remain in Florence for a few days."

"But the deal was that two of you would be coming," the man said.

"The deal has changed." Acker looked into his eyes. "Have you not already been well paid for your services?"

"Yes, but—"

"No buts. Just drive.

A wave of confusion washed over the driver. "Where to?"

"Zurich," Acker replied, gazing at the ponderous Duomo with delight. His thoughts returned to the copy of *Mein Kampf. Did he not think me capable of solving his little riddle? It is I who now command the board!* "I have some banking business there, first thing tomorrow morning."

CHAPTER THIRTY-NINE

Aftermath

Immediately after the shooting, pandemonium filled the Piazza della Signoria. Within minutes of the death of Volmer, the police who were in abundance around the piazza roped off a section of the piazza in front of the Palazzo Vecchio. Guests still in the building were re-routed out through other doors.

The crowd, which only moments earlier had been in a festive mood, now looked on with morbid curiosity. Most of the persons crammed into the piazza knew only that a shot had been fired and a body now lay covered near the replica of *David*. They did not know who was under the small gray tarpaulin, nor the reason for the drama.

Blue quickly grabbed Largo and moved her towards the center of the piazza, away from danger, past the circular plaque commemorating Dominico Savonarola's fiery evangelism in the latter part of the fifteenth century. Where there was very little space in the piazza to begin with, he wedged an opening for them and they fled the area.

Largo, still in shock, looked wildly about for anything that would provide a semblance of normalcy, all the while clutching Blue's arm, as one who was drowning. Everything seemed to be in slow motion, bodies pushing past Largo and Blue, all wanting a more privileged view of the scene in front of the Palazzo Vecchio. Agonizing seconds passed and then the sound of more sirens converging on the nightmare in the epicenter of Florence. The word that came to Blue's mind as he struggled to keep Largo from being crushed by the crowd: *surreal*.

Moments later, they stumbled upon an empty outside table near the Piazza della Repubblica. Blue's arm was wrapped around Largo's shoulders as he tried to ease her back into a state of mind where she

could think more clearly. "It's all right, sweetheart. We are safe now. It's over."

"Volmer?"

"He won't be bothering you anymore. Theo Volmer is dead."

Largo's misting eyes looked blankly at her surroundings as she tried to reconstruct those final moments with the man who had tormented her for so long. "Are you certain?"

"I'm absolutely certain. Can I get you anything? Water, a drink?"

"I want to go back to our hotel, Porter."

On the day following the death of Theo Volmer, Porter Blue and Largo Kopacz wandered around Florence in a state of disbelief. One couldn't avoid seeing newspaper headlines or television clips of the crowded piazza just moments after the shooting. It did not take authorities long to determine the location of the assassin. They scoured the rooftop, finding only an empty shell casing and a cigarette butt. Both were bagged and later examined for fingerprints and useful DNA.

Outwardly, life in Florence continued. Bars and restaurants were soon packed with tourists, fine leather shops continued to lure customers, and the blood-spattered legs of *David* were quickly cleaned and polished.

Blue was especially focused on Largo, relieved to see her slowly turn her keel. They were approaching each other cautiously, tenderly, both aware of the scar tissue. For her part, she was snipping the last of the threads that had bound her to Creed. She was slowly realizing that their time together had been special, but those moments were now behind her. She was finding Porter to be a source of strength, and she was rediscovering the love and trust she had for him.

The final thing troubling Largo was her Memling. With Volmer dead, the chances of ever seeing it again were slim to none. She turned to Blue. "I made the promise to my great-grandparents when I visited Auschwitz that I would find the painting they loved so dearly. It now seems unlikely I'll be able to deliver on that."

He wanted to say something encouraging, but the words were not there. Where would they begin to look? He seized upon what he considered the larger issue. "You're alive, Largo, and you'll never, ever have to worry about Theo Volmer again."

She nodded, knowing this time he was right. Her thoughts slowly returned to his book. The drama surrounding Volmer's demise had all but eclipsed Lucrezia Wildenstein's announcement. "What are your plans now?"

"I'll probably remain here for the next few days and then return to Nashville. You?"

"I don't know. I need to go back to Krakow, settle up with my realtor and then come back and join you, if you would like that." She paused for a moment. "Would you like that?"

"You know I would," he said, draining a glass of beer as she spoke. "There's something I haven't told you, Largo."

"Oh?"

"Prior to coming, I'd thought of it as something of a surprise, but now ... now that everything has happened, I don't know if you will find it all that attractive."

She washed him with a smile. "Why don't you let me be the judge of that."

"Well, for starters, Gladiator wants me to write a sequel. There's no specific timetable, but they want it as soon as I can write it. In the publishing world, that means tomorrow."

"That's wonderful news, Porter. Why did you think I might not be pleased?"

"It's the other part I was thinking about."

"What other part?"

"I've submitted my resignation at Balfour, effective at the end of next semester."

For a moment, Largo didn't know how to respond. "That's sudden, isn't it?"

"There's a little more to it. I've received several calls from some big time universities. I guess you could say I'm being courted, to use an old fashioned term. It's all very flattering."

"What schools?"

"Tulane, Chapel Hill, Brown. They are all offering lucrative writer-in-residence positions."

"Have you made a decision?"

"No, I wanted to talk with you first. Before you respond, let me toss something else on the table. Everything's related."

"The floor is still yours, sweetheart."

"First of all, I gave this a lot of thought while you were gone. When you mentioned you were not attending classes, I revised it a bit. I'm thinking now that we might want to sell the condo and return to Krakow for that doctorate."

When Largo heard him reference having given something a lot of thought, her first thought was that he was about to propose. It wasn't that she was actually expecting it—after all, the scent of Mason Creed was still with them—but had he done so, she didn't know how she would respond. That said, the fact that he didn't do so came as something of a disappointment. She was careful not to show her true feelings. "Sell the condo?"

"Yeah. We'd be free come back to Krakow in June, if you like. You could start all over again at the Jagiellonian and I could work on the sequel."

What had once been her dream, to come to Krakow and attend the prestigious university, was now little more than a footnote. She had paid her respects to her great-grandparents by spending time on Bracka Street and making the painful pilgrimage to Auschwitz. As for the Jagiellonian, perhaps it was best for that to be filed away under What Might Have Been.

"I appreciate your encouragement to start over again, but I'm content now to return to the States. Much of what I wanted to accomplish in Krakow has been realized."

"What about a place like Tulane?" he asked. "Does that hold any appeal?"

A broad smile formed on her pretty face. "It's in New Orleans, isn't it?"

"I believe that's still correct," he replied with a straight face. He knew where she was going with her questioning.

Her face beamed. "Tulane might not be a bad place to pick up my doctorate. What do you think?"

He placed his arms around her shoulders and pulled her close. "Sounds good to me."

EPILOGUE

Nashville, Tennessee

The date was indelibly etched in Porter Blue's mind: it occurred exactly two years ago. On one of their first dates, he had taken Largo to Virago's in downtown Nashville for dinner. It was at a candlelit table that he told her of his plan to leave soon for Florence and write his book. "I've rented a small house for the term, right in the center of town. As for the book, about all I can tell you is that it will be a romance novel set in Florence in the late fifteenth century, a youthful relationship between thirteen-year-old Michelangelo and Contessina de' Medici, the youngest daughter of Lorenzo de' Medici."

He recalled how he had smiled at her response.

"Romance? My, my, I'm learning all sorts of things about my teacher."

"Yes," he had replied. "Even I get interested in the affairs of the heart from time to time."

Two years ago. In some ways it seemed an eternity ago.

Their return to Nashville was uneventful, but pleasant. If Largo was holding any reservations about having to say farewell to the Jagiellonian, she wasn't showing them. Neither was she reflecting any difficulty in letting go of Mason Creed, although Blue knew that somewhere in the remote reaches of her heart tender feelings for the man still carried a pulse.

He, too, was carrying thoughts of Creed. He was working hard to put everything in perspective, but the wounded strings of his own heart had not completely healed. He had his good days and those that were not so good. But she was back in his life now, and he was determined to do everything he could to strengthen their relationship. He loved her—it was as simple as that—and he wanted things to work out. Hopefully, that was happening.

Following their return, they made an early November trip to New Orleans that proved fruitful: he was offered a writer-in-residence position at Tulane for the coming year, one that would grant him ample time to work on his research for the sequel. Largo was pleased with everything she saw at Tulane and was already planning to dive headfirst into their doctorate program in art history once they moved. Almost as a sidebar, the film version of *Tuscan Secret* was about to go into production.

The one issue that cast a dismal shadow over their lives was the Memling, or to be more precise, its absence. Largo had recently taken Pieter Bajek's beautiful copy to UPS for boxing and shipping to Fela. She had scribbled a short note to go in the box, but Porter had not read it. He'd not been asked to read it. They seldom talked of the day the real Memling was taken from their condo, but when they did Largo never failed to mention the ashes. In some ways, it was like she had lost a child.

He could appreciate her profound feelings of loss, not just the painting but the larger fact that it had deep familial ties. Many would find its story hard to believe; that it had been stolen by Volmer's Nazi father in 1939, passed on to him after his father's death only to be discovered by Largo in his Fiesole home, believed to have perished in a fire and eventually rescued from a storage facility in Stuttgart, Germany by Mason Creed. Nothing of that remarkable journey remained, only the nail in the wall of their condo which once supported the small painting of men at prayer.

They had spent the day watching the movers empty the condo at True Opry. Within the hour, Blue and Largo were going back to Virago's for a final dinner. Afterwards, they would spend the night at a Nashville hotel. Then, on to New Orleans.

It was time to begin the next chapter of their lives.

A few minutes after six, Largo was dressing for dinner when the phone rang. She called out to Porter, "Can you get that?"

No response.

She assumed he had stepped out to the car for something. With a mascara brush in one hand, she picked up the receiver with the other. "Hello?"

She could hear some crackle on the line. A bad connection, she thought. Then, a female voice, steady, mechanical, even. "Yes, this is Scotland Yard calling for Largo Kopacz. Will you please hold for inspector Mason Creed?"

Largo's first thought was to simply hang up. It wasn't that she objected to talking with Creed, rather, it was the timing. Her hesitancy came from not wanting his call to upset Blue. This was not the best time to pour gasoline on a still-burning fire.

"Largo, are you there? This is Mason."

The sound of his voice triggered a myriad of emotional associations. "Yes, Mason. It's good to hear your voice."

"I hope I am not catching you at a bad time."

"No, I'm just dressing for dinner."

He assumed it was dinner with Blue. "I'm calling with some good news."

"I can always use some of that. What kind of news, Mason?"

"They've arrested the person they believe shot Volmer."

"Oh, really." Largo tried to sound interested, but the truth was she couldn't care less. She'd hoped he was going to tell her they'd found the Memling. "How did they catch him?"

"Zurich police arrested a young German man who was attempting to sell a certain valuable painting to a prominent gallery there. I don't have full details yet—and I will get them to you as soon as I can—but my guess is that when they take his DNA and compare it with the cigarette butt and the shell casing used to kill Volmer it will be a match. At any rate, your cherished Memling is now in safe hands."

"Mason, I don't know what to say." She struggled to get the words out. "I had all but given up hope of ever seeing it again."

With characteristic British flavoring, Creed replied, "Then perhaps we can agree that two Memling miracles are enough! This time when you get it back, you might consider putting it in a bank vault." His laugher followed.

"I think that's a splendid suggestion." She could envision his smile, the smile that had loved her. "Mason, I don't know how to thank you for placing this call, for all you have done."

"It was my pleasure."

From downstairs Blue was calling to her to hurry up or they would be late for their reservation. Lest he come to the bedroom and find her talking with Creed, she hurriedly ended the call. "Mason, I really have to go."

"Of course, the dinner bell is ringing. My best to Porter."

"Thank you, Mason." She placed the phone in its cradle, fighting tears. She quickly wiped her eyes, made a few adjustments with her makeup, and then joined Blue.

He looked at her and smiled as she entered the living room. "You look lovely. By the way, who called just before we left? I thought you'd never get off the phone."

She washed him with a beautiful smile. "Just a friend calling with a wonderful surprise. I'll tell you all about it on the way to dinner."

The End

ACKNOWLEDGMENTS

As always with a book of this kind, the writer alone cannot make it happen. From start to finish, I received invaluable help from family, friends and colleagues in shaping this story: my wife Suzie, Reggie Gilbert, Rennie Brantz, Sandra Perry, Kay Shields, Bob Darst, Jessica Price and Donna Michael; all read the manuscript (or parts thereof) and offered constructive criticism. Valuable critiques and suggestions were also provided by Bob Bondi, Terry Doherty, Mike Hanley, Carmen Patella, John Cooper, Larry Ellis, Olee Olsen, and Jill and Serge Storelli. Special appreciation goes to Nina Jo Moore for her help with the city of Krakow, Poland, and Auschwitz, in particular. I am most grateful to Joni Petschauer for providing initial proofreading and to her husband Peter for selected translations from English to German. For their parts in making similar Danish, French and Italian translations, respectively, I do thank Carolyn Shepherd, Niki Craig and Matteo Torri. I am especially indebted to my daughter Rebecca Jett for fine-tuning the cover, Luci Mott for the text design, Anita Laymon for her assistance with the galley proof and Judy Geary for her always reliable editing wisdom and advice.

Put simply, I was blessed with a great team!

Noyes Capehart was born and raised near Nashville, Tennessee. He attended the University of the South (Sewanee) before transferring to Auburn University where he received a BA degree in art in 1958. From 1958 through 1960, he worked as a guard and night watchman at New York's Metropolitan Museum of Art. He was called in late 1960 to return to Auburn and fill in for an ailing faculty member. Realizing a love for teaching, he went to the University of Missouri in 1963 for his master's degree in printmaking. He taught at the University of Missouri, the University of Mississippi and at Appalachian State University in Boone, North Carolina until his retirement in 1997; a combined teaching career of nearly thirty-five years.

Noyes Capehart has been exhibiting professionally in adjudicated exhibitions and regional and national levels since 1958, including exhibitions at The Whitney Museum of American Art, The Smithsonian Museum of Art, The Brooklyn Museum of Art, The North Carolina Museum of Art and The Mint Museum of Art. His artwork has appeared in the North Carolina Literary Review and in Symposium: A Quarterly Journal in Modern Literatures. In 2006, Dancingfish Press published The Private Diary of Noyes Capehart, a fifty-year overview of the artist's visual career. That same year, North Carolina's Our State magazine did a feature article on Noyes' Private Diary pictures and UNC-TV followed with an Emmy-award winning program on his uniquely visual and literary approach to picture making.

Noyes Capehart has been writing since the late 1960's. In addition to *Devil's Mark*, Noyes has written five other novels and numerous short stories.

Noyes Capehart is married to Suzie Connor Long, and between them they have six children and eleven grand-children. Noyes and Suzie reside in Boone, North Carolina. Persons interested in the art and writing of Noyes are invited to visit his website:

www.capehart.org.

52488302R00226

Made in the USA
Charleston, SC
20 February 2016